THE

ALSO BY CHERYL ROBINSON

Remember Me

When I Get Where I'm Going

In Love with a Younger Man

Sweet Georgia Brown

It's Like That

If It Ain't One Thing

When I Get Free

THE *One*

CHERYL ROBINSON

ROSE-COLORED BOOKS

ROSE-COLORED BOOKS

The One Copyright © 2012 by Cheryl Robinson.
All rights reserved.

Library of Congress Control Number: 2011918241

Publisher's Cataloging-in-Publication
Robinson, Cheryl.
    The one / by Cheryl Robinson.
    p. cm.
    "The sequel to In love with a younger man."
    LCCN 2011918241
    ISBN-13: 978-0-9847110-0-0
    ISBN-10: 0-9847110-0-7
    ISBN-13: 978-0-9847110-2-4
    ISBN-10: 0-9847110-2-3
    1. African American women--Fiction. 2. Middle-aged
    women--Fiction. 3. Young men--Fiction. 4. Love
    stories. I. Title.
    PS3618.O323O54 2012 813'.6
QBI11-600205

Set in Adobe Garamond Pro
Designed by Ceci Sorochin

Printed in the United States of America.

First Printing, February 2012
10 9 8 7 6 5 4 3 2 1

TO

those readers who encouraged me to continue Olena's story.

⚜

I'VE KNOWN IT FROM THE MOMENT THAT WE MET.
NO DOUBT IN MY MIND WHERE YOU BELONG.
~ADELE

PROLOGUE
COLD SHOULDER

August

It was two thirty in the afternoon. Godiva Hart sat at a large oak desk in her downtown Atlanta office on the thirtieth floor of the Georgia-Pacific Tower on Peachtree Street. She had just finished plucking a Ferrero Rocher chocolate from the cone-shaped shrine inches from her reach. She removed the gold foil wrapper and popped the cream-filled crunchy wafer with a whole hazelnut in the center into her mouth. She needed something to calm her nerves and keep her energized because running a production company wasn't an easy task. Surprisingly, she was able to maintain her slender physique even after devouring so many of the seventy-three-calorie chocolates throughout the day.

Godiva had started Media One with her husband, Smith, seven years earlier in her hometown of Atlanta. She was just twenty-two and he twenty-three. As the cliché goes, they didn't have much, but they had each other and their dreams. He wanted to become a lawyer—the next Johnnie Cochran. She didn't want to model herself after anyone. Her focus was on becoming a trailblazer in the ever-popular reality TV genre.

She studied the plans for the six-bedroom, seven-bath French chateau that she and Smith were building in the north-central Buckhead neighborhood, Chastain Park (the largest city park in Atlanta). Buckhead was the city's most affluent neighborhood and home to the ninth-wealthiest zip code in the nation—30327.

Godiva had set an hour aside to deal with her house plans so that builders would finish on schedule. And it had finally started to sink in just how much she had achieved in such a short time. She and her husband were temporarily staying at The Mansions on Peachtree—a forty-two-story condominium that combined a 127-room luxury hotel with lavish residences. It was an elegant building with plenty of amenities, but she was ready to move out of the twenty-three-hundred-square-foot Presidential Suite and into the home that her dreams built.

A woman burst through Godiva's open office door.

"Deanna, I'm calling the police. You need to leave right now!" said Honey, Godiva's personal assistant, as she trailed after the woman.

"Call them! I don't care. I have every right to be here," said Deanna, who was so frail her collarbone popped out like handlebars. She'd had too much work done; the fish lips, Botox, mounds of blond hair extensions, and double-D cups that were too large for her tiny frame.

Godiva took her time looking up from her house plans. "I don't have anything to say to you. We've already spoken over the phone."

"I was with you from the beginning, and I do mean the *very* beginning. Before anyone even knew who you were, when all you had was a little local reality show that wasn't even syndicated.

Do you remember those days? You were working out of that tiny apartment on Fairburn. Now you think because you've moved on up, you can treat me like shit." Godiva stared right through her and didn't say a word. "You caught a lucky break, and that's all it ever was. You used to be a flunky on a music video set, running errands and kissing everybody's ass."

"Are you finished?" Godiva said in a monotone. Her face held no expression. "I have business to take care of." She plucked another piece of candy from the Ferrero Rocher tower. "I'm the flunky that ended up signing your paychecks."

For Godiva, it was cut and dry—high ratings meant more advertisers, which meant money, which meant more shows and even more money. Did her employees like her? Was she there to be liked? *No.* It was an incredible feeling for her to realize her dreams and so quickly. But not as enjoyable when she discovered that no one aside from her husband and mother even cared.

"You only care about yourself," Deanna raged on. "There wouldn't even be a *Real Beauty* in any other city, if it weren't for me. You got ratings because of me. I was the star, and you still decided to crown Gwen Meyers the new Media One reality-show whore. You promised me *The One.*"

"Things change, Deanna. No one should live their life on promises."

"Well, I am because you *promised* me that new show not Gwen. I was supposed to be the bachelorette, and now I hear that Gwen's not even going to do it. And you're going to recast, for what? It was mine to begin with, so just give it to me, or at least let me come back to *Real Beauty* next season. It's the least you can do seeing as how I made you."

Godiva released a wickedly loud laugh. "*You* made *me?*"

"That's right...*I*...made...*you.*"

"No one wants to see you fall in love. No one wants to see you, *period,*" Godiva said, shooting out the word *period* like a firecracker. "Have you checked your Twitter page lately? How many followers have you lost as of today?"

"I had over three million followers before I closed it down."

"You closed it down after you lost more than half your followers. *Coincidence*? I think not."

"You ruined me. You ruined my fuckin' life, and you know you did!" Deanna shouted as the tears streamed down her pale cheeks. "And you don't even care! You...don't...even...care," she said, stabbing her finger in Godiva's direction after each word. "Are you human? Is it all about the money? What is it? Why would you ruin a person's life...my life?"

"You ruined your own life sweetie, with your attitude and the way you treat people. I feel sorry for that man you manipulated into marrying you. Media One paid for your wedding—that elaborate affair you insisted on having. Not only did we pay for it, but we aired the mess, and you divorced him in four months. I should have put a clause in the contract that if the marriage didn't last for at least five years, we could get our money back. Do you honestly think America cares about who you fall in love with after that? You and your love life are both jokes. The key to reality TV is believability. When viewers can tell it's fake, you've lost them. And, unfortunately, you've lost them *and* us. We don't want to deal with all your drama."

"I still have fans," she sniffled, "and I can go on another network."

"Then that's what you should try and do."

"People still want to know about me. The media contacts my manager every day with interview requests."

"The media," Godiva exclaimed. "You treat the media as if they're your best friends. You're always going to them with lies— nothing but lies. After you started reading the nasty comments that viewers wrote on blogs about you, you went to the media and told them, we scripted all your drama and arranged your marriage. Our writers are good, but not good enough to pen the mess you came up with every season. Do not blame the end of your marriage and popularity on our show. That was all your doing." Godiva's focus shifted back to her house plans. "Now, if you don't mind, I have a French chateau to build."

"Look at me. Look up from that stupid paper and look me in my eyes."

"I don't have time for you, Deanna." Godiva didn't look up.

Deanna lunged toward Godiva, knocking over her twenty-story Ferrero Rocher tower and clawing for her house plans, which she narrowly missed.

Two men from Godiva's production company who doubled as security rushed in to restrain Deanna. "Still acting for the cameras, I see," Godiva said as one of the men held Deanna around her waist. "Well, guess what, Deanna. They're not on, and if they were it wouldn't even matter because viewers are tired of seeing a forty-year-old woman acting like a fifteen-year-old high-school bully. Every week you're in the news talking trash about reality shows, or you're suing a cast member. Either you go, or they go. And we can't have a show with one person, especially one person that no one likes. Now that's the truth. So deal with it, but don't deal with it here. Go home and deal with it the best way you know how." Godiva swiped her hand dismissively as Deanna wiped fresh tears away.

"I don't have any money," she said in a near whisper.

"What?"

Deanna cleared her throat and repeated, "I don't have any money."

"Why don't you? Seasons three and four you made a hundred thousand dollars an episode. Ten episodes, one other season where you were paid almost as much, you do the math. After season one, you started making big money, so you should be set. I don't know what you did with all that money, but honestly, I don't even care."

"I needed it to run my salon."

"Don't you have clients coming through the door?"

"I don't have to explain anything to you—you don't care, remember? I spent it."

"You spent it on a big house and that Bentley, and all the vacations you rush off to. *You* did that. I didn't. The show didn't."

"I just need one more season, and that's it. It'll give me a chance to get myself together financially. One more season and put me back on *The One* like you promised. You owe me that much. I'm begging you." Deanna struggled to kneel down on the floor while being restrained and clasped her hands together as if in prayer. The man removed his grip but remained close by. "If you have a heart at all, please give me another season."

"Get off the floor and go get some help. Another season isn't going to help you. Do you want to go to rehab? Maybe you can get on *Celebrity Rehab*. Call Dr. Drew."

Deanna struggled to rise while she grabbed the pointy end of Godiva's desk.

"I'm not on drugs, you fuckin' hoodrat!"

Godiva darted her hundred-dollar pen—a gift from a studio executive—across the room and sprang from her seat.

"Listen to me, you washed up, Botox-injected, bobble-headed skank. You don't know me. You don't know where I been or what I been through. You don't even know where I'm from. The fact that I've entertained you this long in my office is a reflection of my kindness and goodwill. But I suggest you leave before I call the police and have them arrest you for trespassing. Unless you want to get on TMZ—in that case, stay."

"I still remember the first time we met to discuss the project," Deanna said in a calmer tone. "We were at Starbucks. Yep, I still remember that."

"Let's go," the man restraining her said.

"I guess you don't remember," Deanna yelled as she was led

out of Godiva's office. "But I'm going to do something you'll re-member. Something you won't ever forget. Wait and see!"

Godiva didn't look at Deanna as she was escorted out of her of-fice. Instead, she plucked one of the Ferrero Rocher gold-wrapped chocolate balls that had rolled by her foot and started eating it.

"Would you like your door closed?" Honey asked as she stood and clutched the knob.

"No. She won't be back."

Godiva's day, which started just after six in the morning end-ed at ten o'clock that night. While she drove north on Interstate 85, her cell phone rang. It was her husband calling.

"Did you hear the news?" Smith asked.

Godiva perked up. "No, but I'm ready for it. Which project did we get the green light for this time?"

"Deanna killed herself."

Godiva's heart fell into her stomach.

"What?! When? What are you talking about, Smith? I just saw the woman today."

"It was breaking news at ten. She killed herself. She died from a self- inflicted gunshot wound to the head. I knew the woman had problems, but I never thought she'd do something like that, you know?"

Go home and deal with it the best way you know how, Godiva thought about the last words she said to Deanna.

"Are you still there?" Smith asked.

"I'm here." Her other line clicked. It was Remy, a *Real Beauty Atlanta* producer, calling about the same thing she was sure. But she didn't want to talk, so she didn't answer. "I planned to call her tomorrow and offer her *The One*."

"You did?" Smith asked. "I'm surprised to hear that."

"I wanted to talk to you tonight about it, but my plan was to offer her *The One* because we can always use publicity and she did know how to get press, all the way to the end."

"What was she talking about when you saw her?"

"Nothing really." She didn't tell Deanna to kill herself, but she didn't try to listen to anything she said, either. It was done now. She couldn't bring her back. "Not to sound insensitive, but who's going to be our bachelorette now?"

"I-I really wasn't thinking about that right now. Deanna's dead and right now I'm in shock."

"I guess we can talk about it tomorrow, then."

"Yeah, let's do that," Smith said, dragging out the words.

True, Deanna was dead. But Godiva wasn't. And life still went on.

PART ONE

TAKE IT ALL

ONE

Olena Day lay restless in her king-size bed. Her eyes focused on the white ceiling as her thoughts ran rampant while Lauryn Hill's "Nothing Even Matters" song emitted from the built-in speakers of her iPod docking station. She lived at The Mansions on Peachtree on the thirty-second floor. The late bloomer beauty was successful and in love. But she was terribly conflicted.

She clutched her cell phone and shook it out of frustration. He called again. And again, she refused to answer. She mulled over the times she spent with Matthew Harper, who was eighteen years her junior. Good times mostly. The worst was earlier that day when he tricked her by saying they were going to his frat brother's housewarming, which they had, but he neglected to tell her that his frat brother was also his father. She never wanted to meet Matthew's parents because she had already met his father. They used to date twenty-six years earlier. Back when they both attended Howard University. She was a freshman and he a senior *Date?* Maybe that wasn't the best word to describe what they did, since he never took her anywhere. They used to have sex, and that was all they ever did.

Nothing even matters. Oh, how she wished that were true in her case.

Earlier that day when she was face-to-face with Matthew's father, Andrew, and he accused her of stalking his family that mattered. He said he had forgotten her name until his son mentioned it and that mattered too. He said his son wouldn't settle for his father's leftovers and that really mattered. It was the main reason she wasn't going to see Matthew again—she didn't want to be viewed as any man's leftovers.

She pulled the comforter over her shoulders, snuggled underneath her high-thread count sheets, and buried her head in her pillow. Did she want her relationship with Matthew to end and so abruptly? *Not really.* Eventually, she'd have to choose between him and Jason, and since she hadn't slept with Jason's father, Jason seemed to be her most logical choice. Jason was thirty-two and a twelve-year age difference didn't seem as absurd to her as eighteen years did.

She sat up in bed.

Tomorrow was such a pressing day. She and Jason were flying to Houston to the University of Texas MD Anderson Cancer Center, and, in a few days, Jason would have surgery to remove his prostate.

Naturally, he was scared, and she was also. They'd grown so close over the past few months. When she first met him and found out he was a well-known NFL player, she didn't take him too seriously. She assumed he had several women spread over different states. But he proved to be more consistent with his feelings for her than Matthew had. He was patient with the fact they weren't having sex, but the reason they weren't, at the time, wasn't because she was celibate, which was the lie she told Jason. It was because she and Matthew had started a sexual relationship, and she wasn't going to have sex with both men. But now, even though she was no longer seeing Matthew, Jason's impotence, which was brought on by his treatments for prostate cancer, meant they couldn't have sex.

She removed the book—*Invasion of the Prostate Snatchers: No More Unnecessary Biopsies, Radical Treatment or Loss of Sexual Potency*, by Dr. Mark Scholz and Ralph Blum—she'd purchased a week earlier from Barnes & Noble on Peachtree not far from where she lived and started reading it while she continued ignoring Matthews calls. She kept reading, rubbing her eyes and yawning whenever she started getting so tired she could barely keep her eyes open. And she didn't stop even after Matthew's calls ceased. As she continued turning pages, she felt re-energized because she realized that Jason may not have cancer after all. Matthew liked to say, "Everything happens for a reason," and he was right because the reason she stayed up half the night was to help Jason discover the truth. According to the book, a misdiagnosis was a common occurrence. *Was it too late to do something?* she wondered. What could Jason do, or better yet what could she do?

She rushed over to her desk to turn on her laptop and google "prostate cancer misdiagnosis." She found 498,000 results. Her online research began with a few YouTube videos. In one, a doctor explained the process for detecting prostate cancer along with the great possibility of a misdiagnosis. Those videos along with settlement details she found on a law firm's website in excess of four million dollars awarded to a man who'd been misdiagnosed and had his prostate unnecessarily removed convinced her that she was on to something.

Maybe Jason had another condition that wasn't quite as serious. He was too young to have prostate cancer. The doctors were wrong. "He has to get another opinion," she told herself as she phoned him.

"Did I wake you?" she asked in a voice brewing with excitement.

"No," he said, but she knew she had. It was four o'clock in the morning. "It's late, baby. Why are you still up? You know you have to be over here in a couple of hours. You're not exactly a morning person."

"I couldn't go to sleep, so I stayed up reading."

"Always reading and always writing. Was the book any good?" he asked as he yawned.

"Jason, don't think I'm crazy, but we shouldn't fly out to Houston tomorrow."

"We have to. You know that. I'm having surgery in two days."

"No, we don't *have* to. I was reading *Invasion of the Prostate Snatchers:No More Unnecessary Biopsies, Radical Treatment or Loss of Sexual Potency*. It's a long title. Have you ever heard of it?"

"No, never have," he said, dragging out the words.

"Well, based on what I've read, and what I was able to dig up on the Internet, I believe you should get another opinion."

"Why are you saying that? It's too late for all that."

"It's *never* too late."

"Baby, I'm already scheduled for surgery. Are we going to mess around because of a book and let this stuff spread because I don't want that to happen?"

"And you know I don't either."

"So what do you want me to do?"

"I want you to have your biopsy samples sent to a world-class cancer research—"

"Stop," he said, cutting her off, "it is what it is, baby. I've accepted it, and I'm going to have surgery. Hopefully it all turns out for the best. And if so I'll take it from there."

"It is what it is, but sometimes it isn't. Everything happens for a reason. I read that book so fast. If I'd been able to go to sleep as I wanted to, I would have never read it. Another opinion won't hurt. They'll be able to get the results back fast. Please Jason, you have to do this."

He sighed deeply before moments of silence. "Baby…I've had a second opinion. I have prostate cancer. I've had a third opinion, and was told the same thing; I have it. Now, all I want to do is get better. I know that you're looking out for me, but at this point what I want for you to do is pray and always be here for me. Can you do that?"

"Of course, I can," she said with a reassuring voice.

"Okay then. I'll see you in the morning."

"Okay, I'll be there."

"Hey," he said just before she hung up the phone. "I love you."

"I love you too."

"I appreciate everything you've done for me, baby. I'm going to get through this, and we're going to have a beautiful life together. Believe that, okay?"

"I believe it."

TWO

I t was the day after surgery and Jason was in a private hospital room feeling sleep deprived and experiencing slight pain in his perineum. Dr. Reddy explained to Jason that his discomfort could persist for several weeks and that he may even want to use a doughnut cushion before sitting on hard surfaces. If he experienced any pain after he returned home and was off of the prescription pain meds, she told him to take extra-strength Tylenol. Then, after a couple of weeks, she said he should begin taking hot baths, which would help with the pain, as well.

After the doctor left the room, Jason lifted the small plastic container off the tray that held his liquid lunch and said sarcastically, "Oh look, Jell-o." Since a person's intestines functioned slowly after anesthesia, Jason had been placed on a liquid diet that consisted of water, apple juice, and broth. His urologist, Dr. Reddy, also told Jason to start doing Kegel exercises after his catheter was removed in order to control his urinary incontinence and assist in his return to sexual potency. She explained that contracting those muscles would help squeeze more blood into the penis and should improve his erectile function.

Jason sat in the hospital bed in silence. Olena tried to strike up conversation, but he only responded with a grunt or a shrug.

Suddenly, a loud noise erupted from the flat screen TV that was mounted to the wall. *Real Beauty Houston* was on the air, and two women were fighting, pulling each other's hair and kicking and screaming while four other women tried to separate them.

"Will you look at this mess?" Olena said, flaring her nostrils. "Another stupid reality show with grown women fighting, and they would have to be black." She shook her head, imagining what people of other races must have been saying about black women while they were watching that program. "Why would anybody want to go on national television and make a complete fool out of themselves? I just don't get it."

"For the money," Jason mumbled. "Some people will do anything for money."

"You couldn't pay me enough. This is a prime example of why I hate reality TV. It's stupid, and it makes black women look really bad." She shook her head as she continued watching the program. "Are they in a beauty shop? Look at the hair extensions flying... Oh God, this is stupid. I'm embarrassed."

"Why watch and get yourself stressed out?" Jason said with a strained voice. She could tell he was in pain and trying not to show it. "Turn it off."

"You're right." She picked up the remote that was dangling from his hospital bed by a cord and turned off the TV. "And that solves that."

"This is some way to spend my birthday."

Jason's birthday was six days earlier, but, with his impending surgery, he wasn't in the mood to celebrate. So, he and Olena and Jason's two sons from a previous marriage (seven year old Jason, Jr. and three year old Jamal) had a quiet evening at home. Junior and Jamal were the most adorable kids she had ever been around, and she could visualize herself as their stepmother.

"I'll do something for your birthday when we get back to Atlanta."

Jason shook his head. "I don't need you to."

"I want to."

"Baby, you don't have to stay overnight again tonight. Just go to the hotel and relax in a real bed."

"No," she whined. "I'm fine here. I have my own little area over there with a window," she said as she pointed to the area not far from Jason's bed where she slept the night before that had a sofa bed, lounge chair, and a flat screen TV.

"I want to be alone."

Olena's eyes enlarged. "*Oh*, okay."

"Don't take it the wrong way, baby. I'm glad you're here with me, but I'm getting discharged in a day or two, and we'll be together so much after that you'll be sick of me."

Olena shook her head. "Never." She stood. "But, okay." Her eyes roamed helplessly around the room. She had planned her day all out before Jason evicted her. While he napped, she would go to one of the Family Quiet Areas and write. That's where she was during his surgery, and she'd gotten a lot done in those six hours. The lounge was bright and surrounded by large windows with a perfect view of Reliant Stadium.

"I'll see you in the morning," Jason said.

It wasn't that bad, she told herself. She could go back to their tycoon suite at Hotel ZaZa, order room service, collapse on the king-sized bed, and try not to worry about Jason and how his spirits were holding up.

"I can't believe you're kicking me out, but I still love you." She leaned down and kissed him on the lips.

"I love you too, baby. Be safe."

THE *One*

Olena and Jason had been back in Atlanta for two weeks, and three weeks had passed since Jason's open prostatectomy. She noticed that his spirit had finally started to lift. He had spent three days in the hospital recovering after surgery with a catheter inserted through his penis into his urethra that drained his urine into a collection bag. He started taking antibiotics the morning after his catheter was removed to prevent the possibility of a bacterial infection. He was down from using five to seven incontinence pads a day to only one as a safe measure against wetting on himself or in Olena's bed. He'd already had the misfortune of soaking her sheets on a few occasions, and he seemed embarrassed by it.

His surgeons utilized a bilateral nerve-sparing technique to prevent him from becoming permanently impotent, and he and Olena felt encouraged that it may have worked because the night before he had an erection. She thought he'd finally be able to make love to her, but it didn't even last long enough for him to enter her.

Oh well, sex wasn't everything, she thought. She repeated that saying often. She loved him. If she hadn't realized that before, she certainly knew for sure after this experience.

"Baby, you can't drink that," Olena said as she swiped the lemonade bottle away from a shirtless Jason as he stood in her kitchen in front of her open refrigerator door. "No heavy lifting, remember?"

"Be serious, I can lift that bottle with my little finger." He stood eyeing the bottle in her hand.

"Eighty-nine ounces? I seriously doubt that. And I may love you, but I don't want your spit in my juice; I'm a germaphobe. Besides, you should only be drinking water."

"Did the doctor ever say that I couldn't have lemonade?"

She shook her head. "No, but I'm an overly protective mother. Have you been doing your Kegel exercises?"

"Don't forget that I'm not your child. I'm your man. But let me know when you're ready to have a couple of my spawns because my sperm is in the bank waiting for you. I can tell from the way you are with my sons that you're going to be a good mom."

She shook her head at the thought. No, it wasn't a need for her to consider motherhood. She'd waited too long for that. Olena loved Jason's kids, but she wasn't so sure she had the patience to be a mother at her age. After the diaper and toddler stage, her life would be spent attending PTA meetings, soccer practice, band, basketball, or whatever they decided to participate in. If she were ever to become a mother, she would be a good one like her mother was. But being a good mother meant sacrifice.

"Let me get back to you on that."

"Don't take too long getting back to me because you're already forty-four."

"So Jason's throwing shots now, huh?" she said, poking him softly in his belly button. "You must feel better."

He smiled widely; his dimples caving his cheeks in. "A little bit."

She put the bottle of lemonade back in her refrigerator.

"If you're thirsty, I have prune juice, apple cider, bottled water, but don't touch my Simply Lemonade."

Olena was certainly a by-the-book type. She liked to place checkmarks beside everything she, or, in this case, he was told to do. He had to drink plenty of water to flush out his bladder because, during recovery, it wasn't unusual to find blood in the urine. *Check.* The prune juice and the apple cider would help his bowel movements. *Double check.* One day he'd thank her for her thoroughness.

"I'll be right back," she said. "I'm going to drop something off at Eugena's."

Jason kissed her on the lips. "Tell her to get you a deal, since she's supposed to be all that."

"You really are in a good mood," she said. "Are you excited about your new job?"

He nodded. "Yep. I'm ready."

In a couple of weeks, he would be in California working for Fox Sports as an NFL studio analyst on the pregame show *Fox NFL Sunday*. A move up from his work as a sports commentator mostly covering New York Giants and Jets games, and a step away from his arch-nemesis, Desmond James, a star running back for the Jets. Jason had shared a long and storied rivalry with the running back over most of their years in the NFL.

The night before, Jason told Olena that he felt much better. He had no idea he'd feel that strong so quickly, or he would have never requested a six-month leave of absence from the network. Jason was intent on keeping his illness a secret. The people at Fox assumed it had to do with a past injury of his, and they were ready for his return, so much so that they offered him a better job in Los Angeles. So back to work it was for Jason, and back to work it might also be for Olena. She assumed she'd find out as soon as she returned her manager's call.

She rode the elevator from the thirty-second floor to the fortieth to pay her literary agent, Eugena, a visit. Conveniently, they lived in the same building. And even though they had attended the same high school thirty years earlier, they had only spoken for the first time a few months earlier while they both sat in the English Gardens on the condominium's grounds.

She rang Eugena's doorbell and stood clinging to her manuscript. She had finished writing her book, and Jason was going back to work, so now her days wouldn't be as routine as they had been over the past few weeks.

As always, Eugena flung open her door in a dramatic fashion. *She'd been hanging around her celebrity clients too long,* Olena thought. Most were soap opera stars, and several were reality TV personalities.

Eugena's usually curly dark auburn hair was now bone straight. "Do you like my new look?"

"Wow, I didn't realize your hair was so long." Her hair went from being curly and chin-length to straight and falling to the middle of her back.

"Do you like it? I finally broke down and got a Brazilian blow-out. I didn't like that I had to wear a gas mask. But hey, beauty comes with a price, I suppose. What do you think?" She twirled around, so Olena could inspect her new hairdo.

"It's...*you*," Olena said as she stared at Eugena. The longer length made Eugena's already long and narrow face appear even slimmer. But she wasn't going to tell Eugena she didn't like her new hairdo. Maybe it just needed to grow on her. "Here's my manuscript."

"That's a lot more than the first hundred pages."

"I'm all done," Olena sang. "Let me know when you sell it."

"It won't take long. I am to the publishing world what you are to Lutel. Give me three weeks, and I should have an answer for you."

Three weeks? Olena thought. If it took her that long to close a deal, she wasn't to the publishing world what Olena was to Lutel because Olena normally closed deals the same day. Lutel Industries, where Olena worked, was a leading telecommunications company in the U.S. She was ranked as the number one Senior Key Accounts Manager in the country, which was just a fancy title for an outside sales representative. She wasn't a manager and had no desire of ever becoming one. She'd worked for the company for seven years, relocating to five states; the fifth stop bringing her to a regional sales office in Orlando, Florida, not far from her parents' retirement home in the Villages.

Speaking of Lutel, Olena needed to return her manager's call.

Hopefully, her one-year sabbatical wasn't going to end four months early. Not when she actually wanted to extend her leave. But maybe, now that Jason felt better and was starting work soon, she should too. The book was done, so she might as well go back to earning those insanely large commission checks. Besides, she had read an article on the Internet that stated the following month, in September, the company would unveil a revolutionary new IP phone system for both businesses and consumers; making it the first time Lutel had ventured into the direct-to-consumer market, so it wouldn't be a surprise to her if they asked her to come back early.

"Just get me the best possible deal you can."

"That goes without saying," Eugena said.

Olena strolled toward the elevator and removed her cell phone from her purse to call her manager. She noticed a missed call from Matthew. She'd get back to him after she called her job. She already knew she'd be needed in New York next week for the new product launch meeting and back to work shortly thereafter. She was more than ready.

"I don't know why I'm going here," Olena said as she heaved out a long sigh as she drove westbound on Interstate 20 toward Douglasville, Georgia. She was on her way to Matthew's house. After taking exit 46A, she merged onto Riverside Parkway toward Six Flags. "I don't want to cheat on Jason. I love him. I don't even want to feel like I'm cheating on him, and right now I feel like a cheater. Plus, he's Andrew's son. God, I need help." She let out a heavy sigh mixed with strong emotions. There were needs and wants, and right then she couldn't distinguish between the two. She needed sex, and she wanted sex, too.

"Music...music always helps clear my mind."

She selected an old-school R&B song from her playlist and sang along as the music blasted through her high-end surround sound system while she drove to Matthew's House. " 'When I feel the need of love, I think of you and it eases the pain' Ooh, this is my jam. They don't make music like this anymore. 'Da da da de da la la.' Ooh, Switch, stop, I'm going to have to *switch* from your song. I can't be tempted. Not tonight."

Several minutes later, she pulled her six-series convertible BMW into Matthew's driveway, still feeling conflicted. *Can I remain in a relationship where there isn't sex?* she wondered.

Matthew stood inside the open garage. He had on a pair of dark-washed jeans, his fraternity T-shirt, and some slip-on leather sandals with the thong between his big toe and the next one. She didn't know why, but she loved seeing men in thong sandals, especially when they had feet as nice as Matthew's.

After she pulled her car into the garage, he let the garage door down.

"Thanks for coming. I thought for sure you'd stand me up," Matthew said once she stepped from the car.

"No, I wouldn't do that." She followed behind him.

"Can I have a hug?" he said as he turned to face her.

"Sure, why not?" Olena said.

They stood embracing. "I missed you, baby," he whispered into her ear. "I missed you so much." He nibbled her earlobe, grabbed a firm hold of her butt cheeks, and drew her body closer to him. She was turned on immediately. He held her face with both of his hands and tried to kiss her.

"Let's not go there." She wedged her arm between them.

"Why not? Have you found someone who makes you feel as good as I make you feel?"

"Are we talking in bed or out because there's more to life than sex?"

"But you love sex. Stop trying to act like you don't because you and I both know that you love sex probably more than I do." She took his hand and led him through his laundry room down the small, narrow hallway leading to the living room. "You haven't missed me?" he asked as he took his place on the leather sectional beside her.

"I'm here." She missed him, but she mainly wanted to give him the closure she already had. "But—"

"*But*...but what?"

"I want you to stop calling me. I feel bad when I don't answer; it just needs to stop. I'm getting ready to go back to work. I have to be in New York next week. They're rolling out a new product, which means I'm going to be busy, which means I can't have you calling me all the time." She paused. "*And...*"

"And what?"

"I'm in a relationship."

Matthew tightened his lips and repeatedly nodded his head. "I knew that. Jason Nix, right?" She nodded. "I can't compete with that dude and all his money."

"I have my own money, so it's not about his money."

Olena was an independent woman. She didn't need a man's money, but she respected Jason for what he'd achieved, and she also respected Matthew for all he'd achieved and at such a young age. Did she like the finer things in life? Had she always? *Yes*, but, she didn't want anyone, including Jason, to give those things to her. She earned her own living and a sizeable one. No, she didn't need a man's money, but she did want a man's love. She had made so many mistakes when it came to love in the past that she often second guessed her decisions when it came to matters of the heart.

"You make a nice little living—"

"Stop right there," she interjected. "I make a lot more than a *little* living."

"What I'm saying is you don't have as much money as he does."

"That may be true, but I make enough to pay cash for the six-series BMW I bought from your dealership."

"Yeah, and now I know where you got it from."

"My bank account."

"After he made the deposit."

"You are truly acting your age—"

He grabbed her face and started kissing her passionately.

She pulled away from him. "Matthew, we can't do this."

"Why not? I think about you all the time. What am I supposed to do about that?"

"I think about you a lot, too, Matthew."

"So if we both think about each other, why can't we take it a step further? Come on baby, let's make love. It's not like we've never done it."

"It's just not going to work, and you already know that it isn't. So, what's the point of making love one last time?"

"If we could just do that, it would be the closure I need," he said, scooting closer to her.

"No, Matthew," she said, shaking her head.

"Are you telling me that you don't miss me in that way?"

"In that way...and only in that way, which means all we ever really had was sex," she said. "It's over. I feel bad that I stopped taking your calls. I wouldn't want anyone to do me like that without an explanation. Your father." She shook her head. "I can't...no."

"I don't care if you had sex with him. So what? That was so long ago."

"*So what?* You didn't say so what when you first found out. And it's more than just having sex with him. I was pregnant by him too...with twins...he made me have an abortion. I don't have any kids, and I probably won't have any. And I wonder about those babies, a lot. Why didn't I keep them? I've convinced myself that I don't want kids. But maybe I'm lying to myself because I was pregnant once and instead of listening to my heart, I listened to a man who didn't love me and didn't want the responsibility of raising them. My life would have been different, and maybe it would have been better. I would have been a mother with two kids your age. Sometimes, I feel like God is punishing me for what I did, and that's why I've never been able to find true love." Her eyes bubbled with fresh tears. "I honestly feel that way." She wiped away the few tears that had fallen. "I hate to cry." She looked over at Matthew. He had a distant look in his eyes. "Now, do you understand?" He nodded. "You're going to make some woman very happy."

"I'm not really thinking about that right now. A relationship is the furthest thing from my mind. I'm just going to put all my energy into my new job."

"*New* job? What are you going to be doing?" She wiped her tears away.

"I'm going to be working for my frat brother, Mike Farr."

"*Mike Farr?*" She said with a smile. "I know Mike Farr."

"You know Mike Farr."

"No, but I know the Farr family...*indirectly*. I'm from Detroit. Everyone from Detroit knows the Farrs. My family bought some cars from Mel Farr. But Mike's a lot older than you. He's like my age."

"Yeah and so are a lot of my frat brothers. It's called grad chapter. I know I'm a younger man, but I'm not in college anymore, baby. He owns a car dealership and finance company in Marietta. The dealership is appropriately titled, Second Chance Motors or maybe not since you're not giving me one."

"I'm really happy for you."

"Are you really?"

"Yes...of course. I want the best for you. What are you going to be doing there?"

"The same thing I'm doing now. Working finance as an F&I manager for his company, SCM Credit. This is going to be a great opportunity to get with them while they're still in their growth stage and see where it takes me or where I can take them. I'm excited."

"That's great. I'm really happy for you: change is good."

"Not always, but sometimes it's unavoidable, I suppose."

"I hope you do really well—no, I know you'll do well."

"I know you will too with the new product your company is rolling out. I bet you can't wait."

"I must admit, I'm pretty excited about it."

They sat in silence for a few seconds staring at each other.

Matthew said, "Well, I guess I'll walk you out."

"Okay, I'm glad I came over. We have closure now." She stood and brushed her jeans, which was a nervous habit of hers.

"I don't know about all that. You have closure now. I'm not sure what I have. Oh, a new job. But this is it for us, I guess." Matthew stood right after Olena had and went toward her with open arms. "Know that I love you, always."

They stood in a tight embrace for several seconds.

"I love you too."

"And also know that you've ruined it for me and a younger woman."

"Don't say that. I want you with a young lady your age. It would crush me to know you're with a woman my age."

"What? All bets off. You're throwing me back out there with all those cougars."

"You know I hate that term, but seriously don't date another older woman, even if I have to find you a younger woman myself. I know your type."

"I guess you do."

Olena smiled and stuck out her right hand. "Friends?"

"I'll think about it," he said as he shook her hand. "You have a really firm handshake."

"I'm in sales, and that's a must."

One door had just closed. But others had opened, and still others were getting ready to. It was time for her to embark on another new beginning.

THREE

September

Olena's eyes opened in a flash. She whipped her neck around and looked at the clock resting on the night-stand. "Oh…my…God!" She sprang from the queen-sized bed and fell to the floor taking the Rabbit Pearl she'd used for two minutes the night before right along with her. "It's eight o-frickin-clock," she shouted, unraveling the white bed sheet that was twisted around her ankles. "How in the *blankety-blank* did this happen?" She grabbed the phone from the nightstand to call the front desk and demand an explanation as to why she wasn't given a 7:00 a.m. wake-up call as requested.

She stood pacing, her right hand strangling the ho-tel's phone cord as she shrieked out a grunt filled with disgust. "I don't have time for this." She slammed the phone down and scurried to the bathroom. She was in what had been her home away from home for the past seven years—the Embassy Suites in Manhattan—three months before her one-year sabbatical would end. She was there to attend Lutel's new product launch meeting, and, of course, she still had a sneaking suspicion the company wanted to ask her to help them roll out the new product. And she was ready to make money. But now she was running late for what had been deemed a breakthrough in technology.

A gray pinstripe Brooks Brothers skirt suit and a white cotton blouse with ruffles on the V neckline and around the cuffs awaited her in the closet. For the occasion, she decided to dress conservatively.

Once inside the bathroom, she quickly turned on the water to the shower, but once she began brushing her teeth that she had spent years and money perfecting, her pace slowed. She brushed them as her dentist instructed, for the required two minutes, and flossed between each tooth with a dental pick twenty times, scraping her tongue and then gargling with mouthwash. Not the organic brands, she'd tried those, but it didn't take her long to abandon them for the only one she found that killed the germs that caused her bad breath—Listerine: FreshBurst was her favorite flavor. She spent close to ten minutes brushing and flossing. When, at that time, every second counted. But when it came to her teeth, she didn't rush because the last thing she wanted was to wear dentures.

She wiped the fog from the bathroom mirror with tissue and studied her face in the large circle she'd just created. The two smile lines on either side of her mouth aged her. Even though Olena was forty-four, people often told her she looked like she was in her late twenties. Never mind most of them were young men trying to get her phone number.

She stepped into the shower. She had to admit that she looked a lot younger at forty-four than her mother had at her age, maybe because Olena didn't have kids and not as much stress. Still, she was far from perfect. She had her gray strands dyed black as soon as they surfaced, and the few unwanted hairs that popped up underneath her chin, on her knuckles, and on the skin on her big toes—something she didn't notice before she turned forty—she'd tweeze off immediately. She had a little pouch on her stomach that she sucked in at will. Spanx usually hid her extra belly fat, unless it was that time of the month. There wasn't a body shaper sturdy enough to hide the bloating she experienced while on her period. When she was younger, her hair would grow as fast as weeds. But lately, while she'd been trying to grow out her bob, just getting a half an inch of new growth a month required much work and money on Olena's part. She spent hundreds at Whole Foods on vitamins, organic shampoos and conditioners, bottled water, and leafy vegetables, and even more at a fancy Buckhead hair salon, getting her hair down weekly.

Olena stepped out of the bathtub and dried herself off.

She didn't have cellulite. She didn't have a double chin like some women her age and even younger. She didn't have a loose neck or crow's feet around her eyes. Occasionally, her eyelids did puff, and the area underneath her left eye had a noticeable dark circle. But she didn't worry over her imperfections, and probably wouldn't have thought about any of them at all *if* she liked men her age. Because a man her age, one who wasn't chasing young girls, may not care that the two of them were aging gracefully together. Actually, she never even thought she liked younger men until she met Jason first and then Matthew.

Olena was an hour late when she arrived at eight thirty at Lutel's corporate headquarters on the forty-second floor of One Worldwide Plaza.

At that point, she was quickly ushered into the mid-sized interior office belonging to Joanne Birch, Lutel's human resources manager: a dark haired, thirtysomething beauty whose race Olena had a hard time figuring out. Was she Armenian or Italian? Olena wasn't sure why it mattered.

It was just something she wanted to know, but didn't want to ask.

Inside Joanne's office were two plants, a Peace Lily and a Lucky Bamboo, sitting atop the three-drawer hutch. Atop the credenza and behind her classic cherry wood and black L-desk were framed photos of Joanne crossing the finish line of several marathons.

Olena felt terrible for being late, but she didn't understand why she had to report to HR. The front desk manager at the Embassy Suites had called and explained to Olena's sales manager that there had been a new person working the desk the night before who set Olena's wake-up call for 7:00 p.m. instead of a.m. But the call obviously didn't matter. *Out of sight out of mind*, Olena thought. *Since when does a company drag their best employee into human resources for a reprimand?* Olena had spoken to Joanne several times in the past, usually by phone. Their brief conversations always centered on a mix-up with a few of Olena's large commission checks that Joanne always handled promptly. A few years earlier, Olena was in New York calling on the Loyalty Hospitality Group, one of her largest clients, and she popped into Joanne's office on a different matter. She could've e-mailed the company's request, but hand delivered a letter explaining why she had declined several promotions. Quite honestly, she made too much money in sales. A management position would mean less pay and more headaches.

Joanne was in an unusually talkative mood that day. Off the record, she told Olena that she should change her reason. So Olena stated instead that she still had more to learn in her current position before she could confidently consider herself to be an effective leader. Joanne wouldn't usually advise employees in that manner, even off the record, but that day she'd made an exception because she was ecstatic beyond belief. For one thing, she'd just found out that she'd qualified for the Boston Marathon, which

Olena had no idea was such a big deal. She assumed anyone could run in a marathon if they wanted to, which wasn't at all the case for the Boston Marathon. Joanne was able to qualify by completing The New York City Marathon in three hours and twenty minutes: twenty-five minutes better than Boston Marathon's requirement for her age group. Also, she had finally gotten engaged after six years of living with her boyfriend.

But today Olena felt a totally different vibe.

She sat across from Joanne's desk with her legs crossed and her right foot dangling. Her mind raced. *Had she'd actually awakened, or was this all just a terrible dream?* she wondered. She'd been in Joanne's office a little more than fifteen minutes, and her head was shaking in total disbelief.

Olena listened to Joanne and tried her best to refrain from taking all of her frustration out on her, since she was just the messenger.

"You flew me here to tell me, I'm fired." Olena couldn't believe what she was told. She earned a generous living at Lutel, most of which she invested in stock that had paid off handsomely. But now the tables were starting to turn. She lost money in the stock market months earlier and changed her aggressive portfolio to something with little to no risk. The stock market was one thing, but her job had been her life for the past seven years. And now she had lost that too or was about to lose it.

From the interior designer to the high-end furniture, Olena's list of expenditures seemed endless. All because she thought her job was secure. She wondered about Hugh, her former boss, who she had a six-year affair with. Did he still have his job, or had karma got them both?

"Olena, you're not fired. Technically, you haven't been laid-off of your current position because you're still on sabbatical."

"So you have to wait until I come back, and then you're going to fire me. Thanks for giving me the heads up."

"Actually, I never mentioned firing you. Why would you assume you're fired?"

"I can stay on with a completely different commission scale, but I'd have to be a fool to agree to that."

"Our new incentive plan offers a base salary of forty thousand dollars with quarterly bonuses that max out at twelve and a half percent of your base."

"So what you're saying is that the top salespeople will max out at around fifty-five thousand dollars a year?"

"There will be an additional ten percent annual bonus awarded at the end of the year for those salespeople who fall into the top five percent. Less than three percent of our sales force comes anywhere close to hitting your numbers. You found a way to make our system work for you."

"What's wrong with that? Did the company get tired of cutting me such big checks? Why else would they do this? What's the incentive for your top sales people now?"

"In this current climate, a job is the incentive."

"A job. Do you think I won't be able to find another job?"

"I know you're angry right now—"

"Angry," Olena blurted out, interrupting Joanne. "I'm not angry. I haven't raised my voice. I'm sitting here calmly. I may not agree with what the company is doing, but that doesn't mean I'm angry." But Olena was angry. In fact, she was outraged. But the stereotype that black women were mean and angry immediately came to mind and put her on the defense whenever someone who wasn't black used that word and her name in tandem.

"Please try to see it from our viewpoint; the company has to take strides to remain competitive."

"And those strides mean putting your profits into technology instead of your workforce…the same workforce responsible for the company's profitability in the first place. You're trying to force us to either accept substantial pay cuts or leave. Is that really the best solution? If you think so, I can't see it from your viewpoint."

"We need to go in a different direction as many companies are doing these days."

Olena shook her head slowly. "What kind of different direction doesn't require having your best salesperson with you to help with the transition? Obviously, this company has forgotten about all of the training sessions I've conducted on the company's behalf. All of the awards and prizes I've received. Maybe accepting a one-year sabbatical was more of a curse than a benefit." Or maybe it was the fact that Olena, a sales rep, was the fifth-highest-paid employee in the company right under the top four executives, and yet she wasn't an executive. Maybe the real problem was her refusal to accept a promotion. She didn't actually know. All she knew was come the New Year she would officially become unemployed and thus a statistic.

"We appreciate you, Olena. I can't say that enough."

Olena shrugged. "Well, if I've lost my job, I've lost my job. Look, I know what I'm worth, and you can't expect me to accept that much less than what I'm used to making. I guess now I don't feel bad for missing the launch meeting. I was anxious to find out about the new product, but right now, I could care less. It's time for me to pay a visit to Apple because they don't mind paying their top talent." She stood and brushed her skirt. "Do you need me to sign some paperwork?"

"I just have one thing for you to sign right now, and I'll send out some other paperwork this afternoon for overnight delivery."

"So it'll get there right when I'm getting there."

"Don't you fly out today?" Joanne asked as she frantically checked her computer system. "Because I'm pretty sure, we only had your room booked for one night."

"It was just a figure of speech. I'm not going to cost the company any more money than I already have."

"Olena, we want you to remain with us. If you should reconsider our offer, we'd love to have you. We appreciate all that you've done. I mean that."

"I guess when things seem too good to be true, they really are."

Olena smiled and shook her head as she breezed out of Joanne's office. At least she didn't have to pack a box.

Olena walked out of the Atlanta-Hartsfield Jackson International airport strangling the round leather handle to her Louis Vuitton garment bag. The more she thought about it, the angrier she became. How dare they force her to quit? *No one in their right mind would accept the same job with the same company for a quarter of the pay*, she thought.

Jason was sitting in a two-tone Bugatti Vegron just outside of Delta arrivals. The sight of him behind the wheel of the luxury sports car made her smile. With his black aviator sunglasses and perfectly proportioned biceps bulging from underneath his long-sleeve gray three-button placket Polo.

As she approached the car, he released the front trunk, and she tossed her garment bag and purse inside of the small space.

"I'm gone for one day, and you go buy this rocket."

As he smiled at her, his deep dimples caved in. "It's not mine," he said, leaning over and kissing her after she'd dropped into the passenger seat. "It's Hanny's." Hanny was his sports agent and loyal friend. "I might love nice things, but I'm not paying seven-figures for a car. I don't care how much money I have."

"*Hmm.* Your sports agent can afford to buy a car that cost seven-figures. I might need to look into becoming an agent because being one is obviously better than having one...at least in my case." She reminded herself that Eugena's three weeks weren't up yet. She had to be patient. Eugena would come through with a book deal. She had too many connections not too.

"Could we be any closer to the ground? And I know you're

going to end up buying one of these."

He shook his head. "Nope. I'm going to change my spending habits," he said as he pulled off. "A lot of people in my family lost their jobs and need my help. Money can only stretch so far. And you already know my momma wants it all."

"So what's this mean, instead of buying a pair of dress shoes for fifteen hundred, you're going to spend a thousand?"

He merged onto Interstate 85 north. "You're one to talk. You have so many pair of red soled shoes that I want to take a look at the soles of your feet; they're probably red now too."

"Seriously, you like spending money. But you have it, so I guess it's no big deal. All of us aren't able. That's all I'm saying."

"And seriously, I'm going to bring down some of my spending—private jets are a waste of money. I'm not above flying first-class. When I'm out of town, I don't have to spend eight or nine hundred a night for a room. I can get a decent place for half that."

"*You think*? You can get one for a third of that and still have a very nice room." Money was the last thing Olena wanted to think about. "I thought you'd bring the boys to brighten my day."

"You mean those grown men. Don't forget you promised them a slumber party because they haven't and neither has my mom. She needs a break," he said as he merged onto Interstate 75 north.

"Oh, my God is that next weekend?"

Jason nodded. Even though it had only been a week that Jason had been back to work. His mother had the boys for the three weeks prior while Jason was staying at Olena's recovering. So, Olena decided to step up and split the duty with her.

"I lost my job," she said in a near whisper.

"If you can't watch 'em next weekend that's fine, baby. Does Lutel want you to come back to work early?" He glanced over at her. "Is everything okay?"

She shook her head.

"I can tell something's wrong. I know my baby. What is it?"

"I lost my job." She turned and looked out the window at the cars whizzing by on northbound Interstate 75.

"What do you mean you lost your job? Why? Did the company go under or something?"

"No. The company didn't go under. They just expect me to do what I've been doing for not even half my salary." Her hands began to tremble. She could feel her heart beating rapidly. She loved her job. The only other thing she would rather be was a published author.

"That doesn't make sense. You were their best salesperson."

"Yeah, well, that just goes to show that none of that means anything because at the end of the day corporations run the show not employees. When they're ready to let you go, they will. No one's indispensable. I just wish that I'd planned better. Writing was supposed to be my plan B. I have to think up something and fast so I don't end up homeless."

Being homeless was one of her biggest fears and perhaps what drove her to accomplish so much, sacrificing her social life for career success. She'd seen it happen to one of her cousins. He was married and had three children. For a while, he did well with his own business that supplied auto parts to manufacturers. But a divorce and a class-action lawsuit brought on by some employees alleging unfair labor practices changed all that. A man who never used to drink beer became homeless and addicted to drugs and alcohol.

"Aw, baby." He rubbed her hand resting on her thigh. "It's going to be alright. I won't let you live on the street." He turned back to face her with a wide grin on his face. "I'll rent you a room."

"You don't understand because if you did you wouldn't be grinning and making corny jokes. Everyone wants to do something well. That job was something I did well. Now I don't have anything."

"You have me."

"You don't get it. You don't have money concerns, so you don't understand."

"You don't have money concerns either."

"Why don't I?"

"Because you have me, baby."

She leaned her head against the headrest and closed her eyes. "Everything I love leaves. You better not."

"Is that your lame way of saying you love me? You need to come better than that, Miss Day, much better."

"What am I going to do?"

"Live off of me. I won't even mind."

She grimaced at his words. She couldn't imagine not having her own money. If push came to shove, she knew he'd take care of her. But in her mind that wasn't a consideration. She didn't know what it felt like to receive money or gifts from a man. Jason was the first man to buy her anything—such a sad but true revelation. The diamond cross pendant he'd given her for her birthday was snatched from around her neck three weeks earlier as she sat writing inside a Buckhead coffee shop. The young man who'd stolen it looked to be in his teens. It happened so fast that if someone hadn't told her, she wouldn't have realized her necklace was gone until much later when she went to take it off. She'd wondered why he ran by her so quickly and bumped into her without saying excuse me. But she had no idea he'd snatched her precious necklace. Immediately following the incident, Olena started to reassess her obsession with the "finer things." If just like that, they could be taken away.

"Baby," Jason said as he squeezed her hand, "I got you. You don't have to worry about a thing."

She smiled. She wanted to believe him, and a large part of her did. But the other part that liked to whisper little reminders told her to remember one thing: When it feels too good to be true, it usually is.

FOUR

The next afternoon, at Eugena's request, Olena stopped by her condo. Ironically, they had both flown back from New York the day before. Eugena went for a week to lunch with some of her key contacts at the various publishing houses, and now she wanted to talk to Olena. Good news, Olena prayed.

At least, she still had her completed manuscript, and a literary agent shopping a deal for her love story slash mystery, since love was such a mystery. That's how she told Eugena to pitch the book. But Eugena, who'd been an agent for one of the largest diversified talent agencies in the world before opening her own agency, did what Eugena wanted to do. And she wasn't going to have an unpublished author tell her how to pitch a book. It didn't matter that they both attended Cass Technical High School together. They didn't know each other way back when, and they just so happened to live in the same building now. That's how Olena was fortunate enough to sign on with such a high-powered literary agent who only accepted new clients by referral. But she and

Eugena were eight floors and worlds apart.

"How was your meeting?" Eugena asked, sipping from a cocktail glass. She walked Olena into her sitting room where they relaxed on an ivory lounge sofa and talked.

"I should be asking you the same thing."

"I beat you to it." Eugena continued sipping her cocktail. "Is your sabbatical over? Do they want you back at work ASAP?"

"No, they don't want me back at all."

"Really?" Eugena narrowed her eyes. "I'm sorry to hear that." She fluttered her long lashes, fiddled with her straight hair, and took a larger gulp of her vodka.

"I thought you were trying to give up drinking."

"The key word in that sentence is *trying*. It's not easy. We all have our addictions. For some, it's food. For others, drugs. For me, some Chopin from time to time. What's yours?"

After a shrug, Olena said, "Maybe it's love…*and* food. I do love food."

Eugena shook her head and laughed. "If you were addicted to love, you would have been married two or three times by now. You didn't even date anyone for seven years. A love addict always needs to be in a relationship."

Evidently, Olena had neglected to tell Eugena about the affair she had with her boss. But it might have been during a time Eugena drank too much and couldn't remember what Olena had told her. Olena would leave it at that since that was a time in her life she wanted to leave in the past.

"Maybe I don't have one."

"Everyone has an addiction."

"Getting published. That's my addiction. How's my book deal coming? Did you get me one yet because I really need it?"

"Fiction can be a hard sell."

"*What?* Wait a minute. Why the change in your tune all of a sudden? Just a couple of months ago you were rushing me to get you the finished manuscript because you said you could get me a two-book deal. You said it would go to auction. You loved it or so you said. Now, all of a sudden, fiction is a hard sell. What happened to the editor you said was interested?"

"They're doing a lot of shuffling at these publishing companies. My dearest friend, a senior editor at one of the biggest houses, retired after thirty-five years. She was fed up. She used to tell me the only way she'd leave was in her casket. She went from loving the business to not being able to stand it. I can't even get her on the phone. I've placed most of my new authors with her. She was supposed to buy your book."

"Okay, well, let's not focus on just one person. What did the rest say?"

"Olena, it takes time."

"*Time*? Time is something I don't have. I close deals in a week. Well, I used to—sometimes days, a lot of times the same day."

"We're talking about a book deal. You can't close a book deal in days. Under certain circumstances, you can, but, not in yours."

"But *you* said—"

"I know what I said, Olena. You don't have to keep reminding me. At the time, that's what I meant. How was I supposed to know there'd be so many changes in the publishing world?"

"You've been in the business long enough to have more than one connection."

"I have connections, but for my celebrity books. Straight fiction by a first time author is a hard sell."

Olena shook her head slowly.

"My life is falling apart. I made mistakes in my past, but I really felt as if I'd gotten myself together."

In a matter of just two days, she'd lost her plan A and B. And she refused to make Jason her plan C. She loved him, but she didn't want to live off of him. With as much money as Olena had made over the last seven years, she expected for her savings to put her in a better position. To last long enough that she didn't have to worry as much as she was. Now, she was able to accept that living above her means had been one of her self-destructive issues much like loving the wrong men. And living in Atlanta— especially Buckhead—didn't help matters. She wasn't into the club scene; she was too old for that. But she *was* into the shopping scene, and there were plenty of stores for her to choose from.

Olena got in her own way by trying so hard to prove to people what she had. She knew it all stemmed from her humble upbringing, and her parents never being able to afford the best, but she always wanted it. And now all she had were bills and maybe… *maybe*, between her severance pay and her savings, enough to live on for a year. So what she simply needed Eugena to do was try to get her a book deal.

"I'm still going to try to sell your book. I'll get you some kind of deal. When I say I'm going to do something, I deliver."

"I feel blah. I feel really blah. And I hate feeling like this. I was in my twenties the last time I felt this way." Olena shook her head and took a moment to compose herself. "Did you know J.K. Rowling used to be homeless?"

"J.K. Rowling was not homeless. I wonder where that rumor came from."

"Is it a rumor?"

"She was in a bad way, a single mother, struggling financially. But she had a place to live."

"She didn't have an agent at the time. I have one, and I'm supposed to be right there at the threshold of a book deal. Remember what you saw in my story and what made you so excited about it at first. One of your connections is gone, but there are more out there." Olena shrugged. "Remember who you are?"

"It's not about me, Olena. It's about you. Start blogging. Get about fifty to a hundred thousand followers; then, maybe I can do something."

"Did you just say fifty to a hundred *thousand* followers? I'd be lucky to get *fifty* to a *hundred* followers period."

"Are you on Facebook? Open a YouTube channel and talk about fashion since you love to shop or skincare since your skin looks great. Do you have a Twitter account? It would be so great if you had a celebrity friend."

"What?" Olena didn't want to start making videos about skin care. She loved to shop, but she couldn't imagine making videos about that, either. Call her old fashioned, but she didn't even like texting, so there was no way she would start blogging. "Why do I have to do all of that to get a book deal? I could see if I were trying to promote the book, but just to get a deal."

"It's a new day. You have to get noticed now. Look at all of the YouTube singers who either have deals or received national media attention. Imagine if you were on television. Most books don't sell, because of lack of exposure. These days, word of mouth is through the Internet or television. Put an author on TV and watch what happens."

"Well, I don't know how to sing, and I don't think talking about my skin is going to get me on Oprah. But, if she loves my book, I might get on there. That's *if* I ever get published."

"Listen, I have big name celebrities who can't even get on Oprah, so you might as well throw that fantasy out the window, too."

"Too? What other fantasy should I throw out—getting published?

"I haven't given up. It just might not be with one of the major publishers, and the advances are not what they used to be, let me warn you upfront. If you were expecting six-figures, that's not going to happen. I'll be lucky to get you ten-thousand on your first book."

"Say what? Ten thousand dollars. I have a handbag that cost more than that."

It didn't have to be a seven-figure deal like Olena had fantasized many nights over. But, a decent deal would be appreciated. And to someone like Olena, whose mortgage was twelve thousand dollars a month, ten thousand dollars just wouldn't cut it.

"Writers aren't rich, Olena. There are very few writers doing well enough where they don't have to work a second job. Selling a book right now, in this volatile publishing environment, is a challenge even for people who are already published. I prefer being up-front with my clients. Things are changing quickly, and writers and publishers have to change too."

Olena went home and crawled in bed. On the first day of her shut-in, she got out of bed only to use the bathroom. On the other three days, she would get out of bed to get something to eat and use the bathroom and go right back to bed. She had a pity party and no one was invited but her.

"Snap out of it," Jason said to her over the phone.

"I will…eventually."

"Olena, be thankful for the things you do have."

"Like what?"

"Your health…me…your family, people who love you. It's going to be okay."

She let out a long sigh. "This is the way I deal with things. I don't expect someone who's never been faced with a financial crisis to understand."

"My mother was a single parent with eight boys. She worked two, sometimes, three jobs. We lived in public housing. So, please don't tell me, I never faced a financial crisis. I'm doing well now, but I can still remember the times our utilities got shut off, and we didn't have enough food to eat. My mother had to take two buses to get to work, and she didn't get home until ten or eleven at night. All I ever wanted back then was for my mother not to worry about money and bills…about anything. And all I want to do now is the same for you. I know you're an independent woman, but I'm a man who wants nothing more than to take care of the woman he loves. I love you, baby. And when I say, I got you, I mean that."

Olena was speechless. What could she say after that? When she tried to respond, he said, "End of discussion. My boys and I are going to snap you out of this funk you're in. I'm not going to let you renege on this weekend."

"Is it this weekend?"

"Yes, Olena, it's this weekend."

Olena's doorbell rang. Before she left her bedroom, she had examined herself in the mirror that was in her master bathroom. "I guess I look alright. One thing's for sure, I'm well rested." She got out for the first time in nearly a week, yesterday. She went to Starbuck's for her favorite drink—a white chocolate mocha. Then, she returned home to change her bedding and do laundry. "I'm sure I'm overdressed for the occasion, but oh well," she said with a shrug. She had on a gray color-blocked sweater dress that had a crossover V-neckline and inset empire waist.

She felt as if she were going on a first date with the man of her dreams. When, in fact, it was time for her to babysit Jason's two sons. The time had finally arrived. It was Friday, and she'd be watching Jason's boys all by herself starting the next day—her first taste of motherhood.

"Just a minute," she said in a singsong voice as she scurried down the long hallway leading to the foyer. She took another look at herself, this time in the round accent mirror hanging in her foyer beside the door. Then, she opened her front door and greeted the trio with a smile. "Hi guys."

"What took you so long to open this door?" Jamal, the three year old, asked with a deep-set frown. He stormed in, dragging his backpack with him.

"My…my…my, aren't we dressed up," Jason said. He leaned over to give Olena a hug. "Were you expecting me and my sons or someone else?" he whispered in her ear.

"Ha…ha…ha. Aren't we going out?"

"To the *Cheesecake Factory*. You don't have to dress up to go there."

"Okay, well, I wanted to look nice for my guys. I didn't know we were going to the Cheesecake Factory, *again*." She had gotten burned out after eating there with Jason every day for a week a few weeks earlier.

"That's where the boys want to go."

She threw up her hands. "If that's where the boys want to go, I'm certainly not going to argue with them."

Jason stared into her eyes. "Is everything okay?"

Olena nodded reassuringly. "Everything's fine. I'm just starving that's all. Is anyone else hungry?"

"Yeah," Jamal shouted, "I am."

Junior was quiet as usual. He spoke up when he needed to and when he needed to was usually when he was brutally honest."

Jason took her hand after they all walked into the hallway.

"I don't want you to worry. You never have to worry about anything," he said to her.

"I'm fine. Don't you worry." She wasn't even going to tell him about the book deal falling through. One disappointment after another would make him feel sorry for her, and she didn't want that. "But I am starving."

Later that evening, after the boys were tucked safely in their guest beds, Olena and Jason retreated to her bedroom across the hall from where the boys slept. She needed a release, and she had a man in her bed who doctors had given the all-clear to, for sex, or to at least make an attempt to have sex. He picked up on her cues: her foot brushing against his leg and her arms rubbing his hairless chest.

He said, "I can satisfy you in other ways, baby. That's if you let me. Will you?"

She nodded slowly as his head disappeared underneath the sheets. Her moans started within seconds and grew louder, so loud that he had to cover her mouth and stop pleasing her orally to remind her that his kids were in the nearby bedroom. She'd forgotten. He made her feel so good that she forgot about Lutel and a book deal and her future money problems and his kids who were in the other room. So, maybe she had an addiction after all—sex. She wasn't a nympho, by any means, but she thought about sex often.

Jason had a long tongue, and he went deeper and deeper, alternating between fast and slow movements, hard and soft. She grabbed hold of the flat sheet in her right hand and ripped off the fitted sheet with her left. Then, she used both of her hands to caress the top of his head. "I need you to *fuck* me," she shouted.

The oral stimulation suddenly stopped. He came from underneath the cover and turned on his side with his back facing her.

"I'm sorry."

"My boys are right across the hall, and you were kind of loud. But you don't have to apologize. I know I can't satisfy you."

"Baby, don't say that."

"It's the truth; it's just a matter of time before you leave me."

"I'm not going to leave you."

"Good night."

"Don't cut me off. Let's talk about this."

"No. I don't want to talk. I want to sleep. I'm flying out early tomorrow. And you're going to need all the rest you can get because my boys are going to wear you out, trust me."

He usually flew out on Saturday and returned on Tuesday.

"I love you," she said to reassure him.

"We'll see."

The next morning Jason left for the airport without waking Olena. She was surprised when she opened her eyes, and the space beside hers was empty. She was shocked that he would leave without saying goodbye and that she never heard him getting ready.

"Rise and shine," she said as she tapped her knuckles against the bedroom door Jason's kids were in. She cracked it open. "You boys need to start getting ready because I'm taking you to IHOP."

The room the two boys were in had been the only empty room in Olena's condo. She had been trying to decide what to make of it, so to make the boys feel even more at home after she had volunteered to start watching them, Jason bought the furniture, a flat-screen TV, Nintendo Wii game set, and a chest filled with toys.

"You have to get Jamal ready," Jason, Jr. said.

"*I* have to get him ready."

Junior nodded. "He's only three."

"True. And for you," she said to Jason, Jr, "the bathroom is right across the hall." Olena walked over to the twin bed Jamal slept in.

"Pick me up," Jamal said, stretching his arms out toward her.

"So, you want to be a baby today and not a big boy?"

Jamal nodded. "I am a baby."

"Sometimes you want to be a baby. Other times you act like a grown little man. You're too heavy for me to pick up. I'm not as strong as your dad, so take my hand. But first pick out the clothes you want to wear." He reached in his backpack that was beside the bed and pulled out a pair of khaki pants, a long-sleeved V-neck striped shirt, and Marvel comic briefs. "Perfect, you did a great job." He held her hand and stood from the bed, and Olena guided him into her master bathroom. "How is this normally done?" she asked Jamal as she took a wash cloth and towel from her linen closet. "You take a bath, right?" Jamal shook his head.

"You don't take a bath? Do you wash up?"

Jamal shook his head again.

"So you just go out the house stinky?"

"No," Jamal said, giggling.

"So how do you get cleaned up?"

"I take a shower with my dad."

"What about when your dad's not there, and it's just your grandma?"

"She gives me a bath."

"So that's what I'm going to do." She walked over to the tub and started to run the water. "You're going to take a big boy bath, and I'm going to stay in here with you just to make sure you're okay. But I'm not going to look because if I'm not your mom or dad or your grandparents, I shouldn't look."

"You are my mom."

"I'm not your mom, Jamal. You know that."

"Daddy said you were going to be."

"Your dad said that," she said gushing.

He nodded.

"Well, until I officially become your mom we're going to do it the way I said, okay?"

Jamal nodded.

She turned off the water once it reached his waistline. "Here's your towel and a new bar of organic soap." She looked at his blank expression. "I know you don't know what that means, but it's better for your skin. It doesn't have any chemicals." She helped him take his clothes off and held his hand as he climbed in. She sat on the floor, sinking her toes into her soft, silk blended white bath rug that lay over her travertine marble floor.

"Daddy said you got fired," Jamal said as he sat in the tub, rubbing his arm with the washcloth.

"Your dad told you that?"

He nodded. "Why they fire you? They didn't like you no more."

"I guess they didn't. Do you still like me?" He nodded. "What else did your dad say?"

"Nothing."

"Do you like taking a bath?"

He nodded.

"Daddy said you were sad, and he didn't want you to be sad, and he said he's going to take care of you for the rest of his life."

"Did he really say that?"

He nodded.

"What else did your dad say?"

"Nothing. But my grandma said something."

"What did your grandma say?"

"What's a prenup? Grandma told daddy to get one."

Olena smiled. That sounded just like something Jason's mother would say because she was all about protecting her son's money. "It's a contract. A piece of paper that a wealthy person has another person sign before they agree to get married so if it doesn't work out the wealthy person won't lose anything."

"Daddy said you didn't have to sign that."

"I would sign one. Do you know why?"

He shook his head.

"Because I love your daddy and I love you," she said, poking playfully at his chest, "and I love little Jason and your grandma… and I don't need your daddy's money." Jamal started giggling as he covered his face with his wet hands.

"You're all done, and it's time to get dressed." She stood and held open the ivory bath towel. She wrapped it around Jamal after she helped him step out of the tub.

"Grandma never takes us to IHOP. Grandma always makes us breakfast from scratch because nobody can make breakfast better than my grandma."

"You don't want to go to IHOP?"

He shook his head. "I want to go to grandma's."

What was she supposed to say? You can't go to grandma's because she needs a break. No, she couldn't say that. "Don't you like being here with me?"

"I like being here, but I like being at grandma's more. You don't have snacks," he said while Olena dressed him.

"I do have snacks."

"They're not good like grandma's."

"They're healthy snacks."

"They're yucky snacks."

"I'll tell you what," she said as she helped him step inside his briefs and put his khaki pants on. "After we leave IHOP, we'll go to Whole Foods, and I'll let you boys pick out whatever you want as long as it's not a lot of junk food. Deal?"

He nodded. "Grandma don't shop there. She shops at People's."

"People's. Do you mean Publix?"

He nodded. "Are you going to cook us breakfast tomorrow and take us to church?"

"Church?"

"Tomorrow's Sunday—God's day."

Olena certainly believed in God, but she couldn't remember the last time she went to church. And from what she recalled, Jason attended the same church as Matthew and the last thing she wanted to do was run into Matthew with or without Jason's two sons. "I'll have to give you a rain check on church," she said as she guided a fully dressed Jamal out of the bathroom and into the hallway where his brother stood, waiting.

"Rain check on church?" Junior asked, overhearing the conversation. "God doesn't take those."

"That explains a whole lot," Olena said as she led the boys toward the front door to leave.

FIVE

October

It was Wednesday afternoon. The kids were back with Jason and had been since the prior evening. Olena found it a hard to believe, but she, someone who was never a big fan of children, actually missed the boys. She wanted them to be in her condo when she returned from Eugena's. She didn't miss driving them to school early in the morning *all* the way in Alpharetta, which wasn't actually far. But to Olena, who ran almost all of her errands in or near Buckhead, it seemed like an endless ride on US-19.

Before the elevator door closed, her mind had been racing with so many thoughts: her job, Jason, Jason's sons, Matthew, a book deal, Eugena, ATLTELLS, and even the mysterious woman who she kept running into in her building who was already on the elevator when Olena stepped inside.

After she had caught the young woman staring at her, Olena wanted to ask, *"Do we know each other?"*

The stylish young woman carried herself well enough to make

someone wonder who she was and what she did for a living. Olena wondered if she were one of Jason's many ex-flings. She looked like his type—tall and slender with a big chest and long hair. In some ways, the two of them favored, but the woman staring at Olena was ten or more years younger than her. Instead of black hair like Olena's, hers was light brown. Instead of gray eyes, the young woman's were hazel. Her lips weren't as full as Olena's. Olena's hair wasn't as long as hers. Instead of Louis Vuitton, the young woman showed an affinity for Burberry as evidenced by the checked canvas hobo bag she wore slung over her shoulder; the checked lined walking umbrella she grasped a hold of and the solid-to-check silk scarf bow-tied around her long neck. The last time Olena had seen the young woman was two days earlier while she wrote a chapter to her new book in the mansion lounge that overlooked the English Gardens. The time before—a week earlier—Olena had been in the café of her building drinking cocktails with lewd names and trying to unwind as she mulled over a few of her current dilemmas: her job or lack thereof, the impending sleepover with Jason's kids, and Jason's impotence.

The first sleepover was officially over, but there would be others. She definitely loved Jason but was she in love with him. She certainly had to question herself because there were still times that crept up where she fantasized about Matthew, reminiscing over the many intimate moments they shared together.

Olena inhaled, sucking in her waist after she noticed the eyes of the woman on the elevator glancing at her stomach. Were her Spanx not doing a good enough job of sucking in her belly fat? She may have ruined them in the wash. Were they supposed to be hand washed and line dried? God, she hoped not. She hated hand washing and had stretched out more than a few of her favorite bras by tossing them into the washing machine along with everything else.

Olena wore a belted brown tweed dress with a ruffled surplice neckline and a hemline that hit just above the knee. Eugena said to come dressed for a deal, and that's what she did.

Olena flashed a smile. "Good morning."

"Good morning," the woman said dryly as she turned the corners of her mouth up slightly while she slung her right eyebrow.

Ooh, Olena hated that. How coldly women acted toward each other, at times. It made no sense to her. She had experienced that same attitude at the company she worked prior to Lutel. She was a retail credit analyst there, and many of the women who worked with her were extremely catty. That's why she loved the freedom that her sales job at Lutel had provided; she wasn't stuck inside of an office.

I bet it's that blog, thought Olena. She remembered the Atlanta-based entertainment and celebrity blog ATLTELLS that posted a picture of her leaving Jeffrey, an upscale clothing boutique in Buckhead, with several shopping bags as she headed toward Jason's Bentley. Underneath the photo was the caption:

WORD ON THE CURB: This is the new woman in a popular baller's life. Pop the hood to see which one.

So Olena clicked on the link, and her picture was beside Jason's in his Atlanta Falcons uniform above a paragraph that read:

Our sources tell us that former NFL great and future Hall of Famer Jason Nix is getting some TLC from this woman. If any of my readers know her, please e-mail me her name, so I can get my investigators right on it. My sources tell me that she's a cougar approaching 50. If they're right and she's that old, "She's a Bad Mama Jama", just as fine as she can be, I had to take it old school in her honor. Any who, the reason we haven't seen Jason Nix, our favorite piece of eye candy, on Fox Sports lately, and why we probably won't see him at the Compound any time soon, either, is because he's said to be recovering from a mysterious illness. Let's hope it's nothing too serious. Nothing related to all the years he played the field, and I'm not talking football.

Approaching fifty? Not hardly, Olena thought. She was six years away from that milestone. And how did that person even know anything about Jason being ill? Jason was much better now and was back at work, so whoever wrote that blog obviously hadn't watched Fox Sports lately. Olena had never been on the blog, ATLTELLS, before, because she wasn't one to read those types of things. But it was obviously quite popular, since her niece, Alicia, was the one who called and left a playful message saying, "I thought I was the only soon-to-be famous one in the family. How did you get on ATLTELLS? You better call me before I e-mail your name, age, and cell phone number to the site administrator." That was a few weeks back, and Olena hadn't returned her niece's call. She was still a little upset over the loss of her job and didn't feel like talking, especially not to Alicia, even as close as the two of them were. She considered her niece to be her best friend; she was closer to Alicia than she was her own sister (Alicia's mother) and provided her niece with a lot of financial support while she was in LA trying to land her first big break. She didn't want Alicia to worry about whether or not she was still going to help her with the rent. Olena would figure something out. She wasn't broke yet.

She did confide in her mother about losing her job. She told her not to tell the rest of the family, which included Olena's father. What she hadn't told her mother was that she could have stayed with the company, earning much less. She knew how her mother was and what she would've said, "Some money is better than none at all." Olena needed a whole lot more than some money. She needed a *whole* lot of money. So, instead, she'd told her mom that she was laid off. Lutel could call it a lay-off if they wanted to and give her a flimsy severance package equal to one year's base salary. But Olena felt as if she'd been fired effective the beginning of the year. What a way to start off a New Year?

When the elevator door opened on Eugena's floor, Olena and the mysterious woman exited and turned left. They walked down the long hallway and stopped in front of Eugena's door. Olena felt slightly uncomfortable. Was the young woman a fellow scribe? If so, Eugena better get Olena a deal first.

"Is Eugena your agent?" Olena asked.

"No. She represents you, and that's why I'm here."

Olena's eyes flashed dollar signs. Editors were coming to Eugena's house. She knew Eugena had a roster filled with high-profile authors and was a well-respected agent who'd lived in New York for years, but she didn't know she had it like that.

They stood in front of the door to Eugena's condo, eyeing each other.

Olena couldn't help herself. "Are you with Random House?" That was the publishing company Olena had her eye on because that was the publisher her 4l Maya Angelou was with.

"No," the young woman said dryly.

"Penguin?"

"No."

"HarperCollins?" *Should she continue?* She knew the names of all the major publishers.

"Simon and Schuster…Hachette."

Olena ran out of names, and the woman didn't even blink.

"I'm with Media One," the woman said as she rang Eugena's doorbell.

"*Media One?* Hmmm, I've never heard of that publishing company."

"We're not a publishing company."

At that moment, Eugena's door flung open.

"You two arrived together. What perfect timing. Have you already introduced yourselves?"

"Not really," Olena said.

"Godiva Hart, this is Olena Day. Please come in."

The two women followed behind Eugena—down a long hallway and through the French doors leading to her spacious office.

"Ladies, have a seat. I'm so excited about this."

Olena smiled, but she didn't know why, maybe because Eugena was. She had never seen Eugena so happy.

"Godiva, tell Olena a little something about yourself and your inspirational story?"

"I've told my story a gazillion times."

"Make it a gazillion and one," Eugena said.

Godiva paused for a second while a look of disdain surfaced.

"Godiva is the President of Media One, which is a local production company that she and her husband opened five years ago—"

"*Seven* actually."

"I'm sorry, seven. See, that's why it's best for you to tell your story."

"So you're like Tyler Perry because I have a niece who—"

"No, I'm not like Tyler Perry," Godiva said, cutting off Olena. "We don't produce movies—at least not yet. We're a media company that produces and distributes reality shows for syndication. We produce the *Real Beauty* franchise that airs on VH1," she said as if Olena should be familiar with it. "*Real Beauty Atlanta…New York…Dallas…Detroit—*"

"Detroit, oh, okay," Olena said.

"You've never heard of the *Real Beauty* franchise?" Godiva asked.

"No. I'm sorry I'm not that much of a TV watcher."

"My God, have you been under a rock?" Eugena said. "*Real Beauty Atlanta.* How could you miss those billboards all over the place, including I-20?"

"I've probably seen them but didn't know what the show was all about."

"Tell her how you got started," Eugena said.

"I did casting for some videos. That's sort of how everything got started. I developed a lot of connections. My husband and I sold our first reality show to VH1. Now, we have twenty shows airing across various cable networks with ten more in production."

"That's great," Olena said as she crossed and uncrossed her legs.

"Have you told her yet?" Godiva asked Eugena.

"No, you can. I'm sure you'll do a better job."

"We have a show called *The One* that we're extremely excited about."

"*The One*," Olena repeated with a question mark to her tone.

"That's right. It's our first show on network television. You do know what I mean when I say network."

"ABC, NBC—" Olena replied.

"Right. So far all of our reality shows have been on cable, so network television is a huge opportunity, especially if it does well. Eugena has spoken highly of you, and we have a part that we need to fill quickly."

"*A part?*" Olena questioned. "I thought you said it was a reality show."

"That's right. We're looking for our bachelorette. We had her, but she fell through. So, now we have this opportunity. Obviously, you don't have to accept. And we'd still need to get you approved by the network execs, but hopefully that won't be a problem."

"I'm lost. I'm a writer or at least I'm trying to be. I'm not a reality TV star."

Eugena said, "Olena, sometimes we let good opportunities pass us by that we regret later. And I don't want that to happen in this case."

"Is this an early April Fool's?" Olena said.

"I don't have time to play games," Godiva said. "I take my business very seriously as does my husband and all of our staff."

"I just never expected to be offered a reality show. I don't even know how people wind up on those things in the first place."

"Typically, they audition for them. But, I've worked with Eugena in the past, and she sold me on you."

"First of all, you said the show is called, *The One*. What kind of show is that?"

"It's a dating reality show."

"A dating reality show?" Olena laughed so hard her head flung back and hit the top of Eugena's couch.

"What's so funny?" Godiva asked.

"I'm not looking for a date. I don't need to be fixed up. I'm not single, and I'm very happy in my relationship." Olena wiped a few tears from her eyes. "Whoa, but thanks for the laugh. You just don't know; I needed it."

She glanced back at Godiva who stared right through her. "Are you interested?" Godiva asked.

Olena wondered if Godiva heard what she just said. Just in case, she repeated the most important part, "I'm in a relationship, which means, no, I'm not interested."

"Most people who go on those shows are in a relationship. We don't care about that. What we're looking for is someone with a dynamic personality and universal appeal. Do you think you have those two qualities?"

Eugena said, "Olena, it's an opportunity to get exposure. And the more exposure the better for your book deal."

Olena shook her head slowly. "I can't do that. If I value my relationship at all, which I definitely do, I can't do that."

"Okay, well, why don't you take a few days to think about it," Godiva said as she stood. "We kind of sprung the whole thing on you. I have another meeting to go to, and it's pouring outside. I'm not going to speed, but I also don't want to be late, so that means I got to go."

"Thanks, doll," Eugena said as she planted an air kiss to each of Godiva's cheeks. "We'll talk soon."

Eugena walked Godiva to the front door.

Olena remained seated, going over in her mind what was said and becoming more confused by the minute.

Eugena returned a few minutes later with a glass of vodka in her hand. She sat on the sofa beside Olena.

"For someone who's so good at selling, you did a poor job of selling yourself that time. Did you hear her say the show would be on network television?"

"Yes, I heard her. But I don't care what channel it's on; it's a stupid reality show."

"You want to write. And you want a decent contract. Reality TV is just another way to break you into the business."

"Eugena, are you drunk? Put the vodka down." Olena grabbed the glass from Eugena's hand and placed it on the distressed ionic capital coffee table. "People don't go on reality shows because they want to write. They go on those things hoping they'll become famous. Acting is my niece's department, not mine. Writing doesn't take all that. All it should take is a good book, which I have. Now all you have to do is sell it."

"I can't sell it." Eugena put her right hand on her forehead and huffed out a heavy sigh. "I've tried. No one wants it. They're not going to buy it. They've read that type of story before. It's just not something that they're interested in. I'm sorry."

"*They?* Who are they? How many publishers—"

"I sent it to all the major publishers and even some of my contacts at some of the other houses. I'm sorry."

"They didn't like it."

"It didn't wow them."

"But, I thought you said you'd get me something."

"It wasn't the writing, Olena. Everyone wants to write, and everyone *is* writing—the power of the Internet. Good for them, but not good for us. The big names are protected. Everyone else is left scrambling, and every now and then an unknown writer emerges with a breakout novel. Unfortunately, they don't think yours is one. I wanted to get you something in place of the book deal. I know how much you want that."

"I don't think you know. I've had this dream since I was eighteen years old, actually, before then. I'm forty-four. I don't know. I read about new authors landing deals every day. I don't know what I'm doing wrong."

"When I first started out in the business, writers like you were the only ones I dealt with. People who were writing because they loved creating stories, it wasn't just another piece to their brand. But you can't look back and remember the way things were. You have to change with the times. I understand not everyone who wants to write can just hop on a reality show, but *you* can. Sometimes it's not about what you know; it's all in who you know." Olena's head slowly nodded. "And you know me, and I know Godiva."

Eugena retrieved her glass of vodka from the coffee table and took another sip.

"No offense, but why are agents the gatekeepers to a publishing deal? I can sell my work better than you or anyone else can."

"Why because you were great at selling phones?"

"Integrated phone systems. When you say selling phones you make it sound as if I were at a Sprint store or something."

"I've built a twenty year career in the publishing business. I started off as an assistant and worked my way up, so don't think you can do my job better than I can because you can't."

"I'm not a reality star, Eugena. I can't do something that I dislike, and I *hate* reality TV. Have you seen the way black women are portrayed on those shows? All they do is fuel the stereotype of the *angry* black woman—the type of woman that no man wants. Whether people realize it or not, those images are damaging our youth. I don't want to contribute to that."

"It's entertainment, Olena. Don't make it out to be any more than that."

"At whose expense? Every time a black woman goes on a reality show, she ends up the villain. It sets us back a hundred years."

"A reality show doesn't set blacks back at all. Everyone is made to look foolish on reality TV. Otherwise, no one would even watch. It's entertainment just like writing. If all the characters were happy, you wouldn't have a story. We're talking about network television. We're talking about millions of viewers knowing your name. So when your book comes out it's no longer, 'Who's Olena Day?' It's, 'Oh, Olena Day'. That's called brand recognition and *that* my dear is what sells books these days."

Olena shrugged. "Why me? I'm sure they can get any number of people—models even, so why me? Does she owe you some huge favor?"

"We owe each other favors. But I will be honest, she was a lot more interested after I told her that you were Jason's girlfriend."

"So this is about Jason."

"When he came back to TV, there was some talk about the weight he'd lost. Is he okay?"

"Yes. He's fine. Of course, he's a little smaller. He's retired so he doesn't have to work out every day."

"Most of the retired athletes I see get bigger not smaller."

"He's fine." Olena quickly changed the subject to stop herself from saying something about Jason that she'd regret later. "I guess I have to do what I have to do, and I might just have to do a reality show—*might*—no guarantees. What do I have to lose besides my dignity and self-respect?"

SIX

How could someone Eugena said was so right turn out to be so wrong? Godiva wondered as she sucked on the tip of her Burberry shades and stared across the square table at Olena. This was the woman Eugena sold her on, but somehow she'd forgotten to mention one extremely important detail—her age.

Olena met with Godiva and her husband at close to eight o'clock in the evening. They decided to meet at a neutral spot—The Café—inside of The Mansions on Peachtree, where Olena lived, and the Harts were staying temporarily.

"Forty-four?" Godiva asked, hoping the number would be adjusted like the ratings for some of her shows. In this case, she needed the number to go down, not up. Maybe she hadn't heard Olena correctly. Maybe she'd said thirty-four not forty-four. And even that would be older than she preferred. "That's how old you are?"

"All day every day until June 12th," Olena said with a smile.

"I don't know why I assumed you were a lot younger than that."

"People always say I look young."

"It's because of Jason," Godiva clarified, refusing to issue any compliments. "He's thirty-two, so I just assumed—"

"Well, you know what they say about assuming." Olena picked up a piece of asparagus with her fork. Her attempt at humor fell on Godiva's deaf ears. She'd already begun brainstorming, looking for an upside to having a middle-aged bachelorette, but so far she couldn't find one. Who would want to see that? Week after week, watching a woman who was forty-four, never married, and didn't have kids look for love. The first thing people would assume was something must be wrong with her. A devilish grin quickly surfaced on Godiva's face. "What's wrong?" Olena asked.

"Nothing. Don't take this the wrong way or anything," Godiva said. "Because you'll find with me that I'm pretty straightforward. I'm worried that a forty-four-year-old bachelorette might not be received that well by viewers. Let's face it, if you haven't found love by now, what's wrong with you? We know you're in a serious relationship with Jason, but viewers won't know that. You've never been married, right?"

"Right."

"No kids, right?"

"Correct."

"Are you following me?"

"No," Olena said with an attitude. Godiva had struck the wrong nerve. "Do you know how many single women there are in the world? A lot...let me tell you."

"Yes, there might be a lot, but I think once you get to that point, and you still haven't found the one, you're pretty much resigned to being alone and just writing off your love life."

"Once you get to what point? What do you mean by writing it off? I'm not writing anything off. I'm very much in love—"

"I know you're in love. We know that, but the audience won't. You can't take anything I'm saying personal. I'm simply brainstorming right now. You always have to think like the viewers.

Your clock has stopped ticking. They want to see the fairy tale wedding and envision a happily-ever-after existence with plenty of babies to come. At forty-four, the baby making days are over."

"That's not true. I can still have kids. I'm not sure I'd want to at this age."

"*Exactly*," Godiva said, stretching the word. "That's what I'm saying. But what we could do is fudge your age a little bit…well, a lot. You could pass for thirty-four."

"Age is just a number," Olena said with a dismissive shrug. "That's how I try to look at it. But I could pass for twenty-something, at least that's what I've been told."

"Age is a number that can be changed," Smith added. "Oscar Wilde once said, 'One should never trust a woman who tells her real age. A woman who would tell that would tell anything.' " The long hours and frequent business trips to meet network executives and pitch show ideas had worn on Smith, whose hair was prematurely gray.

Olena yawned. "Oh, excuse me for that. That was rude. I only had two hours of sleep last night. I stayed up writing." Up all night. Well, at least her lack of sleep could help explain why the whites of Olena's eyes were red. Godiva thought it was because of her age. "I went online and googled the show, and I'm confused about something."

"Confused about what?" Godiva said dryly.

"A few things, actually. What kind of dating show is this? Is it basically a clone of *The Bachelorette*; is it like *Millionaire Matchmaker*? What's the premise?"

"We're taking a successful, single woman, such as yourself, and matching her up with ten of the world's most eligible bachelors. It's not a competitive show like The Bachelorette. The men are never all in the same place at the same time. That's why the media is billing it a cross between The Bachelorette and Millionaire Matchmaker minus having the matchmaker. Every time you go to a new city, there's a new date. It's simple, just remember our tagline: Ten eligible bachelors, ten romantic cities, one difficult decision."

"I get that."

"Trust me, when those cameras start rolling you'll have no choice but to get all of it," Godiva said, flashing a fake smile. The other problem Godiva had with Olena was that she wasn't quite sure if she even liked her and that was a significant problem. Not because she couldn't work with somebody she didn't like, but because if Godiva didn't like her, America might not. You have to like someone to tune in and watch them find love. And there was one thing she genuinely liked about Olena, and that was Jason Nix. It was the only reason she even entertained the idea of having Olena become the first bachelorette of the new series. "Any more questions?"

"I also read that some reality show person was cast for the show and had to drop out or something."

"*Reality show person*? Are you referring to Gwen Meyers?"

"Is that her name?"

Gwen Meyers was the poster child for reality TV success. She started off on season one of *Real Beauty Boston* and became known for her love for dogs. She had three Pomeranians: Uno, Dos, and Tres. She started a toy line for dogs and then a doggy clothing line. She opened the dog boutique Bitchy and offered franchise opportunities. Last year, she was the highest-paid reality star, and Olena had never heard of her?

Godiva turned and stared at her husband and quickly turned back and glared at Olena, who sat directly across from her. "You've never heard of Gwen Meyers? The woman is a major brand, and you've never heard of her?"

"No. I've never heard of her."

"Eugena reps her."

"Well, Eugena reps a lot of people. Is she a reality star or something?"

"Do you watch reality TV?" Godiva asked as she buttered her knife.

Olena's eyes enlarged and froze in that position.

"Honestly—"

"Please."

"I've tried watching a few of them, and I just don't get it."

"You just don't get what?" Godiva snapped. "You just don't get being entertained? You just don't get that?"

"*Dexter* is entertaining. So is *Weeds* and *Curb Your Enthusiasm*. I just don't get the public's fascination with reality shows."

Godiva grinned and nodded. "You're one of those HBO/ Showtime fanatics." Godiva was a bit biased against the two networks as they'd turned down more than a few of her pitches in the past. "Gwen was perfect for *The One*, let me just say that."

"What made her so perfect?"

"America loved her already from *Real Beauty Boston*. She runs a huge salon and spa out there."

"Do you think America will love me?"

"*Umm*, I'm not sure, it's hard to predict what America will think of you. America already loves Gwen. She's already been on TV and built up quite a following. And she's young and—" Godiva stopped suddenly.

"And she's young and what?" Olena asked.

"And…she's already been on TV."

"I'd be the first bachelorette of color on a major network."

"I never really put much thought into any of that."

"There's never been a person of color on *The Bachelorette* or *The Bachelor*," Olena repeated.

"Stop, please, let's not play the race card. I can't stand that." Why did blacks always feel so free to talk about race whenever they spoke to Godiva and Smith? Perhaps for the same reason they always assumed the Harts voted for Obama, which they had not. It was because they were black. The last time Godiva checked money was green, and that was the only color she wanted to discuss.

Olena's eyes darted. "Did you just say I was playing the race card?" Olena said with laughter. "It's not a *card* it's a *fact*. Do you think it's a coincidence that there's *never* been a person of color, *any* person of color, on either of those shows?"

Smith said, "ABC says that it's not them, it's that people of color don't come forward."

"No one of another race has ever come forward?" Olena had to stop herself from rolling her eyes. "That's what they want people to believe, but that's hard to believe these days the way everyone's running after their fifteen minutes of fame."

"Do you want to be here?" Godiva asked with attitude.

"I wasn't sure at first. But the more I think about it, this is an opportunity for me to bring something positive to reality TV and prove that black women aren't angry, loud, and ignorant. I mean, some of us are, but you can find ignorance in every race."

"Do you think all black women on reality TV are ignorant?"

"Loud…aggressive…*ignorant*. Yes, that's what I think because anytime we're on a reality show we're turned into the stereotype. We're the ones no one else gets along with. It makes black professional women, such as myself, look really bad."

"I totally disagree. Honestly, I'm not worried about what other people think of me. And I *definitely* don't concern myself with how others feel based on someone they may see on TV who just happens to be of my same race. What does that person have to do with me? *Ab…so…lutely* nothing. If you *ever* watched reality shows, you'd see it's more than just black women acting a fool. That's the nature of reality TV. It's the reason people tune in whether they want to admit it or not."

"Well, I want people to tune in because they like me and they're inspired by me. My age or race shouldn't matter. And it's not about how quickly I can tear another person down or have them tear me down in the process. I won't be fighting. I can tell you that much for sure."

"Fighting? This show is about *finding* love. I hope the men who come on wouldn't be fighting you or trying to tear a woman down they're hoping to connect with," said Godiva.

Smith said to Olena, "So let me make sure I'm clear on what you're saying. You don't like reality TV, correct?"

"That's right."

"Welp, thank you for coming, it was nice meeting you. But we're in the *reality* TV business, and we want someone who's familiar with that genre. It's nice when they're also a fan of it, too."

"No, wait," Godiva said, patting her husband's thigh. "I don't necessarily think it's a bad thing that she's not into reality TV. She'll bring a different perspective. We might even promote that she doesn't like the whole idea of finding love on TV. We've cast the diehard reality TV junkies in the past, and a lot of times they don't work out either. Those are the ones who come in trying to be someone else. Someone they've watched on a reality show. If you don't watch it, that's fine."

"Then, let me be completely honest. I *hate* reality shows. I mean, we have all these campaigns about bullying when all a child really has to do is turn on the TV and see adults acting worse than a lot of these kids do. And a lot of these women on reality shows are mothers themselves. I know what some people would say, 'you're not a mother, so you really can't talk.' So what, I'm not a mother; I'm an aunt, and I have a mother, and I also have an opinion. I have nothing personally against your production company or any of your shows. I just know I could never act the way some of those women do on reality shows. That's all."

"Never say never," Godiva said. The look on her face displayed an obvious attitude. Her perfectly arched eyebrows were blending into the frown lines on her forehead.

"I'm saying never because I know what I'd never do. I'd never go on a reality show and make a fool of myself. *Never.*"

People on high horses fall hard, Godiva thought.

"Have you spoken to Jason yet?" Godiva asked, changing the subject.

"Not yet. He's still out of town."

"Oh, and you can't speak to him while he's out of town? This is very important. It's time-sensitive and somewhat of a package deal."

"I can talk to him whenever. And I do talk to him when he's out of town. But for something like this, I'll need to talk to him about it in person."

Having Jason Nix would be a major move as far as Godiva was concerned. Someone of his caliber would garner high ratings. Athletes did exceptionally well on reality TV shows. *Dancing with the Stars* was one example that immediately came to Godiva's mind. And Jason Nix was a name that most people recognized. You didn't have to love football to know who he was. In just his second year, despite the critics saying he was small for his position, he was named NFL Defensive Player of the Year. In later years, he'd beefed up his six four frame from two hundred and thirty pounds to two-sixty. He was also the second linebacker to win Super Bowl's Most Valuable Player award, which he earned by way of a hundred yard interception. It was a shame that his career had been cut short by an ACL injury. The three-time Super Bowl champion who'd been traded by the Patriots to the Falcons in 2006 had legions of fans. He was also extremely charitable and gave a lot of money and time to St. Jude's Children's Hospital.

What a lot of people didn't know about Jason—that Godiva and Smith and others who read *Bloomberg Business Week* religiously did, was that he was extremely business minded much like Magic Johnson. He had amassed a fortune from not only his NFL contracts and endorsement deals, but also through investing in the right start-ups. So it was worth having her just to get him. Their production company could always use another strong investor if they were ever going to venture into making movies as had recently become one of Godiva's goals.

"We really need Jason to come aboard. Two weeks ago when you and I first met, Jason was out of town, and you said as soon as he returned you would talk to him."

"I'm sorry, I wasn't able to, but I will. Is it a rush or something?"

"As a matter of fact, yes, it sure is. The show airs on Valentine's Day."

"If it airs on Valentine's Day, shouldn't we already be filming?"

"It's a long story that has to do with Gwen and her requirements. Right now it's about you and Jason. If viewers were to see someone like Jason Nix being into you maybe they'll be into you, too."

"Despite my age," Olena jabbed back.

And other flaws like a dry as paint personality, Godiva thought.

"Despite your age. And being a cougar is all that's talked about these days, so who knows, we might not even need to lie about your age."

"I really hate the term 'cougar.' It makes it seem like they're on the prowl for some meat. And enough with the age comments, okay? That's what's wrong with this world. People, particularly women, are made to feel inadequate once we reach a certain age. I don't buy into that. Life doesn't stop at forty-four. I'm young. My life is just beginning. I don't feel old, and I know I don't look old—"

Godiva threw up her hand like a stop sign. "You'll be surprised how old you'll look once that HD technology hits you."

"I'm always being told how young I look."

If Olena mentioned one more time how young someone *said* she looked, Godiva would pick up her steak knife and use the creases on Olena's forehead for target practice. She looked good for her age. But to Godiva's television-trained eyes, Olena looked every bit her age. She was so tired of the whole cougar craze, tired of the young men her age and even younger who were inflating these older women's egos. The whole forty is the new thirty, thirty the new twenty thing, made her sick. So what were the twenties, obsolete? If that were the case, so be it, Godiva supposed. Besides, she'd be thirty soon enough.

"You'll see that there's a provision in your contract about your hair and your weight. Basically, it's a beauty clause," Godiva clarified after noticing a look of confusion surface on Olena's face. "We need you to be as beautiful as you possibly can."

"May I see a copy?"

"I e-mailed you a copy an hour ago and CC'd Eugena."

Olena retrieved the e-mail from her Blackberry. She opened the attachment and began reading, scrolling down to get to the provisions. "So I should lose ten pounds?"

"We need you at one-thirty."

"I'm five-nine. Do I really need to be that small?"

"Television adds ten pounds." *Didn't she know that?* Who didn't know that? Godiva had known that way before she started a career in television.

Olena continued reading silently.

"Okay, so I'm going to read over everything and get back to you. Am I reading this correctly? Does Media One act as my management company for a period that extends one year after the airing of the show?"

"Yes, that's correct."

"I don't understand. Why would that be?"

Godiva's husband Smith chimed in, "Often as a result of exposure from one of our reality shows, the personality receives paid offers. We feel we are entitled to a percentage of those deals resulting from the exposure we provided."

"So if I get a book deal you get a percentage?"

"In your case, we could look at amending that section of the contract because you have a literary agent."

"Right. That part would have to go. Unless you can get me a deal quicker than she can," Olena said jokingly.

"We probably could, but we're not here to undercut Eugena. What we do as a management company is secondary to our bread and butter," Smith added.

"So just talk to Jason about everything because we really need him. Think of this as a package deal," Godiva said.

"May I be honest with you?"

"Yes, please be honest," Godiva snapped.

"I don't think Jason would go on a reality show. He turned down *Celebrity Apprentice* and *Dancing with the Stars*. I don't know if there's some kind of clause in his contract with Fox."

"There shouldn't be," Smith said. "If it's not a sports show in direct competition with Fox."

"I just know he's not a fan of the genre either. We've had lengthy discussions on the subject of reality TV, but I'll still run it by him."

Smith decided to speak up as Olena rose and said goodnight.

"Olena, we don't ever want to produce a boring show. Boring won't bring success. With the right mix of people and the right bachelorette, we'll have a hit. You're going to be meeting men most women would love the opportunity to meet. All of them are going to be successful millionaires or billionaires and some you'll probably find attractive. Put all of that together and we believe that's positive television. But for someone who's not a fan of the genre, you need to ask yourself is this something you want to do and let us know as soon as possible."

"I'll let you know after I speak to Jason," Olena said. "Thank you for dinner."

Godiva remained seated.

Smith returned to his seat after Olena left. He rubbed his forehead. "She wants to bring dignity and class to reality TV. She's delusional. Please help me understand why we're giving this tremendous opportunity to be on network television to someone who doesn't have a personality? This is TV. TV and personality go hand in hand."

"I hear what you're saying, and I don't like her either. And that's a good thing because I won't feel bad when I mess with her life. Is she really trying to bring dignity and class to reality TV? *Please*," Godiva spat. "She wants her fifteen minutes too. Otherwise, why do it? I'll tell you why, for her book deal. I already know how I'm going to spin this. Why is Olena forty-four and single, never married and no kids? There must be something wrong with her. And I really do think she's off. Did you see how small she cut up her asparagus? If she wanted peas, she should have ordered some."

Smith said, "As much as I'm against this tactic, she's somebody I wouldn't mind putting a private detective on to see what he can dig up."

The small grin on Godiva's face turned into a full-blown toothy smile, something that was rare for her. "That might work because I know she doesn't just have designer clothes in that closet of hers. There're some skeletons in there, too, I'm sure. Yeah, some people come alive when it's lights, camera, and action. Hopefully, she's one of those. If not, when all else fails, a little scandal never hurt, either. I can't wait to find out who Miss I-could-never-act-like-that truly is."

SEVEN

Olena was in the Atlanta suburb of Duluth in the Sugarloaf Country Club. She and Jason were visiting his mother, whom Olena affectionately referred to as Momma Nix. She was moving out of the house her son had given her and into his house, so she could watch her grandkids more conveniently while Jason was in California commentating. But mostly because after she divorced her husband, Jason's stepfather, the spacious house suddenly seemed to swallow her up. Jason's stepfather allowed his grown daughter and her husband and three kids to live with them "temporarily," one week turned into six months, long enough for Momma Nix to realize they were all a bunch of freeloaders. If those had been her children, or if they had been respectful toward her that would have been one thing. But they weren't. And her husband, a seventy-year-old, had the nerve to be cheating on her with a woman from their church. She was too old for the drama and too old to be living alone.

There were hundreds of boxes scattered throughout Momma

Nix's home. Boxes that the moving company Jason hired would be removing the following day. Even though Jason was back to work, he was still recovering. Otherwise, he would have moved a lot of the boxes himself. But the doctor still had him under some restrictions and avoiding heavy lifting was one of them.

"What's that look for?" Jason asked.

Olena and Jason were sitting in the kitchen with a plate of pancakes his mother had made. They were both cutting them into several tiny squares, a habit Olena picked up from Jason.

"What look?" asked Olena.

"That Lucy look. Baby, I know you," Jason said with a wide smile. "What did you do?"

Jason calling Olena "Lucy" was a term of endearment that started when she admitted she didn't know how to brew coffee, something that was evident when she poured water into the glass carafe instead of the reservoir and wondered why it took so long to brew. "Okay, Lucy, you've never made coffee before?" Jason had asked, falling out in laughter.

"No, I haven't," she said with a pout.

"Why did you go and buy this fancy Cuisinart pot if you don't know how to use it?"

"Because I liked the way it looked. What did I do wrong?" Olena had asked Jason as she stood in her kitchen beside him, staring at the coffee pot.

"You don't even know, do you?" She shook her head. "You put the water directly in the pot. It doesn't go there, it goes here, baby." Jason flipped the lid on the coffeemaker and pointed to the water reservoir. "And when the coffee brews," he said, falling out in more laughter, "then it drips down into the pot. I can't believe you didn't know that."

"Okay so I didn't know how to make coffee. I buy my coffee from Starbucks. Knowing how to make it was never high on my priority list."

"Aww, poor baby. Come give your man a hug. I'll teach you how to make coffee."

She playfully pushed him away from her. "I'm Lucy. I'm Lucy. I'm such a Lucy, right?"

They were able to have a big laugh at her expense back then. But right now was a different story. Now, she seriously doubted he'd even get as much as a chuckle out of what she would say.

"Say it?" he said, looking serious.

"Do you love me?"

"Yeah, but what's up?"

"Do you love me a whole lot?"

"What's going on, Olena?"

"Do you love me enough to do almost anything as long as it won't hurt anyone and you won't break any laws and get us in trouble?" Olena closed her eyes and blurted it out. "I need you to go on a reality show with me." She opened her eyes quickly. Jason immediately started laughing.

"Did you say a reality show? You need me to go on a reality show with you." Olena nodded. "What, something like *Survivor* or *Amazing Race*? Those are the only two I would consider going on."

"Will you just hear me out? I have an opportunity to be on a reality show, but it's a package deal. You're the celebrity, so they want you to be on it, too. Now, this is the part that's really going to sound crazy. It's a dating reality show."

"Like *The Dating Game* or something? We'll go on there and answer a bunch of questions about each other because I'd win that. I know you well…real well. I think I know you better than you know yourself."

"Not like the dating game. More like *The Bachelorette*."

"It can't be like *Bachelorette* because you're not single."

"Well, I would be going on there as a single woman. I'd go on dates with some men, but you'd be one of them, and obviously I'd pick you."

"Maybe I don't know you as well as I thought because what you just said is making no sense to me at all."

Olena began rambling off her reasons. "You know how much I want a book deal. I want to be successful. I hear about these first-time authors selling a lot of books and readers talking about how much they loved the story and how moved they were and how it touched their lives. I want that. I want to reach people. I've always wanted that, but it's not happening for some reason. And it's driving me crazy. I don't have a job. I've always had a job for as long as I can remember, even when I was in college. I hate not working. I have to do something. I know I can write, and I have an agent now, but I still don't have a book deal. And Eugena acts like she can't get me one. She says these days it's more than just writing a good book. Everyone's trying to brand themselves. So I think if I go on this reality show, it will build my nonexistent brand, and I'll have name recognition."

"Are you serious?"

"Did you hear everything I just said?"

"Oh, I heard plenty. Neither one of us is going on a reality show. My ex went on that stupid show *Ballerwives* and aired a lot of my personal business. That's not going to happen to me again. Besides, why would you want that?"

"I told you why. Honey, I'm not your ex. You can't say no. Please say yes…please."

He shook his head, and his face turned to stone.

"I'm not going to be used like a pawn for someone else's financial gain. Why go on national TV looking for a man when you already have one? Leave that for women who don't. That's why I don't like reality TV because it's all scripted. You're not going on there for a book deal. I'd rather you just tell me the truth, you want to be famous."

"I'm going on there for a book deal. It's on network television—CBS," she said, hammering the table with her fist.

"I don't care what it's on. We're not doing it. Trust me, you will thank me later. That mess is scripted, and they're going to turn you into a fool on network television."

She huffed out a loud sigh and rolled her eyes. "How do you know it's scripted?"

He cocked his head and gave her the duh look. "Are you single?"

"Well, no."

"Like I said—scripted. Baby, I know people in television, so I know how reality TV works. If I want to watch scripted TV, I want to see real actors who've studied and trained and worked hard for their roles and practiced the way I did when I was on the football field." The more he spoke, the more elevated his voice became and the more animated his body language. "You're not fit for reality TV."

"Why not?"

"Don't take this the wrong way, but you need to have a whole lot of personality for reality TV—"

"What are you saying? Are you saying I don't have personality...I'm boring?"

"I love you. I think you have tons of personality, but reality show personality is different. Are you outlandish, the life-of-the-party? No."

"I'm not a fan of reality TV, either. You already know that."

"I thought I did."

"But I have to do something."

Jason pushed his plate of half-eaten pancakes away and sat with his muscular arms folded as he shook his head.

"The more I think about it, the more I feel as if this opportunity is meant to be. They had someone else, but she dropped out. So I feel lucky for the opportunity."

Jason's eyes rolled as he sat slouched down in his chair.

"You were their second choice? Never settle for second place, but then again you aren't an athlete, so I shouldn't expect you to know that."

"Jason, come on, just do this for me, please," Olena's voice strained with anguish.

"What do you think Momma is going to say when she sees you on TV looking for a man?"

"I'm not looking for a man, but let's ask her. Here she is," Olena said as she noticed Momma Nix gliding into the kitchen.

"What's the debate, so I can go on and settle it for y'all?" Momma Nix said as she stood near the kitchen table with her arms folded.

"Okay, Momma listen," said Olena.

"She's so cute calling me, Momma. I just love that. But I'm still listening to both sides before I take one." She pinched Jason's cheek.

"I have a chance to be on a reality show. It's an opportunity to bring dignity to women on television and to sell my book to a publisher."

"*You* have a chance to go on a reality show?"

"Why did you say *you* like that?" Olena asked, turning up her nose.

"I told you," Jason said, sitting up in his chair. "You aren't reality show material."

"I take offense."

"You take offense," Jason said. "You don't even like reality shows, and you take offense?"

Momma Nix said, "I'm just trying to figure out how you found out about it. I'd love to go on a reality show like *Real Housewives of Atlanta*. I'd set that show out."

"My mother is reality show material."

"Is that the reality show you're going on? Please say it is. You can film right in this house and pretend it's yours. I'm sure a few of them are pretending those houses are theirs. They kicked the one with the nicest house off the show. I can't even remember the child's name now. Do you?"

Olena said. "I'm not going on *The Real Housewives of Atlanta*. The show I'm going on is new. It premieres Valentine's Day. It's along the lines of *The Bachelorette*."

"It's about time! I've been asking myself every season when is there going to be a black bachelor or bachelorette. I even wrote a letter to the network saying I would stop watching. But here's my question, why would you go on a show like that when you already have a man?"

"Thank you!" said Jason. "Great minds think alike."

"It's a similar concept to *The Bachelorette* only different," Olena said.

"Momma, what do you think about that? What do you think about Olena going on a dating show trying to meet a man?" He went to the refrigerator, took out the carton of orange juice, and removed a glass from the cupboard. "Do you want some juice, baby?"

"Am I still your baby? Yes, I would love some juice."

He grabbed a second glass.

"So what do you think about that?" Jason said to his mother, who was more preoccupied with the two glasses of orange juice than his question.

"What do I think about that, or what do I think about you not asking me if I wanted some juice?"

"Momma, do you want some juice?"

"No. But thank you for not asking. Now, back to you, young lady, why would you go on something like that when you already have him?"

"Jason would be going on there, too," Olena said. "To meet me."

"Meet you? He's already met you. I'm sure he's more than met you because my son has no problem with introducing himself according to Keena and all she said about him on *Ballerwives*." Keena had discussed intimate details of their sex life on national television. "And we haven't even discussed the most important thing, how much would you be getting paid?"

"I get a wardrobe, my own makeup artist, hairdresser, and stylist."

"Yeah, yeah, yeah, and how much money?" Momma Nix asked.

"It all depends. For the six guaranteed weeks, I'm going to make eighteen thousand dollars."

"I hope that's per episode. If not, you're getting ripped off," Momma Nix said.

"No. It's not per episode. But if the network picks up the other four weeks, I'll get another twenty thousand, plus ten thousand for the reunion show. So I'll make between eighteen thousand to forty-eight thousand. It's not per episode, but I don't have to pay for anything while we're filming—"

"Neither do *The Real Housewives of Atlanta*. I read that they were making thirty thousand an episode. And you're telling me all you would be making is forty-eight thousand dollars for the whole ten weeks." Momma Nix shook her head. "It's not worth it. My son pays more for his watches than they're willing to pay for your time. Foolishness."

"Well, this is a new show," Olena said.

"Olena, if you don't know me by now, you will never know me," said Momma Nix. "That little piece of chump change they're offering you to go and make a fool of yourself isn't worth it. Not to mention, you don't need to go on a dating show because you have my son."

"I'm looking at this in the long term. It's like my job. When I first started working for Lutel, I was paid a base salary of thirty-five thousand dollars for an entire year. I didn't make any commission off of my sales. The next year, I brought home just over five hundred thousand dollars, I'm not even including my bonuses."

"That's not a very good analogy because aren't they the ones that pink slipped you?" Momma Nix said.

"Is that what this is about, money?" Jason asked. "Don't insult me when you already know I'll take care of you financially."

"No you won't," Momma Nix said.

"I want my own money."

"That's right. She wants to make her own money."

"I'm used to having my own money."

"Listen to her. She's used to having her own money. Don't you want a woman with her own money? Because that's the type of woman, I want you to have."

"I don't want a woman with her own money from her own reality show," Jason said. "Look, I don't want you to do it. But at the same time, I can't prevent you from doing it, either. At the end of the day, you have to make that decision."

"But you have to be one of the bachelors, or I can't do it. It's a package deal."

"And what if you end up falling for one of these guys?"

Olena grinned. "Is that what you're worried about? That's not going to happen."

"But he has a point," Momma Nix said. "You could."

"If that were to happen that would mean what we had wasn't real. Besides, all of the rich men I would leave you for are already taken."

"All," his mother said. "Well, is it that many?"

"Well, he already knows about Denzel?"

"Denzel, oh honey, you're going to have to stand in line behind me."

"Who else?" Jason asked.

"You already know about Hakeem Frye."

Momma Nix said, "That is one fine chocolate drop of a man right there. Makes me want to have gastric bypass because I don't think he can handle all of what I got," she said, squeezing her breasts together. "Really, I don't need gastric bypass. I just need a breast reduction. I'll show you young cougars how a real cougar gets her prey."

"I'm not a cougar."

"My son is thirty-two, and you're forty-four, so what do you call that?"

"Wait, I want her to finish naming off all the men on her fantasy list," Jason said.

"Why does it matter?" Olena asked.

"I just want to see what kind of men you're attracted to."

"Okay…well, if we're talking basketball—"

"You have them in categories?" Jason said.

"Ooh, watch out," his mother said. "Gold digger alert—and an old gold digger at that."

"Name my competition. Who do you think looks better than me in football?" Jason seemed fixated on the question.

"Jason, I don't think anyone looks better than you, period. These are just men I find attractive."

"You know just what to say," Momma Nix said. "I mean if you want to start selling books, write you one of those Steve Harvey how-to-get-a-man type books. You're fortysome years old, and you have a rich young man begging you not to go on a reality show. He's telling you, he'll talk care of you. Yep, that's the book you need to be writing because that one'll sell."

"Finish naming 'em," Jason said.

"Kevin Garnett—"

"Another fine chocolate brother and don't dare let me see him in a suit, but just a tad bit too lanky for my taste," Momma Nix said. "But I can fatten him up."

"Momma," Jason said, "these men are the same age as your sons. Some are younger."

"But they're not my sons. And they're legal. And those two things are all that matters. Besides, all I did was agree with her about how good they look."

Olena said, "Okay, enough of this. Jason, will you please just agree to do the show?"

"Wait, what NFL players do you think are attractive?"

"Jason, come on, can we move on?"

"Just answer my question."

Olena hesitated. She couldn't tell him the truth because the truth wouldn't set him free; it would set him off. So, she said, "T.O," and she did think T.O was attractive, but he wasn't the one she thought was the finest NFL player in the history of the sport.

"Who?" Jason asked.

"Terrell Owens. So yes or no, are you going to do it?" Olena asked.

Jason released a loud sigh. "Mom, if you don't mind, could we have some privacy?"

"I mind, but I'll give you some," she said as she scurried off.

He started rubbing his freshly shaved head. He was close to saying yes, she could tell, but he shook the word out of his mouth. "I don't want this to mess us up. Reality shows mess people up. I feel like everything shouldn't be out there for everyone to know. Once it's out, even if it's not true, there's nothing you can do. People will still believe the lies they read because nowadays people believe whatever they read on the Internet."

Olena clasped her two hands together as if saying a prayer. "Please say yes."

"You really had my back when I needed you. So, if this is something you really want to do, yes. But I hope I don't regret it."

"Baby, you won't."

"Don't let that mess come between us. Don't let it change you, okay?"

"You know I won't. Can I call her? Can I call Godiva right now and tell her?"

"Why are you so happy about this?"

"I'm going to turn this all around into something positive. I'm going to end up with a book deal when all is said and done. And I'm going to represent black women in a positive light on TV. I feel good about this."

"Just worry about representing yourself." Jason picked up the phone on his desk. "I need to talk to Miss Godiva, so I can lay down Jason's law. What's her number? Is that her real name?"

"I'm assuming so. Maybe, I should buy her a box of Godiva chocolates. That would be cute." Olena took her cell phone out of her purse to get Godiva's phone number. "Are you ready for the number?"

"Yeah, I'm ready. And a book deal better be all you end up with."

"What else would I end up with?"

"Another man."

"Oh, Jason, please. It's not going to happen."

EIGHT

Was she doing the right thing? Olena wondered as she entered the restaurant behind Jason. Still a free woman until she handed over the signed contract tucked inside the black leather portfolio she clutched. Was this really what she wanted? She and Jason, along with Godiva and her husband Smith were dining at Seasons 52, the fresh grill and wine bar, on Peachtree Road in Buckhead, just a mile from the Mansions on Peachtree.

After they took their seats at a booth near the window, Jason just started firing off questions. "Tell me about this show. I need to understand the full concept. Are you staying locally?"

"Oh, no...no...not at all," Smith said. He was spruced up in a one-button gray velvet jacket, wine shirt, black jeans, and suede penny loafers. "We premiere on Valentine's Day. Olena is going to be traveling to ten of the most romantic cities in the world."

"So, I'm sure Paris is on the list," Olena said excitedly. "Where else?"

"London, Venice, Monte Carlo, Vienna, Melbourne, San Francisco, Boston, New York, and New Orleans."

"Wow, that's spread all over the place," Olena said with a look of concern surfacing. "Those are a lot of places to go in a short amount of time."

"We do have a tight schedule. I'm not going to lie. Twenty-three days to film the first six episodes."

"That doesn't make sense to me," Jason said. "Why would you start filming a month before the premiere?"

"It's hard to explain to someone who isn't in the business."

"I'm real smart and pick things up quickly so please explain."

"Originally, we planned on filming in August, but things happened with our original choice, and January was the best time for us to begin filming. It will be crunch time, but we have experience and we can pull it off. And initially we're only filming six shows. By the third episode, we'll know if they're ordering the other four. As soon as we get the green light for the rest, we'll film those."

The Harts continued going over a few more particulars concerning the filming, and when it seemed as though everyone was relaxed, Smith said, "Should we make a toast?"

"To what?" Jason said. "Nothing's a done deal yet. That's why we're here, right, to meet and discuss things?"

"I wanted to toast to the fact that you are here. We have Jason Nix here."

"And you have Olena Day," Jason emphasized. "Isn't this about Olena? She's the bachelorette."

"Of course, it's about Olena," Smith said.

"So what's your real agenda?" Jason asked.

"To make the show as entertaining as possible for viewers," said Smith.

Godiva was being unusually quiet.

"Entertainment is buffoonery, for some," Jason said. "I don't want anybody making my woman look bad on national television. I'm in television, and I know a lot of people in the industry, in front of the cameras and behind them. I know that sometimes producers have an agenda, and it's definitely not always a good look for the TV personality. Tell me about Media One. Did you just walk into CBS and say, 'I have a reality show?' "

"Fair question. By the way nice watch," he said, referring to Jason's, Louis Moinet. Jason nodded, acknowledging the compliment.

Smith said, "As far as *The One* goes, we made a pitch. We had our storyboards and a fifteen-minute clip, and the studio bought in. We do have several other reality shows running across various networks. So it's a little easier now as opposed to when we first got started and really had to prove ourselves."

"Do you want to know what I don't like about your company?" Jason said.

"What is that?" asked Smith.

"You gave my ex a show. That's definitely not a selling point for me. And I'm glad that show got cancelled."

"I've never been here," Olena said, trying to change the subject. "I don't know what to order now that I'm on a diet."

"Nothing on their menu is over 475 calories," Godiva chimed in. "So you're pretty safe. How's the diet coming?"

"I just need to lose eight pounds and then maintain it."

"Have you ever tried a raw food diet?" Godiva said. "I heard it's real good for the skin."

"Olena already has pretty skin," Jason said. "And she's not fat, so I don't know why you all have her on a diet."

"It's show business as crazy as that sounds, but you're right she looks good, and she's in shape," Godiva said, stuttering through the last few words as if she didn't genuinely want to say them. Olena wasn't sure what to think of the young, ambitious entertainment mogul in the making. When Olena was twenty-nine she was a long way from having it as together as Godiva did and an even longer way from being married. "Do you have your contract?" Godiva asked Olena.

Olena removed the contract from the portfolio and nodded. "Here it is." She slid it across the table.

"Did you happen to bring your signed contract?" Smith asked Jason.

"My attorneys have the contract. I believe it's still under review."

"I know what I'm getting," Olena said in a singsong voice as she glanced over the menu. "I'm going to order the Farmer's Market vegetable plate."

"Are you kidding me? Order something you really want to eat, baby."

"I'm on a diet."

Jason scratched his freshly shaved head. "I guess I'll order the same thing then and take one for the team. I could stand to lose ten pounds."

"No, you don't have to do that," Olena said.

"Actually, Jason, you really don't," Godiva said. "We'd like you to look just like you did when you played football. We'd actually like for you to bulk up a little more."

"Nope. If Olena's going to eat like that, I'm going to eat like that, too. But tonight when I'm cranky, you'll know why."

"I'm not going to get that," said Olena as she continued studying the menu. They'd already sent the waiter away twice while they survived on two rounds of drinks. All with the exception of Jason, who had not drunk any alcohol since his operation. "I'll order the Cedar Plank Roasted Salmon."

Jason nodded. "That's something you would order. And I'll get the filet mignon." He clapped the menu shut and laid it on the table. "Where's our waiter? We're finally ready." Jason said as he looked around the restaurant. "Ready to eat this dinner and go home."

Olena kissed the center of Jason's back and pressed her naked body against his. "It's okay. It's not that important."

"Really, it's not?"

They were lying in bed in his Alpharetta mansion. His back was to hers while his eyes were fixated on the flames steadily flickering from the fireplace. It was late, and Olena decided to initiate the lovemaking, but that rubbed Jason the wrong way. *Was it the dinner meeting they'd had with Godiva and her husband earlier that put him in a bad mood?* Olena wondered. Probably not. Most likely it was his penile rehabilitation program that he'd recently started. He needed to take twenty-five milligrams of Viagra every day for six days without sex and then increase to a hundred milligrams on the seventh day and try sex. They tried it, and nothing happened. He tried the Caverjet Impulse System, which he self-injected into his penis but experienced too much pain and wasn't open to trying any of the other penile injections on the market after that experience.

"I know I have a problem," he said, "but I don't need to be reminded. We've tried several times and nothing ever happens. How do you think that makes me feel?"

"I'm not trying to make you feel any kind of way, Jason." Olena moved her hands over his chest and attempted to inch them downward, but she was met with Jason's tight grip on her wrist.

"Can we use that pump thing the doctor gave you?"

"I'm not using that."

"Why?"

"I don't need a pump."

"Right now you do."

"Can you just shut up? You're getting on my damn nerves. You sound like a sex-starved nympho or something. The more you talk, the more I understand why you never got married."

Olena gasped. "I can't believe you just said that to me. You don't have to be rude. If I had my car, I'd leave right now because I didn't deserve that."

"Well, don't hound me for sex. Have you forgotten that I had prostate cancer? I just had a prostatectomy in August. It's October. It hasn't been that long. How do you think I feel? I'm a man, and I can't make love to my woman. I wish you could put yourself in my position. I've been through a lot in a short amount of time. I didn't know if the cancer had spread, or how long I'd have to live. I have young boys I want to raise. I have you in my life, and I want to grow old with you, but I couldn't think about any of that because my health wasn't right. I'm happy to be alive, but I'm impotent. I'm praying it's not permanent, but what if it were?"

"I'm sorry. I didn't even look at it like that."

She had fallen in love with him without the sex, but when he started talking about marriage she had to ask herself how could she enter into a sexless marriage? She was already forced to keep a steady supply of Duracell batteries for her Rabbit Pearl vibrator, and, at times, she fantasized about, Matthew. She felt fickle, and even remembered one of the men she dated one time calling her that; not that what he said mattered. It always seemed to be a catch-22 with her and the men she fell for. He's intelligent, but he's married. He's a good lover, but she's had sex with his father. He's perfect, but he's impotent. She wanted the man to be great without any ifs, ands, or buts separating them. Jason certainly was a good man. A better man than she initially thought he would be, and she just had to be patient. "If you want to leave, feel free to take any one of my cars. Take anything of mine you want, since I can't give you what you obviously need. I guess soon you'll be getting that from someone who works at a certain dealership, if you weren't already. Were you?"

"Was I what?"

He sat up in bed and looked down at Olena. "If you weren't cheating, how have you been satisfying yourself?"

"Jason, please. You know I'm not cheating. Sex is not—"

"It's not what—important. Don't tell that lie. Maybe once

you've been with the person for a while and experienced a lot with them, it isn't. But not if the two of you have never made love." Jason tugged at the expensive duvet cover on his bed. "Good night."

Olena lay on her back with her eyes glued on the chandelier hanging from the three-tier ceiling. A sexless marriage would never work. Not as strong as her sex drive was. She'd taken Eugena's advice and started writing an erotic novel for her own personal release. And the love scenes she'd written were hot enough to make her reach for her Rabbit Pearl. Maybe, instead of romance, she would change her genre to erotica, or maybe she pulled at too many different straws. Why not just marry Jason and put an end to all of her financial woes? Why not just forget about the reality show and marry him and become a middle-aged, sexless trophy wife? *Independence was as overrated as sex*, she thought as she turned on her side with her back to Jason's.

Halloween. Olena hadn't been a fan of the holiday ever since she was eight years old, and her parents stopped taking her trick-or-treating. They turned off all the lights inside and outside of their house and stopped answering the door when the bell rang. The year prior an eight-year old boy died after eating a Pixy Stix laced with cyanide, which signaled the end of trick-or-treating in the Day household. And now, so many years later, she can't remember what she ever dressed up as. But tomorrow when she took the boys to the Georgia A-scary-um to trick-or-treat at the candy stations in the world's largest aquarium, she would be dressed up like Lucy—a black Lucille Ball. Complete with a red *I Love Lucy* wig that she'd purchased online at a retailer of party supplies and costumes. She was tired of being a stick-in-the-mud. The more she was around Jason's kids the more she understood the reason she'd been so uptight over the years. She didn't have kids of her own. Not that everyone without children was a stick-in-the-mud.

Matthew didn't have any kids, and he certainly wasn't. He knew how to have a fabulous time. But there were some people who needed an added incentive to loosen up; Olena was one of those, and Jason's kids were her incentive.

"Are you boys ready?" Olena playfully shouted after leaving her bedroom. "Aww, look at you two." Jamal was the first to walk out of Olena's guest room. He had on an Optimus Prime costume from the movie *Transformers*. Jason Jr. was dressed up like Michael Jackson from "Thriller"

"Where's your costume?" Jason Jr. asked.

"I'm wearing one tomorrow." Olena had on a black long-sleeve zip up velour hoodie with matching straight leg pants and a gray long-sleeve scoop neck T-shirt underneath. "I'm taking a picture of you two to text to your dad. Follow me." They walked into the living room and stood near the gas fireplace. "Your dad's going to get a kick out of this." Before she could take a picture of Jamal, he sneezed three times. She walked over to him and removed his mask. "Are you sick?" she asked him. He shook his head. "Look at me." She used her index finger to raise his head up and read his eyes. "Yes, you are. We might not be going anywhere."

"I want to go to the zoo," Jamal whined.

"You can't go to the zoo if you're sick."

He nodded. "I can if I want to go."

"Let's take pictures," Olena said, putting his helmet back on. She hadn't mastered the art of dealing with a fussy child. She took three pictures with her cell phone and text each of them to Jason. Then, her cell phone rang. "It's your dad." She answered with a big smile. "I have you on speaker."

"Where are my boys? I see Michael Jackson, and I see a little Transformer dude."

Jamal and Junior were laughing.

"Hi, dad," Junior said.

"Hey, Junior. Are you being the man and watching out for

your little brother and your momma-to-be?"

"Yeah."

"Good, Jamal. Why are you being quiet?"

"I think he's coming down with a cold," Olena said. "And I really think we shouldn't go anywhere, but the sick one is insisting so what do you think?"

"Jamal, you feel okay?" Jason asked through the speaker-phone.

"Um huh."

"Do you feel like going to Boo at the Zoo?"

Jamal nodded.

"He can't see you," Olena told Jamal. "Jason, he's nodding."

"He just wants to go, but I can tell he's not feeling good. Otherwise, he'd be talking a mile a minute. So what did you tell me the agenda was? Today was Boo in the Zoo, and tomorrow you're taking them to the Georgia Aquarium?"

"Yes."

"Why don't you switch it around, since the aquarium is in-doors?

"Whatever you say, Sir."

"Okay, now, take me off speaker, so I can say something else." Olena removed Jason from the speakerphone. "I love that you're with my kids. It lets me see how good you are with them. I love that. You're giving my mom a break, and she really appreciates it. You're a really special lady in my life. Last week when I lost my cool, I never apologized, and I owe you that much. I shouldn't have said what I said, and I'm sorry."

"I understand."

"I should never have been that disrespectful to someone I love, and I love you, baby."

"Did you talk to your attorneys about the contract?"

"Wow, you just blew that. I don't want you to go on that stupid reality show.."

"I already signed the contract. I'm preparing for it. I start working out next week with a trainer that they're paying for—"

"You signed the contract, but it was a package deal, so if I don't sign my contract the package unwraps and you're free."

"But—"

"You want to do it, don't you? Just be honest."

Olena stepped into the hallway just outside of the living room away from the boys, but not too far away.

"Yes, I want to do it. I already told you that. I've never been out of the country, and I'm looking forward to that. Just do it for me, please."

"I can't act like I've never met you. I want you to have this opportunity if it's something you want, but I don't want to do it. Let me think about it some more. I'll let you know soon. I love you."

"I love you too."

When Olena ended the call, she clapped her hands. "Are you guys ready? We're going to go to the zoo tomorrow, which means I don't need all of these cell phones of your dad's." Jason had given Olena four smart phones to hand in for the zoo's recycle program to benefit the gorilla conservation program. "Why does your dad have all of these cell phones?"

"'Cause he had a lot of girlfriends," Junior said, "but now he just has you so he doesn't need all those phones." Olena shook her head, but decided to stop the conversation there.

"Now, you have to put your costume on, since we're not going to the zoo today," Junior told her.

"I will wear it tomorrow. I promise I will."

NINE

November

"**A**re you ready to work out today?" Una Braun said loudly. She had more muscles than most men and an unusually dark tan that made her body shine like a new penny. "I need a serious workout today." Una was born in Calv near Stuttgart, Germany and had lived in the states for forty years ever since she was five. This was Olena's first week of training and third visit. The former Miss Olympia would be training Olena five days a week at her private workout studio, Body by Braun, in Buckhead.

Olena had just two more months—per the beauty clause—to get her body in shape, and make sure her hair stayed healthy and grew a few more inches. *How long did a hair rinse last?* Olena wondered. She didn't want any gray hairs popping up during the filming. And her skin needed to be flawless, or once those high-definition TVs tuned in they'd see a whole other side of Olena Day.

"Yes, I'm ready," Olena said.

"Then act like it. I'm not here to babysit. Just because Media

One is paying me for private lessons that doesn't mean you can slack up. If you weren't with Media One, you wouldn't even be a client of mine because I'm booked solid and I don't take on nobodies."

Olena regretted not having Jason train her. She'd tried to work out with him in the past, but he was a little too intense. She even tried working out to one of his exercise DVDs, but she was left breathless after the first ten minutes of a sixty-minute routine.

"*Nobodies?*"

"That's right, you're a *nobody*," the woman shouted, getting all the way in Olena's face. "You're a *nobody* until you prove you're somebody."

"I'm not a nobody. I'm somebody."

"Then get down and give me twenty pushups and prove it to me."

"What?"

"Get down and give me twenty. You heard me."

"Why are you screaming?" Olena said calmly. "This isn't boot camp."

"Get down on the floor and give me twenty pushups," Una whispered. "Was that better?" she shouted.

Olena dropped to the floor and started doing pushups. "That's one, nineteen more to go. Come on, you should be finished by now." Olena stopped doing pushups and examined one of her nails.

"You're afraid to break a nail? Aren't those acrylics?"

"No, they're not. I'm allergic to acrylic nails, which is a shame because they're so convenient, especially in that I do a lot of typing."

"I don't care about your nails. You can't be prissy in here. You will break a few nails. It takes hard work to be beautiful. Those who take the easy route always take the easy route. Beauty doesn't come in a vacuum or a bottle or a suction tube or a cream. It's hard work."

If she said so, but Olena's aesthetician sold her a cream that she'd been using faithfully for the past two weeks that was like Botox in a bottle. She used to have a couple of creases on her forehead, but those were all gone now. So maybe beauty did come in a bottle. If those exercises didn't work, Olena wanted to see if beauty came in a suction tube, too. Was she actually so vain to consider plastic surgery? *Yes.* Her views had recently changed on the subject. She didn't find anything wrong with it as long as a person didn't go overboard. A tummy tuck was all she wanted; it seemed like the most logical and quickest solution, since she didn't believe Spanx could fool the high-definition TV screens.

"I need you on the treadmill doing an hour of cardio. I'm going to put you on an incline, and you have to run. When you feel your calves burning just run it out."

"Treadmill," Olena huffed. "Mother of God." She needed strength, but she knew she had to do it. She walked to the area where there were five treadmills lining the mirrored wall and stood on one while Una programmed it.

"Run," Una shouted.

Olena took off so fast that she slid off the treadmill on to the floor. "I fell off the treadmill," Olena said, falling out in laughter. "Only I'd do something like that, I'm Lucy."

"Lucy?"

Olena nodded. "But I'm going to get it together. I promise you."

At first, Una didn't seem amused. But Olena's laugh became infectious, so Una started to laugh too. "Let's try that again at a slightly slower speed."

"Please."

The day before she went for her first-ever screen test. The whole reason she was there was to see how she looked on camera. Godiva and Smith were there, too, of course, and Olena met her stylist, Tilley, who was three inches shorter than Olena, and had

a unique sense of style that she accented with handmade jewelry that Tilley told Olena she made herself. Olena had seen her
only one other time at a pre-production meeting Media One held
to go over a few particulars and to introduce Olena to the staff.
But they had so much to cover and such little time that Olena
didn't get to say more than hello to Tilley the first time. The next
time she saw her, she was able to compliment her on the wooden
necklace she had worn and ask her where she bought it. Both
times, Tilley stood out not only for what she wore, but also because she was bald.

Was Tilley sick? Olena wondered. Not that she looked it in the
least. The whites of her large brown eyes were clear, and she seemed
filled with life. But Olena had spent a considerable amount of time
in a cancer center with Jason, and that's where the thought came
from. Her next thought was maybe Tilley was gay. There were a lot
of gay people who worked at Media One, and a lot who lived in
Atlanta; at times, it seemed like just as many gay women as men.
Could she actually be bald out of choice? Olena wondered. *What
woman would want to shave their head completely bald?* Olena
didn't know how to ask, so she probably wouldn't.

At the screen test, Remy, a Media One producer, gave Olena a
few lines to say while she looked straight into the camera. He let her
see herself as she'd appear on TV, and Olena wasn't pleased at all.

Olena continued running on the treadmill. She'd seriously
have to commit herself to those workouts because the more she
thought about it, she realized she wouldn't have time for plastic
surgery, not when the average recovery time was six-weeks.

"Why are you staring at yourself in the mirror? Do you
think you're cute or something?" Una asked. "That fat around
your belly isn't cute neither are those two rolls on your back.
None of that is cute."

"Trust me. I don't think I'm cute."

"You don't? Well, why are you here, then? I prefer training

people who know they look good and want to look even better. If you're insecure, go to a fitness center with the rest of your peers who buy memberships for the sake of saying they have one but are too lazy to use it."

"I don't like to sweat."

"How are you going to work out if you don't want to sweat?"

"It messes up my hair. No one would believe I just got my hair done two days ago." Olena shook her head and glanced at the wall clock. Twenty more minutes and her hour was up.

Olena left the workout with more of her hair out of her ponytail than inside of it. The first thing she wanted to do when she got home was shower. Then, she would go to bed. *Who said working out gave you energy?* She was exhausted.

She smiled when she saw the caller ID on her cell phone light up with the name Jason Nix. "Hey baby," she said with a yawn.

"Hey. It's two o'clock in the afternoon. Are you still in bed?"

"Yes. Can you believe it?"

"No, I can't. Are you alone?"

"That's not even funny? Yes," she snapped back with attitude. "What's wrong?"

"I got the text you sent yesterday about your workout. What kind of workout was it that it wore you out so badly that you couldn't answer your damn phone all night?"

"Pause…rewind. Now, let's start this conversation all over because I don't like your tone."

"It's a lot I don't like. You have never not answered the phone when I called."

"I left my phone in the car."

"*All* night?"

"Yes, *all* night."

"Are you just now getting up?"

"Yes."

"Right…okay, well let me ask you this."

"Okay."

"If you left your cell phone in your car all night, and you're just now getting up, how are you talking on it right now?"

Olena's mouth dropped as she held the phone away from her ear and looked at it. Wow, was she really that out of it. She pressed the phone to her ear. "You're right."

"I know I am."

"Baby, I'm just out of it. Oh my God that workout wore me out. I'm sorry," she said in laughter. "I'm Lucy."

"No, we're not going to blame this on Lucy today. I just called to let you know that I just got off the phone with Godiva."

"Okay?"

"I withdrew my name."

Olena's heart sank. "Jason, why, and why would you tell her before you told me?"

"Don't worry. They love you. I guess they found some interesting men that make me pale in comparison."

"That's not true, Jason. You said you were going to think about it."

"And I did."

"No you didn't. You had your mind made up."

"For one thing, it's football season, and I'll be too busy with commentating."

"They don't film until January, Jason. You'll be done commentating."

"Olena, I learned a long time ago not to do something that I don't feel in my heart I should do. I love you, but I'm not going to chase a woman I already thought was mine. It wouldn't be as good a look for me as it would be for you."

"Who cares how it looks? It's just a TV show."

"Millions of people watch TV. I can't look like a fool. I can't risk that."

Olena's eyes rolled as she slid her eye pillow back over her eyes and lay on her back. "So, Jason, what exactly are you saying because you sound pissed as if I've done something?"

"I'm just letting you do you. That's all. I hope all goes well, and you get a book deal and all the other materialistic things that you want that I already have, but for some reason you don't want to accept it from me. I can tell you from experience that all the fame is cool up to a point, but without your health, none of that other stuff means much.

"But baby, you have your health now. The doctor says you're doing fine."

"How am I doing fine when I can't make love to my woman?"

"Aside from that."

"There is nothing aside from that. Did you really just say aside from that? There isn't anything aside from that. No, actually there is—my career. I love what I do. I'm going to just focus on that. I don't have to worry about branding my name because people already know who I am," he said sarcastically.

"You don't have to be nasty toward me. We've been through a lot, and we love each other."

"Do you love me, Olena?"

"Yes I love you. You know I do."

"Why didn't you answer your phone last night? Who were you with? If it hadn't been raining so hard, I would have driven over there."

"And I would have been here...alone. This is about sex. I know it is. Honey, sex is not that important."

"I'm tired of hearing you say that. Why are you acting? You know you can't go without sex."

"What are you talking about?"

"Have you been seeing anyone else?"

"Have I been seeing anyone else?"

"You just answered my question with a question. When a person repeats a question instead of answering it, they're guilty."

"I just didn't understand your question."

"See if you understand this one. When's the last time you've seen Matthew?"

"It's been awhile. Why? Where is that question coming from?"

"I called him at the dealership."

"You called Matthew at the dealership?"

"That's right. I called him this morning."

"He doesn't even work at that dealership anymore."

"I know where he works. He works at SCM Finance in Marietta. I found that out when I called his old job. But how did you know, unless you keep in touch with him?"

"I'm lost as to why you would even do that."

"You know why I did it. I love you to a level that feels uncomfortable. Love shouldn't feel like this. Last night, when I couldn't reach you all night, it messed with me. This voice inside of me said, call him, so that's what I did."

"Okay, so you called him, *and?*"

"I come from the school of don't kiss and tell. He either dropped out or never attended because he told it all…and I do mean *all*. Now I know what I've been missing out on. I hope you find love."

Olena was silent for a moment, before finally saying, "Wait a minute, Jason. Stop talking in riddles. You're not making sense."

"Why did you claim you were celibate back when I was able to make love to you? You were making me wait, but you weren't making him wait."

"We weren't in a relationship back then."

"But we were in one in August, when you left me to go see him. You drove to his house, and what did you do when you got there?"

"I didn't do anything."

"You're lying. You had sex with him. Didn't you? Tell the truth because he already told me."

"I'm telling you the truth, and if he said we had sex that night, he's lying."

"So tell me this, when you kept saying over and over again, 'I'm celibate,' what was the point of that? Was it true? Who's lying, him or you?" There was a few seconds of silence on the phone.

"Hello."

"It was true…at first—" His laughter burst through the speaker of her cell phone. "Can I finish?"

"No need."

"So what happens now?"

"I still love you, Olena. But I don't think we're going to work."

"Why?"

"If you can lie to me about one thing, you can lie about anything. And the smaller the lie the worse it is. You didn't have to say you were celibate. We weren't in a relationship at the time. That's the first problem. And this whole reality show is the other. I don't know who you are anymore. I know you're not who I thought. And that's my biggest issue because I can't stand a phony."

"I'm not phony, Jason. I can't believe you just said you don't know who I am. We've been seeing each other for almost a year. We were together every day for over a month after we came back from Houston. You peed in my bed."

"Now, you're going to throw that up in my face. I guess I'll read about that in the blogs. 'Jason Nix Peed in my Bed.' I was sick. I'll buy you a new bed if it bothers you that much."

"It didn't bother me at all. I'm saying don't say you don't know me. After all we've been through. Don't say you don't know who I am because that's an insult. You do know who I am."

"No, Matthew knows who you are. I don't."

"I *was* celibate when I first told you that."

"But when you weren't you still said it. It's cool. We don't have to ping-pong it. It's over."

"It's over? Just like that it's over."

"Have fun on your reality show? I hope you find 'the one'. I thought I'd found her."

"Bye, Jason," Olena said, jabbing the button on her cell phone to end the call. She took a deep breath, wiped her tears away, and swiped her hand to dismiss it all. "I'm not going to let you bring me down, mister four-cell-phone-man. *Pssh*."

Her heart ached. The more she thought about it, the angrier she became with Matthew. She grabbed her cell phone and dialed his number.

"What did you tell him?" Olena shouted after Matthew answered the phone.

"Olena?"

"What did you tell Jason when he called you," she asked sternly.

"First of all, why are you talking to me like this? What have I done to you?"

"What did you say to Jason about us?"

"Olena, I'm not sure what's wrong, or where this is coming from, but the dude called tripping. Telling me, he knew for a fact I was with you last night."

"And what did you say?"

"I did end up saying some things I wish I hadn't, but it was just a bad day all around, and I told him the last time I saw you, but that's all I told him."

"So you didn't tell him that we had sex the last time we saw each other?"

"Why would I tell him something like that when we didn't?"

"That's what I'm trying to figure out."

"He asked me, when was the last time I'd seen you, and I told him. He asked if we had sex. I said, no. He wanted to know if we'd ever had sex. And I said I don't discuss my personal business. And he went off. Now, I did say that you came to my house, but that was it. I didn't lie and say we had sex. He just didn't believe me."

Olena wasn't surprised that Jason would try to trick the truth out of her, and his mission was accomplished. Oh well, she thought, another Thanksgiving and Christmas spent alone. Something she had become used to.

TEN

December

Momma Nix loved to eat, and Olena needed answers. So Olena invited her to Bone's, one of Momma Nix's favorite restaurants. It took Jason's mother a few weeks to find the time to accept her invitation, which started to feel like a brush-off to Olena. It was one week before Christmas, and Olena had hoped she and Jason would have reconciled by now. But they hadn't. He hadn't called her. When she tried calling him on four separate occasions, he didn't answer.

"Momma, do you know what you're going to order?" Olena asked while she continued perusing the menu.

"I'm really not sure. Everything sounds so good that I could just kick my shoes off and live here. It's so good not to have to cook. Maybe I'll get the dry-aged Porterhouse for two, but I'm not sharing, so keep looking for your own dish."

"What sides?"

"Truffle butter mashed potatoes, and I need to be healthy and go with something green, so probably asparagus. What are you ordering?"

"Probably a Bone's salad."

"And what else?"

"That's it. I have to watch my weight for the show."

"Eating like that you'll mess around and turn into a bone, and like I said, I'm not sharing my steak."

Olena placed the menu on the table beside her. "That's all I want," she said with a long sigh.

"Girl, what is wrong with you? You look like you lost your best friend."

"I have."

The waiter came to the table and immediately took their order. Momma Nix added a bottle of Black Bart Stagecoach Vineyard.

"Okay, so what's wrong with you?" she repeated after the waiter left.

"Your son is what's wrong with me."

"Oh," Momma Nix said and didn't say another word until after Olena did.

"*Oh*, that's it. You know, don't you?"

"I know a whole lot of things. What are you referring to?"

"That he's not doing the show, and he broke up with me."

"Oh that. He said he wasn't going on the show, but nothing about the two of you."

"You're not a very good liar."

"I just don't want to get in the middle of it, honey. I like you, you know I do, and of course, I love my son. I hope both of you can be happy either together or apart."

"But how could he just give up on us? I mean, I admit I was wrong for lying."

"What did you lie about?"

"When I first met Jason, I had also met someone else, and we started dating. I didn't really take your son too seriously because he was a football player with a lot of money and to me that just spelled out lots of women, which spelled out drama, which is something, at my age, I'm not looking for—"

"And that's why you're going on a reality show because at your age you don't want drama," Momma Nix said sarcastically. "Going on that show is going to backfire on you."

"It's a dating show. How can a dating show really backfire?"

"You're no longer with my son, so it already has, hasn't it?"

Olena's face went long. "Yes, it has."

The waiter returned to the table with their entrees.

"So you were dating another man and?"

"And things progressed between me and this other man and your son knew that I had dated someone else, but he thought I was celibate."

"Oh, yes, I definitely remember that part. I didn't believe it when I heard it, but I definitely remember when we were all together on Valentine's Day and that came up over dinner."

"What do you mean you didn't believe it?"

"That old celibate trick that some women pull just because it's been a few weeks since they've had sex and they think it's going to impress a man. You were forty-something years old, please. You don't have to claim you're not having sex at that age."

"But I wasn't having sex."

"For how long weren't you having sex? Just until you had sex again because, in that case, I'm celibate too."

"Well, at your age, I would hope so...no offense."

"Oh, honey, at my age, I could teach you a few things that would make your man stay, not leave you. So you held my son at bay while you figured out your love life? You're going to be perfect for that reality show."

"Gee thanks, so now you hate me, too."

"I think you're a lovely person. Confused as all hell, but you're my girl. I'm sixty—"she cleared her throat in between the word sixty and the word years, "years old, and I married a broke man and had to figure out a way to get rid of him without jeopardizing my life because folks are crazy these days, so I'm far from giving out Strawberry Letter advice. But I will say this. I think you need to go on that show."

"Now I need it?"

"Once you get around all that fake love, you're going to be ready for someone as real as my son."

"But your son doesn't want me."

"He wants you. If he didn't, he wouldn't care that you were going on the show. He wouldn't care that you lied and said you were celibate. I didn't know my son was gullible enough to believe that mess, but I guess so."

"What can I do, Momma Nix?"

"I want you to work on yourself because you're too old to come across this flaky and next concentrate on that show. Remember your objective. Don't turn into a fool on network television. Don't have us black women embarrassed to tune in because you're making us look bad. Show the world we can be classy and beautiful like we already know. And let me work on my son. He's just being stubborn right now."

"Thank you, Momma Nix."

"I've messed around and talked to you so long my steak is cold. And before I forget, Jason wanted me to give you this." Momma Nix pulled a letter from her purse. Olena smiled. She was excited at first. "Please remember that I'm just the messenger."

The smile on Olena's face immediately dropped off once she noticed the New York address. It was from the law offices of Baker, Stein, & Latham. Olena started reading. It was an official letter issuing a stern warning that legal action would be pursued if their client's name were mentioned during the filming of the show, including the reunion show and any promotional appearances. And it went on and on for four pages.

"Wow, he really doesn't love me. He doesn't even like me." She tossed the letter in her leather handbag and started picking over her salad. "I think I'm going to have this boxed up to go."

"Really, Jason, really," Olena said as she sat on the side of her bed with the legal letter in her hand. The more she had thought about the threat he had issued through his lawyers, the angrier she became. She phoned his cell phone right after she left the restaurant, but he didn't answer. She tried again thirty minutes later and again after an hour. And now just before she headed for bed. Only this time she decided to leave an exceedingly long and detailed voice mail.

"You would sue me if I said your name. And I wasn't even planning on saying your name, but I hate that I have to think about it every time I'm on camera. What if it slips out? I just can't believe that you're treating me like I actually did something to you. Come on now, when we first started dating, you were seeing other women, and you were sleeping around, and you know you were. We weren't in a relationship then. I didn't owe you any kind of explanation. This is not because I told you I was celibate, and you know it isn't. And it's not about Matthew or the reality show. You're acting this way because you're angry because you're impotent. Is that enough reality for you? You're treating me as if I slept with one of your friends, or I stole something from you. I didn't do any of that. I don't understand any of this. But you've made it crystal clear with this letter where I stand in your life. And don't you dare try to take me to court to issue me a gag order. Don't you dare! You don't want me, okay I get it now. I'm no longer in denial, and I hope you have a wonderful life."

As she ended the call, her eyes started to bubble with fresh tears from the frustration of it all. She wiped her tears away. "No, I'm not going to cry this time. Maybe this is for the best…*Maybe*."

PART TWO

HIDING MY HEART

ELEVEN

January

The nonstop Air France flight on the Boeing 777 departed Hartsfield at 5:45 p.m. on January 4th. Olena breathed a sigh of relief when she first viewed the itinerary and realized that she was in business class and wouldn't be stuck in coach for eight hours and twenty-five minutes.

That morning a camera crew, several Media One employees, and craft services arrived at Olena's condo at eight in the morning to begin filming. The show supplied her with Tilley, Christian, and Jean—her own little crew of people whose sole purpose was to make Olena beautiful.

With the help of her personal trainer, Olena had lost ten pounds, and the extra baggage around her waist was gone. However, that didn't prevent her from packing a few pair of Spanx.

She was not going to hold back from experiencing some mouth-watering delicacies from around the world.

Olena grew her hair out three inches past her shoulders and the rest was sewn in by her hair stylist, Christian, so that her hair fell in voluminous curls to the middle of her back.

Since the show premiered on Valentine's Day, for the first day of filming, she wore a svelte red sheath dress with dimensional ruffles and a front bow. She had on understated jewelry: diamond stud earrings and a tennis bracelet. Not the most comfortable outfit to fly in for eight hours. But as soon as they landed, she had to do a photo shoot.

Olena accidentally packed the eye mask that she had grown so accustomed to sleeping in, inside one of her checked bags, and now she couldn't sleep. So while the rest of the production team had their eyes closed, Olena's mind raced.

They'd gone through so many takes during Olena's introduction earlier that Olena didn't think she was cut out for reality TV just as Jason said.

"I'm Olena Day." She sounded like she was an actor on a bad info-commercial. "And I live here in Atlanta, Georgia, but I'm originally from Detroit. I decided to come on *The One* after the one I had got away, and now I'd love another opportunity to meet the man of my dreams. But honestly, I just want him back. Last year, I went on a one-year sabbatical from my sales job, and, unfortunately, with the way the economy is right now, I was laid off. Currently, I'm unemployed, and I finished a book that will probably get published."

"Cut...cut...and more cut," Godiva had shouted. "What was that?" Olena stood stiff and stunned. "What kind of an intro was that? 'I thought I had my soul mate,' Godiva said mockingly, "'but that didn't work. I thought I had a good job, but I lost that too. Oh, and, by the way, I hope I can get published after this.' No, no, and *hell* no. I need you to tell me what that was. What was that?"

"My life."

"Well, it's not going to be your life while you're taping this show."

"It's not?"

"No. No one wants to tune in and watch an unemployed woman try to find the perfect man when what she needs to be looking for is a job. They'll think you're a gold digger. And definitely don't try to promote the fact that you're a writer. That will turn people off so fast."

"How will the fact that I'm a writer turn people off?"

"Not that you're a writer, but that you're trying to play the whole fifteen minutes of fame game to get published."

A puzzled look surfaced on Olena's face. "Okay, if you say so, but I'm obviously not a gold digger."

"All you've said was that you were in sales. You never said what you were selling."

"They can tell from my home that I have my own money."

"They don't know where we're filming. They'll see you sitting in a chair, and maybe they'll be able to tell it's a living room. We don't have a caption underneath that reads: This is Olena's beautiful million-dollar Buckhead condominium."

Olena didn't know whether to be offended or to laugh, so she chose the latter. "Tell me what I'm supposed to say?"

"I want you to be yourself, only different. We need viewers to be able to relate to you."

"Okay, listen. I'm already in love with someone. If I try to act like I'm really searching for someone, I'm going to come across phony. I want people to know I'm brokenhearted. There are a lot of women out there who are—men too, and who are too afraid to try love again because of it."

"That's so bachelor/bachelorette," said Godiva, rolling her eyes.

"It's so true."

"I can work with that idea," Remy said. "I actually think it's a good idea, so instead of doing the introduction here, we can film her in the limo and at the airport. We'll film her first confessional here. Let's have her first confessional about Jason and how much she's in love with him."

"I'm not allowed to say his name."

"What do you mean you're not allowed to?" Godiva asked.

"He had his attorney issue a gag order."

"We need a copy of that."

"You were CC'd."

"Well, maybe they didn't have the right address. So can you make us a copy?" Olena nodded. "Let's film her intro. Then, let's get ready to go to the airport," Godiva said.

They captured footage of Olena being chauffeured from her condominium to the airport.

While they were waiting to board, Godiva asked her if she knew French.

"No. I took Spanish in high school. Beyond counting to ten and a few letters in the alphabet, I can't remember anything else."

"I figured you'd say that so use this." She handed Olena a pocket French-English dictionary. "Most of the people there aren't going to be speaking English, and if you don't at least try to speak French you could come across as a rude American. I e-mailed you a lot of stuff that I'm going to need you to look through sometime between now and, well, right now. Remember, we're trying to give the viewer an experience. We want them to learn about the different places you'll be going to while getting to know you and your date." The more Godiva rattled on and on about the schedule, the customs, what to do and what not to do, important e-mails, and a meeting Olena needed to attend later that day, the more Olena realized how much work reality TV actually was. When what Olena hoped for was an escape from her broken heart.

She didn't want to think about Jason because whenever she did she felt an ache in her heart. She'd gotten over Matthew quickly because of the whole thing with his dad. But she couldn't shake Jason. They hadn't even made love, yet the bond she felt with him was incredible. She missed his sons and his mom. She genuinely saw herself as part of his family. He told her, he loved her, but she didn't understand how his love for her could end as quickly as his did.

How did she end up packing her eye mask? She could kick herself just thinking about it. Otherwise, she'd be sleeping like everyone else. Instead, she listened to music on her iPod—Earth, Wind & Fire's *Greatest Hits* among several others. Every couple of hours, she got up to walk and stretch a little. But every effort she made to go to sleep failed, and she was desperate for her eye mask and a hotel bed.

After the long and somewhat grueling flight into Roissy Airport that was complete with dinner and a movie, Olena couldn't wait to check-in to the hotel and sleep. There was a six-hour time difference, and it was eight in the morning in Paris. Olena's body needed a bed, but production had a different agenda. She was shuttled to the Louvre, one of the world's largest museums and a popular Paris landmark, to take some promotional pictures. In the forty-four minutes it took the shuttle driver to get there, the makeup artist beat Olena's tired face with enough foundation, powder, and blush to make Olena appear wide-awake. Even though she could have fallen over if someone so much as tapped her shoulder.

"We're going to have you stand by the pyramid," the creative director slash photographer said as he signaled Olena to hurry along behind him. The concept was to photograph Olena behind the large glass and metal pyramid that was surrounded by three smaller pyramids. "Are you ready, Olena? Can you look like you're happy to be in Paris and ready to find love? Give me a sexy pose or something."

Sexy pose? The way she felt. He'd be lucky to get a smile out of her. "I'm trying," she said with a big yawn. "I'm really tired. I can barely keep my eyes open. I might just pass out."

"You had eight hours to sleep on the plane. Come on, you need to get it together. Time is money…Media One's money." He snapped his fingers and lifted his camera to his face. "Come on!"

Olena didn't know what was wrong with half the people working for Media One. They had such short fuses no matter what time of the day it was. And they drank Five-Hour Energy like it was water. That couldn't be good for their kidneys. She could only hope they wouldn't be as snappy during the entire twenty-three days of filming.

The photographer lowered his camera and took a deep sigh as if his life, or maybe hers, depended on him composing himself. "Are you ready?" he asked nicely.

Suddenly, something gave Olena an extra shot of adrenaline. She was able to pose for thirty minutes, knowing that when she got to the hotel she would collapse at the first sight of a bed.

A half an hour later, the photographer said, "Okay, we're all done here." Now, Olena was hungry in addition to being tired, and her one wish was to eat while she slept.

"How long is the drive to the hotel?"

"It's nothing from here. Just down the street."

The check-in at the Hotel du Louvre was quick. Olena was surprised that she had a suite. They were markedly pulling out all the stops on this production to make her feel like a forty-four-year-old princess. However, at the moment, she was too tired to notice the beautiful architecture of the 177-room boutique hotel or the charming cafes and shops lining the famous street of Rue de Rivoli. In the five minutes it took them to drive there, she'd closed her eyes and didn't open them until Tilley tapped her on the shoulder and said, "We're here."

The floor-to-ceiling windows inside of her hotel room had

blue floral drapes and faced the Louvre Museum. The bedroom was large enough to fit a sofa, two chairs, and a work area. The bathroom had marble tile, a double sink, and a separate shower and tub.

"Most of the day you'll have to yourself, but we do have a production meeting at three, so rest up," Godiva said.

Olena curled the corners of her mouth to simulate a smile and quickly closed the door after Godiva walked into the hallway. She ran to the bed and collapsed on the king-sized bed on top of the tan duvet. But her eyes still wouldn't close even with her mask over them. She was in Paris, one of the many places she wanted to visit before she died. She'd be traveling to six romantic destinations over the next twenty-three days, meeting eligible bachelors, and pretending to find love. And maybe she would. This was a great way to get over her breakup with Jason; it was the ultimate rebound.

A few hours later, just in time for lunch, her hotel phone rang and woke her from a sound sleep.

Olena removed her eye mask and answered.

"Do you want to go downstairs with me in about twenty minutes to get something to eat?" asked Tilley.

"Sure," Olena said hesitantly. Tilley had been a bit standoffish to her while they were at Olena's condo, and she didn't understand why. Had she felt Olena staring down at her bald head?

Twenty minutes later, she met Tilley downstairs in The Brasserie du Louvre restaurant. They were seated at a spacious booth inside with an excellent view of the Royal Palace (Palais-Royal).

Olena smiled as she looked past Tilley.

"What are you doing?" Tilley asked as she turned and looked behind her at the middle-aged man sitting in the booth two booths behind theirs.

"Why is that man staring me down? And he won't even look away now that I caught him." She and Tilley had already placed their orders and Olena was a few spoonfuls away from finishing her French onion soup.

Tilley shrugged. "Staring is just something French people like to do. I don't know why; it's their culture. Don't take offense to it."

Olena continued to eye the man who wouldn't break his stare. He won. "I quit. Are you excited about being on this project?"

"I've been on tons of projects. It's all just work to me. I don't know why people who aren't in the industry think it's so much more than that."

"It's fun, though, right?"

"It has its moments. But after what happened to Deanna, it sort of puts everything right back into perspective for me. I need to start looking for another job."

"Who's Deanna?"

"Deanna Knox from *Real Beauty Atlanta*. She was the star. Well, for a couple of seasons, until her backstabbing costars got jealous. I loved styling her. Going into her closet was like walking into a Saks Fifth Avenue. She was funny. That was my girl."

"What happened to her?"

"Where have you been? She killed herself. It was on the news."

"I try not to watch the news; it's too depressing. How did she kill herself?"

"She shot herself in the head."

"Oh wow," Olena said and paused for a moment. "I'm really sorry to hear that. That's unusual, for a woman to shoot herself. That's something men do. Women usually take pills."

"Gee, I can really tell you're sorry. You didn't even know who she was, so how sorry are you really? And then you start analyzing how she killed herself. She's dead. I don't want to hear about how women usually kill themselves."

"I really am sorry to hear that. I had a boyfriend who committed suicide when I was in high school. He shot himself. So believe me when I say I'm sorry. Do you have something against me?"

"*Huh*? If I had something against you, why would I invite you to lunch?"

"Okay, allow me to rephrase. You seem as if you do. As a matter of fact, all of Media One seems that way. You all are really snappy around here."

She nibbled on a selection of fine cheese. "Well, I can't vouch for the rest of 'em, but this is how I am, so just get used to it. I don't have anything against you. Besides, those people with the cheerleader-type personalities are the main ones you should be leery of."

"So, I see on the schedule that we're not filming until Wednesday," Olena said, changing the subject. "That's good because the time difference and the long flight have me all discombobulated."

"They were going to film a scene late in the evening tomorrow, but the bachelor won't be able to get here until Wednesday."

"Do you get a lot of the inside scoop?"

"Not a lot, but some."

"So what else can you fill me in on?" Olena said, rubbing her hands together in anticipation.

"Nothing," Tilley said dryly.

"Well, then we'll just eat. The rest of our food is here." Tilley ordered a hamburger in small bites, and Olena decided to try the free-range chicken supreme with pearl onions and mushrooms.

"Bonjour," Olena told the waiter after he set down their plates. She noticed that he eyed her strangely.

"Merci beaucoup," said Tilley.

"That's what I meant to say, merci beaucoup," Olena said.

"Je vous en prie," the waiter said before leaving the table.

"What did he say?"

"You're welcome."

"You know French. Do you know a lot of French or just basic words?"

"I know a lot of French," Tilley said, picking up one of her small-bite hamburgers. Tilley went from hot to cold, mostly cold. But for some reason, Olena liked her—probably because of her bald head. A woman would have to have a lot of confidence to do that, and Olena loved people who exuded confidence.

It was Wednesday night and they officially began filming. Donna, one of the producers, said, "When he walks through the door, we want you to say something to the effect of he's gorgeous, and have your eyes sort of refocus."

"Hey, Donna," Remy said through the walkie-talkie Donna held.

"Yeah."

"Tell her to mention the breakup to him and to seem distant and say, 'I'm not sure I can do this dating thing.' And then, he's going to say, 'We'll just see how it goes. We're in Paris. It's a great date. Let's just see how this goes.' "

"Okay," Donna said, writing notes down on the paper attached to her clipboard.

"Wait, wait, Donna," Remy exclaimed. "We're running off the wrong script. There's a new one. Godiva said she e-mailed everyone. We're not even supposed to be opening at the restaurant. Check your Blackberry. Godiva wants them to arrive at the restaurant together with Nina Simone's version of "I Put a Spell on You" playing in the background. We're going to drop it in during editing, but just so they know the tempo so neither will walk too fast. It's more of a sultry, sexy sway. In the meantime, we need to put bachelor one in the car, get him back to the hotel, and have the car pull up."

"What are we doing? It almost sounds as if we're shooting this scene like a Calvin Klein commercial?" Donna asked sarcastically. "We're already here. Why should we go back to the hotel? Is

Godiva smoking crack?"

"Would you like me to ask her?" Remy said.

"You better not."

Olena didn't know if she would stick to the script. If she were on a date and thinking about another man, she wouldn't tell the man she was with that. There were plenty of times while Olena was with Jason or Matthew, and she thought about the other one.

"But while we're here, we're going to take her to the lobby and film her confessional."

"Did you get all of that?" Donna asked Olena, who shook her head in response.

"A confessional will be kind of hard to do since I haven't said two words to the man," Olena said.

"Make something up. We really don't care what you say, but don't be nice. We're going to tape two confessionals. One we're going to drop in while you're on the date...a sort of first impression type thing. The second one is after the first date is over."

"How can I make a confessional for after the date, before I even go on the date?"

"Trust me, it's easy. They're done all the time."

"How is that possible?"

"Well, look over at him. What's the first thing that comes to your mind when you see him?"

Olena looked over at the bachelor who stood near one of the cameramen.

"He's short."

"Just go with that. Think about some other short guy you dated."

"I've never dated a short guy. I honestly don't know what to say. How can I say something about him before I've even met him? That doesn't make sense to me."

Donna hit her head with the clipboard. "Reality TV isn't rocket science, Olena. You're making this harder than it has to be."

"I'm not trying to make it hard, but I don't want to be a fake, either."

"Do you want to tell Godiva that because I'm not?"

"Sure, I don't have a problem with that."

"Olena, let's not get Godiva involved, okay? Just come with me. I'll help you put together your confessional."

Alright, if you say so," Olena said, following behind Donna

The week wrapped quickly. Olena had imagined the Paris trip to be one way, but it turned out to be something else entirely. She imagined she'd fly in and have a chance to experience the city and definitely go to the Eiffel Tower. How do you go to Paris without going to the Eiffel Tower? It was on her bucket list, and Media One had it on the itinerary. But somehow it was scratched off at the last minute, and Olena felt as if they'd pissed in her bucket. She hoped to eat plenty of tasty Parisian food, but aside from the first day when she had lunch with Tilley, the rest of the days she didn't have time for much more than craft services, and the food Media One had catered. She didn't even get a chance to try authentic French macarons. There was no time to shop or sightsee. It was all about the show and the illusion of love and romance. She and her date went to the Opera Garnier, one of two halls of the National Opera of Paris. She wore an expensive gown and her date was in a suit. But she heard "cut" right before they stepped inside. They weren't going in. They were giving the viewer the impression that they were. Jason was right. Reality TV was scripted.

TWELVE

No chemo or radiation recommended was the good news. Jason was at the University of Texas MD Anderson Cancer Center in Houston for his post-prostatectomy follow-up. He needed to take a PSA test to measure the amount of prostate-specific antigens in his blood and screen for cancer. The pathologist studied Jason's entire prostate that had been removed during surgery and provided him with his Gleason scale numbers of one and two. Adding those two numbers together gave him a Gleason score of three, which was a significantly low number. Any score of four or under was low on the cancer-aggression scale. He looked to be cancer-free. Now, he wanted to talk about the other pressing issue—his erectile dysfunction. If he could start having erections again, maybe he and Olena would have a shot. If not, he'd feel too insecure in the relationship—knowing that she had enjoyed an active sex life and wasn't celibate. He believed she loved him. And she was patient with him. But knowing that she had sex with Matthew—that he could give her something Jason couldn't—was hard for Jason to deal with, so he didn't.

Dr. Reddy stood and looked over Jason's chart, "Let's talk about your other concern. You are still experiencing erectile dysfunction roughly four and a half month's post op, correct?"

"Yes, correct."

"Have you been able to achieve an erection at all?"

"A few times, but they didn't last long, and one of those times," he paused and looked over at her. Maybe, if he were speaking to a man, he wouldn't feel strange about discussing his erections. He had to remind himself that she was still a doctor.

"One of the times," Dr. Reddy said, repeating Jason's last words to prod him along.

"I got a full erection that lasted a little longer when I masturbated, but I climaxed quickly, and it was dry."

"You can have an orgasm post op, but they are dry. Very little if any ejaculation will come out. Of course, you do know this means you are infertile. I see that you've stored your sperm in a sperm bank. You are a very young man...very young to have had prostate cancer. I'm sorry."

"I...am...too."

"It is quite unusual, but definitely not unheard of. You were an athlete. You had a lot of injuries to your body, which could have accelerated some things. Not saying this is the case for you; it could be in your family history, and several factors to consider. But right now, the cancer is undetectable. So that is the most important thing. Now, you're healthy in one way. You look healthy. You have terrific recovery signs. But you're a young man—you want to have a full sex life for sure." Jason heaved out a sigh of anger. Not at the doctor, just at the situation. He couldn't even say if he had a family history of prostate cancer because he didn't know the men in his family. He was raised in a family of women. He didn't know his father, just like his mother didn't know hers. "We can begin treatment or recommend a doctor in your area. No need for you to fly from Atlanta to Houston for treatment."

"Can you tell me what it entails?"

"Sure. Of course, there are oral medications: Cialis, Levitra, Staxyn and Viagra. I believe you were sent home with samples of each after surgery."

"I don't want to use any of that stuff. I don't want to use a pump…a needle…nothing."

"Sure…you're young. You don't want that. I understand. But that rules out just about everything. We do have a suppository that you place in the penis prior to intercourse that you can try." Jason shook his head. "We have penile implants. Maybe that is the solution for you; it won't feel quite as artificial. I would probably shy away from that for now, though. If you were to remove the implant, it might be very difficult for you to achieve an erection on your own. I'd rather hold off. It hasn't been a full year since your surgery. If you can't achieve a sustainable erection at the one year mark, we can discuss the penile implant. Right now, I think it's a matter of time and the body and mind healing."

"It's been a long time already."

"Was your sex life normal prior to surgery?"

"Prior to being diagnosed with cancer, I had a phenomenal sex life. I've never had any kind of problem with getting an erection or maintaining one. This is all new to me, and I don't like it at all."

Dr. Reddy shook her head and frowned. "No…no…of course you don't."

"But, I guess I'll just have to wait it out."

The one-hour American Airlines flight from Houston to Dallas landed at six p.m.

Jason was greeted right outside of the airport at arrivals by a tall, slender woman with long hair who just happened to be his ex-girlfriend, Chevonne. Holding Chevonne's hand was his four-year-old godson, Maurice. "Hey, little man, what's up…what's up?" Jason said as he extended the palm of his right hand toward Maurice, who giggled all over himself.

"Where's Jamal?" Maurice asked.

"At home with his brother and his grandma," Jason said.

Maurice pouted.

"You want me to call him for you. Y'all are like brothers. You have to keep in touch with your brother."

. He nodded and smiled. "Call him right now."

"I see you're like your momma," Jason said, "always telling me what to do."

"Didn't do any good, did it?" Chevonne said.

"Don't start," Jason said as he threw his carryon bag into the back of Chevonne's Cherokee, took out his cell phone, and dialed his son.

Chevonne and Jason were college sweethearts. But he broke her heart when he dumped her and married a one-hit wonder pop star named Keena after a two-month courtship. Chevonne was a general practitioner now and married to Maurice, one of Jason's best friends. Jason and Maurice grew up together and had known each other since they were seven years old. He introduced Maurice to Chevonne a year after he and Chevonne had broken up as his way of righting his wrong. By that time, Chevonne was over Jason and ready to date, and the two of them clicked instantly, and now they were living in a beautiful custom-built home in North Dallas on Waggoner Drive. The last time he had visited Chevonne and Maurice they were in a much smaller home in an entirely different area. That home was nice too, but judging from the pictures Jason had seen, their new home was several steps up. Proof that a couple working together could achieve a lot. They had that white picket fence lifestyle that Jason was indeed ready for.

"J-man," Jason said to his son Jamal through the speakerphone. Jason's mother answered the phone and put Jamal, his youngest son, on at Jason's request.

"When you coming home, Daddy?"

"Monday. Guess who I'm riding in the car with?"

"Who?"

"Maurice."

"Hey…Maurice," Jamal shouted.

"Hey J-man," Maurice said equally as loud after Jason handed him the phone, "What you doing?"

"Cooking with my grandma. It's taco night."

"We havin' that too, J-man."

Jason turned to face Chevonne as she headed east on I-635.

"Are you really having tacos?" Jason asked as his right nostril flickered. Chevonne nodded. "Wrong night for me to come. I can't stand tacos."

"Well, I love the convenience. I'm a doctor. By the time I get home, cooking a big meal is nowhere on my priority list. And you know Maurice isn't going to cook because his hours are just as long as mine."

Maurice was not an athlete. Had never been athletically inclined, but he was a true fan of most sports and especially football. He was an entrepreneur and owned an insurance company that Jason invested in.

Maurice Jr. broke out in laughter.

"J-Man, you so funny."

"Who knew a three and a four year old would have so much to talk about."

It took thirty minutes to drive to Chevonne's house, another hour and a half for Chevonne to cook. By eight-thirty, little Maurice nodded off and Chevonne tucked him in bed, returning a short time later.

Jason, Maurice, and Chevonne sat around the kitchen table with just a few traces on their plates of the tacos Chevonne had made.

"For someone who doesn't like tacos," Chevonne said, "you sure downed enough of them. Tacos aren't so bad, after all, huh?"

"I didn't know they were fish tacos. You didn't tell me that part. I can do fish tacos," Jason said leaning back in his chair. "Man, I did a good job with the two of you. I need to be a matchmaker."

"Yeah, man, thank you for messing up," said Maurice, a tall man with light skin, a slender frame, and bald head.

"No problem."

"Oh really, no problem?" said Chevonne. "It was a big problem at the time. But I'm over it." She pinched her husband's cheek. "Everything happens for a reason. And he is one of the best things that ever happened to me. Of course, my son is the other."

Everything happens for a reason. Jason wasn't so sure about that. What was the reason for him getting prostate cancer? As close as he was to Chevonne and Maurice, he never told them about his battle with cancer. His mother and Olena were the only two who knew.

Jason yawned. "I'm tired. I got up early. For some reason, I couldn't sleep."

"Honey, show him to his room," Chevonne said.

"Where's your bathroom?" Jason asked as he rolled his carryon down the hallway, following behind Maurice.

"There's one in the guest bedroom."

Jason settled himself inside of the guest bedroom, unpacking most of his belongings. It dawned on him; he'd left his toothbrush at the hotel in Houston. Olena was responsible for his obsession with his teeth. Before Olena, he would brush his teeth twice a day, in the morning and again at night. After Olena, he brushed them after every meal and every sugary drink. He flossed once a day before Olena. After her, he not only flossed twice a day, but used those picks between each tooth as she did.

Right after his operation while he was over Olena's recovering, he'd go days without brushing his teeth and showering. He didn't understand how Olena tolerated his poor hygiene, but it didn't seem to faze her. "That was a good woman," he said to himself, but tossed out the thought as quickly as it entered his consciousness. "Oh well, I'm sure she's not the only good woman out there." He walked back to the kitchen where Chevonne and Maurice were.

"Man, you help her clean the kitchen," said Jason.

"Every night."

Jason shook his head. "Before I did that, I'd hire my wife a maid."

"And throw more of your money away," Chevonne said as she put a dish in the dishwasher.

"I need to borrow your car. I have to go to CVS or someplace like that to get a toothbrush, unless you all have an extra soft bristle tooth brush hanging around."

"No, we don't," Chevonne said. "But I'll drive you."

"No, y'all finish cleaning the kitchen. Don't worry I won't wreck your car. If I do, I'll pay for it. Are these your keys?" He picked up the set of keys that were lying on the kitchen counter.

"They sure are. Babe, tell him how to get to the nearest CVS," Chevonne said to Maurice.

"It's real close to here. Just take Hillcrest, which is the street at the corner, make a left and take it down to Royal Lane and make a right and it's right on the I-75 service drive. You can't miss it."

"Did you get that?" Chevonne asked as she stood drying off a plate.

"I got it. I'll be right back," said Jason as he headed toward the door leading to their garage.

Twenty minutes later, Jason called Chevonne and Maurice.

"Hood alert," Jason said through his speakerphone as he took the Skillman Street/Audelia Road exit from Interstate 635.

"Where are you?" asked Chevonne.

"On some street named Skillman."

"Oh, Lord, how did you get over there? CVS is only two seconds from us. Men can't follow directions. I swear."

"I don't know what happened. I just know the houses over where you live, and the ones over here don't look anything alike. Next time I come in town I will be renting an SUV with navigation."

"Well, head back over here. Do you need directions, or do you think you can make it back?"

"I think I know what I did wrong. I can get back. But, I did manage to stumble on a CVS over here, so it's all good."

"Oh, I know you're joking. Don't get out the car."

"This area is several steps up from where I grew up. I'll be fine."

"Maurice, he's going to the CVS on Skillman."

"He'll be okay, baby." Maurice said.

"You're a suburban girl. You don't know," Jason said.

"Weren't you the one who called saying, 'hood alert'?"

"The area can't be that bad with an LA Fitness over here. Okay, I'm parked getting ready to go into the store, so I'll call you back."

Jason pulled Chevonne's Cherokee into a parking spot in front of CVS. He walked in and headed straight down the aisle to the middle of the store. The CVS layout was almost identical to the one near his house in Alpharetta, so he didn't waste much time grabbing a soft bristle toothbrush. When he came out of the aisle, he spotted a fresh-faced woman not wearing makeup breeze through the automatic doors. She had smooth skin and long black hair that was swept back into a neat ponytail with the end swooped into an s-shape. She was a few shades lighter than

Olena with a curvier body and longer hair. As she came closer, he noticed the simple gold cross dangling from her neck, and he also noticed that she wasn't wearing a bra. He knew because he saw the imprint of her nipples through her purple velour jogging suit, which led him to wonder what else she'd gone without. He felt himself become aroused, which was something he hadn't experienced in a while. He watched her in the feminine products aisle looking for a package of tampons.

"Do you need a recommendation?" Jason joked.

"No," she said dryly without looking up.

"I don't mind helping."

After she looked up at him, she began to play with the end of her ponytail and smiled. "I should be fine. I'm looking for the ones on sale."

"I like a woman on a budget."

"Yes, Jason Nix. I am a woman on a budget." Her smile broadened. He had mixed feelings knowing she knew who he was. On the one hand, she didn't seem as excited about him until she'd taken a closer look and realized who he was. So there was always that possibility that she was a groupie. A cross dangling from her neck didn't negate the possibility.

He grabbed a box of Pearl Tampons Super Absorbency Fresh Scent. "This one's on sale. Isn't that what your coupon says?"

She fluttered her long lashes and pointed at the box. "I need unscented, but you stick to commentating, Jason, and I'll pick out my own tampons." He was a sucker for a pretty face, and she certainly had one.

"I'm going to leave you and your tampons alone. But before I go, can I have your phone number."

"Do you have something to write with?"

"I can put it in my phone."

"With all the rest, huh?"

"I'm ready," he said holding his cell phone in the palm of his hand preparing to key in her name and number. "Name or I can just put 'beautiful.' "

"LaRuth Harris." She rolled her eyes playfully and rattled off her number.

"I will definitely call you tonight."

"I hope so."

THIRTEEN

Olena was at the five-star Dorchester Hotel in London. In an airy Georgian style Belgravia suite that was situated above the hotel's front entrance with a perfect view along Park Lane and Hyde Park. She sat on a patterned wingback chair with her back facing the balcony and listened to Godiva complain. Godiva held the emergency meeting in her suite to urge Olena to add excitement to her scenes. Writers desperately wanted to spice things up. Fearing that the footage they had so far—from her time in Paris and what little they already filmed in London—was too dull.

"It seems more like a travel show than a dating show," Godiva said as she paced the sitting room.

"I'm not sure what you're looking for," Olena said.

"We need drama," Remy added. He was seated at the small writing desk directly beside Olena. "You're being too neutral. You seem like you're more into the sights than the men."

"Could it be that the real problem here isn't me at all, but the fact that I'm only meeting one man at a time? Wouldn't it be more interesting if I went on a date with a few of them at the same time?"

Godiva folded her arms and shook her head. "When you go on a real date, do you go with a few men at one time? No. The reason we even have this show to begin with is because it's not like the other dating shows that are on TV. Anyone can make a carbon copy of something already being done. I'm an originator, not a duplicator. Whatever you do...what*ever* you do...do *not* try to make this about us and shift the blame away from you. *You* need to bring it. This doesn't have anything to do with Media One or our concept or our writers or *any*thing on our part. It's all about you, sweetie."

Olena's eyes rolled. "Please don't call me sweetie. My name is either Olena or Miss Day."

Godiva drew her head back and squinted at Olena. "Well, *Olena* or Miss Day, that same attitude you're giving me right now, I need you to show that on camera, and maybe viewers will have something to watch because right now it's a snoozefest."

Olena didn't want any connection to the word attitude.

"I'm not going to be portrayed as an angry black woman. I'm insulted and deeply saddened that someone like *you* would even endorse such a negative image of black women. I'm not going to have people talking about me like a dog because I'm on TV acting a fool."

"If you don't shut up with all that—enough! This is a reality show. *Saddened?* Let me tell you what's really sad. You are forty-four years old and worried about what other people who you don't even know think about you. *Miss Day*, get a grip. People are always going to talk. They're always going to have something to say."

Olena sat sulking with her arms crossed and her face turned away from Godiva.

"Why can't we have more of this attitude when we're filming?" Godiva exclaimed. "That's all I'm saying. I don't want you to act a fool, but can you at least act alive and not like the walking dead. That's all I'm saying."

"And all I'm saying is when there is more than one person conflict occurs naturally. You can't expect me to be the only one creating drama on the show. I'm not the antagonist. I'm the protagonist."

"You need us to create the conflict for you, no problem. We can certainly work on that."

"No," Olena said, shaking her head. "That's not what I'm saying, either."

"What are you saying?" Godiva huffed.

"Maybe what you're seeing on camera is my lack of enthusiasm, which I'll admit I'm not that excited. I've met two men so far. I know I still have a couple dates with the second one, but they just can't match up to Jason."

"You're still in love with Jason. I get that. Again, all we want you to do is show your emotions. Let viewers know you're heartbroken. You can do that without saying his name."

Olena nodded. "True. I can do that."

Before the second day of filming, Olena wanted to take advantage of her free afternoon, so she and Tilley used their Oyster cards and rode the tube—the oldest underground railway in the world—and explored a little of London. Tilley seemed familiar with her surroundings and highly adept at getting around the city. Clad in winter clothing, the pair walked a half mile to Marble Arch and took the Central Line to Oxford Circus, where they exited. From there, they walked east on Oxford Street to the covered shopping center in the West End called The Plaza.

"I'd think you were a native."

"I thought I told you that I lived in Europe for ten years."

THE $O_n O$

"Ten years, really?"

She smiled. "That was when I was a lot younger. My parents like to travel the world."

Olena wanted to ask Tilley so many questions. She wanted to know how old Tilley was and what her parents did for a living. And she still wanted to know why she was bald. Probing was something Olena did well in her former position as an account executive. It was something her clients expected because the information she obtained helped her to recommend the best phone system for them. In real life, many people considered probing questions as somewhat intrusive. Since Olena enjoyed Tilley's company, she didn't want to annoy her, so she contained her curiosity.

Tilley and Olena were on the second level of The Plaza, where a fashion show had just begun. The models—all females—used an escalator for their grand entrance. Olena didn't care too much for the clothes the women had on or the thick black line sprayed across their blond bangs. It was all a little too futuristic—with shoulder pads shaped like oversized balloons, feather skirts that extended outward several inches, and gold or bronze shimmering leggings.

After watching the fashion show for only a few minutes, Tilley decided she was in the mood for fish and chips. "We can't leave London without eating fish and chips and not just any—the ones from The Golden Hind." Not long after, they left The Plaza and started walking back to Oxford Circus. They rode the Central Line to the Bond Street exit and walked west on Oxford Street, turning right on Gees toward St. Christopher Place—another prime shopping area.

"There are plenty of restaurants over here. Do you need fish and chips that badly? We can always get those another day."

"Let me just check this place out," Tilley said as she and Olena walked in the woman's clothing store Ghost and over to a rack of pants. She placed a pair of pants up to Olena's waist. "I think I like this pair better than the one you were wearing on your next date. Let me call Godiva and see if she'll pay me back if I buy them." She dug through the backpack for her phone. "Skip it. She'll pay me."

"If she doesn't, I will."

"Don't do that. They make more than enough money."

She and Tilley left the store and headed over to the nearby Café Rouge.

"Feta cheese and marinated red peppers with French bread sound so good," Olena said as she studied the menu. "I think I'm going to get that for an appetizer. Ooh, but what about these gold-medal green olives, I love green olives—I have to get that too. Spicy beef and lamb sausage with harissa mayonnaise…oh my. Not that, I know what harissa mayonnaise is. But it sounds delicious. Why do I want everything on this doggone menu?"

"Because you're like me, and you love food," Tilley said.

"And you love sweets."

Tilley nodded. "I sure do. And I already know I'm getting the crème brulee for dessert."

"And for dinner?"

Tilley read from her menu. "Probably the traditional French cut of steak marinated in rosemary and garlic served with French fries and melted garlic beurre maison. Best served rare."

"I would never eat rare meat, not even overseas."

"I always get my steak rare. I really wanted some of those fish and chips. I'm going to get some before I leave," Tilley said.

"That sounds good, too. God, everything does."

"You have a serious passion for food. You should be a food writer."

"You mean a critic?"

"Did I say critic? No. Not all writers are critics. But all critics are writers."

Hmm—a light bulb immediately turned on in Olena's head—a food writer. She could eat *and* write, which would be the best of both worlds. Maybe she'd look into that.

"Thanks for that."

"For what?"

"The idea of becoming a food critic...I mean writer. But I don't know how I'd break into that business."

"You mean you never thought about doing that—becoming the next Ruth Reichl?"

"The next who?"

"Maybe not. You better do your research. You have to know the movers and shakers in the business. Can you cook?"

"Well, *no*."

"Hmm. You have to know food in order to write about it. Harissa mayonnaise—you should really know what that is."

"Do you know what it is?"

"No, but I'm not the one who wants to be a food writer. You are. You could always go to culinary school."

"Culinary school to be a food writer? I'm not trying to be a chef."

"You need to know food—various cuts of meat, types of fish, cooking temperatures, and so on." Tilley said.

"How do you know so much about it?" Olena asked.

"During my trying-to-find-myself phase, I looked into several different careers." Tilley started eating a piece of bread she tore from a small loaf.

"Do you like the one you have now?"

"I love my job. Can't you tell?" Tilley asked sarcastically.

"You don't like it?" Olena said. Tilley didn't say another word. She seemed lost in thought. "Tilley, what are you thinking about?"

"The Alexander McQueen outfit getting delivered to the hotel today. It's probably there already. I'm so excited. That crombie coat and that white blouse that I'm going to have you wear underneath it is the business. You're going to have to wear your hair up for that outfit because the collar on the shirt is very high, and it frames the face."

Olena smiled. "You picked the right career because I can really tell you have a passion for clothes."

"Picking out the clothes is the easiest part, and dealing with my clients is easy most of the time. The hard part is for my clients to pull off their looks. You need to exude confidence when you have on an outfit that might be a little edgy. To be honest, I'm hoping to leave Media One soon and start my own clothing line."

"Don't worry, I won't tell anyone anything you say to me."

Tilley shrugged. "I don't care if you do. If I don't want something repeated, I don't say it. They all know I'm not happy, especially after Deanna died. But I can't talk about her right now because I'll get mad at Godiva. Smith's cool. He just wants the business to do well, and he's about his business, not all the extra drama. But Godiva, I can't take her in large doses. You'll understand what I mean once some story you had hidden gets leaked and you're trying to figure out how that happened. You won't have to wonder for too long. She'll do anything for ratings, anything to make sure the number of viewers in the 18–49 range scores a 4.5 or higher."

"Four million five hundred thousand?"

Tilley shook her head quickly and rolled her eyes. "Trust me, she'll educate you on the Nielsen ratings system. *Real Beauty Atlanta* pulled a 4.5 on cable thanks to Deanna, which was why she was paid a hundred thousand an episode. I'm sure for network TV she'll want an even higher number."

"A hundred thousand an episode. Oh, my, I had no idea reality paid so well."

"It pays some people well. But anyway, enough of that, what else do you want to see while you're in London?"

"I definitely want to see Buckingham Palace and Trafalgar Square."

"You'll be seeing plenty. You and your date are walking along the River Thames from Westminster Bridge. Lot of walking on this trip, so I hope those cute shoes I gave you don't make your feet hurt. I'm ready to head back whenever you are. You need to get plenty of beauty sleep, so the camera will be kind to you." Olena stared across at Tilley. "What?" *Should she ask?* Olena wondered. "What?" Tilley repeated.

"Can I ask you something?"

"You want to know why I'm bald, right?"

Olena nodded quickly. "But not if you don't want to tell me. I was just curious."

"Yeah, that's cool. A lot of people wonder. My little sister had cancer—Wilm's tumor, and she had to shave her head, so my mother and I both shaved ours as a show of support. Now, she has her hair back, and I decided to keep mine this way. I actually like it."

"How's your sister doing?"

"Wonderful," Tilley said, smiling. "Thank you for asking."

"Going bald is brave of you."

"Everyone usually assumes I'm either gay or have cancer. The gay part comes in handy because when I had long hair the men I didn't want to be bothered with were always the ones harassing me the most. I don't have that problem now."

"Women probably hit on you now."

"Sometimes, but they're not as annoying."

Tilley and Olena laughed.

"I wonder why a woman has never hit on me," Olena said.

Tilley laughed. "You're my mother's age, but you act so much younger than her."

"What, I'm your mother's age?" Olena asked as she pointed her finger at herself. Tilley nodded. "Tilley?"

"What? Actually, she's a year younger than you."

"How old are you?"

"Twenty-three."

"You're only twenty-three."

Tilley nodded. "Yep, and you seem my age. That's weird."

"Yeah, I've been told that. I guess I need to grow up and start acting my age."

"Not saying that—some people have a young spirit."

"That sounds as if I have ghosts living in me. I just need to grow up. When I was with Jason, I felt more mature. He's a single father, and I would watch the boys when he was out of town on business. But that's over now. Oh, well. Who's the next bachelor?"

"I'm not sure, but I heard at least one is going to be famous."

Was there any possible way? Any possible way that the English actor Hakeem Frye would be the next eligible bachelor, Olena wondered. She would be ecstatic if he were. He wasn't married. He was successful. And he was from Canning Town, East London, which wasn't far from where they were filming. Meeting Hakeem Frye would make the whole reality TV experience worthwhile for Olena.

"Here's to praying my next date is Hakeem Frye," she said, raising her water glass.

The knock on Olena's hotel door came right after she kicked off her shoes and spread herself across the four poster bed, praying they'd forgotten about taping her confessional. "I'm not here," she shouted. But the knocks continued. She jerked her body off the bed. "God, I might as well get this mess over with. I don't have anything to say about the man," she said as she walked toward the door. "Nothing good." She snatched the door open. "He's not 'the one.' How's that for a confessional?"

"We want to go to bed just as badly as you do," Remy said as he entered with the cameraman whose name she had purposely forgotten because he was always flirting with her and every other woman within view.

Olena sat on the sofa waiting for the small crew to set up and begin filming her. She thought the confessionals she did in the hackney carriage would suffice, but evidently not. They needed more. First, she had to give them her first impression. Then, she had to do the confessional that would run after the date.

"If you get this right the first time, we won't have to call Godiva," Remy joked.

"Let's do this." And one take was all it took.

After the camera crew had left her suite, Olena thought about her travels. The next stop was Viena and then Monte Carlo on to Venice and Melbourne before finally heading back to Atlanta and a life without Jason.

FOURTEEN

"Date somebody," Jason's mother said. He had just finished putting his two sons to bed, and his face was long. He missed Olena. With the regular season over, he had a lot of time on his hands to think about her. She was out of the country meeting men, and maybe she'd meet one she liked better than him. That's if she still liked him. The last message she left for him was pretty strong, and her impotency remark hit below the belt. Still, he loved her. But he hated that he'd caught her in a lie. *Without trust in a relationship, what was left?* No need for him to wonder because he already knew—nothing. The way she cared for him when he needed her most was one thing he couldn't forget, though.

"I'm starting to believe all the good women are gone," Jason told his mother.

"And guess what? The good women feel the same way about you men. The only way to know if you had the real thing is to do what Olena is doing—date. Maybe after you start doing that, you'll realize you had the right one all along, and she didn't deserve a letter from your attorney's office."

"I regret doing that, but I did need to protect my name."

"Are you President Obama? Protect your name. Don't be so high on yourself. Besides, Keena already went on national TV and told all your business."

"I said I regret doing it, Mom, okay. What's done is done?"

"Which one—the gag order or the relationship?"

"They're both done."

"Well, then, you might as well date because sitting around here moping isn't helping anything or anyone. You're so irritable lately."

"I can't believe *you,* the woman who thinks most women are gold diggers, is telling me to date."

"I don't think most women are gold diggers. I think most of the ones you meet are. There's a difference. Besides, I'm sure you meet women all the time."

"And I'm sure you're right."

"So go on a friendly date with one of them. Take a woman to dinner. It doesn't have to be anything serious. Just see how the conversation goes. You'll never know how good you had it until you have someone else to compare her to."

"That's not the reason I'm doing it."

"I don't care why you do it. In fact, you don't have to do it at all. I'm not trying to force you to. And if you were to date, please make sure she's not a chickenhead."

"Okay, Momma. I'll definitely do that."

Jason wore the pair of autumn brown double monk strap cap-toed shoes that he'd just purchased from the men's store Sid Mashburn. He paired them with jeans, a black leather jacket, and a stylish blue shirt.

He answered his ringing cell phone.

"I'm here," the young woman said in a cheery voice.

"I'm almost there," Jason said as he made a slight left onto Airport Boulevard.

"I'm right outside of Delta arrivals."

"Alright, baby, see you in a few." He took his mother's advice and decided to start dating. The young woman he already had in mind was LaRuth Harris, the one he'd met while he was in Dallas. They'd been talking and texting several days, but this was their first face-to-face, aside from the time they first met.

As he pulled in front of the Delta terminal at Atlanta's Hartsfield airport, he felt his stomach flutter…like butterflies? *Nah*. He couldn't have been nervous. At least he didn't think he could have been.

He had almost flown to Dallas to visit LaRuth. Coincidently, she had just started her one-week staycation and called him to complain about how bored she was. Jason put on his cape and rescued her. He *loved* being Superman. He booked her a first-class flight aboard Delta Airlines and made arrangements for her to stay in a suite at the Ritz-Carlton in Buckhead. He could've put her up anywhere—closer to his house or right by the airport. Instead, he chose a hotel near Olena's condo. Nothing too deliberate, he liked how convenient the area was. Besides, Olena was out of the country. And it wasn't as if he'd bump into any of her friends because she didn't have any. Olena not having friends seemed strange to him at first; then, he kind of liked it. His ex-wife had too many friends. And when he was gone for the season, she'd hang out with them and meet men. She'd cheated on him, and that was the reason they divorced.

"You didn't have to fly me down here first-class," LaRuth said after Jason exited his black G55 AMG, took her rollaway bag, and held the door to his SUV open for her. "Only the best for you, my dear." She blushed. "Are you hungry?" She nodded. "Do you like wine?"

She shook her head. "I don't drink."

"That's right—you're a good Christian girl. Actually, I don't drink any more, either. I would have one to be social, if you were drinking."

"Well," LaRuth said as she shrugged. "Just because it's on the menu doesn't mean I have to partake."

He smiled at her. Thought about taking her comment left, but decided to be good and stay right. Aside from the cross she wore, she and Jason had lengthy discussions about her Christianity and faith. He'd always been spiritual. He was raised that way. And his recent brush with death certainly drew him closer to his maker. He prayed to Him for strength a lot and attended church more regularly. But it had been awhile since he'd dated a church girl—probably high school. He glanced over at her adoringly. She smiled.

"You have a beautiful smile, but I'm sure you already know that?"

"You do too," she said, poking the dimple on his right cheek with her index finger.

"I made reservations for us at a very nice restaurant. I hope you like it." He switched to Boney James's "Hypnotic"

"I need to change first."

He felt her staring, so he raised her dainty hand to his lips, kissed the center of her hand, and continued driving north on Interstate 85 toward the hotel.

He sat on one of the leather sofas in the lobby waiting for LaRuth to come down in her new outfit. He prayed she didn't pile on too much makeup. She looked perfect just the way she was. He'd gone most of the day without thinking about Olena once, but a thought crept into his mind while he waited on LaRuth. *Did he overreact? Could their relationship be salvaged?*

LaRuth resurfaced in a sexy black dress and a pair of expensive designer shoes that Jason immediately recognized by the red soles.

Her hair was still pulled back in a ponytail. The same amount of makeup on her face as before–just lip gloss.

"You look beautiful," he said as he stood. His knees weakened from twenty minutes of inactivity. "Can I have a kiss?"

"You can have a handshake."

Well, he thought he'd at least try.

"I'll take that," he said, extending his right hand, which she took with her left and shook limply. "Let's try that again. You're supposed to shake my right hand with your right hand."

"Oh, we don't shake hands where I work. We barely speak there."

"So let's do that again with your right hand and a firmer grip."

She stuck out her right hand and shook his hand, but her grip was still flimsy. "Never mind—we're going to have to work on that."

For dinner, he reserved Rathbun's Private Wine Room. He drove into their garage, and he and LaRuth were escorted to the dining room through the private side entrance.

At dinner, he told her again how nice she looked. "If you can afford a pair of those shoes, you're doing pretty good for yourself, because I know all about those red soles."

"I bet. You've probably bought plenty of 'em."

"Quite a few…for my ex-wife."

"Well, I shop at the Clothes Circuit in Dallas. It's a consignment shop, and I get all my clothes and shoes from there for at least half off."

"I'll have to buy you a gift certificate from there, since you like the place so much."

"I don't think they even sell gift certificates."

"Then, I'll just write you a check."

"You just met me. You really like to flash your money around, don't you, Mr. Nix? I already know you have a lot of it, but I don't like you because of your money."

"I hope not because I'm broke now."

"Yeah, right. Jason Nix—broke…I doubt that."

"I'm broke. I lost all of my money after retirement."

"Well, I don't need to know about your financial situation. I want to know about you. Are you a good person?"

"I'm a great person."

"Mmm hmm."

"*Mmm hmm.* Are you?"

"I'm a phenomenal woman."

"Phenomenal—as in Maya Angelou 'Phenomenal Woman'?" He played with the end of her long ponytail. "As in the bend in your hair. The curl of your lips." He moved toward her and tried to kiss her, but she moved away. "That kind of phenomenal?"

"Yep, that's me—a phenomenal woman."

"Are you sure about that?" She nodded. "We'll see."

"I know you have a stable of women. You're just too smooth and too fine not to."

"You think I'm fine, really?"

"Oh, come on, please. You already know you are."

Jason shook his head. "Honestly I don't. But if you say I am, I'm going to have to take your word for it." He smiled, showing his perfectly straight white teeth.

"You never answered my question about your stable of women."

"I don't even have one."

She gazed at him long and adoringly before saying, "And why is that?"

"I guess I haven't found the one, like that reality show that they've been advertising. Are you going to watch that?"

LaRuth turned up her nose. "I don't watch reality shows."

"Good for you. I don't either." He studied her face: how perfect it appeared. Some people just had good genes. "So why don't you tell me about yourself, Miss Harris."

"Ask me whatever you want to know."

"Are you from Dallas? Born and raised? Tell me something?"

"I'm from Fort Worth. The Stop 6 area—have you ever heard of it?" He shook his head. "I couldn't wait to move out of there—away from the gunshots."

"Did you grow up with both your parents in the house?"

"Huh? No one has ever asked me that question."

"I'm asking. Did you?"

"No, I didn't. I never knew my father, and my mother hated men. She wasn't gay, but she hated them. I never saw her date."

"Are you the only child?"

"No, I have a sister and a brother, but I don't talk to them that much. Is that all? I hate being questioned."

"That's all for now."

After dinner, they returned to her hotel. He rode the elevator to the fifth floor and walked her to her room to make sure she got in safely. "I guess this is goodbye for now," Jason said, leaning down to plant a kiss on her cheek. She turned her face so that her lips would touch his.

"It doesn't have to be."

"It doesn't?"

"No," she said. "I really like you. Do you like me?"

"Of course."

"Then, why should it have to be goodbye?"

"I guess it doesn't."

She took his hand, swiped the card key to the door and was met with a cold burst of air as she entered. "It's so cold," she said, rubbing her shoulders.

"It's going to heat up real fast. Trust me. Real fast."

In under a minute, they were both undressed.

"I don't know," she said, admiring his erection.

"You don't know what?"

"I don't know if I can handle all that."

"I'll give you a progress report."

"God forgive me," she said, tumbling on the bed on top of

him. Her words caused his erection to soften, but once the fore-play began it stiffened, and their loud moans grew intensely.

At nine in the morning, Jason's eyes opened. He turned and saw LaRuth lying beside him with a look of disappointment in her eyes.

"What's wrong?"

"Last night you called me, Olena."

"I did?"

"Yes, you did. Who is Olena?"

"I was moaning—'O,' like that."

"O...*lena*. That doesn't sound like a moan; it sounds like a name, and I feel like a fool."

"Don't feel like a fool. You should never feel like that."

"Well, I do," she said, sitting up in bed with her arms folded. "Who is she, your woman?" He had to admit to himself that he loved the sound of Olena's name. Whenever he masturbated, he thought of Olena. When he came, he'd say her name. The name Olena sounded so much better than the name LaRuth. Saying LaRuth's name over and over again sounded too much like the song, "The Roof is on Fire."

"She was my woman, but we aren't together anymore. She's off doing her thing, and I'm here doing mine. I'm sorry for that slip up. And trust me, it'll never happen again."

"Why won't it happen again, you're not going to see me any-more?"

"I never said that. Did I?"

"No, but I'm pretty good with reading between the lines."

"Obviously, you're not. After last night, I'd be a fool not to want to see you anymore. You really know how to blow a man's mind."

"Is that all I know how to blow—a man's mind?" She giggled.

"You have skills. But you know what they say, practice makes perfect. Have you had a lot of practice?"

She shook her head. "Very little."

"You're just telling me what you know I want to hear."

She shrugged. "I'm telling you the truth. Believe whatever you want to believe."

"I know strippers who don't know the tricks you were doing."

"So you sleep with strippers?"

"Not intentionally, but I can't say one or two didn't slip by me. I only know what a person tells me when I meet them, whether or not what they're saying is true eventually comes out. I'm a true believer of that."

"So what are you saying, Mr. Nix?"

"You have a real innocent look about you. It's sexy but sweet. In bed, though, you're far from innocent. Did reading the Bible teach you those tricks?"

"Why did you have to go there? You don't think I feel bad enough about fornicating. Those without sin cast the first stone. I got a good vibe with you, and I let my guard down. That's all. But now you're making me regret that I did."

"Any secrets you want to tell me? Speak now while you have the chance."

"No secrets on my end. What about yours?"

"Do you have any kids?"

She shook her head. "That's what I should be asking you. Any kids, Mr. Nix?"

"I have two boys by my ex-wife. Junior is seven and Jamal will be four soon. *And you?*"

She shook her head. "No kids," she said as she straddled him. "You're still in timeout for calling me that other woman's name. I'm so mad at you."

"Yeah, I can really tell," he said, lying on his back enjoying the view her naked body provided. *Was she too good to be true?* He wondered. Right now it was lust, and he'd experienced that many times before. But none quite like this.

While she was in the bathroom, he called down to the concierge. "I need some assistance. I'd like to purchase a gift card, and I hope someone at your hotel can help me with that."

"Certainly, Mr. Nix."

The shower water stopped running, so he quickly provided the young lady with the details. "Can you purchase a thousand-dollar Neiman Marcus gift card for me?" He felt that Neiman's was an excellent choice. For one thing, the Lennox Square Mall was across the street, so the concierge would be able to get there and back quickly, and Neiman's flagship store was in Dallas. He assumed LaRuth, being a Texan, would appreciate the gesture.

"I will personally get right on that and bring it up to you, myself, Mr. Nix. And we'll add it to your room or would you like for me to come up and get your card?"

"Add it to the room."

"Of course. The gift card will be up to your room in less than thirty minutes."

"Thank you so much."

"Who was that?" LaRuth asked as she walked out with a bath towel draped over her body and another over her hair.

"Room service."

"Oh, what did you order?"

"Nothing yet. I decided to wait and find out what you wanted. Too bad it's Saturday. They have a great Sunday brunch here."

"Waffles? I love waffles."

"You don't like pancakes?"

She shook her head. "I hate them."

"You hate pancakes?" he asked, looking at her as if she'd just committed a cardinal sin.

She nodded as she removed the towel from around her head and used it to scrunch her wet hair dry.

"So you're a curly head."

"Yes, before I blow dry and flat iron my curls straight."

"But it looks good just like that."

She turned and walked back into the bathroom. A few seconds later, the blow dryer came on. He realized something about LaRuth. He'd made a mental note of it the day before. But the sex had blown mind to the point that he didn't have any recall, until she'd just done it again. She had yet to say, thank you to any of his compliments. And he'd given her plenty. And when he'd mentioned the brunch, she didn't comment at all aside from asking if they had waffles and that she hated pancakes. Not that he compared her to Olena, but Olena always said thank you, and she got excited over small things. When he first told Olena about brunch at the Ritz-Carlton, her eyes glimmered at the mere mention of icy crab claws, oysters, and shrimp; caviar; fresh organic salads; traditional breakfast favorites; and classic summer desserts. LaRuth came off as robotic, even in bed. As much as he enjoyed the sex, he missed something. Maybe it was because they didn't really know each other, and there didn't feel like a real connection between the two. When they weren't having sex, he found himself bored with her. Olena made him laugh. He realized he would never be satisfied until he made love to Olena. Even if they didn't work out, he had to experience her in that way.

While she was blow-drying her hair, he ordered room service—pancakes for him and waffles for her, and they were delivered at the same time the gift card was. He'd asked room service to bring up an extra plate with a lid, so he could hide the gift card there.

LaRuth resurfaced a few minutes after the concierge left. Her hair was straight again and pulled back into her signature ponytail with the S-shaped tip.

"So our food is here now?" she said as she glided from the bedroom to the living room, over to the sofa and the coffee table where Jason set up everything. "Aren't you going to eat?"

"Ladies first. Start with that one."

She pulled off the lid to the one he'd pointed to. "Neiman Marcus, what's this for?" she asked as she picked up the envelope."

"Merry Christmas."

"This isn't for Christmas. Christmas was last month. This is your way of apologizing for calling me that other woman's name, isn't it?" He nodded. "Baby, you don't have to buy me. You're too sexy to do that."

She handed him the gift card. "Take it back. I forgive you."

"You can't return gift cards, so you might as well take it."

She nodded. "I'm not the Neiman Marcus type. I told you the Clothes Circuit is my store."

"Then, I'll have to take you shopping there one day."

"You don't have to."

"I want to."

She earned some major points for not taking the gift card and for saying she'd rather shop at a consignment store than Neiman's. Maybe she wasn't a gold digger after all. He removed the lid covering his breakfast and went through the ritual of cutting his pancakes up in several tiny squares.

"What are you doing?"

"Cutting up my pancakes."

"Do you really have to go to that extreme?"

"Yes."

"Okay, if you say so."

"So you're absolutely sure you don't want the gift card?"

She nodded. "Give it to your mother." He smiled when she said that. She may not have resembled Olena, but she did something Olena had done the first time he tried to give her a gift. She didn't take it and had him give it to his mother, which was what he did, and what he wanted to do that time also. Maybe that was a good sign. Maybe all the good women weren't taken. But, then he reminded himself that they had sex on the first night, and she initiated it. He tried not to overanalyze the night they shared. They just had chemistry. That's all. And even more importantly, he had an erection. "I hope I see you again," LaRuth said as she poured more syrup over her waffles.

"Why wouldn't you?"

"Because we slept together on our first date, you probably think differently of me."

"You probably think differently of me too."

She shook her head. "You're protected under that double standard rule."

"If it weren't good, and you weren't fine, I might have to hold it against you. But you're protected under that double standard rule."

She bit down on her bottom lip as she stared at him seductively. She picked up a strawberry from her plate and fed it to him, sticking her finger in the little silver cup filled with syrup. She put her finger in her mouth and sucked the syrup off. "This syrup tastes so good I could pour it on anything, and I do mean anything." She reached for Jason's belt buckle.

She had some kind of magical powers because the erections he achieved with her were like the ones he had before his cancer diagnosis. Sex wasn't everything, but right now it was. She knelt down on the floor between his legs and unbuttoned his jeans. His head fell back against the sofa cushion. She blew his mind and made him feel like a man again. He didn't feel embarrassed that she knew he was impotent because, with her, he hadn't been. She provided him with a much-needed clean slate.

FIFTEEN

Olena and Tilley stood in a junior suite of the Grand Hotel Wien unpacking their suitcases.

"I guess I won't be wearing these," Olena said as she folded her jeans over her arm. "Viennese people don't wear jeans." She tried not to think about Jason. But when her mind wasn't on him, it was usually on his kids or his mother. She wondered what they were all doing, especially now that Jason was done commentating for the season. She had imagined spending Christmas and New Year's with all of them. Instead, she never even received a call from him to wish her Happy Holidays.

"It's good to know somebody's been reading the e-mails Godiva sends out because I haven't," Tilley said. On the two-hour British Airways flight from London to Vienna, Olena discovered that Tilley's full name was Chantilly and that she and Tilley would be sharing a suite for the next leg of the trip because production had run over budget. *All good things must come to an end,* Olena thought, and having her own suite had certainly been a good thing. Not that she was anti-social. But she was pro having her own space. "They wear jeans, but not that much. They're dressy here."

"I just don't want to be viewed as being disrespectful. I usually prefer to dress up. But when I'm not filming, I just want to be comfortable. After this experience, I never want to see a pair of five-inch heels again, let alone wear a pair." Olena tossed her jeans on the chair beside her.

"Those don't actually look like jeans, and you're not going to the opera. You'll be fine."

At least, Olena and bachelor number two had the opportunity to visit a few of London's landmarks. Unlike in Paris where she and bachelor number one had dinner once and pretended to go to the opera.

"I just realized it's been a few days, and I haven't thought about losing my job, my man, and my book deal. But now, I just did, and I'm depressed."

"Chocolate cake will make you feel better. I'm not leaving Vienna without getting a slice of Sachertorte."

Once they left Vienna, there were three more stops; then, she was Atlanta bound. But she was no longer anxious to return home. She could imagine living the life she led now minus the cameras—a nomadic lifestyle traveling from one place to the next never settling down permanently in any of the places she visited. Somewhat like her parents were doing now that they were traveling the Western states in their RV after their retirement. Not that, she could afford to do so, but she appreciated the experience she was given for free. She'd miss her family, but only a little bit. As long as she could talk to them from time to time on the phone to catch up on everyone's life, especially her niece, Alicia, she'd be fine. So the reality show exposed her to something different. But she missed writing. She was too busy to think about characters, hadn't heard from Eugena since she'd left, not that she expected to. No news, in that case, was bad news, though. Her career seemed doomed before it even had a chance to spread its wings and take off. Days like today when she had a few hours of free time were days she spent with Tilley seeing the sites they wanted to see, not the ones in the script; those were the best days.

The place to go for the Original Sacher-Torte was the Café Sacher next to the Vienna State Opera house and just a short walk from their hotel. "Guten Tag," Olena made sure to say when they entered the coffeehouse.

After waiting in a long line at the busy café, they were finally seated at a small round table for two beside a window.

"Welcome to the Café Sacher," the waitress said as she stood at their table. "What would you like?"

For lunch, she and Tilley both had Sachertorte, mélange (coffee with milk), and water. To Olena, there was something sinfully satisfying about eating only cake for lunch. Something that she would have guilt-tripped herself out of if she weren't overseas. The torte had layers of dense chocolate cake with apricot jam mixed in and was iced with dark chocolate and a generous serving of whipped cream on the side.

"Where did Godiva dig up her information about these different places we're going to?" Olena asked. "She said they didn't speak English here, but they speak English and very well."

"Godiva has her assistant do all that stuff, so there's no telling what website she went on to get her information. Like I said, I don't even read her e-mails. I'll figure out what the places are like once I get there. The only reason they send them out is to protect the company from a lawsuit. If you eff up, they want you to know it's your fault and not theirs, or I guess I should say, *Godiva* wants you to know that. She didn't even go to Deanna's funeral. Just issued that same standard two sentence statement to the media that they all issue, 'We here at Media One are saddened by the passing…blah…blah…blah.'"

"But she was right about the city being animal-friendly," Olena said, observing several dogs lying underneath tables inside of the café. She tried to change the subject because every now and then Tilley would go on a Godiva rant that Olena found very uncomfortable. Not that Godiva was Olena's favorite person by any means. They'd bumped heads quite a few times while on the trip. But, she didn't have to like a person to respect them, and she also knew running a business wasn't easy, so in some ways she sympathized with Godiva. Not in a lot of ways, but in a few.

"I respect Godiva. She has a lot to be proud of."

Tilley said, "I respect Godiva too…for what she's achieved, but I don't like her nor do I have to pretend to. I like Smith, but I don't understand how *he* ended up with *her*."

Olena took a sip of water. "This water tastes like bottled water."

Tilley shrugged as she looked at a map. Olena assumed Tilley was thinking about Deanna at that moment and blaming Godiva for her suicide. Olena, on the other hand, tried to understand people and figure out why they acted the way they did. "With Godiva, it's something in her childhood probably. Maybe something happened to make her so distant or appear to be that way. You can tell a lot about a person based on how they were raised and things they went through. Do you know anything about her background?"

Tilley shook her head. "I just know she's from Decatur, but she tells people Atlanta. I don't know what's up with that."

Olena sipped her mélange and thought back over her own childhood. She blamed a lot on her high-school boyfriend, Stan, who committed suicide, and even more on her college fling, Andrew, Matthew's father. The common denominator was they were both men. If Jason didn't come around, his name would be added to her list, as well. She'd tried calling him the night before, but his cell phone went straight to voice mail.

"The only thing more irritating than a grown woman whining

about something that happened a long time ago is a grown man doing the same thing," Tilley added. When my sister was sick, I realized that most of the things people worry over and bicker about are so irrelevant. Move on."

"A lot of people talk about their childhood, Tilley—the good and bad. Oprah does it all the time."

Tilley spit out laughter. "A lot of people want to know everything about her. She can talk about her childhood all day every day. She can talk about her bowel movements and people will listen. I know I will. I love that woman."

"Uh, let's not discuss bowel movements while I'm eating chocolate cake."

"One of the best things about being successful is that people care about what you think. They value your opinion. They listen to you. I was a dental hygienist and quit my job after Oprah said people should do what they love; I hated cleaning people's teeth. Some people have really bad dental hygiene."

"I don't want to talk about that while I'm eating, either."

"I didn't have any experience in fashion other than I always loved putting outfits together. I taught myself how to sew. I didn't have any celebrity clients. I just knew I could do it, and I had lived in Europe for close to ten years before coming back to the States. I used that to my advantage. That sort of thing looks good on a resume. No one needed to know it was when I was a child."

"I understand what you're saying."

"You seem insecure. You can't do this show and be insecure. The audience will be able to tell. You have to project confidence at all times even if you don't have any. Men like confident women."

"I'm very confident...I mean I was. I'll admit losing my job has set me back a bit, but I'll get it back together."

"What did you use to do again?"

"I was an account executive for a company called Lutel, and I sold phone systems to major corporations."

"Ugh, sounds boring. Be glad you lost it."

"Are you kidding me? I *loved* my job. I was so good at it and made so much money. Everyone in the company knew my name, because I was the best. But no need to dwell on what was." *And that included Jason,* she told herself. "What time does filming start…seven?"

Tilley shook her head. "I thought you read Godiva's e-mails. Even I know filming starts at four. They're shooting you and your date going to the opera."

"But we're not really going."

"Exactly. It's going to be shot out of sequence. I'm sure you can already tell they do that a lot."

"I figured that out in London. I met the bachelor for the first time, and he was talking to me like we'd already been on a date. They forgot to fill me in. Then, in the next scene, I had to act like I was meeting him for the first time."

"I'm thinking they're using men who are somehow connected to Media One. Because Jeff Sterling lives with Kate, she's a salon owner and part of the *Real Beauty Miami* cast."

"Who's Gordon connected to?"

Tilley shrugged. "I'm not sure about him, but they'll use friends for small parts, and, if the part is a larger one, they'll do an open cast for that or go through a modeling agency."

"So you mean Gordon isn't real? My short Frenchman with the sexy accent is a fraud." Olena shook her head as her eyes rolled. "I'm devastated," she said sarcastically.

"Couldn't you figure that out when they were telling him how to say his lines?"

Olena nodded quickly and sipped some more coffee. "I was in denial, though. I wanted Gordon to be real. I didn't care about the other one. After you've had as much bad luck with men as I have, it feels really good to be pursued by a bunch of different men— rich at that. But I guess these men aren't really rich, either." Tilley had just finished eating her second slice of Sachertorte. Olena looked down at her clean plate. "Are you ready or do you need a few minutes to let that chocolate digest properly?"

"I'm fine. But I'm not even ready to go back to the hotel. Let's take in a few sights. I brought a map from the hotel with the ten must-sees while in Austria."

"Which is the closest?"

"The Staatsoper is right across the street, and that's where you're going tonight. Let's go here."

Tilley pointed to the picture of St. Stephen's Cathedral that was on the front of the map. "That's only one point seven kilometers away. By foot it takes nine minutes. That's a nice little walk to burn off some fat. I just hope we don't get lost."

"Burn off some fat? Are you trying to say, I'm fat?"

"You might want to step on the scale because your clothes are fitting a little snug."

"Shh, don't tell anyone, but I gained two pounds. And even though I probably do need to walk, it's too cold. My ears are still numb from the walk over here. I'm going back to the hotel and take a cat nap before my date, so I won't look tired on TV. I can burn some extra calories while I sleep."

"You won't burn that many, only about forty-eight calories an hour."

"How do you know so much?"

"I thought about being a trainer."

"Tilley, is there any job you didn't think about doing?"

"Yep." She nodded. "Selling phones."

"Ah, a comedian, too. Why not add that to your list of fledgling career options?" Olena stood and tugged at the waistband on her jeans. "Do you really think I'm fat?"

"Not *Biggest Loser* fat. Just be careful. Two pounds can quickly turn into ten. And if you were to gain ten pounds while you're filming this show, Godiva would beat the fat off of you with the contract you signed."

They both laughed as they strolled out of the café.

Olena stormed back into her hotel suite with the cameras following. It was hard for her to believe that, after two dates with Fitz the day before, the necktie designer would act a fool on their third date. The adrenaline caused Olena's heart to beat rapidly—an effect of the cameras and the pressure to perform. And for the first time, she understood her niece a little better.

"You've got to be kidding me, Auntie. A reality show? I've been in LA for thirteen years trying to break into the business and my aunt, who sold phones for a living, gets cast to do a reality show. Unbelievable, I'm now convinced that anyone with a pulse can get their own reality show. I don't want to talk about this anymore." And Alicia hung up. She was upset. *But, oh well,* Olena thought, *she'd get over it.*

"He's a jerk," she told Tilley. "And the worst part about the whole evening was that I didn't even get to finish my Wiener Schnitzel."

Tilley tried to contain her laughter but couldn't and she burst out.

"Why are you laughing? Nothing's funny."

"All you think about is food," said Tilley. The writers had decided to add Tilley to the cast because Godiva liked the interaction between Olena and Tilley. So Tilley was officially Olena's best friend. The only part she and Tilley didn't like about that was now the cameras would always be following the two of them too.

"Me? You're the one who had me running around town for Sachertorte."

"Just tell me what happened."

"True, the guy who waited on us was rude, but that doesn't mean Fitz had to go ballistic. I was embarrassed." She sat on the edge of her bed. "All I wanted to do was finish my Wiener Schnitzel."

"Cut," Godiva said. She walked up to the sofa where Olena and Tilley were sitting. "Here's the thing. You know how you date someone, and you come back and tell your girlfriend how you had a terrible time. You'd tell her exactly what you thought of him. Don't sensor that. 'He's a jerk.' We don't need to hear that. How do you think he looks? Did he have body odor? Did you think he was gay? That's why we added Tilley. She's your confessional. Got it?"

Olena nodded. "I think so. Tilley's my confessional. So I don't have to do any more confessionals?"

"Yes, you still have to do confessionals. You're talking to us when you do those...and to viewers. In fact, let's tape the confessionals right now," Godiva said.

Olena sat on the sofa in her suite and let her hair and makeup team work on her for a few minutes before the camera started rolling again.

Olena tried her best to give them what they'd asked her for while trying not to look at Godiva, who stood beside a monitor with her hand on her hip.

As usual, she started with her confessional before the date and immediately followed that up with her thoughts on the bachelor after the date had ended.

I was excited about my date. Really excited. Fitz looks good. He's taller than I am with my five-inch heels on. His eyes aren't scary. He needs a stylist, though. I hate his outfit. What's that saying? Clothes don't make the man. The man makes the clothes. He's a designer with no style. He doesn't need to be making clothes for men or for anyone for that matter. He's tall. But some attractive men I'm just not attracted to. I hate his name—Fitz. Growing up, I had a dog named Fitz. No, wait a minute. My dog's name was Fritz. But still, his name reminds me of my dog.

Fitz is an extremely rude man. He feels he's entitled, and everyone's supposed to kiss his you know what just because he has a little money. And by the way, I didn't like his tie, which wouldn't be a big deal IF he weren't a tie designer. What was that thing he had around his neck? Was it a leather tie? Are they bringing those back? I guess he's trying to. I hope not. That's so circa 1980s— an era I wish to forget. I don't like him. There's no love connection there. So what is this now? Oh for three. I don't think I'm going to find love on this show. My ex has impeccable taste. But then again, he dumped me, so maybe his taste isn't all that impeccable.

The hotel phone rang, and Tilley reached over to answer. "Hello, yes, okay, one second." Tilley pushed the mute button.

"Why is Gordon in the lobby?" Olena asked.

"Cut," Godiva said. "That's perfect. We'll do a quick set change for the Gordon scene. You need to get into a different outfit and get makeup and hair."

"Seriously, do they sell Wiener Schnitzel in the restaurant downstairs?"

"Please get her some Wiener Schnitzel," Tilley said. "This woman is serious about her food. Please get her some."

Olena met Gordon in the Grand Café on the first floor of the hotel. They sat at an intimate table that overlooked Ringstrasse, Vienna's most famous boulevard. Olena was content now that she was able to enjoy a fresh plate of Wiener Schnitzel.

"So tell me about your date," Gordon said as he rubbed her hand and gazed lovingly into her eyes. *Hmm*, what was it about French men that she loved so much? And yes, she made her assessment based solely on one man. He genuinely seemed to care about her. He was expressive, romantic, and extremely sexy. But didn't they have a reputation for being womanizers? But she had to keep reminding herself that more likely than not, he was a fraud, acting for the cameras.

"Am I going to have to follow you everywhere you go?" he asked her, raising her hand up to his lips and kissing it. He was extremely attractive. *Why did she have to be tall?* She wondered. In the long run, she was certain their height difference would get in the way.

"You might? I wouldn't complain," she said as she started to smile.

"I'm sorry," he said, and she still wasn't clear about what he apologized for. "It was stupid and silly and very reckless of me. Do you forgive me?"

To which Olena was to reply, "I probably shouldn't, but yes, I forgive you."

Something would happen in one of the other cities. Vienna was the third stop overseas, but when edited it would end up being the sixth episode, so they could end with the impression that she'd found love abroad. There was a method to all of their madness, Olena figured out. And now, if she were to turn on a reality show, she'd surely never look at it the same. But she might at least look at one, now. She couldn't believe she said that, but she just might give a reality show a shot, and take it for what it was—pure entertainment.

After dinner, they quickly headed into the Ringstrassen-Galerien Shopping Mall that connected to the hotel's lobby. It was an hour away from closing, so the crew filmed the pair walking through the mall.

The next three stops were Venice, Monte Carlo, and finally Melbourne. From what Tilley continued to hear, at least one of the men Olena would meet, either abroad or in the states, was famous. She was still working on getting the details from her sources. While Olena just wanted to keep the delicious food and interesting men coming. Even if they weren't a love connection they were still the perfect diversion from Jason.

SIXTEEN

A town without cars in and of itself fascinated Olena. The transportation in the city of Venice, Italy was by water bus, water taxi, or a flat-bottomed Venetian rowing boat called a gondola because the city stretched across 117 small islands along the Adriatic Sea.

"This kind of reminds me of D.C.," the man said to Olena as they floated in a gondola through the light mist of fog cast over the Grand Canal. "That building looks like the row house I was raised in," he said, pointing to one of the buildings lining the Grand Canal.

My first thought when I saw him was, he doesn't look familiar, but his name sounds very familiar. Then, I looked at his shoes and you know they say you can tell a lot about a man from the shoes he wears. I can tell his feet hurt. And I can also tell that's him—a blast from my past, if I want to call him that.

For years, Olena had been trying to remember his full name,

but it wasn't until a Media One writer and researcher sat down and asked Olena several questions about her life and past loves that it all came rushing back. Stephon Mason. Was it a coincidence that there he was? It couldn't have been because she'd told the writer Stephon's name and where he'd attended college, his age and the street he grew up on—Elm Street near Third in a light red brick row house. She remembered the house well and the street because of the movie *Nightmare on Elm Street*, and going to his house eventually turned into a nightmare. Nothing too frightening, just another one of Olena's many reality checks when it came to men.

In that moment, Olena felt like the character from one of her favorite movies, *The Girl Most Likely To*.

She had a smirk on her face once she realized that Stephon didn't recognize her as the young woman he'd dated long ago. Well, not really date…and they didn't have sex, either. She wasn't sure what to call what they did. *Waste time?* It had been twenty-six years since she'd seen him last, so she wasn't too surprised that he hadn't recognized her. She looked entirely different. Just like the character Stockard Channing played in *The Girl Most Likely To*. Only Olena's transformation didn't come as a result of a car accident and plastic surgery.

How could he not remember her name? Olena wasn't that common. She'd never met another Olena. Matthew's father, Andrew, had said he'd forgotten her, and evidently so had Stephon.

Before she became infatuated with Andrew, there was Stephon. And like most of the men Olena dealt with, she convinced herself that she was in love. Last year, out of mere curiosity, she'd thought about looking him up on Facebook, so she could see what he'd been up to. Even though, she didn't have a Facebook page.

But now thanks to a reality show, he sat right beside her.

She'd met him the week before her freshman year at Howard

began. She and her cousin Candice were riding the Metro bus downtown to the department store Woodward & Lothrop or Woodies as the locals called it. They were headed to the salon that was there. And Olena would be the first to admit that she wasn't looking her best that day. On the bus, she didn't sit beside Candice because Candice was a fat, and she needed the extra seat to be comfortable. From out of nowhere, a tall, lanky, fair-skinned young man with a full head of shiny black curls walked up from the back of the bus and sat beside Olena. He smiled and introduced himself and didn't stop talking. Not even after they got off at F Street. He walked her to the escalator inside of Woodies that Candice had already taken to the second level where the hair salon was. The salon Olena desperately needed to get to. The new growth around the nape of her hair and the crown were screaming for a touch-up.

Olena gave him her number after he asked for it, and he called that night. They talked for almost an hour. He was nineteen and in his second year at George Washington University. He lived just a few blocks from Howard's campus, so she started spending a lot of time with him and his family over at their small row house.

The last day she saw him was on a day she'd skipped classes. This was after she'd seen him almost every day for nearly a month.

His mother came outside and stood on the porch not long after Stephon had walked inside of the house telling Olena he'd be right back. Olena heard her mother saying to him, "You need to tell that girl the truth because what you doing ain't right, and you know it ain't." He never came back outside. She never saw him again before now, all these years later.

His mother sat down beside Olena on the porch step and said. "My son ain't been honest with you or with me either. He said the two of y'all was just friends. But you feel like you his girlfriend, don't you?"

Olena nodded and said, "Yes," meekly. They'd kissed a couple of times. Hadn't had sex, but she knew if he had tried, she would've given in. He never tried.

His mother released a heavy sigh. "These young mens need to stop playing games with you girls' feelings. I be telling them boys they gonna mess around with the wrong one. I love my son to death, but wrong is wrong."

"It's okay. I understand," Olena said. Not fully understanding anything since his mother hadn't yet said much. *What had Stephon done wrong?* She wondered.

"What do you understand? Do you understand that my son has been making a fool outta you? You understand that?" she asked, puffing on a Newport. Olena shook her head. "Listen, he can't be your boyfriend because he already has a girlfriend, and a baby too. They broke up, but they always breaking up. Now, he's starting to feel bad. He thinks you're a really nice person, but—" she paused.

"I understand. He wants to get back with her," Olena said with her voice breaking apart. She stood up ready to run to her dorm and buy a pack of cigarettes from the vending machine and puff on them the way Stephon's mother was. Even though she'd never smoked before, she was too young to buy liquor and couldn't afford any anyway. So nicotine would have to calm her nerves instead.

"No."

"He doesn't want to get back with her?" Olena asked with hope still lingering.

"You might as well say he's already with her. I told you they break up all the time. But this is the part I wanted him to tell you. I wanted him to face you and tell you the truth, but he said he couldn't. Like I said, he feels bad. I'm not telling you this to hurt your feelings. I'm telling you this to make you a stronger woman. Sometimes it takes us gettin' hurt in order to make us strong...a lot of times it does. I used to have this *same* mess done to me." Olena nodded her head, egging her on. She wanted his mother to tell her whatever it was that would hurt Olena and make her stronger.

"He's got some silly ass friends. They think they grown, but they just silly boys still playing tricks on people. Some of them same silly friends had him pick out a girl on the bus to meet and pretend to like." That really did sound silly. Too silly for Olena to believe was even true. *Pick a girl out on the bus and meet her? Why on the bus?* "He had to pick out the ugliest girl on the bus and make her feel pretty."

Olena's heart fell to her stomach. She was too stunned to respond, or maybe too embarrassed to. He felt Olena was the ugliest girl on the bus. The same bus her obese cousin was on. It was one thing for Olena to think she wasn't all that attractive. It was another thing to have her suspicions confirmed by, of all people, the mother of the boy she'd convinced herself she loved.

Stephon's mother continued, "As you can see, I ain't exactly Jayne Kennedy myself. When I was your age, they called me ugly too. I know how it feels to be laughed at. But ask me if I care. I never cried a day over it. Not one." Olena couldn't imagine Stephon's mother crying over anything. All she seemed to care about were cigarettes and beer. Olena watched Stephon's mother as she continued puffing on her cigarette and cracking open a second can of beer.

Something came over Olena and she started to cry.

"What's so wrong with me?"

"Nothing!" Stephon's mother shouted. "Girl, you need to think more of yourself than that. You're in college now, honey. This ain't high school. Get some self-esteem about yourself. Don't ever let a man bring you down. Ya hear me?" Olena nodded and Stephon's mother continued. "Men can tell when a woman don't think nothin' of herself. For some men that's a turnoff, but for others that's the exact type of woman they looking for. You

(THE)

have to tell yourself, I'd rather be alone than be abused. And hittin' ain't the only way a person can abuse you. Tell yourself. Go 'head. Say it!"

"I'd rather be alone than abused?"

"Say it with meaning. Not like you're asking a question."

"I'd rather be alone than abused."

"Say it with some meaning, girl. Put your back up in it."

"I'd rather be alone than abused," Olena said much louder.

"There you go. Like I said, I love my son, but if he's doing wrong, he's doing wrong, and he did you wrong. And I'mma tell you something, and I might just be the only one who's ever told you something like this before. And if so, so be it. You got to learn the truth from somebody. I'mma tell you the same thing my momma told me. If a black man ain't treating you right, move the—" His mother nodded her head— "on." There are more colors in a rainbow than just one. Get you a white man."Olena wrinkled her brows at Stephon's mother. She was right. No one had ever told Olena that. "That's what I did." She took a long swig of beer and a longer drag of her cigarette. "Let me tell you about white folks and how they operate. True, some of them are prejudiced and do some sneaky stuff sometimes. But all of 'em ain't like that. In fact...*in...fact*, some of them ain't as shallow as some of us. You know how some of us can be toward each other. We can be some ugly acting folks. Talkin' about, how the white man done us wrong. Well, what about how we doin' ourselves? Yeah, I said it." She threw both of her hands up and dropped her beer can. Olena jumped back expecting a splatter, but instead heard a hollow beer can bouncing down the short walkway. "I'm just telling the truth. We all about the looks and the flash, you know how we are. We don't help each other, and it's a damn shame. You know I'm telling the truth. If you don't, I guess you're too young and you haven't found out yet."

"Well, white people are into blond hair and blue eyes—"

"True…some of 'em are. My children's father is white, and I don't have blond hair *or* blue eyes, do I? I hardly have any hair at all after I take this wig off."

"Are the two of you still together?"

She nodded. "But he's in prison right now. But as soon as he gets out in the next…mmm, fifteen years, he gonna be right back here with me."

The conversation somehow ended, and Olena walked back to her dorm to the break room to buy a pack of cigarettes from the vending machine.

She went back to her dorm room and sat thinking about what his mother had said. She coughed after taking her first cigarette puff. Smoking wasn't going to remove the word "ugly" that had been permanently etched in Olena's mind as of that day.

So now here she was face-to-face with Stephon. She could pretend she didn't know him, had never met him before that day, or she could try to jog his memory.

"We've met before," she said.

"I know."

"You know?"

He nodded. "Olena Day…I know."

"Were you going to say something?"

"I wanted to wait a few more minutes to see if you said something. By the way, you look beautiful. Time certainly has served you well."

Unfortunately, she couldn't return the compliment. He looked different but not in a good way. His shiny black curls were now gray. Some men looked sexy and distinguished with gray hair. And some just looked old. He fell in the latter category. His hair was short and stuck straight up instead of curled. He looked tired and unhappy, and he was fat, especially his cheeks. For Olena, the idea that someone who had been so skinny could get that large was the most shocking part.

"I hope you're willing to give me a chance to make up for all of this lost time. There must be a reason why none of my marriages worked. Maybe you're that reason."

"Me? I doubt I had anything to do with it. How many times have you been married?"

"Don't fall off the gondola when I say this—four times."

"*Four times*? Well, can't say you don't believe in love or marriage one."

He stared deep into her eyes and smiled without showing any teeth. "I just think I never found the right woman, and I definitely thought about you through the years."

"Really?"

"I'm so glad to be given this opportunity."

"So you've had four marriages and how many kids?"

"Just one."

Olena looked shocked. "You only have one child?" He nodded and continued ogling her as the gondola came to a stop.

The easiest route back to the Hotel Rialto would have been by gondola. But they wouldn't have been able to walk down narrow streets trying to find their way back. They wouldn't have gotten lost while the small camera crew followed closely behind them.

Stephon didn't seem the least bit fazed by the cameras and attempted to kiss Olena while they stood at the door to her hotel room, but she refused.

"Well, how did it go?" Tilley wanted to know as soon as Olena entered the suite.

"Get this. I used to date him," Olena said as she sat on the sofa with a dazed look on her face.

"No," Tilley said, taking a seat beside Olena on the sofa.

"Yes...well, wait, I can't really say date because we never went anywhere but his mother's house. He sure was a blast from my past."

"So what did you think?"

Should she insult him on camera by talking about his weight

and how he wasn't her type? How he looked so much older than he was and any man with four exes was a man she wanted to stay away from? She'd save that for her confessional.

"It was good to see him."

"Cut," Godiva said with a frown. "You need to give us more than that. Wasn't he the one who made you feel self-conscious? Now, after all these years, and after you have yourself together and he doesn't, 'it was good to see him' is the best you can come up with."

"I thought all the men on the show had it together?" Olena questioned.

"I'm not talking financially. He's fat. He looks old enough to be your father. He can't dress. You need to say all that. Do you know we haven't had to beep you one time? Don't you curse?"

"I try not to."

"It's normal to curse. You don't have to be a sailor."

Olena shrugged. "I don't want to say what I'm thinking."

"What are you thinking?"

"He does look really bad. Honestly, I took one look at him and thought karma's a bitch; time has definitely not done him any favors. This is the same man who called me ugly. My...my...my how the tables turn."

"Then say that," Godiva said.

Olena shook her head. "I don't want to say that. I could say it about the other guys, but not Stephon because I feel like I know him. His mother might be watching."

"Okay, Olena, forget it. This show is going to get cancelled—"

Olena's eyes bulged. "Why would you say that?"

"Because I don't lie, and you're boring. You just don't have a personality. Off camera, you don't seem as bad, but when it's lights, camera, action, we get nothing. Maybe I've just been around too many over the top personalities, but you seem like a zombie to me. On camera, you going to have to start saying what's on your mind and not worrying about how it translates."

"You mean when you're not telling me what to say?" Olena said sarcastically.

"We wouldn't have to tell you what to say as much as we do, if you would say more."

"Let me explain something about myself—"

"I don't need you to explain anything about yourself. Right now, I don't care about you. It's about this show. Now, we're going to turn the cameras back on, and you're going to give us something to work with. Something other than, 'it was good to see him.' "

It was a sunny fifty-eight degrees when the plane landed at the Côte d'Azur International Airport in Nice, France—fifteen miles from the Principality of Monaco. With the cameras rolling, Olena and Tilley boarded a helicopter and arrived in Monaco in six minutes. Once there, Olena, Tilley, and one of the cameramen hopped in the back of a white mini-van that shuttled them to the Hotel De Paris.

Olena and Tilley were upgraded to the larger Churchill suite, a two-bedroom apartment with a private elevator, two lounges, a dining room, two bathrooms, and a terrace with a panoramic view of the Mediterranean Sea.

After Olena guided herself through the maze of luxury the suite offered, her thoughts kicked in. "There's only one Churchill suite in this entire hotel, and it's given to us and not Godiva. How is that possible?"

"I'm sure this was Godiva's suite. Maybe she's trying to make up for blasting you."

"When did she blast me?"

"Not really blast you, but she did call you a boring zombie and told you that the show would get cancelled because of you."

"I guess she did blast me."

Olena sat in one of two white wingback leather chairs near the door leading to the terrace.

"Is something wrong?" Tilley asked as she stood in front of Olena with her arms folded.

She shrugged. "I sort of wish I didn't have to go back. After we leave here, we go to Australia and then home."

"I thought you were ready to go home."

"What I would give to be your age knowing what I know now?"

"What does that have to do with going back home?"

"Nothing. I'm just trying to change the subject."

"Well, let's pretend for a second that you are my age again. What would you do differently?"

"Tilley, more than half the things I did when I was in my twenties, I would not do over. None of the men I dated would I date over. I'm just so proud of you. To be so young you really seem to have your life together."

"*Me?*" Tilley asked.

"You are so mature to be twenty-three. Have you ever had your heart broken?" Olena patted the cushion of the seat beside hers, a signal for Tilley to take a seat, which she did.

"No."

"You probably don't take any mess."

"You could say that, or I could say I've never had any mess to take. I'm a virgin."

"Tilley, you're a virgin," Olena said with a gasp, "oh, my God, that is so special."

"*It is?*"

"Are you kidding? What I would give to be a virgin still at my age?"

"Seriously? I feel like something's wrong with me."

"Tilley, there's nothing wrong with you. Promise that you won't give up your virginity until you get married."

"I'm bald, so you don't have to worry about it. I'll be a virgin for a while. And as long as I'm bald, I doubt I'll get married."

"Tilley, so what you're bald. Weren't you the one who called me insecure? You're beautiful." Tilley shook her head. "Yes you are."

"I'm not shaking my head because I don't think I'm beautiful. Don't think I'm conceited, but I know I'm beautiful. I have pretty eyes, nice skin, straight, white teeth. But I know that men stare at me in a different way now from when I had hair down my back. But this isn't about the trials and tribulations of Tilley." There was a knock on the door. "We need to start getting you ready for your date tonight." Tilley walked to the front door to let the makeup artist and hairstylist in.

"While you're out doing your thing, I'm going to be gambling at the casino. If you come back and I'm not here, I hit the jackpot."

"I need to be going out with you instead of whomever," Olena said. "I need to hit a jackpot."

Bachelor number five, the retired race car driver from Milan, Italy, went by one name—Amanzio. He had driven for Ferrari and had several wins under his belt. He was half French and half Italian. He was average height and very stylish and physically fit. She loved the casual jacket he wore with a plain white T-shirt underneath, a pair of stonewashed jeans and navy leather lace-ups. His look reminded her of an updated Sonny Crockett from *Miami Vice.*

Their evening started off on restaurant alley at the Cosmopolitan Restaurant and Wine Bar where she had the grilled veal and he had the grilled Argentinean beef tenderloin. After dinner, they went to Zelo's, a chic restaurant and club with a terrace that overlooked the Mediterranean.

Amanzio ordered a bottle of champagne, and they danced the night away. There were lots of businessmen inside throwing money around and mingling with beautiful women. Olena tried to pay attention to her date, but the pulsating techno music prevented conversation. Instead, she sat and people-watched as her head swayed and her fingers snapped to the beat of the music. She sipped on champagne and became hypnotized by the bluish-green strobe light. Zelo's was so different from anything Olena had been to in the states. But, she couldn't remember the last time she'd been to a nightclub in the states.

The view and the Miami Vice vibe put her in a whole different mind frame. She felt sexy, even though she regretted Tilley's wardrobe choice. She'd wished instead of the eggplant stretch-satin flutter-sleeve Grecian dress that she had worn the light moss with gold sequined scoop-back mini. She would've felt even sexier and glowed in the dark.

After a few drinks, she was in the partying mood. She grabbed Amanzio's hand and pulled him up and led him to the dance floor. She knew she'd had too much to drink after they sat back down and Olena went from swaying her head to the music to bouncing her boobs in Amanzio's face, and of course the cameras were rolling.

Amanzio. Even his name is sexy. He's tall, dark, and handsome. I love his accent. I love his eyes. I loved his shoes. I loved his tie. The man definitely has some style. But he parties too much, and I'm too old for that lifestyle. I'm not old, but I'm too old for that. I didn't go to a club when I was in my twenties and it was age-appropriate. I can imagine what my life would be like if I were with him. Jet-setting, booze, threesomes, and Botox. Not that I would do a threesome. But I probably would do the Botox. I'd have to do something so my face wouldn't slide off. He was good eye-candy, but not much beyond that, at least not for me. America, will I ever find love?

SEVENTEEN

At the last minute, Jason decided to book a nonstop Delta flight from Atlanta to Dallas and surprise LaRuth. His plane touched down at 1:30 p.m. on Friday. And even though he didn't know where she lived, he knew where she worked. She talked about her administrative job at First Financial Services. She mentioned it was in Westlake, far from where she lived. He used Google to get the Roanoke Road address and the navigation system, in his rented Cadillac Escalade, did the rest. He drove past rolling pastures, a herd of bison, ponds and an old-fashioned house, before pulling into the entrance. The modern two-story building, with Texas flags waving in the wind, was set off the road out in the middle of nowhere.

It was 4:45. She said she worked until five, so he backed into a spot in the front lot within full view of the main entrance and waited for her to come out, if she even would. He had dated a woman for six months back before he and Olena got serious. She told Jason that she worked for Delta Airlines in reservations. Well, one of Jason's sisters-in-law was a manager there, so he asked her to confirm the young lady's employment. She called promptly with the news that no one by the name Suelette Powers was on Delta's payroll. When pressed, the young lady admitted she was a stripper. He couldn't get serious with someone who took her clothes off for a living and then lied about it. But he tried not to judge her. She said she liked dancing, liked the attention she received from both men and women. She loved her body and loved showing it off, and she made decent money. So, he tried to help her out. Since stripping was her passion, he used one of his many connections to help her improve her employment from the lowbrow Decatur strip club to the upscale Cheetah Lounge. He hoped LaRuth wouldn't have a similar story. But, if he could catch Olena in a lie, he felt as though he could catch anyone in one.

It was five o'clock and people started rushing out of the building in droves. Some were literally running. After fifteen minutes, when he didn't see her and wasn't sure if he'd missed her in the crowd, he let his window down to speak to the man who walked up to the Dodge Ram parked beside him.

"What's up, man? Do you know LaRuth Harris?"

The man who looked to be in his mid-thirties took off his prescription glasses.

"Jason Nix?" he asked with laughter. "Ah man, I don't even believe this. You're one of my favorite players. Man, I wish you were still out there. What are you doing down here, man? I just watched you on Fox a few days ago. You know you're a straight-up fool on that show, right. You should go into acting."

"Thanks man."

Jason had appeared on Fox the week before, calling a playoff game while he filled in for another commentator who was out with the flu.

"But yeah, LaRuth, I sure do know her. Great lady. I just saw her at her cubicle, so she should be down any minute."

"Alright, man, thanks."

"It's good seeing you, Jason. It's really good seeing you. I would ask for your autograph, but I already know you don't like giving those out, so I can understand that."

"I don't have a problem with autographs, just pictures."

"Oh, okay, yeah, I can understand that. Ah nah, I don't need a picture. I don't blame you on that one. People try to take videos and all that stupid stuff. But your autograph would be real nice, man, for real. You wouldn't happen to have one of your football cards on you, would you? My son would love that."

Jason shook his head. "Sorry, bro. I don't have any with me."

"I understand, man. Maybe I can get it from LaRuth. If you give it to her, and she can give it to me, so I can give it to my son, you know."

"I can do that."

"Thanks." The man flicked his nose and then tried to shake Jason's hand.

"Good meeting you," Jason said without extending his hand.

"Yeah, we're cool, okay. And here comes LaRuth walking out the building right now. So you take it easy," the man said as he opened the door to his pickup. "By the way, my name is Quincy. I'm the only Quincy in the building so LaRuth will know exactly who you're talking about. I can't wait to go home and tell my wife and son about this."

"Okay, Quincy. Take it easy."

"Jason Nix," Quincy said, smiling as he stepped inside his pickup. "You've made my day, for real." Quincy blew his horn as he pulled off.

LaRuth was sandwiched between an extremely large black woman and a Mexican woman with a medium frame. She held onto a black case that he initially thought was her purse before he noticed her purse slung over her shoulder. She looked the way she had every time he'd seen her—conservatively dressed and makeup free.

LaRuth was a little peeved at Jason. She didn't understand why she couldn't meet his mother or his children. Things between them did seem to be progressing well. But Jason wasn't ready to bring a new woman around his kids. His ex-wife hadn't been the best mother to them, choosing her career over them. And they'd grown attached to Olena. It was hard enough trying to explain to them where she was and why they couldn't spend the weekends in Buckhead anymore. So, he didn't exactly tell them the truth. But he didn't really lie either. Because she was on a trip, and she would be back—just not back to him. He wanted to introduce LaRuth to his mother by taking them out to dinner so they could get to know each other. The way he did with Olena. But when he mentioned it to his mother, she didn't want to meet her. She needed time and advised him not to get too serious with a woman he barely knew. She reminded him of who he was and how much he stood to lose if he made a mistake, stressed to him that he need-ed to be careful. Not all women have it as together as Olena. Not all women can afford their own fabulous lifestyle. "You should always try to date a woman who has her own," she'd told him. But he didn't listen to her lecture because he had enough for him, his sons, his mother, and whichever woman he chose. So far, LaRuth had made a pretty decent go of it.

After LaRuth got into the passenger seat of the black woman's Saab, he phoned her, and after exchanging greetings told her where he was.

Jason followed behind the Saab as he drove out of the parking lot.

"Where are you?" LaRuth asked.

"I'm driving right behind you, baby."

"Seriously."

He watched as her head turned to look back at him from inside the Saab.

"That's you in that black SUV."

"You don't know what I look like."

"Not through tinted windows. I'm going to kill you." A second later she exited her co-worker's car and walked swiftly over to Jason's rental. "I'm going to kill you," she repeated after she'd climbed into the SUV. She placed her purse and whatever the black thing she held in her hand on the floor, buckled her seat belt, and turned to look at him.

The car behind them blew its horn several times.

She turned to look at the line of cars behind them.

"There's a long line of cars, and you're holding them up. Drive, baby, hurry up. People are serious about getting out of here on Friday. I'm going to kill you," she said with a smile that wouldn't leave her face.

Jason pulled out onto Roanoke Road. He turned off the radio when he heard a familiar song.

"Why did you do that? I love that song."

Jason did too. In fact, he and Olena had seen George Benson perform "Turn Your Love Around" live at Symphony Hall in Atlanta last year. But some songs evoked memories and some memories were reminders of mistakes. Letting go of Olena was a mistake, which was another reason why he tried so hard to immerse himself into LaRuth. She was an escape, undeniably a physical one. LaRuth turned the radio back.

"I didn't know you listened to secular music."

"As long as it isn't rap or rock."

That song felt eery to him. Music had a way of making a person relive a moment in time. That's part of what made songs special. The concert was right after he had regained a lot of his strength after the operation. She'd bought the concert tickets and took him to South City Kitchen in Midtown for dinner before-hand. She looked so sexy that evening in a black wrap dress, and she smelled lovely. He had no idea what perfume Olena wore be-cause she switched fragrances so often that he stopped asking. He kind of wanted her to ground herself with one scent, but she had trouble making up her mind. She'd told him she liked variety, and now he wondered if that were also true with men.

"Are you hungry?"

"Not yet. Maybe later."

"I fly out in the morning."

"You fly out in the morning, baby, why?" she whined, which turned him on. Made him feel wanted. "What was the point of you even coming, then? I want you with me longer than a day. We're still in the getting to know each other phase. How am I going to get to know you if you rush in and out like that?"

"I made a promise, and I like to keep my promises. The name of that store was the Clothes Circuit, right?"

LaRuth looked puzzled. "Yes. Why?"

"I'm taking you shopping. That's your store, right?" She nodded. "I want to make you happy."

"Ahh, you already do, baby. You already do," she said, rubbing his thigh. "So happy."

"How do I get there from here?"

"It's on Sherry Lane."

"Help me out. I have no idea where that is."

"Take a right here, and just ride this to 114 East, and you're going to be on that for a minute, so I'll tell you the rest as you drive." She smiled again. "You are sweet. What did I do to deserve you?"

Jason grinned. "You put it on me."

"So it's just because of the sex? Is that what you're saying?"

Jason shook his head. "Nah, you're a sweet girl." She did seem to be. He just had to get used to her ways, which wasn't necessarily a bad thing, but something different.

Thirty minutes later, he turned left onto Westchester. A Wells Fargo, one of Jason's banks, was on the corner.

"I think I'm going to stop in here."

"For what?" she snapped.

"Because I need to go to the bank, is that alright with you?"

"I guess, but the Clothes Circuit closes at seven and it's already six."

"Actually, it's a quarter to six and the bank closes at six. It'll be fine." He pulled into the only available space in front of a Jamba Juice shop. "Don't talk to any strangers while I'm gone. Keep the doors locked. If anybody messes with you, I have a three-fifty-seven in the glove compartment."

"You have a gun in here," she said, twisting her nose.

"It was a joke. Last I checked you can't board a plane with one. Be right back." His face turned to stone as he turned away from her. He liked LaRuth, but he didn't like her snapping over him going to the bank because she was afraid the store would close: the store she said he didn't have to take her to. That rubbed him the wrong way, and he was reminded that he hadn't known the girl that long, not even a month.

When he returned fifteen minutes later, she had the black case open in her lap and was reading while she slurped on an Orange Carrot Karma fruit smoothie. "Did you get me one?" Jason asked after strapping his seatbelt on.

"You like smoothies?"

"I love 'em."

"Well, we haven't left yet, go get one."

"You're missing my point. Why didn't you get me one? You're supposed to be my woman. Aren't you supposed to take care of me?"

"Are you saying I don't?"

"It's more than one way to take care of your man, remember that." He started up his engine and pulled out of the tight one-row parking lot in silence.

"What are you reading?"

"The Bible."

"I know that much, baby. I do know what one looks like. I go to church, too."

"You do?"

"Yeah, you didn't think I did."

"You never talk about it. We should go to church together, sometime."

"We can do that. What book are you reading?"

"First Corinthians." LaRuth closed the Bible on her right hand and said, "God spoke to me the other night."

"And what did God say?"

"That you're my husband."

Jason tried not to frown, but he couldn't prevent his eyes from narrowing. He didn't know how to respond to that, so he didn't. A freak in the sheets and a lady in the streets was a turn on to a certain degree. But marriage material? Would she make a good mother? The verdict was still out for her in those areas. It was too soon for her to be thinking about marriage.

The Clothes Circuit was a few streets down from the bank on the left side of the street and sat on the corner. He handed her the bank envelope with ten crisp one hundred dollar bills inside. "Aren't you coming in?" she asked, placing one hand on her purse and the other on the knob.

He shook his head. "I need to make a business call."

"Business call? You retired over a year ago, and you still have business."

"Actually, I have more business now than I did when I played ball."

"Alright, businessman, but I might be a minute."

"Take your time, baby."

He reached for his Blackberry after LaRuth walked in the store.

"Hello?" Olena said hesitantly.

"How are you?"

"I'm okay. How are you?"

"Could be better?"

"What's wrong?"

"I'm missing you."

"Missing me? The woman you put your legal pit bulls on. That's a little hard to believe."

"Where are you right now?"

"Monte Carlo for another two days and onto Melbourne and then finally back home. I can't wait. I miss being in my own bed and my condo."

"Wishful thinking on my part, I hoped you'd say you missed something else. "I miss being in the bed with you in your condo."

"I'm really surprised you called."

"Did you get my other message where I apologized?"

"You didn't call me on Christmas, and you didn't call me on New Year's. And now you up and call me while I'm overseas. How much is this call going to cost?"

"I don't know, but whatever it is you know I'll pay for it that's if you'll let me. You don't let me do anything for you. I'm surprised you even answered."

"I'm surprised I did too, but I had a break in filming."

"How are the men you're meeting?"

She let out a long sigh. "This is a production. It's not about finding love. It's about hopefully getting ratings. Honestly, I can't even remember too many of them.

"I told you it was scripted."

"Did you need anything specifically, or are you just checking to make sure I didn't say your name during filming?"

"Why are you being so cold toward me?"

"That letter slapped some sense into me."

"Forget that letter. Tear it up. I don't care if you mention my name. I was angry at the time—"

"See that's the thing that scares me about you. When you're in your defensive mood, you snap even at those you love and who love you. This isn't football, and I'm not on the opposing team. You don't have to tackle me."

"You're right. I don't, and I didn't mean to."

"You have to start realizing who has your back, Jason. I was on your team."

"You're right. I do and I will. Are you still on my team? Are you going to give me another chance?"

"No."

"*What?*"

"No."

"*No?*"

"Nooooooo," Olena said stretching out the word.

"How can you say, no?"

"Jason, I love you. I'll probably always love you, but—"

"But you let a reality show ruin us. So just keep on doing you."

"Is that it?"

"Yeah, that's it. Enjoy the Down Under."

"Mmm hmm. You too."

When he ended the call, he was surprised to see LaRuth coming out of the store at just six thirty, and with only one shopping bag. "Are you finished shopping already?"

"Yeah, I'm going to wait a week or two and come back. They're always getting new stuff in. But I did find some cute things I can wear to work. Do you want to see?"

"Show me later."

"What's wrong?"

"Nothing. Are you hungry?" He checked the navigation system in the Escalade for nearby restaurants. "Have you ever been to Texas De Brazil?"

"Never."

"Do you want to try it?"

"Sure. You now I love trying new things."

They sat at a table for four on the first level of the restaurant. She didn't look at herself once in the huge accent mirror affixed to the deep red wall that was directly in front of her, which he found surprising. Olena would have tried to sneak a look the entire time they were there, and he would have caught her each time. At first, he thought she did that because she was vain. As time went on, he learned that it was actually for the opposite reason—she was insecure. That was one thing that bothered him about Olena. Any woman he spent time with would have to know they looked good. Jason wouldn't bother with a woman who he didn't feel was beautiful. But as he thought about it, he realized it was his attempt to find something more redeeming about LaRuth than Olena.

The hostess invited them to help themselves to the salad bar, which he did, but she didn't because she didn't like salad. *Didn't like salad? Didn't like pancakes? Who was this woman?* He filled his plate with gourmet artisan breads, imported cheeses, Brazilian hearts of palm, spicy surimi sushi, and several other items that were on the forty-item salad bar. When he returned, he offered her some items from his plate, at which point she barked her reply. "I said I didn't like that stuff."

He nodded. "I'm going to have to talk to you a little later."

"About what?"

"Not here, but a little later," he said as the meat-bearing gauchos made their way over to their table with grilled meats on sword-like skewers. They carved off slices of beef, pork, lamb, chicken, and Brazilian sausage. He took a little of everything, but she took only lamb and chicken. "You don't like the food."

"I would have rather gone to Pappadeaux."

"Why didn't you say so? I could have taken you there."

"I just didn't want to make a big deal. I thought I might like this place." He shook his head. "What?"

"We'll talk about it later," he said with his voice dragging and his face turned away from hers.

He made the mistake of not booking a hotel and instead spending the night at her apartment. Curiosity had gotten the best of him. He wanted to see how she lived and make sure she was there alone. The apartment was off of I-635 near Skillman. First sign of trouble was the wide-open security gate at the entrance. Overall, it looked decent enough, even though it was an older building.

Her apartment was clean and well furnished. Nothing he'd ever buy, but he didn't expect her to have the type of furniture he had. She was neat and that mattered to him more than how much her furniture cost. One thing he couldn't stand was a messy woman.

Before he barely had a chance to get through the door, she asked, "What do you have to talk to me about?"

"I don't even remember now."

"You don't remember? Why did you make it seem so important?"

He shrugged. "It must not have been." He just didn't feel like getting into an argument and having a lousy evening. He had just finished a great meal, at least he thought it was. And now he was tired. "Which door is to the bedroom?"

"You can't wait can you?"

"I'm tired. I just want to go to sleep right now."

"That's all you want," she said, rubbing the crotch of his pants.

"That's all I want tonight. The morning might be a different story."

She led him into her bedroom to the queen-sized bed. All he brought with him was a small carry-on with toiletries. He wasn't in the mood for sex, and he doubted that would change in the morning.

"I'm going to take a shower," LaRuth said. "You don't want to come?"

"No," he said, shaking his head.

"You don't want to come?" she repeated.

He knew what she meant, but he still said, "No."

In the morning, he was awakened by LaRuth's head buried between his legs and her mouth sucking away. It was semi-pleasurable but mostly uncomfortable. He was not a man who enjoyed be awakened with oral sex. He would have preferred the opportunity to urinate first, and would have rather washed up because he was sweaty, and even though she didn't seem to mind, he was getting turned off by the suction noise her lips were making.

"Okay, you can stop," he said, prying her from between his legs.

"You're not even that hard. What's wrong? I don't turn you on any more."

"It's not that."

"Well, what is it?"

"Let's take a shower," he said, leading her into the bathroom attached to her bedroom. He noticed the Cosmo magazine while he urinated. She stood in her bathtub with the shower water running; the sight of her naked body aroused him. It was a small tub, but he could make any space work when he was in the mood. He joined her. They stood facing each other. She hugged him and wrapped her left leg partially around his waist. He put his right hand on her thigh for leverage while he entered her, stroking her face and wet hair with his free hand.

"Pull on my hair," she said, but he didn't. "Pull my hair!" she shouted. That's when he eased himself out of her, stepped out of the tub, and dried off with the towel that hung over the shower stall. "What's wrong with you?" she said.

"I'm running late. I need to be at the airport in forty minutes, so I'm going to go ahead and get out of here."

"You were thinking about your flight while we were making love."

"I thought about a lot of stuff."

"Such as?"

"Sometimes, baby, I don't get you."

"What do you mean you don't get me?"

"I'm trying to get to know you better. Maybe we moved too fast in the beginning. I don't know. Never mind." He left her in the bathroom and returned to the bedroom. On her nightstand was a picture of LaRuth with two young children. He picked it up and studied it. Those were her children. Had to be. The girl looked just like her. The youngest was in LaRuth's lap and the older one at her side. He was still holding the 3x5 frame when she came back into the bedroom. "Are these your kids?"

"That's my niece and nephew."

"They look just like you."

"They look just like their mother who looks just like me. I'm an identical twin."

"You have an identical twin sister?"

"I told you that."

"No, you said you had a sister and a brother. You never said that your sister was your identical twin. Usually twins talk about the other, a lot."

"We're not that close."

"Really? You're not that close to your own twin?"

"She's in Afghanistan, so the distance prevents us from being close. She's a civilian contractor. She does data entry and makes ninety thousand dollars a year tax-free."

"My mom's a twin and my aunt lives in Memphis, and they talk on the phone every day, several times a day. They see each other on every holiday. You're not a twin, for real, are you? And those are your kids, right? Just be honest."

"What, do you have a degree in twin-gineering or something? I don't have to lie. I *am* a twin."

"Who has her kids?"

"Her husband."

"Why didn't you ever mention any of this? You seem like an only child to me. Okay, twin, show me some pictures of the two of you together because I don't believe you."

"Okay," she said, huffing off to her closet where she pulled out a box with some photo albums. "Here, since you don't believe me." She shoved a photo album into his chest.

He opened the photo album and looked at page after page of the two women from childhood to adulthood.

"*You* are a twin."

"Who would lie about something like that?"

"There are two of you. Beauty duplicated."

She smiled.

"It doesn't change who I am. It just means there's another person out there who looks like me." Now, even more than before, he felt like he didn't know who she was. Who doesn't talk about having a twin? He really didn't understand her now.

EIGHTEEN

Gone was business class. After the first flight from Atlanta to Paris, all of the others were economy, which wasn't a concern for Olena until the last leg of the trip. She was actually jetlagged and couldn't imagine how she'd feel after another seven hours of air travel. She'd already flown two hours from Nice, France back to Heathrow, where they waited an hour and a half before departing to Changi, Singapore. The nearly thirteen-hour flight arrived into Changi the next day. There was a two-hour-and-thirty-five-minute layover, but the time passed quickly after she and a few others went for a free fifteen minute foot massage at the foot and calf stations in terminal one and on to GoGo Franks for some cheese balls. She and Tilley eventually moved away from the Media One crowd gathered by Gate 13 and all the inane conversation that didn't translate well in either one of their worlds, where the topic of discussion was Media One reality stars and stories being reported on blogs. The most recent—a big conspiracy theory that Deanna hadn't actually killed herself; she'd been murdered. She'd been dating some guy in the mafia, and her house was wiretapped by the FBI. The woman had been dead for months, but the lies were still alive. Tilley had enough and started walking away from them without Olena, who didn't stick around much longer either.

They made their way to the Cactus Garden on the third level and sat on a bench in a forest of more than forty species of cacti.

"Do you want me to take some pictures of you by those cycads?" Tilley asked in a glum voice. "You can send them to Jason, so he can see what he's been missing."

Olena smiled and shook her head. She'd be the first to admit she looked like death without makeup. Her hair was wrapped in a headscarf, and she had on a fleece top and animal print pajama pants.

"I'll admit I kind of threw myself together."

"The only thing missing is a pair of fuzzy house slippers," Tilley said.

"I seriously thought about wearing a pair." Tilley raised her right eyebrow and shook her head as she grinned. "*What*, didn't you look at the itinerary? I read my e-mails. We're in for another long day as if yesterday weren't long enough."

"Enjoy your anonymity while it lasts; after February 14th, it'll be all over. And you won't want to see yourself on a blog looking the way you do right now."

"The only way a blog will do a story on me is if I were still with Jason."

"What? Are you kidding me? You're getting ready to do reality TV and on a major network. You could be the next reality TV star. Who knows?"

"Olena Day...*Olena* Day...Oh-ley-na Day. I guess it has a ring to it."

Tilley shook her head and burst out laughing. "You are so goofy."

Olena smiled. Goofy and gumpy were two staple words often

used to describe Olena, and she used to take offense, but now she just embraced her quirky nature as being who she was.

The Qantas Airways flight they boarded departed Changi at 7:45 p.m. and arrived in Melbourne at six the next morning.

Olena wasn't sure one day would be long enough to recover from all the air travel.

Tilley, whose youthfulness accounted for some of her energy, only required a few hours of sleep, and she was ready to explore another new city on the lookout for a good place to eat and a fantastic place to shop. Tilley spread the map across Olena's bed as she sat on the edge of the bed and pointed out the GPO, a place that had restaurants and shopping. It was on the corner of Bourke Street and Elizabeth, which was walking distance from the hotel. Clothes weren't nearly as crucial to Olena as they used to be now that she was unemployed. If she never stepped foot in a mall again, she'd have more than enough outfits to hold her over for years to come. Olena grumbled and swiped the map off the bed.

"I really need for you to go with me. I need you to try on the outfits I pick out for you."

Olena could barely open her eyes. She rolled over on her side and flung the comforter over her head. She had other plans for her evening. Room service would be Olena's best friend that day, since Tilley left with the makeup artist and hairstylist in the mid-afternoon to explore the city.

Olena had a three course meal brought up to her room. A fricassée of seasonal mushrooms, smoked bacon, asparagus, and egg mollets were her first course. For the main entrée, she had crispy-skin New Zealand king salmon with spinach and pear salad with orange balsamic dressing and crème brûlée for dessert.

After dinner, she showered and went directly back to bed, so she'd be refreshed for the early morning shoot.

The next morning Olena and Tilley stopped for coffee at the Quarter, a café along Degraves Street in Melbourne and sat outside underneath a black umbrella at a tiny table for two. Tilley studied the map she'd picked up from the Melbourne Visitor Center in Federation. They weren't alone. A camera crew was within inches of their every move.

"Why don't we go to Centre Place and then to the Block Arcade and then Howey Place to do some shopping, and then we can go to Skydeck 88 and then to Chinatown for dinner." Tilley slid the map over to Olena. "What else do you want to do?"

"That's sounds like more than enough. I doubt we'll have time to do all that."

Tilley shook her head. "We'll have more than enough time. Look at the map. Everything's right around here. It's so close we can just hop on the tram or walk." She leaned back, sipping her cup of coffee as if she had it all figured out. "Don't worry about how we're going to do all this; you need to figure out what you're going to tell bachelor number six about standing him up." That was the lie that the producers wrote into the script. "Do you have a fear of commitment?"

"I definitely don't have that. I just might stay single for the rest of my life."

Olena was never given the name of bachelor number six because there never was a bachelor number six to begin with. They auditioned some men in hopes of finding one, but none measured up. He had to either be strikingly attractive and camera ready, or oozing in personality, which meant he was able to perform the role. Some of the bachelors who'd made the cut were unknown actors who'd never appeared in anything not even a commercial. Finding ten of the world's most eligible bachelors to agree to be filmed pursing a woman wasn't the easiest task. Those men were too busy running their businesses and had enough girlfriends that they didn't want to pursue one. Olena would meet four eligible bachelors when they were back in the states, if Media One were given the go-ahead to film the final four shows. But until then, viewers were left to assume that Olena stood up bachelor number six, so she could hang out with her best friend and go on another date with Gordon, the Frenchman who had popped up on each leg of the trip.

Olena and Tilley rode the free city circle tram while they explored some of Central Melbourne's alleys and lanes, deciding to bypass the museum for an early dinner in Chinatown, stopping on Little Bourke Street, where a small debate ensued between Chine on Paramount and the basement-level Japanese restaurant Nihonbashi Zen right across the alley from Paramount.

"Since we're in Chinatown, I want an authentic Chinese meal. I love Chinese food," Olena said.

"Well, I like the way this place looks. I love basement restaurants."

"Just pretend you're stepping down," Olena said, pulling her into Chine on Paramount.

It was during lunch that Olena muttered the words producers would use for the promo. Something she'd said without any prompting.

"I'm forty-four, and I still don't have anyone who loves me. Everyone deserves love."

She thought of Jason. How they were much more alike than different. How both could be difficult when they felt they needed to be. She knew when she got back to Atlanta she could see him if she wanted to, and she probably would break down and call him, since she was a little harsh when he reached out to her. She didn't expect to be, but he'd caught her at a bad time, after she'd just finished having a meeting with Godiva—that woman had some serious problems.

After a long day of filming with Tilley, Olena was exhausted and ready to head back to the hotel after dinner, but there was still one more stop.

They walked the first part of the way until Flinders Lane, where they caught the tram, making their way over to the Eureka Tower—the tallest residential skyscraper in the southern hemisphere that sat on the southern banks of the Yarra River. There they took in the best views of Melbourne. Remy told Olena to pretend to be deathly afraid of heights. But she'd told him how difficult that would be seeing as she was someone who loved to fly and who lived on the thirty-second floor of a forty-two story skyscraper. But then she saw the building, and it had more than double the number of floors as her condo, and she was a little frightened to go all the way to the top.

It took just thirty-eight seconds to go from the ground to the eighty-eighth floor. A young woman in a black polo shirt uniform with a bright smile welcomed them to the sky deck as soon as the elevator door opened.

It started to hit Olena. She'd be home soon. It was fun, but she was so ready to curl up in her own bed. She'd been away for only nineteen days and it felt longer than her sabbatical. She had become jaded by all the travel. She realized it in Monte Carlo after she walked into the suite, looked around, and didn't even flinch. A suite that was larger than some people's homes and had a spectacular view of the Mediterranean Sea.

She was forty-four and numb, not a pleasant feeling.

Olena and Tilley walked around Skydeck 88, peering out of the floor-to-ceiling windows at the 360-degree views across Melbourne and the Port Phillip Bay, stopping at several spots to look through one of the many viewfinders that were placed around the sky deck floor that captured the city's landmarks.

"Do you want to go on that?" Tilley asked, noticing the long line of people waiting to go on The Edge, a glass cube that moved ten feet away from the building, leaving the people who were inside suspended 984 feet above the ground.

There was a sign posted that people should not ride with the following conditions:

Fear of heights

Fear of Enclosed Spaces

Sensitivity to Loud or Sudden Noises

Pregnancy

Heart Problems

Fear might be the jolt Olena needed, so she gladly took up the challenge. After slipping blue surgical booties over their walking shoes, Olena and Tilley, along with ten others, walked inside of the glass cube, leaving the camera crew behind. Although, it was Tilley's idea to go on the ride, she was the one grabbing firmly to the metal bar along the edge. She stood on the metal bar after the opaque glass became clear enough for her to see the city streets below. Tilley removed her hands from the bar and started clinging to Olena's right arm, screaming louder than the five-year-old-girl beside her.

Before they left The Edge, she and Tilley had their picture taken by the camera that was inside and went to the gift shop to pick it up and then headed back to the hotel.

"Guess what I found out," Tilley said after they'd made it back to the hotel. "They just booked two bachelors for the episodes filmed in the US, and they're famous. So, pray that the show gets four more episodes."

"Do I know them?"

Tilley nodded. "They wouldn't give me names, but they said

you definitely know who they are."

"Did they say it just like that? Did they use the word, definitely, or did you add that part? If they said definitely, then it's Hakeem?"

"You're determined to meet Hakeem, aren't you?"

"I told Tommy that Hakeem was one of my celebrity crushes." Tommy was the Media One employee who had interviewed Olena. "So I know it's going to be him. My God, I'm going to finally meet Hakeem."

"Don't get too excited. It might not even be him."

"Do you already know who it is, Tilley? If you already know, you have to tell me."

"I don't know," she squealed. "If I knew, I'd tell you."

"It's going to be him. If it's him, this whole experience would be totally worth it. I wouldn't even care if I got a book deal. Well, wait a minute. I would still care. I'd start writing movie scripts that my baby Hakeem could act in. We'd be the new power couple like Will and Jada, baby."

"I wish I hadn't said anything."

"No, I'm glad you did. I'm going to sleep good tonight."

"Hey," said Tilley, "can you believe that we're just a couple of weeks away from airing? You're about to be on national television, and everyone's about to recognize you and ask for your autograph. Are you going to be ready for that?"

Olena shrugged. "No one's going to recognize me. It's a reality show. A dating reality show that I'm going on one season. It's not a series." Olena had been practicing her autograph for years, by signing the inside title page of books she'd purchased, all in preparation. But to sign one for being a reality star instead of an author wasn't something she wanted.

"Good night," she said as her voice pepped up with thoughts of Hakeem.

It was a five-hour drive from Melbourne to Port Campbell National Park in Victoria. They started out early, at seven in the morning, and drove 190 kilometers (118 miles) southwest along the Great Ocean Road, one of the world's most scenic coastal routes. The winding cliff-top road, with its sharp corners, at times, was difficult to handle.

January in Melbourne was considered high summer. The temperature was a blazing forty degrees Celsius (104 degrees Fahrenheit) the day Olena and the rest of the cast and crew arrived. Just a couple days later, it was twenty degrees cooler.

Olena was in the front passenger seat of a red 1963 Ford Falcon convertible with crisp white interior, her date Gordon was in the seat directly behind hers and beside a cameraman. A professional driver dressed in the same clothes as Gordon was behind the wheel.

Godiva was behind them, riding in the white van with a camera crew.

They were being chauffeured most of the way until the driver pulled over as they approached the park so cameras could film Gordon pulling into Port Campbell and viewers would assume he drove there. On the drive to Port Campbell National Park, Olena thought about the day before when she and Gordon were filmed in the afternoon enjoying high tea at the Hotel Windsor in Melbourne, the same hotel where the cast and crew were staying. They had a pleasant time while they sat in a dainty booth, sipping house blend tea while nibbling on freshly baked scones, pastries with fresh fruit, and Black Forest cake, along with finger sandwiches that had the crust removed. Everything was presented elegantly on a three-tiered silver stand as sparkling wine, freshly brewed tea, and coffee were brought to their table throughout the afternoon.

It was one of the first dates that producers didn't cut short, and Olena was actually able to finish an entire scone and a few finger sandwiches along with two cups of tea and a complete thought—she actually liked him. Gordon was intriguing. Olena was a sucker for an accent, or was it the fact that he'd invented something, which made him creative and meant they had something in common. It could have been the endearing way he stared at her. He was exceptionally polite, always opening the door for her and pulling out her chair. Jason opened the door for her too but never pulled out her chair. And there were times with most of the men she'd dated that she'd catch their eyes wandering over to an attractive woman; even if only for a second, she still found it rude. But not with Gordon because he kept his full attention right where Olena wanted it to be—on her.

Now, she and Gordon were together again. But she wasn't in the best mood. Two days after flying into Australia, Olena was still jetlagged from the long flight and the nine-hour time difference between Monte Carlo and Melbourne. But she looked pretty in an Australian-designed printed dress that Tilley picked up at Myer, Australia's largest department store chain. Her makeup and hair were flawless. *Everyone should have the opportunity to travel with their own beauty team,* Olena thought.

After she and Gordon arrived at the park, they took a helicopter tour, flying over limestone stacks called the Twelve Apostles that rose a hundred and fifty feet above the waves. After the tour, they ate on the deck of the 12 Rocks Café and Beach Bar, Gordon still acting smitten over her, and Olena still wondering if it were all just an act as he ordered glass after glass of Victoria Bitter beer that he quickly guzzled down. She hadn't seen this side of him.

The cameras stopped filming after Olena took a few bites of her stuffed lamb.

"We're not going to drive back to Melbourne today," Godiva said, pulling out a map as the professional driver and a few key members of the crew gathered by the table where Olena and

Gordon sat. "We're going to stop in Yuulong, there's a nice bed and breakfast there." Godiva told Olena and Gordon they could wait for their driver in the car. Olena looked back at Godiva going over the map with the driver while the driver's head nodded continuously.

"He can't drive. He's drunk," Olena said, pointing to Gordon, after noticing the professional driver climb in the backseat with the cameraman.

"He's just going to start it off," Godiva reassured her. "And we want you to object just like you're doing now."

"But he's really not driving, right?" Olena pressed.

"He won't be driving for too long," Godiva said.

Gordon started off the drive for four miles, and when instructed, he pulled over and the professional driver took over, at which point Olena took a Herculean sigh of relief and even closed her eyes for nearly an hour as they headed toward the bed and breakfast in Yuulong.

"Olena, I need you to wake up, I'm going to start filming," the cameraman said as he got his camera into position.

"I'm up," Olena said, prying her heavy eyelids open. She lowered the vanity to inspect her makeup. "My eyelash is coming off," she said as she peeled it off. "Can we stop, so I can get my makeup refreshed before you start filming?"

"You don't need your eyelash for this scene."

"I don't?"

"Hang on," the driver said.

At a normal rate of speed, the car suddenly lost control around a curve at a tricky hairpin corner along Great Ocean Road near Yuulong. They plunged down a steep slope.

"Ah...ah...ah," Olena screamed the entire way. "Oh, my God!" Olena cried hysterically as the car continued its descent.

In that flash of a second, she was powerless.

She braced herself and prayed.

And suddenly, the car stopped.

A few men from the crew rushed down the slope with cameras.

A medic and a tow truck driver were nearby.

"Okay, Gordon, we need you behind the wheel," Remy said. "Makeup," he shouted. "Can you make it look like he has a gash over his forehead? By the way, your scream was great, Olena, which is why I decided not to let you in on what we were planning so we could get a natural reaction."

"What's going on?" Olena asked.

"We're not sure which way we're going to go with this. At the same time, we're showing the consequences of drinking and driving," Remy told Olena. "Or we're going to have him apologize to you in Vienna, which we already recorded. It all just depends."

"What?" Olena said, wiping away fresh tears from her trembling cheeks. "Wait a minute, are you saying that our car going off the road was written into the script?"

"We needed a little drama. The more you give us the less we need to make up on our own."

"I could have died."

"He's a professional driver. Nothing would go wrong."

"I'm sure professional drivers have died in car accidents before."

Olena unclasped her seatbelt, flung her door open, and trekked up the slope to Godiva.

"You're sick," Olena said to her.

"Excuse me."

"You heard me. You're sick. What if I would've died? I want a driver to take me back to the hotel right now, and I want to leave first thing in the morning. It's not worth my life."

"Olena—"

"I don't want to hear anything you have to say. I thought I was here to find love."

"Is that why you're here? I thought you wanted exposure, so you could find a publisher."

"If you were going to pull this stunt, you could've at least told me. I could've had a heart attack."

"This is why doing favors for people don't work. I'm doing you a favor by putting you on the show. You read your contract and signed waivers. Element of surprise, period—that's all it was. Take her to the hotel," Godiva told her driver.

Olena turned and started storming off. As she got away from Godiva, the corners of her mouth turned upward into a smile. As crazy as it might sound, she felt something. The desire to live that she thought she'd lost while on the trip, but just like missing baggage, it was returned to her. But she wasn't going to thank Godiva for that because what she'd done was still irresponsible.

Seconds later, she climbed into the back of one of two waiting vans and was whisked off.

Olena had been overseas for twenty-one days and had met five men: an inventor, the heir to a greeting card company, a retired race car driver, a software developer, and a necktie designer. Five men and so far not one of them was the one. Not that, she expected to meet him on TV, but an attraction that developed into a friendship was a welcomed diversion from Jason. In two days, she would be in Atlanta sans a book deal. By the third episode, she'd know about the outcome of the four remaining shows. If the network decided to pick those up, she'd make a lot more money and meet four more men. If not, it was back to a life filled with uncertainty.

PART THREE

ONE AND ONLY

♥ ～

NINETEEN

February

"I'm Rich O'Conner, the host of the all-new series *The One*," the young man in his mid-thirties said as he stood near the Eiffel Tower. He was fitted in a black suit with a red pocket square with small white hearts neatly positioned inside of his front breast pocket, and a white shirt and red tie. "Tonight is a special two-hour Valentine's Day series premiere. I'm here in the breathtakingly beautiful city of lights, Paris, France, awaiting the arrival of this year's bachelorette.

"This season we will travel to ten of the world's most romantic cities. In each of these cities, our bachelorette will go on three dates with a different eligible bachelor. After our bachelorette has met all ten bachelors, she will narrow down the list to her top two and announce her choice during our series finale. So here's a quick recap: one bachelorette going to ten romantic destinations to meet ten of America's most eligible bachelors. After she's met all of the bachelors, she'll choose two. From there, she'll pick the one live on our series finale.

"Along the way, there will be plenty of uncertainty as each

week we unveil a new bachelor, and there will also be a major twist that our bachelorette won't even see coming. Each of the bachelors' profiles can be found on our website, where you can also enter our sweepstakes for a chance to win a trip to Atlanta, Georgia for the live taping of the reunion show. With that, are you ready to meet this year's bachelorette? She'll introduce herself right after we take this short commercial break."

"A twist I didn't see coming." Olena said. "What does he mean by that, Tilley?"

"It's a twist you don't see coming," Tilley said. "If you don't see the twist coming, what makes you think I will? But I'm sure it's something you haven't taped yet."

Olena rushed to the kitchen to get some snacks before the show returned from commercial break. Although, she'd been supplied a DVD of the episode a few days before the broadcast, she opted to wait and watch it with Tilley and Eugena when hopefully everyone else was.

Tilley was there. But Eugena called a few hours before to say she couldn't make it. She had a last minute surprise date. And Olena understood, of course, after all it was Valentine's Day. She wondered who Jason was with. This time last year the two of them were together.

"I can't wait to see how it came out after the edit," Olena said as she darted from the kitchen with a plate of finger sandwiches. "Everything went by so fast that I can't even remember the men I dated. Oh, I'm nervous. What are people going to think of me?" Olena looked over at Tilley who was shaking her head. "Oh that's right. I don't care what people think of me. I wonder if Jason's watching." Tilley's shook her head again. "Why can't I wonder if he's watching?"

"Today isn't about Jason. It's *your* day. You have a show premiering on Valentine's Day."

"I wonder how I'm going to look. I hope my face doesn't

look fat."

"Welcome back to the series premiere of *The One*, where this season we're giving one lucky bachelorette the opportunity to choose between ten eligible bachelors in the hopes of finding the one. I'm your host, Rich O'Conner, and it's time to introduce our bachelorette. This native Detroiter resides in Atlanta, Georgia, and the rest I'll let her tell you." The cameras faded away from Rich and into Olena's condominium. She was sitting in her living room looking directly into the camera.

"Last year, I moved here from Florida and didn't know a soul. I'd heard a lot of things about Atlanta and how the people were down here. Let's just say, I've met a lot of strange characters. Don't get me wrong, Atlanta is a great place for a single person, *especially* if you're gay."

"Wait a minute, I need to rewind this," Olena said as she took the DVR control to rewind the episode. "What is going on? I didn't say any of that." She paused the DVR. "I never said I met a lot of strange characters in Atlanta. I said I met a lot of great people. I never said Atlanta is a nice place especially if you're gay."

"Trust me," Tilley said, "At some point, you said it. You just didn't say it that way. Did they have someone interview you?"

Olena nodded. "It wasn't really an interview. We just talked."

"And when you talked they taped and voila there you have it. Get used to it. The story department carves up audio bits like a turkey. They just take two or three bits and put them together to create something they feel is more interesting."

"They're mixing up my words. I *never* said Atlanta is a great place especially if you're gay. Can they twist my words around?" Olena asked. "Is that even legal?"

"They sure can, and they sure will keep on doing it. Read through that novel you signed, otherwise known as a Media One contract. They don't leave out anything." Tilley shrugged. "Get used to it."

"Wow, I really didn't think they could take what I said at different times and put it together and manipulate my words like that. And she told me that I would be a role model to young girls all across America—"

"She's so full of it. And you should know better. Basically, she told you what she knew you wanted to hear. That's her specialty. She's probably got a team staying up all night looking through hours of footage for whatever makes you look the most psycho. If I had known you were going to turn out to be as cool as you are, I would have given you a heads up. But I didn't know, so my bad."

Olena was upset, but she didn't want to show her anger. She wanted to be a pleasant hostess for Tilley's sake.

"Pray that we get the green light for the other four episodes, and now that you know their game try to play it in your favor. Not sure if that'll work. It's hard going up against an editor who's one of the best in the business."

"What are you doing?" Tilley asked when the volume suddenly cut off a few seconds after Olena started her introduction.

"I muted it. I don't want to hear myself speak."

"Why not? You can't invite me over to watch the show and then put it on mute."

"I didn't think I was going to do that, but I sound like I'm speaking through my nose and I hate that." Olena twirled a long, wispy curl that was resting on her shoulder. She was still getting used to having all of that hair.

"Take it off mute, please."

"Alright," Olena said begrudgingly as she picked up the DirecTV remote and pressed the mute button. "Ugh, I don't want to hear myself."

After a few more scenes that included Olena's intro, the Air France plane landing at Roissy, and Olena checking into the hotel, the first bachelor was introduced.

"What am I expecting?" A man's voice was heard coming from

behind a dark screen, and only his shadow was seen. "Just to have a great time with a beautiful woman, laugh, and get to know her."

The camera brought the man's face into focus. He had deep-set dark eyes, smooth skin, a thin mustache and beard, and short dark hair.

"I want her to know that I believe in love, and I know how to love." Olena walked out of the hotel. She was wearing a one-shoulder red matte stretch jersey dress with an asymmetric sweetheart neckline and a ruched waist with a beaded brooch. Her hair was swept into a feminine updo, and Tilley had accessorized the outfit with a pair of dramatic art deco earrings.

Gordon, who had just exited the chauffer-driven Maybach, stood a confident five-seven, and with Olena's five-inch heels, she towered over him by six inches.

He was wearing black slacks, a white shirt, and a black blazer.

"Bonjour," he said, kissing her hand.

Olena blushed and said, "Bonjour."

"You look beautiful."

"Thank you. You look very handsome. I hope it doesn't bother you that I'm so much taller than you?"

"Yes, it does."

Tilley blurted out during the scene, "French people are more honest than Americans. If that had been an American man, he would've said, 'Oh no that doesn't bother me. I love a tall woman.' Gordon told the truth, 'Yes, it does bother me.' "

Back on the show, Olena was shown stepping into the car followed by Gordon. They were then whisked off. It was time for Olena's first confessional.

Gordon is a nice looking man, but he's short—too short. I'm five-nine, and I wear five inch heels. He's probably five-seven. And for me that's just not a good look. You have to at least be my height. And you can't have small hands and small feet. Don't judge me.

They dined at La Maison Blanche, a contemporary restaurant with white-and-purple décor that was situated on the seventh floor of the art deco-style Theatre des Champs-Elysees. They sat at one of the best tables in the house beside a window overlooking the Seine. The food was presented like a work of art on their plates. They ate and sipped wine with a beautiful red-purple hue that flowed steadily from the Chateau Gloria St. Julien bottle into their wineglasses.

"You don't talk much," said Olena.

"No need to talk a lot," Gordon said. "But I will say that you're beautiful. I feel lucky."

Olena smiled and said, "Thank you. That was sweet."

"May I plan our next date? Will there be one?"

"Of course, but you came on not knowing who the bachelor-ette was going to be. It's not really as special. I mean, maybe I'm not your type."

"Type? I'm not sure what you mean."

"Maybe you're not attracted to me."

He wrinkled his brow. "I told you that I was. I can say I am again if you need more reassurance. You're beautiful, and I feel lucky."

Right before the commercial break, Olena was on the TV screen with a confessional.

The date wasn't as enjoyable as I imagined my first date in Paris would be. Don't get me wrong, the man is very easy on the eyes and ears. I adore his accent. It makes up for a lot. I'm not sure it makes up for seven inches. And just to clarify, I'm referring to his height. But something was missing. I don't know what it is, but I just know that he's not the one.

Tilley said, "I meant to tell earlier when I first walked in that your place is the business, like for real. When we were here for the first day of taping, I had no idea this was your place. I guess I assumed it was Jason's, and you were just living

with him. You must have sold a whole lot of phones, huh?"

"I surely did."

Tilley stood craning her neck. "Do you mind if I look around? I want to live like this when I grow up."

"You're going to live better than this. You're going to be a great designer. I just know it."

"I hope you're right."

"If that's what you really want to do just put your mind to it and believe. Don't let anyone tell you otherwise. And it'll happen for you. So many people give up right when it's about to happen for them."

"Is it really just a matter of believing?"

Olena nodded. "It is. When I accepted that job at Lutel, my parents thought I was crazy. Why would I want a job working for a company that only pays a base salary for six months and after that I'm on straight commission? Why wouldn't I? That was back when I worked for a company that paid a set salary, no incentives, and my annual raise averaged twenty-five dollars a paycheck. I wanted more. I felt so proud of myself when I earned my first large commission check at Lutel. I had that job down. I could do it in my sleep. I knew all of my clients extremely well and had a terrific relationship with them…" Olena paused, placed one hand on her chest, fanning her face with the other.

"What's wrong?"

"For the first time in a long time, I'm scared about my future. I became successful once, but can I do it again."

"You can do it again. You can do it with your book. Believe in that."

"Thank you," Olena said as she smiled at Tilley. "I needed to hear that."

TWENTY

"So fake," Jason said as he sat in one of several large leather recliners in his custom home theater. "That show is so fake. Chantilley isn't her best friend. Olena doesn't have friends. The only best friend that I know of is her niece, Alicia."

"What do you mean she doesn't have friends? Why doesn't she?" Momma Nix said as she sat tooling with her laptop.

Jason shrugged. "I have no idea. All I know is, if she weren't going out with me, she wasn't going out. Let me correct that, if she weren't going out with a man, she wasn't going out because I wasn't the only man she dated."

"I don't know about that…a woman with no friends. But then again, I have a lot of phone numbers, but how many of those women do I really consider my friend?" Momma Nix mulled over her own question. "Maybe three."

"And that includes Aunt Thadie, right?" Aunt Thadie was his mother's identical twin.

"Of course, she's my best friend."

"That's still two more than Olena has."

"Well, I don't know why she doesn't have friends. I like her. She's a sweet girl."

"Ooh, I'm so glad I didn't go on there. The show and Gordon Landry are both fake."

"From what I've seen so far, he doesn't look all that fake to me. I know one thing his money's not fake. He's an inventor, and his net worth is over five hundred million."

"Did I miss something?" Jason asked his mother. "I never heard him mention his net worth."

"I went on the show's website and viewed his profile."

"That's probably fake too," Jason said laughing. "Show me his financials. The whole thing was fake and scripted. I know Olena. Not only did she look nervous, but the way she phrased some of her words didn't sound right. It was scripted. I'm not worried."

"Worried? I didn't think you were worried. Why would you be? Weren't you the one who said you didn't want to deal with her anymore? Didn't you say that? You don't want her. Haven't you moved on to that girl in Dallas?"

It was Valentine's Day. Last year he'd spent the day with his two favorite women—his mother and Olena. This year it was with his mom and his boys, who were in the nearby recreation room playing video games.

He had two dozen red roses delivered to LaRuth's office, and she called right after she received them to tell him how much she missed him. They had seen each other two weeks earlier. He had flown her down to Atlanta. But they didn't have sex. He could have, if he had wanted to. He didn't want to.

"What did you say?"

"The girl in Dallas. What am I supposed to call her, a woman?"

"Before that. How would you know what I said to Olena."

Momma Nix's eyes enlarged.

"Momma, how would you know? All I told you was I changed my mind about going on the show. I didn't tell you anything about our relationship."

"Maybe a little bachelorette bird told me. Just because you

don't like her anymore, doesn't mean I won't. I'm her friend. It's no different with her than it is with Chevonne—once my girl, always my girl."

"What did she say about me?"

"Don't worry about what she said. Besides, that was before she went off to film her show. What if she married one of those guys? I mean, you don't want her."

"Stop saying I don't want her, and stop acting like this mess is real."

"Stop saying it's fake. You don't really know that."

"Well, she's not marrying one of 'em. I do know that."

"How do you know that?"

"I just do. She's so much better than that. She's better than meeting a man on a reality show. All they're looking for is fame. Did you hear that corny music playing in the background?"

"That was Nina Simone. There's nothing corny about Nina Simone."

"I'm not talking about the singer. I'm talking about the scene. 'I put a spell on you, because you're mine.' " Jason fell over laughing, his right arm hanging off the chair. "You couldn't pay me enough money to make a fool out of myself on national TV."

"Those men are some of America's most eligible bachelors, so I don't think they need the fame. In 2005, Mr. Landry invented an all-purpose organic cleaner."

"He invented an organic all-purpose cleaner. What was the name of it?"

"It didn't say the name."

"It didn't say the name. Hmm, maybe because the only thing he invented was that lie, and he probably didn't even invent that. Media One did."

"If the man said he invented it, I believe him."

"I'm your son. Believe me. He's a fake."

"You don't have to like any of them, since you're not the bachelorette. Why don't you just admit that you want her for yourself, and you're just being stubborn? What's that song?" she asked, snapping her fingers. "You never miss a good thing till it's gone. That's it, but Monica's version." Momma Nix started singing the song, "Now I'm Gone," by Monica.

"First of all, I wasn't busy kicking it with my boys, and I definitely took care of my woman so sing that song to someone else. Thanks for the viewing party, but I won't be watching with you next week."

"Uh-huh. Don't be jealous."

"I'm not jealous. I have a woman, remember?"

Momma Nix cleared her throat and rolled her eyes. "Well, don't bring her over here. I don't want to meet her." Jason walked out of the room. "And check on the boys."

"Be sure to tell Olena that it's a no to that Landry dude the next time you speak to her."

"Why don't you tell her?"

"On second thought, I don't want you to tell her anything. It's her life."

"See you next week."

"No, you won't be seeing me next week. I'm done with that show."

"Like I said, I will certainly see you back here next week."

It was the following Sunday, and Jason was back, just as his mother predicted. Only this time they weren't watching in the home theatre. His mother had only gone in there the week before because it was the season premiere, and it was Valentine's Day. But for the rest of the episodes, she wanted to curl up on the sofa and get as comfortable as possible, so she retreated to the family room with the fireplace lit in the background.

"Now, I'm about to set some ground rules before my show

starts. When I say, 'shh' that means just what it means—no talking. You can talk during a commercial break. I don't want to hear you saying, 'it's fake' through the entire show like you did last week."

"It's whatever. I'm not really watching it."

"Okay, whatever you say. *Shh*."

Brick Lane was the first meeting place for Olena and bachelor number two while in London. It was a street in the London borough of Tower Hamlets, in the East End, which was world famous for its graffiti featuring artists such as Banksy, D Face, and Ben Eine. On Sundays, it was packed. Olena and bachelor number two, whose name was Jeff Sterling, walked the busy street until they arrived at a flower market on Columbia Road, where he bought Olena some fresh cut roses. There were hundreds of people walking along Brick Lane, sitting on the sidewalks while several others entertained those passing by with live music, singing, juggling—almost any and everything imaginable.

After Brick Lane, they went to the London Eye, the tallest Ferris wheel in Europe situated on the South Bank of the River Thames, where they were able to get to know each other a little better. There they enjoyed priority boarding and a glass of Pommery Brut Royal Champagne inside one of the thirty-two sealed capsules that took thirty minutes to rotate and moved at a pace slow enough to allow Olena and Jeff to stand and walk around.

The first thing I thought when I looked into Jeff Sterling's eyes was serial killer. He has intense eyes. The way he stared at me was scary. I felt like I could read his mind. He was thinking, "I have this shed on the back of my property that I'm going to chain her up in. You have to be careful with people who have never had to work for money

"Has your family been in the greeting card business as long as Hallmark?"

"No, I'm afraid not. Hallmark's been around for a long while. My grandfather started the company in 1940. When he passed away it went to my dad, and when my dad passed away it went to me. Have you ever bought one of our cards?"

Olena hesitated. "I've bought Hallmark and American Greetings. Are Sterling cards the ones they sell at all the dollar stores?" He nodded. "So no, I don't buy those." He looked down, and there was an awkward silence. "What I really like about Hallmark is the line of cards Maya Angelou writes for them. I love her, and I always have. And then American Greeting cards are sold everywhere. I don't frequent too many dollar stores. I do love Walmart, though. To me, that's like a dollar store."

Jason blurted, "No, you don't Olena. You love Target. Walmart must be one of their sponsors."

"Shh," his mother said loudly.

"We're making great strides with e-cards," Jeff said.

"I don't see digital greeting cards taking over actual greeting cards. Books going digital is one thing, but people want to display greeting cards. I think the digital market is for lazy people who don't feel like going to the store, but they don't want a person to think they've forgotten the occasion. It's an add-on business. Having been so successful in sales in my former life, I can predict trends." Jeff nodded and grinned.

"Look at him," Momma Nix said. "He's pissed, putting down the man's family business.

"Olena wouldn't say that to somebody for real. This mess is scripted."

Momma Nix darted her eyes at Jason. "Didn't I tell you not to talk while the show is on?"

"Oh, so you can talk, but I can't?"

"That's right. Now, *shh!*"

The next scene Olena was in the sitting room at the Dorchester Hotel, enjoying fish and chips when the phone rang.

"Hello, Olena, guess where I am?"

"Gordon, are you in London?"

"Are you hungry? Would you like to go get some dinner?"

"Umm, sure," Olena said, dropping her plastic fork and closing the lid to the carryout container.

After the commercial break, the next scene was of Olena and Gordon having dinner at a nearby restaurant.

"Gordon, what made you come here?" Olena asked.

"I wanted to see you. We went to eat a few times in Paris, but there were other things we could have done there as well. I needed another date...a few more."

Olena smiled widely.

When the hour-long show ended, Momma Nix turned off the large screen TV and said, "I want to go to London, too. Why haven't you already taken me to these places?"

"Because you don't like to fly, Momma, and it's an eight-hour flight to Paris. Can you handle that? If you can, I'll take you. "

Jason had just gotten home the day before from a midweek trip to Dallas.

"I really like Gordon. But Olena was right about that other one. Those eyes. You can tell a lot about a person from their eyes, and Jeff has that crazy look. "

"I don't want to hear about it. Love was made for me and you, really? That was the second time they'd seen each other, and that's the song they decided to play."

"He's French."

"What's that mean?"

"Men from France are romantic. I need a Frenchman because American men are nothing but a bunch of lying, cheating scoundrels—at least that's what my ex-husband was. I hope Gordon follows her around to every city. I love a persistent man."

"He's also short, and Olena doesn't like a short man. Momma, I know what you're doing."

"What am I doing?"

"You're trying to use psychology on me, and it's not working. You better hope they stay on the air the full ten weeks. Six million viewers for a series premiere on a major network isn't very high, especially not for that type of show."

"Now you're pulling the show's ratings."

"I was just curious."

"I bet you were. Why don't you worry about Dallas, since you're sending for her nearly every weekend?"

"How do you know what I'm doing?"

"I opened your credit card statement by mistake."

"How was it by mistake when I pay all your bills?"

"It was an honest mistake, but I'm glad I did. You flew that floozie here first class. Next time she comes down here it better be coach. In fact, there shouldn't even be a next time? I bet she's no different than Keena. Are you helping this one with an album too?

"No, she has a job."

"And it doesn't pay enough for her to buy her own plane ticket? Why does a man have to pay for everything all the time?"

"Momma, you're a woman. Shouldn't you be taking up for women?"

"I'm a woman with eight sons and some of them been through some mess with some women, and I know some women can be just as trifling as some men. You can hit on my son, spit in his face, stab him in the arm, but if he tries to defend himself, he's getting arrested. *Oh really*? But I'm wrong for saying that because I'm a woman." She was referring to an incident that had happened a few days earlier between her youngest son and his girlfriend. "If a man doesn't want you, leave. If a woman doesn't want you, leave. It's no need to be violent."

"We've sorted all that out. The charges are going to be dropped."

"And they'll be back together, and what kind of sense does that make? I mean, I know I raised my sons to be respectful but don't be stupid."

"You heard about being a gentleman, haven't you?"

"Yes, I sure have. I've heard about that and being a fool, so don't be one. It's a pattern you sometimes fall into. You had a nice woman, and you dumped her for a woman who used you to pay for her studio time."

"Can we please stop talking about Chevonne and Keena? I made a mistake, but LaRuth isn't like Keena," he said, coming to her defense. The last few days in Dallas turned out better than expected, and the sex was incredible, as usual. She opened up to him and talked a lot more. She talked about God and the Bible, but not in the sanctimonious way she'd done so many times before. In a way that showed him that she honestly did love and understand the word. And in a small, but extremely kind gesture, she took him to Pappadeaux for dinner, and they had a pleasant time. He had never been there, so he let her order for him. She made all the right choices down to the bottled water. He loved boudin. *How did she know?* And the boudin was pretty tasty, not like it was in New Orleans, but close enough. She shied away from ordering him any fried foods, letting him know she had been listening, and she ordered the Texas Red Fish with Maine lobster—one of the most expensive entrées on the menu. Though, to him, the menu wasn't pricey at all. Still, it was the thought that counted.

"La who? I don't like her. I don't know why, but I don't."

"She's not for you to like. She's for me to like. Ooh and I like it," he said, and then he started singing the Debarge song, " 'I like it…I like it…I really, really like it…I'm for it…adore it…so come let me enjoy it.' " Jason continued singing as he walked up the long, winding staircase.

"And how many other men in Dallas like it too, huh? You're probably not the only one singing that song. You gonna like it all the way to bankruptcy." Jason slammed his bedroom door.

TWENTY-ONE

March

Olena and Tilley had just walked into their balcony suite at the Fairmont Hotel in San Francisco—the first stop on the last leg of filming. From there they were going to New York, Boston, and finally New Orleans. As it stood, ratings had improved significantly from the series premiere. The thought being that since they premiered on Valentine's Day the numbers may have been low because people were out celebrating with their loved ones. When the network re-aired the first episode the following Saturday, it garnered two million more viewers. By the time, Sunday's new episode aired the numbers were at fifteen million, which was better than Media One and the network even expected, so the final four episodes and the reunion show were ordered two weeks after the Valentine's Day premiere.

That was the great news.

The not-so-great news was after thirty-three days back home, she had to head back out again, and they had ten days to shoot everything except for the live finale and the live reunion show. Ten days in four cities with so many sights to showcase. There was so much product placement and sponsorship that the money flowed into the network from everywhere. Every place she ate, every hotel she stayed in, every airline she flew on, rental car agencies—subtle things that the average viewer would see as being part of the show, in most cases, was actually product placement or sponsorship. Right down to what she drank. There were times a bottle of water had been taken out of her hands right before the cameras rolled and replaced with one of their advertised brands. This took a little getting used to, especially when she was forced to eat or drink something she despised.

Her newfound notoriety also took some getting used to. All of a sudden she was on all the Atlanta nightclubs' VIP lists. She couldn't go to the mall without people asking to take pictures with her and for her autograph. Everyone had his or her own opinion of who Olena should pick, and so far the consensus was she needed to keep looking.

Finally, at her hair salon, one of the clients said what she'd been waiting to hear, "Thank you for not making black women look like a fool." She'd probably made the blogs, but at Godiva's urging, Olena didn't read any of them. Media One had Olena open a Twitter and Facebook account. Within days, she was at half a million followers. She didn't tweet or post on her Facebook wall. They hired someone for that. Olena earned income for some of those tweets, a percentage of which went to Media One. She earned a thousand dollars a tweet before they took out their sixty-five percent. Four hundred and fifty dollars to do nothing wasn't bad.

"You don't know yet, do you?" asked Tilley.

"What am I supposed to know?"

"Let me start with what's going to make you smile. I did some snooping, and I know who the famous man is, and you're meeting him tonight."

"It's Hakeem, isn't it? I don't need to be surprised, just tell me." Olena covered her face with both hands and shook from the excitement of it all.

"It's not Hakeem."

She dropped her hands. "It's not. Then, who is it?"

"He's a musician who hails from your hometown."

"I need you to be a little more specific. There are a lot of musicians in Detroit."

"He's a saxophonist."

"Is Boney James from Detroit? I don't think he is. Who?"

"Porter Washington."

"Are you sure?"

Tilley nodded. "He's the next bachelor."

Olena pulled her suitcase on the bed. "Hmm, I'm not sure how I feel about that."

"I'd feel excited if I were you. He's so fine."

"I think he's here to promote his album, because he already has a fiancée. What else? You said there was something else."

Tilley reached in her tote bag and took out a supermarket tabloid.

"I meant to show you this at the airport, but since I got there late I didn't have time. You're famous." She tossed the tabloid on top of the clothes in Olena's open suitcase and pointed to the headline above Olena's picture.

WHAT YOU DON'T KNOW ABOUT AMERICA'S SWEETHEART

She's already said "I Do" once

Read the shocking details of the secret wedding inside

Olena let out a loud shrill that sounded like a dying animal.

She threw the paper across the room, hugged her knees, and placed her head down as she sat on the bed.

"So I guess that means, it's true," said Tilley.

Olena tried to shake away her feelings, but she felt so violated that so many people would know her little secret.

"Olena, it's not really a big deal if it were true. So what, you were married. If I knew you were going to act like this, I wouldn't have said anything. Let's just order room service and wait for episode three to air. We only have two hours to wait." But the more Olena thought about it, the more she cried. Her parents would find out the secret she'd hidden for years. They always read the tabloid headlines as they waited in line at the grocery store, and so would her niece and nephew and her sister and brothers, and would Olena ever move past the Olena Day of old? She was embarrassed. What would her mother think?

Everything made sense now—the strange look on the production team's faces while she waited inside the airport for the plane to board. Olena had sat beside Godiva on the plane and Godiva never said a word to her about the tabloid.

"Does Godiva know?"

"Do pigs eat slop? She's the one who probably sold the story."

"Why would she do something that was so damaging to a person?"

"If you have to ask, you haven't been listening to anything I've been saying for the past couple of months. Godiva doesn't care about you or your feelings. Media One does a complete background check. They know all your business, and they'll throw some out whenever they feel the need. "

"I'm embarrassed. I thought it was my little secret."

"Olena, you're not the only one in the world with secrets."

What could Olena tell herself to feel better? Where did she start? With her marriage, the one that lasted six months and no one knew about other than the man who was just as stupid as

she was for saying "I Do". Her biggest regret, apart from agree-
ing to the nuptials, was not getting the marriage annulled after
it fell apart.

She was twenty-seven, and he was thirty-five. She met
him at the gas station, of all places. He stood at a pump at the
Chevron station on Grand River near Fenkell in Detroit, fill-
ing up his black Camaro Iroc-Z. He worked the line at General
Motors. On their first date, he obsessively discussed his ex-wife.
They'd divorced because of her bad attitude. She was selfish and
thought she was the finest woman in the city of Detroit and sur-
rounding suburbs. She never wanted to have sex and just wanted
to hear him tell her how good she looked. Mr. Iroc-Z and his wife
moved into a big house in the suburbs, and his wife didn't have
to work. But after the divorce, they sold the house, paid off the
bank, and divided what little was left between the two of them.
He moved back to the city. To a two-story brick home with a
red awning that sat on the middle of Ilene Street on the northwest
side of Detroit.

Mr. Iroc Z told Olena that he didn't believe in dating. If he
were to see someone he wanted and they hit it off, why wait? Their
relationship moved quickly, and she couldn't totally blame him
for that. By the time she turned thirty, she wanted to be married
and have one child. For her, marriage was the ultimate validation
of being a woman. If she were married, then, she was normal. It
meant a man loved her and wanted her for his wife. She would
be just like many of the women who worked with her, who loved
talking about their husbands and kids, and Olena loved listening. So about two months in and numerous mind-blowing sexual
encounters later, they went down to the Justice of the Peace to
exchange vows.

Her first impression of married life was that it felt like what
she'd been searching for. She was more confident as a woman. Her
husband was one of the good guys; therefore, her life was great—

at least for a short while. Then, nearly four months into the marriage, things changed. First, he started complaining about his job. Soon after about her and her lack of cooking skills and then any little thing he could find wrong from the way she wore her hair to her boney frame and crooked teeth.

"You go to that beauty shop that's supposed to hold some kind of secret to making a woman's hair grow, but yours hasn't grown an inch. You're wasting your money. You need to use it on some braces. It's going to take a lot more than hair to make you look like something," he said out of the blue one day. "I wish you could see the women I used to date. Every last one of them look so much better than you."

Olena didn't understand why he had suddenly become so mean and nasty toward her. The day before, they'd made love and everything was fine. Less than twenty-four hours later, he looked at Olena like she was trash and told her how ugly she was. Soon after, he started spending hours away from home. His explanation was always the same. He had been working out at the Northwest Activity Center. After getting up the courage to question him further, she asked why it took him three or sometimes four hours to work out. He began to stutter as he told her that he had fallen asleep in the steam room.

The first thing he did when he got home from work was put on a jogging suit, grab his duffle bag, and rush out the side door.

"I'm going up to the Northwest Activity Center to unwind."

So, one day, a fed-up Olena waited nearly ten minutes and headed out after him. To see, for herself, if he actually were where he claimed he would be. Either he was in the steam room, or he wasn't. She'd have to see him there in order to believe him.

When she entered the Northwest Activity Center, she immediately asked the young woman sitting behind the welcome desk where the steam rooms were. Her heart sounded like a drum roll as she walked down the long hallway. Her answer was less than five minutes away, and something inside of her said she was not going to like it. Something told her that he wasn't unwinding at the Northwest Activity Center. He was at some woman's house doing she could only imagine what. She took a deep breath and went through the set of double doors leading to a row of three doors and three separate steam rooms. She walked down the narrow hall to each door, opening them as she came to them. No one was behind door number one. Behind door number two, there was also no one. She stood in front of the last door and took a deep breath before she turned the doorknob. This was it. If he weren't on the other side, he had lied to her all along.

"Open it now," the tiny voice inside of her said just before she barreled through.

There was someone inside...*two* people and a lot of steam.

When the fog cleared, she saw the open condom wrappers on the wooden bench and a naked man frantically trying to leave. The other man was still sitting on the bench on top of a white towel. His legs spread widely. He remained seated with a dazed look in his eye.

That man was her husband.

She was stunned.

He was gay and pretending not to be. Now, so many things made sense. She never considered herself to be a beauty queen. Not by a long shot. But what man would marry a woman only to use every opportunity to put her down—a man who was unhappy with himself and hiding who he truly was.

"I'm on my way home," he told her. Did he think she was blind or stupid enough to pretend she didn't see the condom wrappers and the other man rushing out the door?

She took off her wedding ring. The one she hated wearing because the diamond was embarrassingly small and the band too large for her slender fingers, and she hurled it at him. "Since you like small round holes, maybe you can find some use for that."

Why did he have to drag her into his life and his lies? she had wondered. It was 1993. A long time before the subject of down-low men was discussed. She thought of the fashion director back in college that she'd had a crush on. He was gay, but at least he didn't hide the fact. He even kissed a man out in the open at a party, where there were more straight people than gay ones, and he didn't care what anyone thought.

Well, at least, she found her answer.

She rushed home, tossed her most valuable possessions, which at the time were just her clothes and shoes, into a couple of suitcases and threw them in the trunk of her car. She left the door key on the kitchen table and drove off.

The next time she saw him or thought she had was a few months later while she stood in line at the party store on Lahser. She glanced at the man in the wheelchair. He looked like her ex-husband. But, she didn't want to take another look to confirm whether it was him. Olena had never been one who dealt with the truth well. If *her ex had HIV or AIDS, did she?* Olena didn't get tested, at first. A couple of years earlier Magic Johnson made his HIV-positive announcement at a press conference, and she remembered how shocked she was, and how scared she assumed his wife must have been. She didn't want to go through that. She didn't want to know. Instead, she decided to assess her health by other things, such as a Pap smear and urine analysis. The results of both were always normal. Wouldn't someone with HIV have an abnormal pap? Maybe that was HPV? She wasn't quite sure. The more she learned. The more she realized the only way to find out if she were HIV-positive was to get a blood test.

It wasn't until nearly ten years later that she found out the truth. Lutel required a complete physical before granting her insurance coverage. After nearly ten years of wondering, she had her answer in a matter of days. Everything she tested for was negative, including HIV.

It could have been worse. Big deal, she was married once. And yes, the article mentioned that her husband was now openly gay. The writer even made a joke that Olena turned a straight man gay. Fortunately, for Olena, what they hadn't uncovered was the six-year affair she had with Hugh, a married man and her manager at Lutel. Jason and his mother would have a harder time forgiving her for something like that then a secret marriage she had almost twenty years ago that lasted only six months.

"There's another one," Tilley said.

"Another one?"

"I saved the worst for last."

"America's new darling a homewrecker," Olena said, reading the headline. On the cover was a picture of her between Matthew and Andrew with an X over Andrew's head and a heart drawn over Matthew's. She quickly flipped through the newspaper pages to the story and scoured each word.

"They mentioned the abortion. That I was pregnant with twins." As she read the rest of the story, her eyes welled up. Seeing her life in print was worse than living through it.

"Andrew did this to me, either Andrew or Matthew."

Tilley shook her head. "Godiva did that."

"She couldn't do this." Olena held the tabloid in one hand and slammed it on the bed. "She could *not* do this. That was twenty-six years ago. I don't even remember the name of the clinic I went to for the abortion, so I know she couldn't find it out. Nope. Andrew did this."

"You have to know *her* the way I do," Tilley said, bouncing the word her. "She finds ways to F-people up. I swear it's that woman's favorite pastime. She probably reached out to Andrew or Matthew or maybe even one of their friends. There are so many things she could've done. But either way, neither one of those stories is a big deal, so don't worry about it."

"Tilley, I don't want my family to see this...or Jason."

"Are you still thinking about Jason?"

"I mean not all the time, but—"

"Almost all the time."

"Slightly more than that."

"I knew you still loved him."

"Well, *duh*…Yes, I love him. He broke up with me. I didn't break up with him."

"Don't worry about what Jason thinks. I'm sure he's made mistakes just like everyone else."

"Keena."

"I worked with her on *Ballerwives*, but I didn't consider her a baller. I can think of another word that begins with the letter b that describes her best," Tilley grinned.

"I heard she wasn't very friendly."

"And whoever told you that was being very kind. She puts on way too many airs. I wanted to ask her, who does she really think she is? She lucked up and married Jason Nix and had two babies by him that she doesn't raise, but still collects child support for them. I don't even want to be on that plan because that's just trifling. But, I'm going to leave and give you some space so you can call your family." Tilley headed for the door.

Olena picked up her phone to call her mother, but quickly made an excuse of why she shouldn't.

"This can wait. If she already knew, she'd call me or Alicia would. Alicia must still be mad. Mom and Dad are probably off somewhere in their RV. It's not important. My date—I need to get ready for my date."

TWENTY-TWO

For Olena's date with Porter, she wore her hair straight with a part at the center. Tilley styled her in a black flirty halter dress made of rayon that draped at the neck. It had some edgy metal mesh around the waist and revealed half of her back. She paired the dress with a pair of purple suede five-inch peep toe heels with a one-inch platform.

Hopefully, her date with Porter would be one she'd remember, so she'd be able to forget about what the tabloids had written.

She stood across from him and welcomed his sensual stare down.

Porter Washington. And to think, I have his song, "Rebound" in my iPod. I listen to it all the time That and Lauryn Hill's, "Nothing Even Matters." I discovered his music a while back. And he's from Detroit as I am...so that makes him my homeboy. When I first heard the single, "Rebound," I thought I was listening to Boney James. I'm a Porter Washington fan and excited to get to meet him. I love his music, and I've always thought he was a handsome man. Young, but, for some reason, those are the ones I meet these days. I like everything about him. He's tall and muscular without being the Incredible Hulk. And I love his sense of style. But, what I truly want to know is what happened to Winona. Why aren't they together?

Porter used his tongue and wet his lips when he first looked at Olena. Was that a coincidence? Olena thought not, or maybe she was just getting too carried away with that new book she'd started writing that teetered on erotica. As a result, her mind was always going in one direction, and sex was all she'd thought about lately. It had been so long since she'd had sex that she could safely refer to herself as celibate again.

"We already filmed one of Olena's confessionals. So what we're going to film now is your introduction," Remy said to Porter while Godiva stood glued to Remy's side. "We're going to film in The Tonga Room. They have a live band that floats in a boat on the lagoon and enters to thunder and a rainstorm, so we thought it would be great, since you're a musician, if you could play along with the band. We already have it set up with the band. Are you okay with that?"

"I'm not okay with that," his young female manager said. "Nothing against the Tonga Room, but as you may already know Porter performs in large venues now. It's been a few years since he's played at small clubs and restaurants."

"I don't mind meeting Olena in there," he said as his eyes remained focused on Olena. "If we were on a real date and I was actually meeting her for the first time, I'd probably meet somewhere small and intimate like that. But floating out on a boat with a band seems a little lame to me. No offense, Tonga Room."

"How do you see the Tonga Room fitting into the courtship?" Godiva asked. "We're here to accommodate you. So tell us how you'd prefer to have the introduction filmed, and we'll find a way to make it work." She flashed the biggest smile Olena had ever seen on her. In fact, she rarely saw Godiva smile. The way Godiva was with Porter startled Olena. She saw how she and the rest of the crew catered to him and let him tell them how he wanted the scene to play out as opposed to the way they dictated what Olena would and wouldn't do and say. But Tilley had already told Olena they always treated entertainers better than the cast.

"We can just meet here in the restaurant or in the lobby," Porter said.

"That doesn't make for good television," Godiva said. "We've done a lot of restaurant meetings."

"Dinner is a standard first date," Porter said. "What makes the experience different is the person you're on the date with, not the location."

"Give me thirty minutes so I can go over something with the story team and I'll be right back," Godiva said and then marched off with Remy on her heels.

Olena and Porter stood silently for a few seconds as they stared across at each other.

"Would you like to go to the bar?" Porter asked.

"Sure."

He took her by the hand, something she didn't expect, and led her to the Tonga Room, leaving his manager behind.

There was a bright blue lagoon in the center of the restaurant where the boat with the band aboard floated in.

"Were you trying to get away from your manager?" Olena asked after he pulled out one of the bar stools for her and she sat comfortably on it with her legs crossed. "Vanity is cool, she's just high strung, which is the exact reason I hired her. We go back a long way." They ordered a round of Tonga Mai Tais, which were served in a fake coconut cup garnished with a pineapple wedge, cherry, and yellow umbrella.

"So should we hurry up and get through the awkward, 'Tell me about yourself' phase?" Porter asked after his second Mai Tai and Olena's third.

"Sure," Olena said, pushing her half-finished cocktail away from her.

"Do you say anything other than sure?"

"Yes."

"Sure and yes—that'll work."

"So I'm curious about something," Olena said.

"And what's that?"

"How does Winona feel about you appearing on this show? Aren't you two engaged? You said in one of your interviews that she was the love of your life. " What fascinated Olena about his relationship with Winona was the fact that Winona was HIV-positive. She remembered on a few occasions wondering why a man who wasn't, or so she assumed wasn't, would take such a risk.

"As a rule, I don't discuss past relationships," Porter said. "I hope you understand."

"Sure."

Porter smiled. "But I'll tell you anything you want to know about me.I can tell you about my daughter, Portia. She's six and she's really smart and pretty. Did I mention she's smart? And she can sing."

"She has musical talent like her dad."

"She's my heart. She wants me to get married."

"She told you that."

Porter nodded. "Her mom's married. She wants her daddy to be married and happy too."

"And what do you want?"

"Right now, I'm just looking to chill with a cool person. That's what I want right now." That's all Olena wanted once she took the time to actually think about it. Not a relationship because she'd just gotten out of one. "My life is hectic right now. I go from a plane to a hotel room to a concert hall back to a hotel room and the cycle continues. When I'm at home, I'd love to have good company. Are you good company, Miss Day?"

Olena smiled. "I think so."

"Wrong answer. Don't buck the trend. You were supposed to say either *yes* or *sure*."

"Okay, yes."

"Keep that up, and we'll get along just fine."

Olena reached for the drink she'd pushed away. "So, Mr. Washington." She took a sip from the straw.

"Miss Day."

"Tell me about yourself."

"What would you like to know?"

"What I really want to know you probably won't tell me."

"About Winona?" he asked. She nodded. "No, I don't want to talk about Winona. There's nothing else you want to know."

"Well, there is, but I don't really know how to ask you my other question that's indirectly dealing with Winona, but it's also about you."

"No, I'm not HIV-positive."

"How did you know I wanted to ask you that?"

"If I were you, I'd want to know the same thing. It's a valid concern since Winona was. But, no, I'm not."

"Weren't you concerned about getting that?"

He nodded. "But I didn't think about it as much as you would probably assume I would. There were times that I didn't think about it at all. I loved her. I wanted us to work and be like any other couple. And sex is a big part of most relationships. I can't imagine being in a relationship without sex, even though I found myself in one. No, I'm not HIV-positive, but I'm willing to take a test if you need me to prove it, only on one condition. Do you want to hear it?"

"Sure."

He smiled. "We will be making love once the results come back negative."

"Seeing as how this is our first date, sex is the furthest thing from my mind right now." Which wasn't quite true because, in actuality, she was sitting beside him at the bar trying to imagine how he'd look naked.

"That was just a joke," Porter said, "with a little wishful thinking attached."

"But how can you be so sure that you're not HIV-positive?"

"We never had sex, and I've also been tested before."

"How long were the two of you together?"

"Three years."

"And you never had sex."

"We never had sex. She wanted to hold out for marriage, but I don't even think we would've had it then."

"How did you go three years without sex?"

He shook his head. "I don't know, because I didn't. I couldn't do it."

"Oh," Olena shook her head. "So typical."

"Who's typical? I'm not. I had needs. That's all that was. Yes, I cheated, but I didn't have feelings for those women."

"*Women*? Plural?" Olena shook her head. "Men...I'll never figure you all out."

"What do you mean? What was I supposed to do? I had needs, but I loved her, so that was what I did to stay in a relationship where I wasn't being fulfilled sexually."

"You're having sex with a woman, or excuse me *women*, plural, so I'm sure you developed feelings for at least one of them. One-night stands are one thing, but if you keep going back for more that's something else all together."

"You have a good point...you have an excellent point, and we can talk about that."

"Let's," Olena said as she smiled and twitched her nose.

"Okay, lets," Porter said smiling back at her.

Olena felt so comfortable with him. It felt as if she'd known him for years. With the other bachelors, it was hard for her to have an enjoyable conversation while the cameras rolled. But right now the cameras weren't there. It was just Olena and Porter. He felt familiar in a good way.

Porter nodded. "Let me break it down for you."

"I'm listening, go ahead and break it down...all the way down."

"Do you own a vibrator?"

"What kind of question is that? Okay, maybe not all the way down...maybe halfway."

"Just answer my question. What's the big deal? We're both adults."

"Yes, I own a vibrator—a Rabbit Pearl."

"Of course, isn't that supposed to the Rolls Royce of women's vibrators?"

Olena shrugged. "I don't know about all that, but it's the only one I've ever owned."

"Do you have feelings for it? Do you want to marry it?"

Olena laughed. "Why would I want to marry a vibrator?"

"Because it makes you feel good, and you keep going back to it, and, by the way, I think it's hot that you have one. Can I watch you use it?"

"No. Okay, I get your point. Where is Godiva?" Olena looked around the bar. "What's taking her so long?" Olena said playfully.

"You don't enjoy my company?"

"You know I do. You're very easy to talk to," she said and then mumbled, "and look at."

"What was that last part?"

"Oh nothing."

"You're very easy to look at also, but this will have to be continued later tonight," Porter said as Godiva entered the restaurant.

"Later tonight, I'm going to be in the bed," Olena said. Porter's smile widened. "Don't go there."

"What, I just smiled? That was your mind with those dirty thoughts. You should be ashamed of yourself," Porter said playfully.

They stared at each other for a few seconds as Godiva glided up to them with Remy and one of the writers.

"Okay, if you don't mind, let's go to the lobby to discuss what we have so far," Godiva said. "I'm really excited with the new direction we're about to take."

Olena stood from the bar first, stumbling after three Tonga Mai Tais and barreling into Porter's chest. "Umm, wait a minute," Olena said as she used her hands to feel around his muscular chest. "Solid as a rock…that's what our love is," she sang while she snapped her fingers. Porter smiled and shook his head. Olena stopped singing when she noticed the irritated look on Godiva's face. "Maybe not."

"Are you drunk? We won't film if you're drunk. Are you?"

"I'm not drunk, Godiva. Lighten up…oh, you're already light. Darken up then." She slapped Godiva's arm.

"Get it together." Godiva said.

"She's okay," Porter said, coming to her defense. "She had kiddy drinks."

"Which might not be a bad thing," Remy said as they all walked out of the bar. "Maybe it'll loosen her up while we film."

"Maybe so," Olena said, snapping her fingers.

"Oh yeah, she's feeling that buzz," Remy said.

They sat in one of the sitting areas in the elegant hotel lobby.

"We want viewers to have the impression that the two of you are instantly attracted to each other," Remy said.

"We are," Olena said as she looped her arm with Porter's. "Okay let me stop because I don't want you all thinking I'm drunk for real. I'm not buzzed. I'm just high on life."

"For the song, we want to use your cover of 'I'll Be Good,' " Remy said.

"That's cool," Porter said. "I'm not authorized to release it, but

I'm sure the label will."

After the success of Porter's single "Rebound," which Jason's ex-wife Keena sang vocals on, the pair recorded a cover of Rene and Angela's song, "I'll Be Good." Keena and Porter were label mates. Maybe instead of asking Porter about Winona, she should ask about Keena.

Remy continued, "The last scene we shoot will leave a question mark in the viewers' minds. Did they or didn't they?"

"Did they or didn't they what?" Olena questioned.

"Have sex. Porter will convince you to invite him up to your room, and he'll tell you how attractive he thinks you are and how he never thought he'd find the perfect woman again."

"Which is true," Porter said. "All of that is true."

Olena released her arm from Porter's.

"I don't want to give the impression that we're going to have sex on the first date," Olena said, sobering up quickly. "My parents are going to be watching this.

"How old are you again?" Godiva asked.

Olena shrugged. "In my mother's eyes, I'm fifteen."

"Olena, it's just for the cameras," Godiva said.

"And that's what I don't like about it. We're sending the wrong message to young girls. I wouldn't be setting a good example by doing that. I don't want the young women watching to think it's okay to sleep with a man on the first date because it isn't." Porter grinned at Olena as she spoke.

"So far you haven't even kissed a man on any of the dates, which is pretty tame for a dating reality show," Remy said.

"I'm not going to kiss every guy I go on a date with."

"The only one she needs to kiss is me," Porter said. "We'll figure all the rest out."

Godiva said, "Just make the scene sexy. The comments on Facebook are saying it's a show about dating and finding love, but all they're seeing are dates gone wrong. So we need to show more of the love connections."

"And, we can do that, but without a sex scene," Olena said.

The hotel phone rang at 6:30 a.m.

Olena yanked off her eye mask and snatched the phone from the hook.

"Hello," Olena snapped.

"I hope I didn't wake you."

It was Godiva.

"It's six-thirty in the morning. Yes, you woke me. What do you want?"

"Olena, Porter called. He wants to take you to breakfast and needs to find out your schedule. I told him that you had a few hours this morning, so if you could meet us in the lobby in an hour."

"*Us…lobby…breakfast.* Wait a minute…Hold up. I'm tired. When I'm tired, I'm irritable, and when I'm irritable I don't respond well to something like an early morning call. Do you know what time it is? I don't want breakfast. And *if* I did, I wouldn't want a camera crew following me. Right now, all I want to do is go back to sleep."

"The restaurant opens at eight, and we want to get there before the doors open. Porter said the place wasn't that big, and it gets crowded fast."

"Hey…hey. Are you listening to me? I don't want breakfast. I'm tired."

"And I can appreciate that, but it needs to be done, so I'll see you in an hour."

"You can appreciate that I'm tired and not hungry, but you're still going to try to make me go?"

"It can count as one of the three dates. It's perfect."

"I don't want it to," Olena shouted.

"Calm down and get ready," Godiva said and then hung up without saying goodbye.

An infuriated Olena slammed down the phone and stumbled out of her bed. She was on the hunt for her cell phone, so she could retrieve Porter's phone number.

"I like you, *but*," she said to him as soon as he answered.

"What did I do?"

"Did you really have to call Godiva in order to ask me out?"

"That's not how it happened, Olena."

"How did it happen, Porter? Please explain, since I'm up now."

"Calm down."

"I was in the middle of having some of the best sleep ever."

"Whoa. My heart stopped for a minute. I'm glad you said sleep."

"But I was blasted out of it by the loudest ringing phone I've ever heard. I'm in such a bad mood right now. So, I might be taking this out on you. If I am, I'm sorry."

"Let me explain what happened. Godiva called me to follow up on our evening and to make sure I got her email about the tapings today…at six in the morning she called. I was asleep also. So, since she'd already waken me, I asked her what your schedule looked like for this morning. I know of this really nice place that serves breakfast. She kept saying it's no problem she'd call you and call me back. I really apologize about this whole thing. I definitely want you to continue liking me, and I'd still like to take you out to breakfast."

"I don't want a camera crew following us."

"I don't either. But do you want breakfast?"

"I'd love to have breakfast."

"So I'll call her back and tell her something came up, and I can't go. Then, we'll still go. I'll just have my driver come pick you up."

"Porter, you really are big time now. You have your own driver."

"Can you be ready in an hour?"

"For *you*, yes I can."

The driver pulled up to the quaint restaurant with the dark green awning and white lettering that spelled out the name—Mama's on Washington Square—with a red heart replacing the apostrophe.

The inside was small with an adorable country style ambiance. Since they were there on a Tuesday as soon as Mama's opened at 8:00 a.m., there wasn't much of a wait, as was typical, especially on weekends.

Olena attempted to order pancakes, her personal favorite.

"They have really good food here you might want to try something new. The French toast is the bomb and the Pandora is good too."

Olena looked down at the menu to find a description of Pandora. "I don't like apples, so I'm going to stick to pancakes."

Porter ordered the chocolate-cinnamon French toast that came with fresh seasonal berries and bananas. They both had a side of bacon and a glass of orange juice. "So where are you flying to tomorrow?" Porter asked.

"New York. While I'm there, I might try to get my old job back. Nah, I won't."

"I'm sure you won't need your old job after this. I'm sure you'll be writing full-time pretty soon."

"I hope so, but I need to stop putting all my eggs in one or two baskets. I have to consider my other options. I want to write, but what if God has another plan for me."

"Yeah, He may want you to be a reality star."

Olena's eyes rolled as she took a long gulp of orange juice.

"Whoa, someone's thirsty."

"I love orange juice."

"I need to get my name changed to orange juice. When you're

in New York meeting this actor they hired—"

"How do you know he's an actor? Did they hire you?"

"Let me explain how I came about getting on the show. I get this call from my manager—"

"By the way, your manager is very pretty. Are you sure she's not more than your manager?"

He nodded. "She's just my manager. I've known Vanity for a while. She's not my type."

"I know you're trying to make me feel better. She's beautiful."

"She's nice looking. But…I guess I can tell you. Nah, forget it. Nothing."

"I *hate* when people do that."

"Do what?"

"Start to tell you something and then stop and say they can't tell you. Basically, what you just did. If you can't tell me, don't bring it up because I would have never known the difference."

"I guess I could tell you; I just don't want to."

"Please just keep your secret. Next subject."

"Ooh, you're kind of feisty," Porter said with a smile and a nod. "I like that. I need a woman to keep me in line. That's sexy to me."

"It is?"

Porter nodded. "I don't like doormats. You have to have some fight in you. I think that's why I prefer to date older women. They've lived and learned." He stared across the table at Olena. "When can I see you again?"

She shrugged. "You're the one on tour, Mr. Washington. And, by the way, I love your last name."

"You can have it if you like."

"I'll let you know."

The reason she loved it was because it was the same as Denzel's, but she wasn't going to tell him that part.

"*When?* On the season finale?"

She shrugged. "I'll let you know."

"Don't forget about me when you're in New York with that actor."

Olena smiled. "I'll try not to."

TWENTY-THREE

Olena arrived in New York at 3:30 p.m. on Wednesday. There wasn't any filming scheduled for that day, but there was an emergency meeting.

"We're not going to tell you what to say. I'm not even going to be on the set," Godiva told Olena at the meeting. "Neither is Remy or any of the producers. It's just going to be you, your date, and the camera crew. I want to try something different."

Something different like having Olena guess the first meeting place. That wasn't different. Putting clues in the taxi cab left Olena to wonder if she were on *The One* or *The Amazing Race*.

Olena hoped that Porter would pull a Gordon and just show up because she couldn't stop thinking about him. They'd been exchanging several text messages and the night before spoke to each other via Skype for nearly two hours. She would love to see him again and have three dates with him without Godiva around.

"Olena, how are you this morning?" Rich O'Conner asked. He'd met up with her in Central Park the next morning to give her the clue.

"I'm excited."

"Good. We're going to do things a little differently today. I hope you like trivia."

"Not really, but I'll give it my best shot."

"I'm going to give you three clues, and you'll need to guess the location you'll be meeting the next bachelor. Here's your first clue. It was declared a national historic landmark in 1987." Olena had no idea. "It was first opened to the public in 1933." She still had no idea, a better clue would help. "And finally, its address is the same name as a popular American television comedy."

Olena smiled. "I know what it is."

"Don't tell me," Rich said. "Tell your cab driver. And there's another clue inside."

She rushed over to the waiting cab. Not because she wanted to rush because she didn't like running. But Godiva made sure to leave her with a few instructions.

"Take me to the Rockefeller Center, please. The entrance to the Top of the Rock." Olena said.

The cab drove to Fiftieth Street between Fifth and Sixth Avenues and stopped in front of the entrance to the Top of The Rock. Once inside of the building, she ascended a winding staircase to the mezzanine, passing a small theatre as she headed for the elevator. Olena had never been inside of the building, but she used the additional clues that she found in the cab and headed to the observation deck on the seventieth floor.

Just her luck, she was trapped inside the high-speed glass-top elevator with a bunch of screaming teens.

"This is so cool," one of them shouted.

"It's just like a rollercoaster," another said as blue lights illuminated with each passing floor. While music played, historic holograms of the Beatles, President John F. Kennedy, Dr. Martin Luther King and President Richard Nixon flashed atop the glass ceiling, ending with an image of President Barack Obama.

In sixty seconds, they had reached the sixty-seventh floor. When the elevator doors opened, the teens shouted and clapped.

Olena was nervous about meeting the next bachelor. What if it weren't Porter as she had secretly hoped? She would be upset.

She huffed out a deep breath that made her feel a little better as her nerves continued traveling downward from the center of her chest to the pit of her stomach. She heaved out yet another breath as she walked to a standard elevator without music and video that took her from the two-story sixty-seventh floor to the observation deck on the seventieth-floor.

As the elevator door started to open, Olena quickly assessed her outfit. She had on a pair of low heels with rubber soles, black jeans, and a gray cashmere military jacket with black trim. She was pleased with what she had on and the way she looked in it.

A cameraman was with her in the cab but not in the elevator. But there was a camera crew waiting on the observation deck along with bachelor number eight.

He stood with his back facing her and turned around slowly. She actually felt as if she were on a blind date. Her stomach felt the same way now as it did when she had first met Flint Michigan, who had been a blind date. Hopefully, the result would be different.

"Olena," he said with a smile. Her eyes darted, but she didn't respond because she was in shock. "Olena," he repeated. He was six-three, completely bald, no facial hair, and a diamond stud earring in both ears. He smiled even wider the next time he repeated her name. "Olena. Are you okay?"

"Yes."

Was this a dream? Standing before her was the celebrity crush she could never tell Jason about. The one she had mentioned to Remy after a night of drinking.

"I'm Desmond James."

Desmond James was her NFL crush and Jason's biggest rival in football.

"Nice to meet you," she said, barely squeaking out the words. "Are you nervous?"

"No…well, a little," she said as she laughed and blushed. To her, he looked better in person than he did on TV.

"What do you think of this view?" he asked as he stretched one of his arms out toward the Empire State Building. "Isn't it something?"

"He's beautiful," she said without taking her eyes off of him.

He turned and grinned at her. "*He?*"

"He…as in the Empire State Building," Olena said, trying to fix her slip up. "Doesn't that building look male to you? It's so tall just like a man. Just like Central Park. Look how massive it is." Okay, maybe she was talking a little too much, so she stopped.

He walked up to Olena and placed his hands firmly on her shoulders. "Let's get this out of the way." He leaned down and kissed her lips. "Now, we've had our first kiss, so you can't be nervous anymore."

She buried her face in her hands and screamed with excitement. Then, she told the camera crew, "please edit that part out."

"Are you really that nervous?" Desmond asked. "Come here, give me a hug. Don't be nervous." She hugged him and placed her head against his hard as steel chest and was reminded of Porter's chest. He whispered into her ear, "Don't be nervous. I'm not going to bite. Not yet." She felt as if she were cheating on Jason, even though they were no longer together. Still, she knew he would consider that to be the ultimate betrayal.

I don't know what to say right now. I can't believe I just met Desmond James. He's one of my celebrity crushes. And I'm not one to go overboard on the whole celebrity thing. Look at my hands, they're shaking. I feel like I'm back in high school, and the popular guy asked me for my number. And, by the way, that never happened to me in high school. The popular guys never even spoke.

She said Katz's Deli. He said Eisenberg's. The debate was over which had the best pastrami sandwich. In order to settle it, they agreed to go to Eisenberg's after Olena admitted she'd never been because she was such a staunch Katz's fan. She had heard of the place that was directly across from the Flatiron Building. One of her clients loved it, and she'd made plans to take her as soon as she came off her sabbatical—so much for planning ahead.

"There's a Russian Bookstore on the second floor," Desmond said as they exited the cab and looked over at the sign on the building beside Eisengberg's. "Or you can buy another pair of jeans."

"Lucky Brand doesn't fit me too well."

"The jeans you have on do."

"Thank you," she said partly to him and mostly to Cookie Johnson for designing them. They sat at the counter in the extremely narrow restaurant and ordered hot pastrami sandwiches on rye, two sides of coleslaw, two orders of fries, and two cans of Dr. Brown's Cel-Ray soda. While they waited for their food, he asked her if she followed football.

"Not really."

"So you didn't know that I was a football player?"

"Well, I did know that."

"You don't follow football. What, you just follow me?" he asked, giving her the sexiest grin.

"Sort of," she replied as she sweetly batted her eyelashes at him.

"Explain."

"I mean, it all started with that one movie that you were in, I don't really remember the name of it, *Badder*, I think it was."

"I thought you didn't remember the name of it."

"It just came to me all of a sudden. You're a good actor."

"Thank you. I plan to pursue that career after my football career ends. Hopefully, that won't be anytime soon. But, continue."

"Then, from there, I googled you and found out you were a

football player and I started watching your games. I didn't know what I was watching, but I did know your number and I knew that you were a—"her mind went blank.

"Are you talking about the position I play?"

"Yes, it just escaped me."

"No problem. I'm a running back."

"Exactly… a running back, I knew that."

"That movie came out five years ago."

"Yep."

"So you've been watching me for five years?"

"Maybe not five whole years."

"Five seasons," he said playfully. "What other football players have you been watching?"

"Just you, you're the only football player that I know, or I knew, or you know." Olena looked over at the cameraman and suddenly remembered everything she was saying was being filmed, which meant Jason would see her all googly-eyed over the man he hated, so she snapped out of her high-school crush antics and tried to do away with all of the gazing. She had to remind herself that Jason could potentially see this episode. She had to tell herself to get it together.

The date was pleasant. And that's all I think I'm going to say at this point. No, actually, I'm going to say more. I didn't like my vision being blurred every time I looked at him, which means I'm infatuated. I don't want to be infatuated over a man when I'm forty four. I shouldn't say that because it may be a good thing to have that same feeling I used to have when I was a teenager. I'm fifteen just times three minus one.

Olena practically skipped into her suite at the Waldorf Astoria with a smile that hadn't left since the moment she accepted that meeting Desmond wasn't just a dream. "You knew," she told Tilley, after slamming the door. "You knew I would meet Desmond James, didn't you?"

Tilley shook her head. "No."

"Why don't I believe you? Why don't I care?" Olena placed the small gold Godiva gift bag on the table in the sitting area. I'm so happy right now I could do the cabbage patch," Olena said as she broke out a few moves.

"Whatever you do, don't dance when you're around him. If he's attracted to you, he won't be after he sees that. You are one of the few rhythmless black people who exist."

"I'm sure there's a lot more out there like me."

"I doubt they're as bad as you...My God. And what are you doing with that Godiva bag."

"Oh," Olena said, holding it up by the rope handle. "There's a Godiva store at 30 Rock, and while I was there I thought it would be cute to buy something for Godiva. Isn't that a cute idea? Look it has her name on it."

Tilley closed her eyes momentarily and shook her head. "Whatever you do...let me repeat this...what*ever* you do. Do not give her that."

"What are you talking about? Her name is Godiva, and it's spelled the same way as this." Olena ran her finger across the chocolatier's name on the gift bag. I've seen it enough times in my email. So what actually is the problem?"

"The problem is she has been given Godiva chocolate or something from Godiva ever since she was a child, and she has convinced herself that she is allergic to it."

Olena frowned at Tilley. "Allergic to it."

Tilley threw her hands up as if in surrender. "If it were up to me, I'd say give it to her. Let her break out in hives and leave us all alone. But I've seen too many people make the same mistake and get cussed out. Something seriously comes over the chick. But it won't go to waste because you know I love sweets." Tilley swiped the gift bag from Olena.

"How do I know you're not lying? It's no secret you can't stand her."

"I could be lying, but why would I lie. If you don't trust me, go for it. But I'd wait until after my date because if you do it before, you're day will be ruined."

"You can have it."

"Thank you." Tilley sat on the bed and opened the biscuit gift tin.

"Are you going to share?"

Tilley shook her head as she bit into one of the hazelnut praline biscuits. "I'm just looking out for you. You're under contract, remember. You need to maintain a certain weight."

"And she hasn't weighed me once."

"Trust me, she weighs you every time she looks at you. She's a lot of things, but a dummy isn't one of 'em. The girl knows her stuff. She just needs to stop being so cutthroat."

"Help me find something to wear," Olena said in a singsong voice. "We're going to the Comedy Cellar in Greenwich Village tonight. Desmond asked me out. Can you believe it?" Olena widened her smile. "Ooh, I just wish the cameras didn't have to follow us. At least Godiva won't be there."

"How is it that a forty-four-year-old woman gets more play than me? Oh, that's right you have hair."

"Tilley, you don't have hair because you don't want to have hair. And besides, you represent women in this country who have lost their hair for an untold number of reasons and what you have done is shown the world you can be beautiful without hair."

Tilley's head shook all while Olena spoke. "I don't want to be a role model or represent anyone but myself. I did this because of my sister. Then, I did this because," Tilley paused, shrugged and then said. "I am not my hair."

"I am not this skin," Olena sang the India Arie song, "I Am Not My Hair as she danced around the suite.

"You can't dance *or* sing…tragic."

"Hey, it happens. Help me find something to wear."

"Do you want to be sexy?"

"I have a date with Desmond James. What do you think?"

"Nah, you don't want to be too sexy. Not with a football play-er. They see sexy all the time. Come with something different." Tilley walked over to the rack of clothes she had for Olena. "You wore jeans earlier, so let's do a dress tonight. How about this one?" Tilley removed a black jersey dress with an asymmetric slit from the rack. "It's sexy, but not too much." Olena stared at the dress in silence. "It looks much better on."

"I hope so because I have a date with *whom*?"

"Desmond James," Tilley said.

"That's right," Olena sang in an off-pitch operatic voice.

"We picked a great night to go to the Comedy Cellar," Desmond told Olena right after she'd hopped into the back-seat of the black SUV without a cameraman trailing behind her. Desmond wouldn't allow cameras in his vehicle. So the camera crew followed behind the chauffeured SUV in a van.

"We did? Why do you say that?" Olena asked.

Desmond was relaxed in the backseat beside her in the same clothes he'd worn earlier. Any minute now, he would compli-ment her, tell her how pretty she looked and how nice her dress fit. Any minute now, she was so sure of it.

"Chris Hill and Ryan Parks perform at the eleven o'clock show along with five other comics, but I don't know any of them."

"Are we going to see Hill or Parks?"

"We're going to see all seven of 'em," Desmond said. "They each perform a twenty-minute set."

"At eleven? What are we going to do in the meantime?"

"Have a few drinks, I guess."

He took her to a nightclub in Greenwich Village called the Bitter End, where they ordered two drinks per the bar's minimum drink policy. It was too loud to hear so they didn't say much, mostly listened to the live music. Olena had never heard of the performer before. "She's from Detroit," Desmond said, and Olena nodded with a smile.

Olena said, "That explains why I like her. There's a lot of talent in my city."

The highlight of her night was when he squeezed her left thigh, leaned over, and said, "Don't think I didn't notice how beautiful you're looking tonight." She smiled and thanked him for the compliment. "You officially have me as your fan."

Olena picked up her drink and took a long swig.

She leaned into him, placed her hand on his thigh, and said, "I don't want to sit in the front row at the comedy club."

"Are you telling me, you'd rather take a backseat?"

When he put it like that, it didn't sound as good to her.

"No, I just don't want to get heckled."

"Look at you. Do you honestly think you're going to get heckled?" He put his hand on top of her hand when she started to rub his thigh. The second drink loosened her up. "If you keep rubbing my thigh, instead of taking you to the Comedy Cellar, I'm going to take you to Desmond's Cellar. Are you down for that?" Olena shook her head. He shrugged. "I'll check back with you later just in case you have a change of heart."

Olena didn't say a word. She just shook her head and smiled.

They left the Comedy Cellar a little after one in the morning, but he wasn't ready to take her home, so he had the driver ride them around the city. "Is there anything you'd like to see?"

"I want to go across the Brooklyn Bridge."

"Steven, did you hear her?"

"Yes," the driver said while he looked at Desmond through the rearview mirror.

"Steven's my little brother."

"That's nice. Keeping it all in the family."

"What do you like to do, besides go on TV looking for love when you know you don't need help?"

"I don't need help. Well, you definitely don't, so how did you end up on here?"

"I'm signed with CAA."

"Creative Artists Agency."

"That's right."

"I sent my manuscript to them. I was thinking big. I guess a little too big."

"I like that. Better to think big than small."

"So this is sort of like an acting gig for you."

"It is, but I'm not acting. At least, I don't feel as if I am because I am an eligible bachelor. And I think I'd date you in the real world."

"You think?"

"I think so. I need a few more dates. One day together doesn't prove much."

"So do you have lines you have to rehearse for later today for our last two dates?"

"Not really lines. Just topics. Things they want me to talk about."

"Such as."

"You'll just have to wait and see," he said as the SUV merged onto the Brooklyn Bridge after turning left from Centre Street.

Olena and Desmond were at The Neue Galerie—housed

in a renovated brick-and-limestone mansion on 86th and Fifth Avenue along New York's famed Museum Mile. On exhibit were early twentieth-century German and Austrian art and design. She and Desmond were amongst a small group gathered around the shiny gold 54 x 54 inch "Adele Bloch-Bauer I" painting of the wealthy Viennese society woman from the turn of the century displayed in the first room on the second floor of the museum. The Gustav Klimt painting had been acquired for a reported $135 million by the museum's owner, Ronald Lauder. Olena stood beside Desmond and listened to an audio tour that detailed the Austrian Symbolist painter's most known portrait, which took him three years to complete.

Olena seemed more impressed by the painting than Desmond was.

"This is such a beautiful masterpiece," Olena said in a tone that was low and respectable enough not to disturb the other patrons.

"I'm not into all that," he said much too loudly. A few others in the group darted their eyes at him in a disapproving fashion. "I'm hungry," he said. "Let's go." Clutching firmly to Olena's hand, Desmond led her out of the room, down a white marble asymmetrical spiral staircase. He bypassed Cafe Sabarsky that was on the ground level and headed to Café Fledermaus in the basement.

"The other one looked nicer," Olena said as they settled into a small, low table.

"I don't pay for the way a place looks. I'm sure the menus are the same. There's a line up there and no line down here, so this makes more sense. Don't you think?"

"These low tables don't make sense, at all." She repositioned her legs by turning them sideways. "But this does remind me of Vienna." Olena smiled when she spotted a familiar item on the menu. "I know what I want."

"What's that?"

"Wiener Schnitzel and two slices of the Sachertorte so I can take one back to Tilley and make her night, and then a glass of Almdudler Limonade."

"Cool. I'll get the same thing," he said without picking up the menu.

After what felt like several minutes of silence, she said. "So, tell me about yourself."

"I thought you already knew. Didn't you google me? All you have to do is google me."

"I want you to tell me."

He shrugged. "I'm thirty-seven."

"And still playing football?"

"Yep, George Blanda played until he was forty-eight, so I should be able to at least get three more years in."

"Forty-eight, are you kidding me?"

"Most of us would stay out there for as long as we can. I love the sport. I love everything about it except getting tackled. But nobody wants to be brought down."

"Did you make any enemies out on the field?" she asked to see if he'd mention Jason. She's not sure why she cared. Maybe because she realized she no longer cared about Desmond. He was her celebrity crush. And while they hadn't been around each other a lot, the times they had spent together were enough for her to know there wasn't a love connection. And she doubted there would ever be one. Desmond was too in love with himself.

He shrugged. "Nah, I go out there and do my job. I'm sure there are dudes out there that don't like me. But I don't give them a second thought, and I'm definitely not going to breathe any life into them by mentioning their names." He paused for a second. "One more date, huh?"

"Yep...one more."

And that's all he said, which let Olena know that he wasn't any more interested in her than she was in him.

"You're everything I need and more…" Olena sang the popular Beyonce song "Halo," as she strangled the cordless microphone. She twirled around the private room at Biny, a popular karaoke restaurant in lower Manhattan's SoHo neighborhood.

It was almost two in the morning. Olena had been with Desmond, three of his teammates, and their significant others for a few hours. They ate sushi and drank green tea mixed with whiskey. And after consuming two such drinks, Olena's channeled her inner Beyonce. She felt sexy in her royal blue pleated jersey dress with cutaway sleeves and a fold-over collar. But she lost her footing a few times and tripped over her six-inch open-toe patent leather sandals. She couldn't handle the extra inch in her heel. And it had nothing to do with her buzz because she had started taking baby steps as soon as she reached the lobby in the hotel to leave for the evening.

When Olena finished her song, she curtsied, and the small group cheered and clapped.

"That was so much fun," she said with a big smile as she walked over to Desmond. He grabbed her waist, drew her body into his so that their sides were touching, bent over ever so slightly and kissed her on the cheek.

"You did good, baby," he said as he looked into her eyes adoringly. "Are you ready to go home…with me?" She nodded. Olena never imagined that she would sing outside of her shower, let alone in front of Desmond James, six of his friends, and a Media One camera crew. But the green tea with whiskey removed all of her inhibitions.

The camera crew followed Olena and Desmond back to his four-bedroom, four-bathroom condominium at the Rushmore on 64th and Riverside. The cameras rolled until Olena walked into Desmond's home and from behind the closed door, he said, "I want you to stay with me tonight."

She flew to Boston the next morning with the cast and crew. And Olena met the most unmemorable bachelor of them all. It didn't even matter that their flight had been delayed, and the schedule for filming was cut in half. Three dates in one day and she wouldn't have had it any other way.

She checked into the Marriott Boston Long Wharf on State Street and changed quickly, so she could meet her date for lunch directly across the street from the hotel at Legal Seafood.

Bachelor number nine was another actor slash model. No one told Olena he was. But he looked a little too much like a Malibu Ken doll, someone who'd be perfect for a Ralph Lauren commercial. He was young, much younger than her. She'd be surprised to learn he was any older than twenty-two.

Her confessional was short:

Date? I don't think I'd call that a date. His name doesn't have to be added to the list because it's just going to get scratched off, so that would be just a waste of ink.

After lunch, they had boarded an orange-and-green Old Town trolley and went on a tour of Boston. They went by ancient burial grounds, Old North Church, the Old State House, Bunker Hill, and the site of the Boston Massacre. She couldn't remember any of that. But she did remember riding in a Swan boat. She just couldn't remember that he sat beside her.

TWENTY-FOUR

Jason took LaRuth to the Cheesecake Factory for brunch even though he wasn't a huge fan of the place. But that's where she wanted to go, and they could walk there from the Hilton in the Southlake Town Center, where he was staying.

On the same day, LaRuth insisted he go to church with her, the bishop's did a sermon that covered marriage, commitment, and love. At first, he thought LaRuth had set him up. She had to have known that the bishop was beginning a four-week series on love and marriage. But the more he listened to the bishop's words the more he was convinced had she known she wouldn't have rushed him out of the hotel room that morning. Because the bishop said a lot of things that made Jason think about not only his life, but the lives of those he loved. The bishop said that anyone who abused their partner actually hated themselves. He thought about his younger brother and wondered whether or not his brother's girlfriend had told the truth. He knew his younger brother had difficulty controlling his anger at times and sometimes even directed it toward Jason. It didn't matter what Jason did for him because Jason could never do enough. His brother always wanted more, and somehow it was Jason's fault that his younger brother didn't get drafted into the NFL.

During the sermon, LaRuth rose to her feet, stretched her arms upward and outward, and began speaking in tongues as her tears began to flow.

Jason had been raised in the church. Her actions weren't shocking, in the least, but her tears were. There were just so many of them, and he wanted to know what was behind them all. So, later that evening, after they arrived back at the hotel, he asked her why she had been crying.

"I don't know, for a lot of reasons. For one, I don't want you to judge me."

"I'm not a judgmental person. I know no one's perfect." And as soon as he said that he thought of Olena. *No one is perfect.* But for some reason he had expected Olena to be. Or maybe it was just like Olena said in the voicemail message she'd left for him. Because of his impotence, he couldn't handle having a relationship with Olena. He wanted to make love to Olena and knowing she had sexual needs that he couldn't fulfill was too much for him to deal with at the time. "I've definitely done some things in my life that I'm not proud of. I also know people can change. Honesty is my big thing. I need the woman in my life to be honest with me and not just some of the time. All of the time."

"I feel really guilty about having sex with you because we're not married. I shouldn't have gotten so weak to the flesh."

"You didn't do it alone. And was it really so wrong?"

"You don't get it because you're a man and society expects that from men."

"God is going to judge us both the same. But what's so wrong about having sex before you're married? I'm willing to bet most of the people in your congregation are. A lot of people say one thing and do another. And I've learned that the very ones who have the most to say are also the ones doing the most. We have a good time together. You're twenty-seven. I'm thirty-two. We're grown. I don't think we have anything to feel guilty about."

She didn't respond. Instead, she picked up the remote and started flipping through channels, stopping at *The One*. "I can't believe they finally have a black bachelorette."

"You sound like my mother."

She kept watching.

"Do you think she's pretty?"

"Why ask me a question like that?"

"Because I want to know." He hesitated before answering. LaRuth turned to look at him. "You can be honest."

"Yes I think she's pretty."

"I figured that much, since you used to *fuck* her." She turned away from him and focused her attention on the TV.

"Hold up."

"No you hold up. I stumbled on this show last week and started watching it and put two and two together. Her name is Olena, and she's from Atlanta."

"Okay...*and?*"

"And? And I googled her and found a blog post on ATLTELLS. That's the woman whose name you called out the first time we made love. No big deal. You all obviously aren't together if she's on a show looking for love. So how did y'all meet?"

He wondered how much he should say.

"Why does how we met matter?"

"It matters because I want to know," she said angrily.

"We sat next to each other on a flight. I was attracted to her, and I loved that she didn't know who I was—"

LaRuth interrupted, "How do you know she didn't? Some women like pulling that trick."

"She didn't."

LaRuth pursed her lips and rolled her eyes. "So what happened? Why didn't it work since she's so perfect?"

"That's you calling her that not me. It just didn't work."

"Why didn't it?"

"Because she's self-conscious about our age difference."

"You don't look that much older than her."

Jason smirked. "It's the other way around. She's older than me."

"How much older?"

"Twelve years."

LaRuth had waited a few seconds before she spoke. "She's twelve years older than you, and that was fine with you."

He shrugged. "She looks good. I don't care if a woman is older than me if they look good."

"But what happens when she gets in her sixties, and she doesn't look good anymore?"

"I know women in their sixties who still look good. Besides, Olena has a real young spirit. She was a late bloomer. I don't think she even dated that much, at least not seriously."

"I'm sure she did. And, I bet she's had plastic surgery. I bet those breasts are fake and that nose too. She's wearing contacts, and that hair isn't real either."

"Her hair is the only thing that's fake, but her real hair is a nice length."

"So she has green eyes."

"Actually, they're gray. But I don't want to talk about her."

"Why not?"

"I just don't. Can you please change the subject? Do you mind if I turn off the TV?"

"I wanted to watch the rest of it. It's cute. Even though most of them seem like bad actors. Olena looks okay, for her age. But I'm sure she's had some work done. I know those big ole boobs aren't hers."

"Oh no those are definitely real. I can provide a certificate of authenticity," he said with laughter.

But LaRuth didn't find his comment the least bit funny. "How are you going to disrespect me like that? Her boobs are no bigger than mine. In fact, mine are probably bigger."

"I can't believe we're having this conversation right now. I don't really care whose boobs are bigger. I'm not with a woman because of the size of her boobs or her behind."

"I guess not because her behind isn't that big."

Jason scrunched his face. "Why are you being like that?"

"How am I being?"

"Jealous. And it's not cute. You don't even know Olena, and you're sitting up here talking about the way she looks. It's nothing wrong with the way she looks, and you know it's not. She's beautiful. Our relationship didn't work for other reasons. But the way she looks wasn't one of 'em because if I were judging our relationship solely on that, we'd still be together. One thing I can say about her, she never put down another woman. You have to be real insecure to do that."

"I'm not putting her down. She's pretty. I know that. I guess I'm just jealous like you said. Jealous of the ex."

"No need to be." He turned off the TV and said, "I want to do something for you. I want to help you get a place that'll be closer to your job. There're some nice-looking apartments around here."

Jason had pulled a uniform crime report on LaRuth's apartment community and found extremely high rates of robbery and burglary. There wasn't much aggravated assault, and the incidences of theft had been low over the last few months. There weren't any reported rape offenses either, which was a good thing. But still, she clearly didn't live in the best area.

"The rent is real high out here."

"And that's why I said I'd help you. Just start looking for a place. You can do that next weekend. That way you'll be busy enough not to miss me."

"Are you serious?" she said, climbing over him. "You're going to get me a place." He nodded. "I'm gonna miss you. Let me show you how much."

He could help her by moving her into a decent place. And he didn't mind doing that. If anything happened to her, he would be the one feeling guilty knowing he could have helped out but didn't.

"I found a place," LaRuth said over the phone. That was the most excited Jason had heard her since they'd started dating a few months earlier. Was it only a couple of months? he wondered— closer to two and a half. He shook his head at the thought because it seemed so much longer. He guessed that was a good thing. It spoke to his comfort level with her, he supposed.

"You did? Okay, good. So now what? What do you need for me to do?"

"Can you cosign, and give me the move-in money? It's going to cost fifteen hundred and seventy-five dollars to move in."

"That's all?"

"I might need help with the rent. It's more than double what I'm paying now."

"How much is it?"

"A thousand-fifty, but they're running a special. I'll get one month free prorated over my first year's lease. So nine-hundred and sixty-two dollars and fifty cents a month."

"So a thousand dollars."

"No. Nine hundred and sixty—"

"Right, I got you. Yeah, I can do that. No problem." In his eyes that was cheap. He'd bought a woman he'd dated a top of the line Range Rover before and never missed the eighty thousand from his bank account. "It's in a real good area and everything, right? You're sure you like the place."

"It's in a real good area and only five minutes from my job. One of my coworkers lives there. And I'll have my own garage."

"That's the other thing we have to work on, getting your car out the shop." He wasn't going to offer up a new car just yet. Just because he had it to give didn't mean he wanted to be used. He wasn't saying LaRuth was using him, but he couldn't say for sure that she wasn't. The rent money he could do in his sleep. It was less than the monthly interest he earned from one of his many accounts. Getting LaRuth out of the apartment community she was living in was a must.

"Oh, yeah," she said as her voice dragged. "My car. Those mechanics always find something wrong with it. I'm ready to abandon that Sable on the side of the road. But don't worry about that. I'm not really worried about a car right now."

"Just have the manager fax me the app, and I'll get it right back to 'em."

"We can do it that way, or you could fly down and help me move, and stay a little longer than usual. Please, baby," she moaned. "I need to see you."

Jason boarded the nonstop first-class Delta flight to Dallas. Since it was a short trip, he brought only one carryon. He lowered the retractable handle to his rollaway luggage, lifted his medium-sized bag over his shoulders and into the overhead bin and sat down. He looked over at the woman who sat beside him and was reminded again of Olena and how they first met on the airplane with her falling asleep on his shoulder. *Why was he thinking about her so much these days?* he wondered.

If he were being honest about LaRuth, it was her body and the sex that kept him motivated. He was a man. Not quite a typical one, but he had his moments like last weekend when he ran into one of his ex-girlfriends. One thing led to another, and they ended up back at her condo—the one he had paid the down payment on. Her credit was good enough that she didn't need him to cosign. She was a teacher with a masters degree, so her income was sufficient. Not six figures, but enough to handle a thirteen-hundred-dollar mortgage. They kissed and groped, and she tried her best to arouse him, but nothing happened. She was offended, and she told him that it was obvious he was no longer attracted to her. Was it because of the fifteen pounds she'd gained in the two years since they'd dated or because she cut her hair? It had to be something wrong with her because she remembered Jason's sex drive while they were together and there was no way it was something wrong with him. All that incident did was prove that there was something about LaRuth that turned him on more than any woman he'd been with, with the exception of Olena. He couldn't forget a woman who'd taken care of him in his darkest hour, watched his children and treated them the way he imagined she would treat her own, if she had any. Olena got along with his mother, and Momma Nix was not an easy woman to get along with. Sex was an important part of a relationship, but it would never replace those other attributes that Olena had demonstrated. Perhaps, eventually, LaRuth would adapt into his family the way Olena had.

After he landed at DFW airport, he rented an SUV and headed to LaRuth's job to pick her up. Since the Hilton he regularly stayed at was beside a Truluck's restaurant, they went there for dinner after he dropped off LaRuth's overnight bag. He ordered a sixteen-ounce ribeye and a twenty-dollar glass of red wine. He told himself that one glass wouldn't hurt him, and since it was red wine it might actually help. LaRuth remained consistent by not drinking any alcohol and ordering her favorite entrée—shrimp. After the waiter left, LaRuth sat shaking her head.

"What's wrong with you?"

"You promised you'd help me move," LaRuth said through

sighs.

"What are you talking about? I'm here, right?"

"Physically help me. You were supposed to be here on my moving day."

"Stop. You told me over the phone that you were moving this weekend. It wasn't until I got here that you said it was next weekend. Do you think I can just stay here for a week? I have two kids and other responsibilities."

"Excuse me. I thought I was a priority in your life."

He sat and bit down on his bottom lip. "I'll be back."

"Where are you going?"

"To the bathroom. Is that okay?"

She shrugged.

He had to leave before he said what he was thinking. Sex wasn't worth the extra hassle. He wanted a relationship, but only if it were drama free. And the fact that what she was angry over wasn't that major made it all the worse. What would happen if something major were to go down in their relationship? Sex was complicating things. He didn't want a relationship where he wasn't having sex. He'd already been there and done that. What he needed was a happy medium, and LaRuth didn't seem to be that.

Now he just wanted to hear Olena's voice. Something he'd thought about during his two-and-a-half-hour flight. So, as he stood in one of the bathroom stalls, he phoned her.

"Hi. This is Olena, I'm sorry I missed your call. Please leave a message, and I'll be sure to return your call as soon as possible."

"Hey, baby, are you surprised? I hope you still remember my voice. Give me a call when you get this message. I really miss you." He ended the call, huffed out a sigh of disappointment, covered his eyes with his left hand and started massaging his temples. He certainly wanted to talk to her. A few seconds later while he stood in the stall, his cell phone rang. It was her.

"Hey," she said.

"Hey?"

"It's good to hear from you."

"Do you really mean that?"

"Of course I do."

"So why haven't you tried to call?"

"I didn't think you wanted to hear from me again. It's been how long, and you're just now calling," Olena said.

"Our last conversation didn't end so well."

"True. So, have you been watching the show?"

"Not really…I watched a couple of times just to see what it was like, but it was hard for me. Is it still on?"

"Yes," she laughed.

"So, did you meet, 'the one' yet?"

There was a few seconds of silence. "I don't believe I will. It's all scripted as you said."

"I knew that."

"I think it's going to be episode seven or maybe eight, I'm not sure because they've been switching some of these episodes around, but that episode is totally scripted. It's going to look like…I'm embarrassed to say."

"What happened?" Jason said firmly.

"I can't really talk about it. I signed a contract. I can't discuss it, but just don't believe what you see."

"I thought the saying was, don't believe what you hear; how can I not believe what I see? Is this something I'm really not going to like?"

"You probably won't care, since you don't want me."

"I want you, baby. I want you, so I am going to care."

"You were in my dream the other night. It was the weirdest thing, but it felt so real," Olena said. "We made love, but after when I went to the bathroom and looked in the mirror, it wasn't me. It was some other woman's face. I know you've moved on, and I just want you to be happy."

"If it weren't you, it was because you didn't want it to be. I haven't moved on. We're going to make love one day real soon, baby. My heart aches for you. Did you hear me? It aches."

"Why does your heart ache, Jason?"

"I never should've let you go. Tell me what happened that I'm not going to like? You met somebody, didn't you?"

"It's not real. That's all I want you to know. I don't know why I still care so much what you think of me since we're not together. Just like the stuff they wrote about me in the tabloids. I know if you see it, you're going to think poorly of me."

"I already saw it, and I don't care about any of that."

"You saw both of them?"

"Both. The thing about your marriage…and the other thing about, well, you know. I don't care about any of that. That was you then. I know you now."

"God," Olena said with a sigh of relief. "How did we let our relationship get like this?"

"It's not your fault. It's mine." He sighed as he cast his eyes downward. "My ego…my stubbornness. Blame me, I don't care. I just want to fix it. Are you going to let me fix this?"

"Where are you?"Olena said. Jason hesitated. Her question came out of nowhere. "Hello?"

"Yeah."

"Where are you?"

"I'm in Dallas."

"What's in Dallas? Or should I say *who*?"

"I'm just taking care of some business here."

"I'm sure you are." More silence before she said, "Well, I'm literally just getting in from the airport—"

"Where are you coming back from?"

"Boston. I have almost a month off, and then I'm off to New Orleans. We filmed three cities in ten days. It was crazy. It feels so good to be home."

"Home? That's cute you adopted Atlanta as your home." He tried to make their conversation last longer. But he could tell she wanted to get off the phone.

"Okay, well, enjoy Dallas. I hope you have a productive trip."

"I want to see you when I get home."

"Yeah, right," she said through laughter.

"Yeah, right. I do. Can I?"

"We'll see."

"I might have a surprise for you."

"What kind of surprise is that?"

"You'll just have to wait and see."

"I don't know."

"Don't say you don't know yet. Think about it."

"I'll *think* about it.

After Jason ended the call and returned to the table, his mind was still on Olena.

LaRuth looked agitated. "The food is cold now."

"Why didn't you eat it when it first came out?" he asked with a slight attitude.

"Because that's rude, I'm from the South, and we don't do that."

"I'm from the South too, and yes we do. It's not rude. Besides, you've been rude before, Miss I'm-from-the-south."

"How have I been rude?"

"I'm just saying you're not perfect."

"I never said I was. What's wrong with you?"

"Nothing," he said curtly.

"Why were you in the bathroom so long?"

"What? That's a strange question."

"You were in there for a long time. Were you on the phone?"

Jason cleared his throat and shook his head. "Let's try to enjoy our meal. Can we do that?"

"How can I enjoy my meal when it's cold?"

Jason removed the silverware from the cloth napkin resting

beside his plate, put the napkin across his lap, and cut into his ribeye. After taking the first bite, he said, "My meal isn't cold at all."

She looked across the small table at him. "Who were you on the phone with?"

"Really, I'm not in the mood."

"This is why I never wanted to date an athlete. Do you think you can talk to me any kind of way just because you have a little money?"

"By telling you, I'm not in the mood? I just want to enjoy my meal. What's wrong with that."

"I get it. You have money, and you can fly first-class. You can fly me first-class. You can rent fancy cars and book suites. But that don't mean I have to deal with you and your attitude because of it."

"*My* attitude." He laughed a bitter sound. "That's funny. I'm not the one bringing up my money, you are. As for who I was on the phone with, it's not relevant."

"It's very relevant to me, because I want to know."

"Olena. Are you happy now?"

She leaned back in the chair, crossed her arms, and rolled her eyes. "I figured that much. Well, if you want to be with some old-ass woman go right ahead. You don't have to co-sign for my apartment. I can stay right where I am, which is where I've been living without any problems. I'm moving trying to please you. And this is how you do me."

"I've lost my appetite dealing with you." He tossed his white cloth dinner napkin on top of his uneaten food and left to find his waiter.

"You're just going to leave me," she said, trailing behind him.

He held her wrist gently and drew her into him, "Don't make a scene in here," he whispered. "People know me."

"I just need to get my bag, okay, that's it. You can go on back to Atlanta and be with your *grandma*."

He stood near the entrance and didn't respond, didn't look in her direction either. He waited while the hostess went to get his waiter. A few seconds later, the hostess returned.

"He'll be right out."

Jason nodded.

"You're not going to talk to me?" LaRuth said.

"You're not interested in talking. You just want to argue."

The waiter glided through the swinging double doors.

"I'm sorry, something came up, "Jason said, "and we have to go, but I wanted to give you this." He handed the waiter two hundred dollars.

"I'll be right back with your change."

"No change. The rest is for you."

"Thank you," he said, perking up.

Jason left the restaurant with LaRuth on his heels.

"I don't even understand what I did to make you storm out the way you did."

"You're never going to understand."

"What? That you love some woman named Olena? I get that. I just need my bag, and I'll be out of your life."

They were in a king-sized bed. She lay on her back with her legs straddling his back. Most of the bedding was on the floor, at the foot of the bed and off to the sides. He moaned out his last passionate sigh, a sound that vibrated through the room like bass from a stereo. Jason grabbed the sides of her face with emotional force and sucked her bottom lip. "Olena…ooh, Olena… oh, baby…oh you feel so good."

"Yes, yes," she screamed out in ecstasy, "Jason, yes. So do you, baby."

"I love you…Olena. I love you. Oh, baby, I've been waiting so long for this."

"I love you too," she said, her voice trailing off.

He opened his eyes and turned on the light to the lamp on the nightstand.

He looked down at her, hoping he'd somehow made his ultimate dream come true. But he hadn't. "Why did you want to do that?" Jason asked LaRuth.

"I wanted to be her. For one night, and see how it felt. I felt loved." He rolled off of her and lay on his back with his eyes fixated on the white ceiling.

LaRuth was on the phone sobbing, her voice trembling as she spoke to Jason, who was at the hotel. "Calm down, and tell me what happened," Jason said.

"I was robbed at gunpoint."

"What?" Jason said as he sprung from the sofa. "When did this happen?

"Almost three hours ago?"

"Why are you just now calling me?"

"I had to file a police report, and I just got back."

"I'm on my way. Tell me exactly what happened." He grabbed his wallet and his key to the rental car off the coffee table.

"There were two men and a woman," she said with a trembling voice. "I heard a knock on my door, and I answered. I didn't look out the peephole because I'd ordered pizza and I thought it was the pizza man."

"You always have to look out, baby." He rushed out of the room and headed for the elevators. "You should have come back to the hotel after work and none of that would have happened. I hate to say I told you so, but didn't I tell you that place where you're living is dangerous."

"I want you to love me the way you love Olena. I just needed to be by myself and think all of this through because I don't want to lose you and then this happened."

"Just be thankful that you're alive, and you're getting ready to move out of there. I told you that wasn't a good place."

"I know. You told me, and you were right. I'm thankful to be alive. You're so good to me. I really appreciate you."

The next day, after he dropped LaRuth off at work, he headed to the precinct to get a copy of the police report. The female clerk was extremely helpful, despite the fact that Jason didn't have a police report number. He needed to understand what happened for himself because LaRuth, with all of her nervousness, wasn't making much sense. She would say one thing one minute and contradict herself the next minute.

"Let me have her name and address," the female clerk said to Jason as he sat across from her desk. "This happened last night, right?"

"Right."

"You said it was a home invasion," the female clerk asked, checking her computer

"Right."

She shook her head as she scrolled through her computer.

"I don't see that."

"You don't?"

"I don't see a home invasion. I see a domestic dispute. Could that be it?"

"With a LaRuth Harris?"

The woman nodded. "Yes, with a LaRuth and Kelvin Harris, her spouse…or ex. Could that be it? It's not at the address you provided, but I cross-referenced it with her address."

"That must be it," he said, trying to keep his composure. *Spouse?* Jason thought. *How was that even possible?*

"I just need to collect the six-dollar fee, and I can run you off a copy."

He couldn't get the money out fast enough. "Here you go."

She took the ten dollar bill from him and walked to the printer to retrieve the copy of the police reported she'd printed.

He was in shock. Not hurt. He just wanted to get to the bottom of whatever it was.

The clerk walked back to her desk and proceeded to fold the report to put in an envelope.

"I don't need an envelope."

"Okay, here you are then." Jason grabbed the report and rushed out of the precinct without getting his change.

He sat in his rental in total disbelief as he read over the report.

Firstly, she was not twenty-seven; she was thirty-eight. And that wasn't all. The incident didn't happen at her apartment, it occurred at the home of the complainant, Kelvin Harris.

Offense Narrative

Comp. Kelvin Harris called 911 to report that his ex-wife, LaRuth Harris, refused to leave the premises and was both verbally and physically abusive to him as a result of his refusal to allow her to see their two children. Comp. Kelvin Harris states that LaRuth Harris has no visitation rights to said children and is past due on child support and, as a result, has had her driver's license suspended. Comp. Kelvin Harris stated that LaRuth Harris threatened to have someone hurt him badly if he did not amend the terms of custody. She began throwing items found in his house, at which point he grabbed her firmly by the arms and began to shake her. She spit in his face, kicked him in his groin, and attempted to grab their youngest child. Comp. Kelvin Harris's wife,

Thelma Harris, also called 911 to report the disturbance. When police arrived LaRuth Harris had already calmed down and did not remove the child from the home. Comp. Kelvin Harris does not want to press charges at this time.

Jason called the number listed in the police report for LaRuth's ex-husband. The phone rang four times before a woman answered.

"Is Kelvin in?"

"Yes, one second."

"Hello," a man said.

"Is this Kelvin Harris."

"This is he? Who is this?"

"Ja—mie…Oliver, and I'm calling about LaRuth Harris." He'd started to use his real name, but he didn't want to take any chances. So he just pulled a name from out of nowhere. Better to go by a made up name than one most people would recognize. "I've been seeing her, and she's been lying quite a bit. I'm just trying to find out the truth."

"The *truth*. How funny. You can't use truth and LaRuth in the same sentence I don't care if the two words do rhyme. The truth about her is that she's a liar."

"Yeah, I'm figuring that out."

"A little too late I'm sure."

"She lied to me about her age. She lied to me about having children. She even went so far as to say she had a home invasion."

"That's because she's a *pathological* liar. How long have you been seeing her? " Kelvin asked. "I hope not too long."

"Around four months…not even."

"I'm sure you already slept with her. She doesn't exactly make a man wait for that."

"How long were the two of you married?"

"Six years too long. Unfortunately, I have to deal with her

until our children are old enough to live their own lives, and then they'll have to most likely deal with her too. She lied to me about the same things too—her age...having a child."

"She has more children."

"She has a twenty-year-old daughter who lives in Louisiana with relatives. LaRuth's from Bossier City. Did she lie to you about that?"

"She told me that she was from Fort Worth."

"I'm not sure what's up with that. But again I'm definitely not surprised because she's told me a whole bunch of things that weren't true. It took me some years to figure out who that woman was, and I was married to her. She kept me away from her family. It was crazy."

"What kind of person doesn't claim their own kids? I'm having a really hard time with that."

"Trust me, there's more that you'll have a hard time with. I met LaRuth at a club in Houston. She's a beautiful woman as you know...physically speaking. I left my job, relocated to Dallas just to be with her. You couldn't tell me, I didn't have a prize. I was ready to settle down and have a family with this God-fearing woman. She was the one. Yeah, she was the one, alright. We got married three months after we met. She was pregnant with our first child. But I married her because I loved the person she claimed to be. Did she tell you about her twin?"

"Yeah I saw pictures, so I know she's not lying about that."

"Nah, she's not lying about having a twin, but they're complete opposites, and LaRae hates LaRuth, and for good reason: She slept with LaRae's husband."

"LaRuth slept with her twin sister's husband," Jason asked for clarification. He'd heard what Kelvin said, but he couldn't believe it.

"That's right. She tricked him. Of course, LaRuth said he knew, but my ex-sister-in-law and her husband have the best marriage, and they're still together now. I don't think he knew. I think LaRuth pretended to be LaRae. They have a brother too who's just as shady as LaRuth."

"What's wrong with that girl?"

"A lot…trust me. Are you driving?"

"No."

"I don't know how to tell you this other part, but bro, you're going to want to go to the doctor and take a blood test. Get yourself checked out." Jason's heart sank as he took several deep breaths.

"Why? Does she have an STD?"

"Herpes. She gave it to me. Who knows what else she has by now? That's why we're no longer together. That cross she hangs around her neck is all for show. She may go to church, but it's obvious she's not getting anything from it. Are you still there?"

"Yeah, I'm here." Jason had zoned out after the word "herpes."

"Just wait until you hear this part. One of the dudes she used to mess around with tried to kill me after she lost custody of the kids. He's in prison right now for attempted murder."

"What?!"

"Man, you don't even know, that is one evil woman. In my heart, I know she put him up to it. He pled guilty and never brought her name into it. After this last incident, my wife and I have decided we're moving. We just can't deal with her anymore. I think God every day that I was fortunate enough to find a woman who loved me, and understood that I got mixed up with the wrong woman. She had the same thing happen to her with some no good man. Her ex gave her Herpes. So we just deal with it and try to move on. I love my wife. Things happen for a reason, and I'm glad I'm with her."

Jason buried his face in his right hand and shook his head out of frustration.

"Just get yourself checked out, man. And if she gave you anything get treated for it. Start taking medication. It's not the end of the world, but it does suck. And definitely make sure you have them check you for everything."

It took everything in his power not to storm inside the call center and snatch LaRuth out of it. He was there thirty minutes early, waiting anxiously for five to arrive so he could ask her why. Why did she lie? He didn't love LaRuth. He enjoyed having sex with her. That was it. He loved the sex, and the fact that he could maintain an erection. It was as if she was his miracle drug, or so he had thought. And she seemed decent enough. She never really asked him for anything. But she rarely turned down anything he offered, either. And what did she give him in return? Possibly herpes. She was a liar. They were over. Done. The next time he came to Dallas it would be to visit Maurice and Chevonne.

He watched her as she walked out of the building at a quarter after five sandwiched between the same two women she was always with whenever he came to her job. She looked happy, laughing and smiling. *How could a person filled with lies laugh about anything?* Jason wondered. She waved goodbye to them as she headed to the passenger door of his rental that was already unlocked and climbed inside.

"Hey, baby," she said leaning over to kiss him.

"Don't." He edged his body away to establish distance between them. He didn't say anything just looked straight ahead through the windshield, stone faced and ready to explode. He had actually met someone more trifling than his ex-wife.

"Are you okay? What's wrong?"

"I'm going to take you back to the hotel," Jason said calmly, "so you can get your stuff and go. However you get home from there isn't my problem. We're done."

"But baby what's wrong? What happened?" The panic rose in

her voice.

"I'm not your baby. I'm just some man you were trying to trick. You have some serious issues. Now I understand why you were crying so hard in church."

She inhaled and then exhaled. "What are you talking about? Just say it," she said through gritted teeth.

He turned to face her. "You're a lying ho."

She swiftly slapped him across the face.

"What else you got? Don't answer that. I already know what else you have—three kids, right? Or is it more? *Herpes.*" He shook his head. "If you gave me that, if you ruined my life—"

"Someone ruined mine."

"Did *I* ruin yours? I was always nice to you. I would have moved you into an apartment."

"Oh, so you're not now."

"Are you smoking crack? Have you heard anything I've been saying? No I'm not now."

"You said you would help me get an apartment."

"You are crazy."

"I'm not crazy. Stop saying that! You said you were going to help me, and I already gave my notice, and they already re-leased my place. So now what? I'm going to be homeless."

"I'm not going to help someone like you. How old are you? Why do you have to lie about your age too? And you slept with your twin sister's husband. What kind of person are you?"

"I don't have listen to this." She grabbed the door handle and jumped out of the parked SUV. He eyed the black case resting on the floor of the passenger seat. "Oh, don't forget your Bible." She pulled the black case off the floor by its handle and darted her eyes over at him. "Why don't you have custody of your kids?"

"Don't worry about why. I'm going to have custody of the one I'm carrying. The one I'm having by you."

"Not by me. Trust me."

"Trust me. Yes I am."

"I'll see you in court on that one. There's no way I'm the father. I'm not going to be your meal ticket, sorry."

 "Oh you are the daddy."

Before she closed the car door, he drove away, and the door swung shut a few feet later. *Her things*? That's what she screamed about as he pulled off. He'd leave them at the front desk. It was over. And he was out, and just like she lied about her age, her kids, and who knows what else. He knew she was also lying about being pregnant by him. He had a prostatectomy; what would be the odds? Jason knew there were none.

The day after Jason returned to Atlanta he went to his doctor to get screened for every imaginable STD. His doctor drew his blood and used a swab to take a sample from his urethra. It took a few days for the results to come back. He didn't have herpes. But he did test positive for Chlamydia, which his doctor told him was the most common sexually transmitted disease in the United States. Hearing those statistics didn't make Jason feel better. He just wanted that bacteria out of his body. The doctor prescribed him an oral antibiotic to take once a day for two weeks, and he'd made up his mind when he was done taking the medication, he would be ready to get back Olena who he so foolishly gave away.

TWENTY-FIVE

It was Throwback Thursdays at Gladys and Ron's Chicken & Waffles—an opportunity for Olena to enjoy one of her favorite meals—the Midnight Train (four large chicken wings and a waffle), four-dollar martinis, and old school hip hop and R&B. And she couldn't leave without taking home a piece of sweet potato cheesecake—her favorite. The first time she ate a slice she went home and literally dreamed about it. And since Olena had a taste for chicken and waffles, and Porter was in town specifically to see her, that's where he took her. Funny, she didn't even like waffles that much, but she loved eating them with fried chicken, especially the fried chicken at Gladys and Ron's place. And despite the fact that she'd been to Gladys and Ron's several times in the past with Jason, and the last thing she wanted to do was run into him, she resolved her anxiety by going to the one in Union City that was inside of Citizen's Lanes Bowling Alley and not the one downtown on Peachtree, which was all for the better because they were able to bowl and play arcade games at the Union City location.

Since there was a line of people waiting to be seated to eat, they bowled first.

"Have you ever bowled before?" Porter asked Olena after her second gutterball.

"Once when I was around nine, but I did so badly I never wanted to pick up a bowling ball again."

Porter stuck his fingers inside the bowling ball. "Next time try a lighter ball and don't focus on the pins. Keep your arms straight and throw your ball with a curve. Did you take all that down?" He made his way toward the line, threw his bowling ball with ease, and another strike was the result. "That's how it's done."

"And now we're done," Olena said.

"You're going to quit on me," he said as he walked up behind her and hugged her. "You can't quit on me." He kissed the side of her neck.

"I can quit on you if I suck, which I do."

"No you don't. Don't be so hard on yourself. Practice makes perfect."

"Well, I guess I won't make perfect because I'm not going to practice." She stared at him staring back at her with a smile. "What?"

He shook his head. "Nothing. I'm just happy to be here."

They had bowled four frames and Olena ended with an embarrassingly low score of six, and soon after their table was ready. Olena wanted to talk to her new friend and enjoy some comfort food. She took his hand and led him over to the restaurant. A half an hour later, after their meals were on the table and they were between topics, Olena said, "Did Winona move out of state?"

"What? Where did that question come from?"

"I was just wondering if that's why the two of you are no longer together."

"I, for one, don't have a problem with a long distance relationship. If I did, would I have flown down here to see you?"

"I was just curious."

"Don't worry about why we're no longer together. We're just not. Believe it or not, sometimes people really do grow apart."

"Oh, I believe that. I'm just trying to make sure I'm not your rebound."

"Just because I wrote a song about a rebound doesn't mean you're one."

"I'm just making sure."

"I see you're saving room for dessert," Porter said as he looked down at Olena's plate that she'd barely touched. "I can't believe you're not finishing you're food. I don't know about yours, but mine was the bomb, and we had the same thing. I'll eat it. I'm like that kid Mikey from the commercial. 'I'll eat it. I'll eat anything.'" Olena smiled. Then she started laughing. She couldn't help herself. "You're nasty."

"What are you talking about?" Olena asked as she continued laughing until tears formed in the corner of her eyes. "You don't even know why I'm laughing."

"Yes I do. And they say men have one track minds. Shame on you, Miss Day."

"You don't know why I'm laughing, so stop it. Your mind is going that way, not mine." She wiped the tears from the corner of her eyes."

Olena couldn't eat anymore because she was full of excitement from her first date with a man who had potential to mend her broken heart. She couldn't finish dinner, so she asked the waitress to box it up, and she ordered a slice of sweet potato cheesecake to go.

In the forty minutes it took to drive from Union City to Buckhead, they talked about a variety of subjects. Porter held her hand most of the way as he drove. Even though, he was only slightly familiar with getting around the city, he preferred doing the driving. He told Olena that he never liked being chauffeured by a woman—just one of his pet peeves.

"You seem resolved," Porter said.

"In what way?"

"You're single. And you don't have kids, and you seem okay with that."

Olena shrugged. "You have to remember I'm forty-three. When I was younger, I was very idealistic about marriage and having children. But now, I'm a little bit jaded. It hasn't happened, and I can't force it to."

"By the way, you're forty-four."

"What did I say?"

"You said I had to remember that you're forty-three, and you can't even remember that you're forty-four."

Olena looked over at him as he started laughing. His dimples reminded her of Jason. "Love just hasn't worked out for me."

"Believe it or not, some men get dogged just as much as some women. Some men experience just as much heartache."

"I don't believe that."

"I'm a man, and I'm telling you that it's the truth."

"We're born and then we die," Olena said. "And in between the time of our birth and our death our purpose isn't just to coexist. It's to make a difference. That's my focus now. Not men. Not marriage. Not motherhood. I want to make a difference. My dad had his own business doing what he loved. He worked for himself. I just feel like I don't have anything for myself."

"I thought you were a writer."

"I'm not even a hundred percent sure that I want to be a writer anymore."

"What do you mean you're not sure? You're not giving up on your dream, are you?"

Olena shook her head. "I don't think so. Writing was a way for me to express myself. It was therapy in a way. I just feel like—"

"You don't need as much therapy now."

"Not so much that…I keep hearing that writing is a business, and I genuinely viewed it as more of an art. For me, that's what it will remain. I'm going to stay true to myself. I'm not going to be writing erotica. I may not get published, but I'm okay with that."

"Are you really, or are you giving up on yourself? You have to believe."

"At forty-four, I still have to…oh my God. I can't believe I just said that. I'm the main one who's always complaining about how people of a certain age are made to feel."

"So why did you say it?"

She heaved out a deep sigh. "There are just some things in my past that I'm so ashamed of."

He had stopped at a red light at an intersection not far from her condominium. "People make mistakes, Olena. You're not the only one." He looked into her eyes, and she could tell he wanted to add more. A few seconds later the light turned green, and he pulled off. "You've had a lot of disappointments, and so have I. I think that's why our spirits connected so quickly. I don't want you to give up on love or on your dreams. I think you can have it all, or most of it, if you work at it. But you need someone to love. Don't close the door on that," he said as he pulled into a parking space at Olena's building.

"I won't."

"Pinkie promise."

"I don't do those."

"You're going to do it tonight."

As Olena intertwined her pinkie with his, he leaned across the center console and kissed her lips softly. "I'm really attracted to you, Olena, everything about you not just physically. But you have that going on too."

"Thank you," she said, blushing.

"Are you going to invite me up to see your place?" She shook her head. "Why not? When I picked you up, I had to wait in the lobby. Now, I'm dropping you off, and I can't come inside. Are you married?"

"No, silly. You know I'm not."

"No, silly doesn't know that. Men run into the same mess that women do, I told you."

"I'm very much single."

"Well, I fly out tomorrow, but I am free the rest of the night."

It was close to midnight. Olena considered inviting him up, a fleeting thought.

"Skype me as soon as you land tomorrow."

He grinned. "Okay, Miss Day. I'll do that. Hopefully, we can see each other soon."

"I'd like that."

"Then I'm going to make it happen."

"Are you're sleeping?" Porter said to Olena as they spoke over the phone.

"I was," Olena said as she turned on her back and put on a huge smile after removing her eye mask. It had been a few days since she'd seen him last, but they talked to each other often.

"You go to bed this early? Who, aside from a senior citizen, goes to bed at eight-thirty? Wake up and talk to me."

"Are you drunk? You sound so hyper."

"I'm high on adrenaline. I always get like this before I perform a set."

"Oh," Olena said while taking a long yawn.

"Wake up. I'm not getting off the phone until you do. Are you sick?"

"No, Porter, I'm not sick." She sat up in her bed in her flannel pajamas and matching eye mask. "Why is it so loud wherever you are?"

"I'm in my dressing room about to do a set. I want to see

you again."

"Do you have any tour stops in Atlanta?"

"I already did those dates. But I do have one coming up this weekend at the Fox Theatre in Detroit. Do you want to come out and see me? I'll fly you down, and I promise you'll be given the red carpet treatment."

It only took Olena seconds to consider the offer. "I'd love to see you in concert, but there's one problem."

"What's that?"

"While I'm filming the show, I can't do that kind of stuff without approval."

"You've got to be kidding me."

"And knowing Media One they're going to want to film it all. They don't understand that people have lives outside of their reality show."

"If they want to film it, they can film it. I don't care. They can't film my whole concert. They'd have to pay me quite a bit to do that, but they can film a few minutes. If you don't care, I won't care. I just want to see you."

"You look like a princess," said Tilley who tagged along with Olena to Detroit. Media One sent out a skeleton crew since the concert wasn't part of their storyline, but they were confident they could work it into the plot somehow. "I need to pop my collars because I know what I'm doing."

"Yes, you do," Olena said. "I really love this outfit."

Olena was in a flowing French gray beaded-bodice silk gown with a charmeuse skirt that was raised and revealed her right leg. She was in a pair of five-inch silver T-strap peep-toe sandals.

Porter's concert at the Fox Theatre in Detroit began promptly at 8:00 p.m. on Saturday. Olena had the option of watching back-stage or in the front row of the Fox Theatre. For the sake of Media

One's desired behind the scene access, she chose to watch from backstage. However, her preference had been to watch his concert from the middle section of the front row.

Olena was finally able to see Jason's ex-wife, Keena, in person. She'd heard so much about her, mainly from Jason's mother. She was on stage with Porter performing his biggest hit, "Rebound." And even though the pair appeared to have a great deal of chemistry, Porter had assured her during one of their Skype conversations that they were just friends.

After Keena had left the stage, she brushed past Olena without establishing eye contact. Olena wondered if she knew that she'd dated her ex-husband and babysat her kids. *Probably not, she didn't seem like the kind who read blogs or kept up with her children's lives, either.*

Porter stopped blowing his saxophone and said through the microphone, "I have a special guest here with me tonight that I'd like to introduce to all of you. Some of you may recognize her name. She's on a show called *The One*. Well, I flew her all the way down here to convince her that I'm the one, and I want you to help me welcome Olena Day to the stage."

Olena strolled from the backstage to the main stage and over to Porter, who opened his arms to her for a quick embrace as one of the stagehands pulled a chair on stage for her to sit in.

"I wrote a song that was inspired by this beautiful young lady, and I want to share it with her and all of you. It's entitled 'The Only One.' "

He had on a brown fedora and a pair of loose-fitting light-washed jeans, a dark gray T-shirt with a Superman decal underneath a two-button brown blazer, and blue suede sneakers. He put the saxophone up to his lips and started blowing. As he swayed his head and body to the beat of the music, his fingers worked each note while he raised and lowered his instrument while the rest of his band played on. His female guitarist was wickedly good. He let her have her shining moment midway through the song. He stepped back and motioned to her to take center stage, and her fingers exploded against the strings. Olena swayed her head to the rhythm and moved her shoulders. She felt seduced by the sound of his music.

He held the last note long to provide a climax.

The last concert Olena went to was with Jason. Before that, it had been years. But she thoroughly enjoyed herself.

"Did you like it?" Porter asked after she joined him in the dressing room an hour later. The show didn't end when the last song was performed. There was backstage mingling, autograph signings, and pictures to be taken with the fans.

"I loved it," she said. "I...absolutely...loved...it," she repeated, she repeated, squealing out the words. "That last song gave me goose bumps. I mean I knew you were good, but you're really good."

He stood in front of the sofa that Olena sat on. "Thank you for coming, and I'm glad you enjoyed it." He wouldn't break his stare. "Am I going to have to take you home tonight?"

She shook her head. "But you are going to have to take me to the hotel and drop me and Tilley off."

"Wow," he said as he pulled her off the sofa. "You really are going to make me wait." He kissed her on the cheek and held her in his arms.

"Porter, we just met a few weeks ago."

"So there's a time limit? How old are you again?"

"So you think my age makes me easy."

"*Easier,*" he said jokingly.

"I'm going to get you for that."

"You know I was just joking," he said, widening his eyes.

"Sure you are. I know young men probably do think that."

"I'm thirty-four. I'm not a kid. I just don't want you to put time restrictions on us. Why can't we just go with the flow? Our chemistry should make up for a few months if not a year. We should be planning our wedding next month."

There was a knock on the dressing room door.

"Come in," Porter shouted.

"Hey, you got a minute," Keena said as she cracked the door open and poked her head through the small opening.

"What's up?"

"Can you come out here?" Keena asked with a strange expression on her face.

"Have you met, Olena?" Porter asked.

"No, I sure haven't," Keena said, dragging her voice.

"Olena, this is Keena, my label mate."

"Nice to meet you," Olena said.

"Mmm," she said with a grin. "Porter, I just need to see you for a minute."

"Can you excuse me for a minute?"

Olena nodded. "Of course." When Porter walked out, she shook her head. *Mmm* was right because they seemed like much more than label mates.

He returned five minutes later.

"Are you hungry?" Porter asked.

"I am. But it's one in the morning. Unless Detroit has changed, I don't think anything's open."

"Are you staying at the MGM Grand?"

"Yes."

"They have a food court that I believe stays open all night. We can go there, or I can take you ladies to my favorite spot."

"Take us to your favorite spot," Olena said.

"Ten two on ones, two heavy onions, two chili cheese fries and two Cokes," the waiter yelled out to the kitchen then walked away and immediately returned with their order.

It was two in the morning, and Olena, Tilley, Porter, and some of Porter's band members all ended up at Lafayette Coney Island downtown, Porter's favorite spot that stayed open until four in the morning on weekends.

The cameramen who flew in with Olena and Tilley were kind enough to cut the cameras off after the concert. All but Chalston headed back to the hotel, and Olena felt like a free woman.

"Porter, can tell us where to go," Olena said. "He still lives here. But do you know, I don't even know where you live."

"I guess that never came up in our conversation. I live at the FD Lofts, it's at the Eastern Market."

"What's the FD stand for?" Olena asked.

"Fire department. It used to be the Detroit Fire Department's repair shop."

"You must really miss being a firefighter."

"I didn't mind it. I felt as if I had a purpose."

"That really is a purpose—saving lives."

"I like the place because it reminds me of my past, which motivates me to stay on track for my future."

"Well, Tilley loves sweets, but I haven't been to Detroit in awhile to recommend a place. What's a good restaurant to go to for dessert in Detroit?"

"It depends," Porter said. "What kind of dessert do you like?"

"It doesn't matter as long as it's sweet and it's good," Tilley said.

"Do you like sweet potatoes? I know Olena does."

"I literally like anything as long as it's sweet."

"I should probably take you ladies to Sweet Potato Sensation. They have sweet potato everything: cookies, cake, of course, pie, and Olena's favorite—cheesecake. I'll take you all there before you fly out tomorrow evening."

Olena smiled.

"I'll be right back, ladies."

"I like him for you," Tilley said as she watched him walk to the restroom.

Olena nodded. "He's nice."

"And he left his cell phone right on the table, which means he has nothing to hide."

"Or it could mean he has another one in his pocket. I know someone who had five cell phones at one time."

"My God," Tilley said. "That person had no excuse to miss a call."

"That's one way to look at it. But no, Porter doesn't strike me as someone with more than one phone. I'm not sure why I think that, but I do."

He returned a few minutes later, and as soon as he sat down he leaned over and pecked Olena on the lips.

Olena seemed embarrassed.

"You don't like PDA—public displays of affection," Porter said.

"I know what PDA is. And I don't mind it. It just takes some getting used to."

"I think it's cute," Tilley said as she stared across at the pair. "And I think you two make a cute couple."

"Tilley," Olena said, flaring her nostrils.

"What?"

"Thank you," Porter said. "I think we do to."

"I'll leave you two alone. I'm going to talk to Chalston."

Olena and Porter both took a bite of their Coney dog at the same time. The chili and onions fell on their plate. Juice from the chili splattered onto the bodice of Olena's outfit, so Porter used his napkin to wipe the small red stain off of her dress. "I'm sorry you're all dressed up, and this is where I took you. But you know what that means, right?"

"What does it mean?" Olena asked.

"Raincheck. I have a free weekend next weekend. Isn't that when our segment airs?" Olena nodded. "I'm coming to see you, and we can watch it together. Of course, I'll take you out, too.

Anywhere you want to go." Olena looked helpless.

"What's wrong?" Porter asked.

"I'm so exhausted from all the travel I've been doing since January that I don't want to go anywhere. Coming here was a stretch, but I really wanted to see you again."

"I know what I'll do. I'll cook for you. You won't have to do anything. I'll be your chef for the day."

"Can you cook?"

"Can I cook? Put it this way, Wolfgang Puck doesn't have anything on me."

"Is that right—some would say Wolfgang Puck is the greatest chef in the world—he has nothing on you?"

Porter shook his head. "The greatest chef in the world," he said, using air quotes. "That's just a title. My mom owned a restaurant in Detroit for years. I can throw down. That's if you like soul food."

"I love soul food, even though I'm somewhat trying to become a vegetarian."

"Put that on pause," he said as he downed one hotdog and reached for another.

Olena smiled at the thought of Porter cooking a meal for her. "I can't wait. And you know what? Do you already have somewhere to stay?"

He perked up. "No. I sure don't."

"Well, there's a hotel right in the building—the Rosewood. So it's perfect."

His shoulders dropped. "Not perfect, but I guess it'll have to do." He stared at her the way she stared at him. "What?"

She shook her head. "Nothing. I'm just glad we met."

"I can't wait to spend some one-on-one time with you, finally. Please don't tell Godiva I'm coming to see you."

"You know I won't."

"They don't have to follow you everywhere."

"They didn't follow us to Gladys and Ron's, and they won't be following me to my place either."

She stood in her foyer, waiting for Porter to arrive. One of the men from building security had phoned up minutes earlier to let her know Porter was waiting in the lobby. He decided not to rent a room at the Rosewood, opting to stay with a friend instead.

Olena wore a red sleeveless jersey Valentino dress with a ruffle trim and a bow around the collar. Tilley had purchased the dress in Italy for one of Olena's dates that never happened. But Olena was allowed to keep her wardrobe, one of the perks that made up for the low pay.

Porter had flown in early that morning and arrived at her place at noon. He needed a jumpstart because it would take him a few hours to prepare the traditional soul food meal he had in mind.

Her doorbell rang.

She peered through her peephole at the handsome man on the other end holding a bouquet of roses and a small white gift bag with red hearts.

"What's all this for?" Olena said after opening the door. She spotted the doorman coming down the hall toward her with several Publix shopping bags.

He extended the box of roses toward her. "Happy belated Valentine's Day. I wanted to do something special since you love Valentines so much, and I didn't know you back then."

"Aww that's sweet."

She'd mentioned to Porter during one of their Skype calls just how much she loved Valentine's Day and how much of a disappointment the last one had been, aside from the fact that the show aired on that day. He handed her the gift bag. "You can't open this one until later."

"You are too much."

THE *One*

Porter took the four plastic shopping bags away from the doorman, tipped him a twenty dollar bill, and walked behind Olena into the spacious kitchen.

"Okay," she said, taking the gift bag and the flowers into her kitchen, arranging the dozen roses in a vase she set on top of her long center island in the kitchen.

"Perfect—a kitchen with two ovens—just what I need." He stood behind her and wrapped his arms around her waist and whispered into her ear. "You smell wonderful. What are you wearing?"

"Don't laugh, but I have so many bottles of perfume that I can't even remember."

He embraced her tighter. "I could go to sleep standing here holding you. That's how good you feel." He kissed her shoulder and then her neck, and turned her around to face him, so he could kiss her lips too.

"Not right now."

"Are you nervous?"

She shook her head. "No…just."

He nodded. "Okay. Well, I hate to kick you out of the kitchen, but this is like my second stage, and I have to perform alone, sorry."

"What's on the menu?" she said as she headed out.

"Smothered pork chops, collard greens, macaroni and cheese, and spicy black eyed peas."

"Wow."

"I'm not finished."

"You're not finished," Olena laughed as she stood on the other side of the granite kitchen counter.

"I also have corn muffins, and you haven't had corn muffins until you taste my mom's. And I have sweet tea with a little vodka mixed in to give it a little kick."

"I guess I'll see you tomorrow because it'll take you forever to prepare that holiday meal."

Porter shook his head. "I'm an expert. It won't take me long. I'm good like that. And it'll be well worth the wait, just like you are."

"You're a charmer."

"I'm just telling you how I feel. So just relax and get comfortable. Why are you so dressed up? Don't get me wrong, I love the outfit, and I especially appreciate a woman who keeps herself up. But you're at home, high heels and a dress. You don't need all that."

"Thank you because my feet are killing me."

"Get comfortable."

She left him in the kitchen and walked into the large walk-in closet in her bedroom and changed into a red Aphrodite gown with a V neckline and empire waist with pleating. And she went barefoot because after weeks of wearing five and six inch heels she wanted the luxury of feeling her own soles. She'd gone to the spa in the building earlier for a French pedicure, and her toes were sparkling.

His eyes popped when she returned to the kitchen.

"I like that look much better. Barefoot and pregnant."

"Excuse me?" Olena said. "What are you trying to say? I look fat."

"No," he said, elongating the word. "That's just what I think of when I see a woman's bare feet. Sorry. You look sexy not pregnant. But I do think pregnant women are sexy."

She stood in the kitchen observing his skills with food preparation. He was a neat chef, highly efficient and fast. He was almost ready to put the greens on the stove. "Give me ten minutes," he said with his back to her, "and I'll be all yours for about an hour."

"You don't have to rush."

"I'm not rushing," he said dividing his eye time between her and the greens. "Ten minutes."

Olena walked into the living room and relaxed on her sofa.

He was the perfect replacement for Jason, who'd never once cooked for her, all except for one thing. "How come you never call me, baby?" Jason always called her baby in the sexiest tone.

"How come I never call you baby?" he repeated from the kitchen. "Is that what you just asked me?" he said with a laugh.

"Yes."

He walked into the living room, drying his hands off with a paper towel. "I'm going to let you in on a little male secret. A lot of men prefer calling women baby, so they don't have to worry about calling you the wrong name. So every woman they deal with is baby. I love your name, so I'd rather call you that."

"Is that okay?" She nodded. "But I'm sure that I've called you, baby." She shook her head. "I haven't?"

"No," she said.

"I'm sorry, baby. If that's what you like, I'll have to do better." She became immediately aroused and felt a throbbing sensation like a mini orgasm. "Let me throw this napkin away, and I'll have an hour to spend with you before I finish up the rest." He darted into the kitchen and returned with her gift bag. "Are you ready for your appetizer?"

She nodded. "What did you make?"

Porter held up the gift bag. "It's in here."

"It's in the gift bag. Is it chocolate?"

He walked over to the sofa and handed her the gift bag.

Olena pulled out the pink wrapping paper and looked at the package. "The JimmyJane Form 2," she said reading the packaging. She looked up at him. "You bought me a vibrator?"

"A cordless top of the line one according to the reviews...I did my research."

"This is my appetizer."

"It sure is," he said as he ran his fingers through her hair. She was so glad she'd removed her hair extensions a few days earlier. "Are you going to let me use it on you?"

Their eyes locked. She had the word, no, on the tip of her tongue, but nodded instead.

"Yes?" he asked.

She nodded. "Yes."

He closed his eyes and let out a deep breath that turned her on more than imagining how her new toy would feel.

She stood and reached for his hand, led him into her bedroom, and lay on the bed on her back.

He kicked off his shoes. He wasn't wearing socks. A fashion statement that many of the younger men were into, Olena had learned from Jason.

He took off his T-shirt but left on his jeans and removed the vibrator from its package.

"Doesn't it need to charge?" Olena said. Her voice reduced to moans in anticipation.

"I took care of that this morning."

"You think of everything."

"When it interests me, I do." He walked over to her and sat on the edge of the bed. "And you definitely interest me, Olena." He hiked her gown to her waist, inserted the plastic fluttering ears inside of her vagina, focusing on the clitoris. After a matter of seconds, Olena's eyes closed, and her legs began to swim. She moaned from the satisfaction. "Let me know when you're ready to have your meal because it's more than ready," he said placing his hand on his crotch.

The sun shone bright through the open blinds—afternoon tea. For some reason, that's what popped into her head that moment.

She opened her eyes and took pleasure in watching him watch her.

"May I make love to you, Olena?" he asked.

"May you?"

He nodded. "May I?"

"What about all the food on the stove? This is just an appetizer."

"We still have forty-five minutes." She used both of her hands and placed them on the side of his face to bring him closer to her. "Is that a yes? I need to hear you say it."

"Yes."

He stood and unbuckled his pants and stepped out of them quickly after they dropped to his ankles.

She didn't want to share her thoughts as she stared at his naked body. She'd save the dirty talk for dessert.

He was a patient lover and entered her slowly, allowing her to climax before he did. The first time lasted ten minutes, but it felt as though it had been much longer, and their lovemaking continued all throughout the night.

After her first orgasm and his, he stopped and finished preparing dinner. They ate and made love after dinner. This time on the floor in the living room, but eventually they ended up back in her bedroom. "Am I the one, Olena?" he asked while they were making love.

"Yes," she moaned.

"Say it. Say, 'you're the one, Porter.' "

"You're the one, Porter," she repeated. "You're definitely the one."

His body erupted with pleasure at the sound of her words. Minutes later, the room was filled with the sound of him snoring.

She'd never had a meal like that one, she thought as she clung to Porter's side.

She kissed his chest and shook her head as her mind raced. As tasty as the actual dinner was that he prepared for her, she couldn't concentrate on pork chops or collard greens, not on those small, sweet corn muffins that, on any other day, she would have devoured. He was much better than the food on her fancy plate. She'd been starving for months—celibate for real that time and not by choice. She had gone so long without sex that she'd lost count of the days. *Almost a year*, she thought, *maybe not quite that long, but close.* And to Olena, it had felt even longer.

Porter's eyes opened. He grinned as he watched Olena look at him.

"I'm knocked out. What have you done to me?" He kissed her forehead. "Why aren't you tired? Oh that's right. I did all the work. I cooked, I cleaned. And I made love to you over and over again," he said as he took a wide stretch. "And all you did was lay back and enjoy it all."

Olena nodded. "I like that arrangement."

He smiled and kissed her forehead again. "Do you like it enough to make it permanent?" She nodded. "Don't say it if you don't mean it."

"I haven't said anything yet."

"I read sign language. You nodded—that means yes."

"Guess what?"

"What?"

"We're missing our episode," Olena sang as she picked up the remote from her nightstand and turned on the TV.

"I don't need to watch that when I have all this to look at," he said as he peeked underneath the bed sheets. He took the remote control out of her hand and snuggled closed to her. He turned off the TV, and the room blacked out.

TWENTY-SIX

Rich O'Conner was on Jason's TV screen. Over the weeks, Jason had grown tired of the host, who seemed to be trying too hard to be someone he wasn't. He resembled the host of *The Bachelorette*, only younger, with better suits, and an accent that to Jason sounded like an American trying to sound British, who, at times, sounded Australian.

Jamal turned back toward the TV and shook his head. "Ooh, you in trouble now," he said pointing to Olena as he walked right up to the large TV screen. "You're going on punishment when you get back here. You're not going to be able to go outside. You're not going to be able to talk on the phone or watch TV or use the computer or see daddy."

"She don't care about seeing daddy," Junior said.

"Excuse me?" Jason said to his oldest son.

Junior smiled.

Jamal continued, "You're not going to be able to do nothing but eat and sleep."

"Okay, son, is that a punishment or prison? She can't get in trouble for acting."

"She's not acting," Junior said.

"Shh, it's back on," Jason said.

He wondered if this were the episode Olena said would upset him.

He had his boys in the room with him so he hoped not. His mother was out with her girlfriends. She was in her sixties, and she had found a club that catered to the fifty and over crowd.

"She can't even act," Junior said. "'Cause it seems too real."

"I know who that is," Jamal said. "That's my momma's friend. He sang a song with her."

"He didn't sing, he blew the saxophone," said Junior.

Jason muted the TV. "Alright, now, listen you two, your daddy is trying to watch Olena, so we can't have all of this talking."

Jason pressed the mute button, and the sound returned. He started to rewind to the few seconds he had missed, but he wasn't that interested in seeing the woman he loved batting her fake lashes at another man.

"He could have dressed better than that," Jason said. "Pssh, my woman's dressed up looking good like Cinderella on her way to the ball, and you got on jeans, bro, pssh. And she's acting like she's okay with that. Wow."

"Is Porter Olena's man?" Jamal asked.

"Her *who*? Her man?" Jason said. "Where do you pick that up from?"

"Daddy is her man," Junior said.

Jason grew angrier by the second, not at the interruption but at Olena and Porter's chemistry.

"No, he's not. Grandma said you put Olena down for a floozie in Texas," Jamal said. "What's a floozie?"

"First of all, no matter what your grandma said I did that's not true. And she shouldn't be talking to you all like that."

"Well, why come we don't see her no more?" said Jamal.

"You're going to see her. She's going to be your other mother soon."

"Yeah, right," Junior said. "She going be Porter's kids other mother, not ours."

"Okay boys, I have an important call to make so don't get into anything while I'm gone. I'm coming right back." Jason walked from the theater room into a guest room on the lower level to call Olena.

The phone rang several times before going to voice mail. "I'm over here watching your little show, and, honestly, I can't believe you right now. You seem really into this dude. Didn't you just meet him? I know this is all scripted, but of all the shows I've seen so far, this is the one that seems believable. If I didn't know for a fact that he were only on there to promote his album, I might be a little jealous. So baby, please, don't fall for the okie doke. It's not real. I'm real. And I've been calling you for over a week, but no answer. I'd appreciate a return call, please. I love you, baby. Please call me."

A week passed, and Jason still hadn't heard from Olena. If they couldn't be together, he wanted them to at least be friends. It was better than nothing at all, at least, until he could convince her otherwise.

He was in the kitchen, and hadn't noticed the time to realize *The One* was on. He'd told himself last week that he wasn't going to watch again, but he'd told himself that every week it aired, and he hadn't missed an episode yet, and the season was almost over. He may not have watched them all the way through. Might have done more talking to the screen and complaining about the show being scripted, but he still tuned in."

"Oh no she didn't," he heard his mother yell from the great room. He could see the large TV screen from the kitchen, and an image of a woman and one of a man but couldn't make much more out. "Desmond James."

Did he hear the name he thought he heard—the name of his nemesis?

"What about him?" Jason asked as he walked from the kitchen into the great room.

"That's the next bachelor," his mother said, pointing to the TV screen.

Now he understood what Olena wanted to tell him.

Jason stood with an evil grin on his face and a constant shake of his head. *Desmond James. Not him. Anyone but him.* Not the running back he felt was responsible for Jason's career ending injury after blocking Jason on a blitz pickup. He underwent season ending surgery from a torn right hamstring, and then the Patriots traded Jason to the Falcons. Physically, he was never the same afterward.

"Maybe Olena and I didn't have what I thought," he said with his voice trailing as he replayed the image of Desmond kissing Olena and the thought of Olena making love to the only person he could honestly say he hated. Even before the injury there were plenty of times when he and Desmond would get into it on the field, and over the years, the media covered their rivalry.

"I don't think she loves me?"

"What happened to all your talk about the show being scripted? So every episode was scripted except this one?" Momma Nix asked while she held the phone up to her ear. She was on the phone with her twin sister.

"This one and the one before it."

"Yeah, that last one didn't seem scripted at all," Momma Nix said.

"I think he knows she's my woman," he said, burying his hands in his jeans pocket.

"If he does, he knows something that I didn't. Since when

did she become your woman again? I thought you two broke up. What happened to the one in Dallas?"

"There isn't one in Dallas, so please don't bring her up ever again. Yep, he knows she's my woman. That's why he's doing this."

"I'm sure he doesn't know about you. Remember, you had your lawyers issue her a gag order."

"Okay, Mom, okay. Don't remind me."

Desmond James wasn't going to wife Olena. He wasn't going to marry anyone. Didn't Olena know about his playboy reputation? He said in numerous interviews that he didn't believe in marriage. The only loves of his life were his parents and football. *Didn't she know that about him?* Jason wondered. If she googled him after seeing him in that movie, why didn't she read about more than what he did for a living? Why didn't she read about the models, actresses, and singers he'd bedded, or the trouble he'd gotten into when a jump-off accused him of sexual assault. His star power got him off, but Jason believed the allegations.

Jason turned to walk out of the room.

"You're not going to watch the rest."

"No. I don't want to see that."

The next morning Jason phoned Olena after leaving several messages for her the night before.

This time she answered.

"Yes Jason."

"I don't want to talk over the phone. I want to talk to you in person. Will you meet me for lunch at Bones?"

"Is it safe? You might kidnap me and fly me off to a deserted island." That was one of the messages he left for her the night before. After he watched the show, and it ended with what appeared to be Olena spending the night with Desmond. "That is what you said you were going to do if I picked Desmond."

"*If* you picked him, but I know you better than that, and I know you won't pick him, right?" After a few seconds of silence, he said, "Right?"

"It's just a show, Jason."

"Will you please just meet me…for lunch? I won't take up a lot of your time."

He saw Olena as she pulled in front of the restaurant on Piedmont Road and valet parked her car. It was a few days before the airing of the live finale and a little more than a week before the live airing of the reunion show.

A few people came up to Olena to take a picture with her and to ask for an autograph. Shocking Jason, who hadn't quite accepted how popular the show and Olena had become.

"Thank you for coming," Jason said as he kissed her on the cheek. He wore a classic suit in charcoal with a black shirt. "You look beautiful."

Olena's hair was down and fell just below her shoulder with a center part.

"You cut it?"

"You know all of that hair wasn't mine. That was the show's idea. But I had to come out of those extensions. I had enough hair on my head for five women. My neck started to hurt."

She had on a long-sleeve color block dress with an asymmetric black faux-leather banded waist and black patent leather platform pumps.

The maître d held on to two menus as he led them to a cozy corner table.

Jason pulled out a chair for Olena.

"Are you paying for this?" Olena asked.

"You never have to ask me that. Ever," he emphasized.

"Because I changed purses and forgot my wallet, so I don't have any cash. I have to borrow the tip for the valet, too."

"Borrow, be serious."

He slid a twenty dollar bill over to her.

Olena started focusing on the menu. "Oh, I finally finished listening to all twenty-seven of your messages. Have you thought about speaking to a professional because you have problems?"

"I need to apologize for some of the things I said."

Olena started concentrating on the framed caricatures of Atlanta's well-to-do, and the autographed photographs of celebrities and political figures that lined the walls, anything to divert her attention away from Jason's many Desmond James questions.

The waiter came to their table and took their order.

"I'll have the *Porter*house," Olena said, emphasizing the word Porter. "Well done."

"And you, sir?"

"Let me have a bottle of your Penfold's Grange."

"And what would you like for dinner, sir?"

"Let me have the dry-aged bone-in ribeye."

"Very good."

"Not funny," he told Olena after the waiter left.

"What?"

"Porterhouse. I got the little joke. And, by the way, he looks like me."

"Who looks like you?"

"Porter."

Olena shook her head. "He does *not* look like you."

"Not as good as me, but we favor."

Olena fell out in laughter. "Not as good as you. That's funny."

"Oh it's funny. I remember a time when you said no one looked better than me."

"That was when I was with you. As they say, love is blind. I'm sure you've heard that expression."

"Okay, you got me good," he said with amusement. But inside he was torn apart. "But seriously, Olena, we could be brothers. Don't be that obvious. You want me, and you can have me, the real me, not my knockoff."

Olena shook her head and smiled. "You and your ego, that's what I can't take."

The waiter returned to the table with the bottle of wine, two wineglasses, and bread.

He poured wine into each glass and left the bottle on the table chilling in a bucket of ice.

As soon as the waiter left their table, Jason said. "I want you back, baby. I hate not having you in my life."

"It's too late for all of that now."

"Why is too late? We're both still alive, so it's not too late. It's never too late. It is what it is, but sometimes it isn't. Remember that?"

"No," Olena said shaking her head. "Jason, listen, you had your opportunity, and you decided that you didn't want to be with me. That was your decision, not mine. I loved you—"

"*Loved?*" he questioned, interrupting her. "Past tense." His head shook at the thought. "So you don't love me anymore."

"I still love you. You know I still love you."

"Stop because I hear a *but* coming, and I don't want to hear that. You still love me. That's all I need to hear you say." He leaned forward and took her hand. "We've been through a lot."

"*But*—"

"But what?"

She shrugged. "I'm not *in love* with you anymore. You broke my heart. If I hadn't had the show to distance myself from the hurt, I would have still been devastated. Thankfully, I didn't have enough time to think about you."

"I don't want to talk about that show because if it weren't for that show, we'd still be a couple and probably married by now. So don't talk about that show."

The waiter returned with their meals, and, for a few seconds, their conversation ceased. Long enough for Olena's mind to go to

Porter. She had feelings for him. Not love, but something pretty strong. If not for the show that Jason couldn't stand, she and Porter would never have met. *Everything truly does happen for a reason,* she thought.

"You're eating fast. What's the rush?" Jason asked.

"I have a meeting with Godiva, and I don't want to be late."

"What is it about this time another reality show?"

"I hope not."

"I'm sure she's going to offer you a spinoff. Would you take it?"

"I honestly don't think she will, and if she did I doubt I'd take it, but I do need to figure out what I am going to do."

She checked her cell phone for the time. "I've gotta run. Thanks for lunch and for the money for the tip."

"Are you leaving already?" he asked as he watched her stand and grab her large shoulder bag from one of the empty chairs.

"Yes, I have to. I owe you twenty dollars. I'll get it to you soon."

"Don't insult me," he said as he watched her rush off. He knew what he had to do. He had to win her back, but it wasn't going to be easy.

TWENTY-SEVEN

Olena sat stiffly on the infamous antique brown Derby Chesterfield sofa that Godiva had imported from Southwark, a district of Central London, England. She spread her right hand over the buttoned leather cushion and rested her left arm on the rounded scroll arm. She had to admit it was an extremely nice sofa. But from what Olena was told, Godiva paid almost as much for shipping as she did for the sofa. It wasn't that nice.

"Godiva is ready for you, now," Honey told Olena.

Olena had no idea what Godiva wanted. The only thing she knew was that in a few days they'd be flying off to New Orleans to film the finale.

"Welcome…welcome," Godiva said as she unwrapped a Ferrero Rocher chocolate. Godiva's eyes followed Olena over to one of two leather chairs that she also had imported from England. "By all means, do have a seat and make yourself comfortable."

Olena sat down and crossed her legs. "I love your furniture."

"Thank you. I wanted to bring a few reminders back from our trip…such fun times those were."

Olena didn't exactly consider them to be "fun times." They had the potential to be without Godiva's presence.

"So, I'm sure you're wondering why I called you to my office. And I'm not going to keep you in suspense much longer. I've been reading some blogs and Facebook and Twitter…basically all of the social media sites. And I just have one question for you."

"Okay?"

"Who are you choosing?"

"Am I supposed to tell you that right now, or can it wait for the live finale?"

"You don't have to tell me now. But it's pretty obvious to me and everyone else that it's going to be Porter. Am I right?"

"I'd rather not say. I haven't made up my mind just yet," Olena lied.

"Good. I'm glad because I'm hoping I can persuade you. You could really help make this a much better finale, if you picked Desmond."

Olena's face dropped. "*Desmond*…why Desmond?"

"Well, if you didn't pick Porter, the only other logical choice would be Desmond because of the obvious attraction you had for him. If you pick someone other than Porter or Desmond, viewers will swear it was scripted. Desmond is not an obvious choice as only five percent of those surveyed feel he'll be, *The One*. But he's a believable choice and selecting him will make for great television. It also gives Media One the option of bringing Porter back next season."

"Bringing him back for what?"

"To be the bachelor. It's called, The One, and it won't always be a bachelorette. It's going to rotate from season to season. Season one we had a bachelorette, which means season two we'll have a bachelor. Women really love Porter. Not to mention, if I can track down Winona and bring her on the show next year that will be a major twist, especially with her being HIV-positive. I can only imagine the advertisers we can get for that episode. Not to mention the publicity."

"He has a music career. I doubt he'll have time for reality TV."

"We've already looked at all that. He has a new album coming out next year on Valentine's Day. *Hmm*." Godiva placed her index finger under her chin. "I wonder if you were the inspiration for that."

"I doubted."

"Anyway, I see season two with Porter being the Bachelor. As attractive as Desmond is, he just doesn't have that extra umph that we women love. He's not a Prince Charming sweep you off your feet type of guy like Porter."

"I don't think any man is truly that."

"It's not about what he is in real life. It's about viewers' perception. Perception becomes reality never forget that. And that's especially true with reality TV."

"If he has an album coming out next year, he'll be on tour."

Godiva shrugged. "And that's even better because instead of flying all over the country, which was massively expensive, we'll have the cameras follow him on his tour…in his tour bus even. That'll be real cute. And he'll meet a different woman in each city. I'm salivating at the very thought of how great this angle is going to be. But there's no pressure on your end…really. Choose whomever you feel is *The One* as long as you don't choose Porter. That's all I'm saying." Godiva plucked another piece of candy from her candy tower.

"And if I choose Porter. What happens then?"

"You'll be in breach of your contract. You did read your contract, right?"

"*Every* line."

"You must have skipped over the ones that said management has the right to alter the outcome of any show based solely on their own discretion and then it goes on from there and explains that it could include selecting the bachelor for entertainment purposes and the shows best interest...so on and so forth...yadi...yadi..ya."

"I didn't see that part at all."

"I have a copy with your signature. Trust me, it's in there. We don't miss anything. So, I trust that we are now on the same page, right?"

"Yes, Godiva we're on the same page." How did she know Godiva was going to do something to piss her off? Because she knew Godiva; therefore, she came prepared. Olena stood. "Oh, I almost forgot. I have something for you."

"For me?"

"Yes, a little token of my appreciation for believing in me enough to cast me as your first bachelorette."

Godiva smiled and perked up. "How sweet."

"Olena reached into her oversized Louis Vuitton bag and pulled out a gold Godiva chocolate box with a red ribbon tied around it. "Godiva chocolate. Thirty-six assorted pieces." Godiva's eyes bulged from its sockets. "I hope you enjoy." Olena said with a wide smile as she inched her way over to her.

"Thank you, but give it to Honey, please."

"But it's for you."

"I *said* give it to Honey," Godiva snapped as she pushed her chair back, away from the desk.

"Is something wrong? You're acting strangely."

"Yes, I'm allergic to Godiva chocolate, so don't bring it near me."

"But you eat chocolate those chocolate balls all the time. How can you just be allergic to one kind of chocolate?"

"Did you hear what I said, I'm allergic to it? Don't bring it near me." Godiva swiveled her chair so that the back of the chair faced Olena.

"I'm sorry. I didn't know. Maybe you also should put that in your contract." Olena dropped the box of chocolate on Godiva's desk, and then walked to the sofa and retrieved her purse before hurrying out of the office.

"We're going to put you through our version of speed-dating," Remy said as he stood inside of Olena and Tilley's hotel suite. They were in New Orleans, staying at the Hotel Monteleone in the French Quarter on Royal Street. Olena was excited after reading the hotel's history. The fact that Ernest Hemingway, Tennessee Williams, and William Faulkner immortalized the hotel in their works and had each stayed there. Maybe their spirits were present, and she'd be motivated to write because it had been awhile since she picked up her pen and moleskin notebook. Eugena still didn't have a book deal for Olena, and Olena was at the crossroads, trying to decide if becoming a published author was even in the cards for her. It was probably going to be time for Olena to move on. Perhaps look into becoming a food writer as Tilley suggested. She liked Eugena, but business was business. She loved to write and would do it for free if she were able to, but without a j-o-b, she needed some c-a-s-h and enough of it to pay her b-i-l-l-s. She detested dipping into her savings and didn't have enough of it to last forever. *The arts were more respected back in the days of Hemingway*, Olena mused. Now saying you're a writer meant very little if you hadn't yet been published, and Olena wondered what it would mean once you had. It didn't seem like people read as much now as they once had. So many people watched TV. Reality shows were taking over, and she was sad that she was contributing to that dumbing down trend.

"You didn't get to meet a bachelor on the first leg. It's been so long I can't even remember which city we were in," Remy said. "And we promised viewers you'd meet ten bachelors so ten it is. Your next date will be with two men instead of one. Both are native New Orleanians. One's a record producer. The other is a writer."

"A writer?" Olena perked up. "What did he write?"

"I have no idea," Remy said dismissively. "That's something you can ask during your speed dating."

After Remy had left, Tilley flung her suitcase on the bed and in the midst of unpacking said, "I did what you told me not to do."

"What did I tell you not to do?"

"Think about it."

"Honestly, I can't remember what I told you not to do." Olena kicked off her flats and sat on the edge of the bed. But then it hit her. "Oh no, Tilley, I hope it's not that," Olena said as her voice cracked. "Are you still a virgin?"

Tilley shook her head. "I'm not."

"Tilley," Olena said and then gasped. She covered her mouth with her right hand and felt like crying or slapping Tilley or both. "Why?" Olena snapped. "You haven't even been out of my sight for that long. Where did this happen?"

"Atlanta."

"With whom?"

Tilley hesitated.

"You don't want to know."

"Do I know him?"

Tilley nodded.

"Not Smith."

"I wish."

Olena shook her head. "Don't say that. Don't ever want to commit adultery. Trust me. Karma is alive and doing very well. So who was it with?"

"Chalston."

"Chalston? Chalston who? I know not the cameraman Chalston Reed."

"Yep."

"Tilley, he flirts with everybody, including me. Tell me that you didn't."

"I did, okay, I did."

"How old is that man?"

"Forty-two."

"Why would you want to have sex with a man that old?"

"He's younger than you."

Olena paused. "Wow, you're right. Why do I always forget my age?" She shrugged. "Well, the difference between me and *Chalston* is that he's forty-two going on eighty-four, and I'm forty-four going on thirty because I don't want to be going on twenty-two. I have to get past the twenties. He dresses like an old man, talks like an old man, and I don't even want to imagine what else he does like one."

"He does that like an old man too."

"Stop before I throw up. I just had a mental image of him naked. Yuck. Did he use protection?"

"Yes, we used protection. I wasn't that dumb."

Olena took a sigh of relief. Okay, so she had sex. It was Tilley's life, after all, and not Olena's. Olena was just hoping to live vicariously through the eyes of a virgin for a few months if not years, but now that was no longer possible. One time certainly didn't make her experienced. "How was it?"

"Were you the one who said sex is overrated, or maybe that's what my mind told me while I was doing it? I wish I wouldn't have done it. He couldn't exactly keep an erection either, and he's the size of my thumb. I do mean that literally."

"Why Tilley why?"

"I don't know. I think it had something to do with Porter. I can tell he really likes you. I think it's so cute you all Skype each other all the time. I guess I wanted someone like him. I don't know why."

"Well, don't beat yourself up over it. He's just one guy. You made a mistake. You don't have to continue making them." Olena said. "We all make mistakes."

Like sleeping with Porter? Was that another Olena mistake? It didn't seem as if it were one. Could she truly start over with him, or was he just a rebound?

The first round of Olena's speed-dating took place at Olivier's, an authentic Creole restaurant on Decatur Street in the French Quarter. She was more enamored over the Louisiana BBQ shrimp than either of the two bachelors. The writer was short, but not a sexy short like Gordon. And he didn't write fiction. He was a technical writer for a multinational information technology corporation, whatever that was. The record producer was also a rapper, writer, and composer—a little bit of everything, which, for her, meant he was probably a whole lot of nothing. He was tall and muscular, and his neck and hands were covered with tattoos. Olena assumed his entire body was covered with them, but she didn't want to picture him naked.

Oh God, are those diamonds on his teeth? If so, he has one expensive grill. The best thing about the writer is that he's nerdy, and he's wearing a bowtie, so he's already in the lead.

"Mmm, I want to know their secret family recipe," she said after popping a barbecue shrimp in her mouth. She studied the menu and ignored the men. Female viewers liked Olena's nonchalant attitude toward the bachelors. "Creole rabbit, hmm. I don't think I want to eat a rabbit." She continued perusing. The men discussed sports after being ignored by her for several minutes. "Sorry guys, I can't concentrate when I'm hungry. Do you both already know what you're ordering?"

The writer nodded. The record producer blurted out, "Ribeye steak."

"How does it feel to be famous?" the record producer asked. "I can't go anywhere without seeing your face on a magazine. Mostly tabloids. Why they hatin' on you so much?" *Was that written in the script?* she wondered. For him to bring up that tabloid. She'd almost forgotten about that before he brought it up. Not really. But she'd been trying not to dwell on the past for too long before that man with all of his tattoos and a diamond grill in his mouth said what he did.

"That's in the past just like your criminal record."

"Criminal record?" he said. She didn't know if he had one, but the script told her to say that. "I don't have a criminal record." *Oops*—so much for her assumptions or the script's. "Why did you assume I did because I'm a rapper? Did you know most rappers didn't get a criminal record until they got a record deal?"

"I've heard someone else say that. *Hmm*," she placed her finger on her chin. "I think it was Jay Z." She'd never heard it, but she said what the script told her to. "I'm getting the taster's platter. 'Superb Louisiana seafood, battered and deep-fried, is a staple of the Creole table. We dip the seafood into a milk-egg wash then roll it in yellow corn flour seasoned with garlic and salt'—I love garlic—and deep fry it in light, pure vegetable oil. This platter includes fish shrimp crab and salmon cake and Creole gumbo.' Yum." She glanced up at the two men and their blank stares. The record producer talked on his phone and made deals while he was eating. The technical writer tried to make small talk with her, but the more he spoke the more Olena thought of the womp-womp-womp of Charlie Brown's teacher. Luckily it was a speed date, which meant she didn't have to go on two more with them. They were just fillers. Viewers knew who Olena's two picks would be. And Media One knew who *The One* would be.

A rapper and a writer. I was excited to meet the writer. I thought we'd have something in common right off the bat. But as it turns out he writes instruction manuals. Not knocking what he does. I mean, we need someone to do that. He just didn't have much to say. He was unusually quiet. Very reserved. The rapper, or is he supposed to be a music producer, I honestly don't think he's as successful as he claims to be. I think he may have tricked some folks and gotten past the screening process because I googled him while we were at dinner—Big Groove Music Group, BGM...I don't think that company exists. I can't stand all of his tattoos, the saggy jeans, and the diamond grill. Maybe it's the era I was raised in, but someone needs to bring the distinguished look back because I couldn't wake up next to that. Not one night. Let alone every night.

Rich O'Conner stood in the middle of Decatur Street in the French Quarter as the episode began to air. "Good evening, I'm Rich O'Conner, the host of *The One*—the show that matches one lucky bachelorette up with ten eligible bachelors and takes her to ten romantic destinations, so she can make one difficult decision. Tonight, our bachelorette, Olena Day, will make that difficult decision. "If you've been with us all season you may have some idea of who she's going to select. Porter Washington and Desmond James seem like front-runners, but you just might be surprised. Don't rule out Stephon Mason. She might want to give a former fling a second chance. Or Gordon...well, maybe not Gordon. But I'm sure viewers will be in for a few surprises. We want to thank the millions of you tuning in each week and making *The One* the most watched program on Sundays."

Rich walked across the street and into the Café du Monde and approached Olena as she sat at one of the small round tables inside the crowded coffee shop.

"It's good to see you again, Olena."

"You too, Rich."

"Well, tonight is the night. You're going to pick the man whose impressed you the most out of all the bachelors. Are you ready to make your decision?"

"I think so."

"Over the past several weeks, we've asked viewers to go online and vote for the bachelor they felt deserved an extra date. Our viewers have spoken. Do you have any idea who they chose, or maybe I should ask who do you hope they've chosen?"

"As long as it isn't Gordon, I'm okay."

"Not feeling old Gordon. I can't say I blame you. But, unfortunately, Olena, I'm sorry to say. . ."

"No," she said, shaking her head.

A man walked up behind her and placed his hands on her shoulder. She dropped her head back and looked up and smiled. "Porter."

Porter smiled down at Olena and then sat across from her at the small table inside the café.

"Porter Washington was our fan favorite, but before I leave you two alone I'm going to leave these three questions that fans of the show would like for you to ask Porter." Rich placed a small card in front of her.

Olena bit her bottom lip and continued batting her eyes at Porter.

"What?" Porter said with a tender smile pronouncing his deep dimples.

"Nothing."

"Are you glad to see me?"

She nodded. "Very."

"How's our friend doing?"

"Our friend? Oh, our friend," she said with a shy grin, realizing he was referring to the vibrator that he'd given her as a gift. "He's doing great."

"Did he come on the trip with you?"

"Yes, he's here."

"Good. I wouldn't want you to travel alone."

A server brought café au lait and an order of beignets with powdered sugar to their table.

"Let me go ahead and dive into these questions," she said as she looked down at the index card. "Okay, Missy from Chicago wants to know what is your favorite time of day, day of the week, and month of the year?"

"Hello Missy, my favorite time of the day is the morning. My favorite day of the week is Sunday, and my favorite month of the year is December."

"And why?"

"Let me see that question. Did she really ask why?" Porter said. "I'm just kidding. I'm a morning person even though I have concerts at night. Even when I stay up late I still like to start my day no later than eight in the morning, preferably seven. I used to be a firefighter, and I've worked around the clock, and there would be times when I would have to sleep during the day when the sun was out. I just felt like I missed out on a lot, almost like I slept my life away. As for Sunday that day is really peaceful. I'm more relaxed on that day than any other day. It goes by slower than other day. Almost like God slows the time down. And December is my favorite month because it's a month of celebration, people seem happier and friendlier, and I love seeing all the decorations. And it's the last month before the New Year so I get to reflect on what changes I'd like to see in my life."

"Good answers. Let's see what the next question is. Angie from Detroit would like for you to name a song that best describes what you're looking for in a woman?"

"Hello Angie, my home girl. Well, I want somebody to love me for me...for me," he sang.

"Heavy D," Olena said. "I love that song."

"Read the lyrics…story of my life. Hopefully, that chapter is coming to an end soon."

"Okay, last question comes from Jasmine of Upper Marlboro, Maryland. What defines you as a person?"

"My choices define me. The choices I make for my life…the choices we all make define our lives. The choice you make at the end of this show will define yours."

Olena said, "Those were all really great answers and I definitely feel like I know you better. Thank you for being here."

"Thank you for having me."

The camera switched to Rich. "Who will Olena choose as *The One*? It's time to find out." The camera switched back to Olena and Porter inside of the café as Rich walked up to their table. "Well, Olena, I don't mean to pull you away, but it's time to let America know your decision, so if you could say goodbye to Porter, and please come with me." Olena waved goodbye to Porter.

"I'll see you soon," Porter said with a wink.

Rich walked Olena out of the café and over to an area in front of the St. Louis Cathedral in Jackson Square, the historic park named after General Andrew Jackson, a hero in the Battle of New Orleans.

"Olena, we thought you might need help in determining which one of the ten bachelors is the right one for you. So in the spirit of New Orleans, we're going to leave you in the hands of a psychic for a tarot card reading."

"Oh, no," Olena said, shaking her head. "I'd rather not know my future."

"Don't be scared," the woman said as she motioned for Olena to sit down. Olena sat at the small round table directly across from the woman, whose long bright dress draped her meaty shoulders. The woman shuffled the tarot cards before she set them down on the table, cut them, and laid four cards down in a diamond formation.

"I'm going to read only one card; point to the one you want me to read."

Olena pointed to the one closest to her.

"This one on the top of the diamond formation speaks of romance," the woman said as she turned it over to reveal a jester in bright clothes with a white flower in one hand, a staff over his shoulder with all of his possessions tied up, and a dog at his side.

"The fool card. I'm getting a very strong vibration from this card also the other three as well as your presence. You have a very strong presence."

"Is that a good thing?" Olena asked, assuming it was.

"Not always."

"*No?*" Olena said, looking confused.

"You have never been truly happy, have you?" Olena shook her head. "Not even when you were in a position where you made a lot of money. And now that money has left you as have a lot of other things in your life. Now, you are making decisions out of fear instead of logic.

You think over things too much. And you care too much of what others think of you and say about you, people who don't even know you. But I'm feeling through the vibrations of these cards that the money is coming and a lot more than you've had, but not in the way that you expect it to or want it to come, and you have some choices to make, life-changing decisions. Someone is going to ask you to do something that you won't want to do. Don't be afraid to make a decision. Trust yourself for once because if you don't, your ship will sail. You are being led to believe that you have only two, but actually there are three. This card is in reverse, and since it's not facing you, I'm afraid that means that the decision you make will most likely be the wrong one."

After the tarot card reading, there was a commercial break, but before they went to break, Rich told viewers that they'd be back with Olena's decision. When the program returned from commercial, the camera was focused on the crescent shape of the Mississippi River. The next shot was of Rich and Olena standing in front of Washington's Artillery Park with the Mississippi River behind them, Jackson Square in front of them, and the ten eligible bachelors all wearing black suits standing in a straight line behind Rich.

"Olena, over the past ten weeks, viewers have had an opportunity to get to know you along with the ten eligible bachelors, and while it hasn't always been a smooth ride, and I do mean that literally, did you have fun?"

"Absolutely, I've had so much fun here. In a way, I hate that it's almost over, but most women don't meet ten great men in a lifetime, and I was able to meet them in a matter of weeks, and I'm very grateful for that."

"Olena, now it's time to let viewers know the name of the one you've chosen."

"This was a pretty easy choice for me. He was clearly the one for me."

"Are you sure?"

She nodded. "I'm two-hundred-percent sure. It was a wonderful experience that became even better as time passed and this man is definitely, *The One*."

"So tell us who you've chosen."

"Porter Washington," she said with a big smile.

"What?" Godiva screamed. She must have forgotten it was a live taping.

"Porter Washington," Rich said, looking stunned. "You chose Porter Washington."

"That's right. Porter Washington."

"Okay, well, um, I can't say that's a surprise. Porter, please come join us."

"I sure will," he said as he stepped from the line.

"Well our bachelorette has spoken. She's chosen Porter

Washington. Join us next week for our live reunion show and who knows possibly a proposal?" Rich said into the camera. "Until we meet again." The camera zoomed in on Olena and Porter in a warm embrace.

The limousine pulled in front of Atlanta's fabulous Fox Theatre on Peachtree Road. The driver got out to open the door for Olena whose hair was swept off her face into a French roll. She had on a black-and-nude strapless lace bodice with a black feather satin skirt and a satin belt that fell naturally at her waist.

As she was exiting the limo, she hiked her dress several inches, so it wouldn't sweep the ground. The live reunion show was tonight. And she was anxious to get to it. One week without speaking to Porter felt like forever.

She walked through the front door making her way to the entrance to the theatre.

The cameras followed Olena's every move as she walked down the side aisle toward the stage where the show's host, Rich O'Conner, waited.

"It's good to see you again, Olena. As always you look stunning."

"Thank you," she said as she tilted her head quickly to one side and smiled.

"And how has your time away from the show been?"

"It's been good."

"Are you missing all of those flights and hotels?"

"Umm, not so much the air travel, but all of the hotels we stayed in were absolutely beautiful."

"And did you do as instructed and not speak to any of the bachelors this week?"

"I did as I was told."

"Good. Well, we know why you think you're here, but during

the season premiere, we told viewers there would be a twist that you wouldn't see coming. Do you remember that?"

"I do now that you mentioned it."

"Why do you think you're here?"

"I'm here for the reunion show…to talk to the guys and go over the season and to reunite with Porter."

Rich shook his head.

"No?" Olena said.

"That's what's usually done on a reunion show. Just not ours. Are you ready for the twist that you didn't see coming?"

Olena shrugged. "I'm not sure if I'm ready for this or not."

"Did you see this coming?"

The red curtain pulled open and behind it was Jason dressed in a classic black tuxedo.

"What are you doing here, Jason?" Olena asked as he approached her.

"I'm here for you."

"Do you know we're taping? It's live. You're on the reality show."

He nodded. "Yes, I know. That's fine."

"It is?" Olena said in shock. She never thought he'd voluntarily appear on a reality show. "And you still came on."

"Olena," he said as he got down on one knee.

"Why are you getting on one knee?"

He pulled a Tiffany ring box from his tuxedo pants. "Olena, I'm here to let you know just how much I love you. How much I've missed you. How much I need you in my life and my sons' lives. You are everything to me, and I would be the happiest man in the world if you'd marry me. I would honestly feel as though I was the luckiest man alive. Will you marry me, baby?" She hesitated as she stared into his eyes. He repeated his question. "Will you marry me, Olena?"

"Yes, I'll marry you," she said gushingly.

Confetti fell from the ceiling, and minutes later they were whisked off to the Egyptian ballroom to celebrate their engagement among family, friends, and select viewers who'd gone online and entered the sweepstakes to win a spot in the audience during the live reunion.

There was a live band and so much catered food that everyone could eat three times. Drinks were flowing steadily from the bar. And Olena and Jason were on the dance floor slow dancing to Savage Garden's "Truly Madly Deeply." Jason whispered into her ear. "I'm your new beginning. I always was."

She stroked his right cheek and said, "I know."

Their evening concluded at the Four Seasons hotel. They were on the nineteenth floor in the Presidential Suite. He stood on the marble foyer as he carried her through the door and pushed the door closed with his foot. "I think you're supposed to do this after we get married."

"I'm going to do this every night."

He carried her into the bedroom and over to the king-sized bed, sitting her down gently on the bed. She wasn't expecting much to come of the rest of the night. It would be perfectly fine with her if they lay next to each other cuddling, kissing, and talking the night away. She did miss him and his family—the kids, his mother. But she'd be lying if she didn't admit to herself that she missed Porter more. He slipped off her satin sandals.

"How did you get in your beautiful dress?"

"There's a hidden zipper in the back," she said, reaching for it as she sat on the bed. He removed his tuxedo jacket first and then his bowtie. Next to go was his white tuxedo shirt and then his patent leather derby shoes. He unlatched his tuxedo pants, pulled down the zipper and allowed them to fall to the floor. He didn't have any underwear on. "So I see a lot has changed," she said, focusing on his erection.

"A whole lot." He took both of her hands and guided them toward him. "I just want you to feel how much I want you." And she did, and that was the extent of their foreplay. Their moans traveled throughout the twenty-two hundred square feet of the suite.

"I love you, Jason. I love you so much."

"I love you more, baby."

"Call me, Olena, not baby, please."

"Olena," he moaned. "I love you more."

EPILOGUE
NOW AND THEN

One month later

Olena sat at one of the banquet tables inside of the Grill Room at the Horseradish Grill restaurant on Powers Ferry Road. She placed her right hand on the center of her chest. She ate her food too quickly, and now she felt like some of it had gotten stuck.

Jason stood beside her. He was in the midst of making a toast.

"Love makes you do some crazy things; things you say you'd never do," he said to the crowd of fifty friends and family, all there to celebrate Jason and Olena's engagement. "I've heard that said many times before, but I never imagined I'd experience it firsthand. I never thought I'd go on a reality show and let Olena know just how much I love her. I can't stress enough how much I love this woman. She's been there for me through a dark time in my life. There's nothing about her I would change. And—" He dropped his face in his hand as tears rolled.

"Take your time," one of his brothers said.

He looked at the crowd. "I can't wait for her to become my

wife and for us to spend the rest of our lives together."

Olena felt sick.

She ran from the table as her mouth began to water. She could feel the food easing its way back up. Quickly, she made her way to the ladies' restroom and into one of the stalls with Tilley following after her. She dropped to her knees and stuck her head inside the toilet bowl with her arms clinging to the basin. Seconds later as her head and chest jerked, she heaved up every bit of food she'd eaten.

"What's wrong?" Tilley asked, rubbing Olena gently across her back. Olena flushed the toilet and sat on the floor in her burgundy and black strapless tufted dress with her back against the stall. Sweat poured down her brow and mixed with her tears. "Did you get food poisoning?"

"I don't know what's going on. I just know I don't feel right." Tilley helped Olena up from the floor and over to the sink. She took a few paper towels from the holder affixed to the wall, wet them, and wiped Olena's face off.

"Poor baby is sick."

Olena nodded. "Can you please get Jason for me?" Olena was out of breath.

"Okay, I'll be right back."

Tilley rushed out of the bathroom, and a few minutes later Jason knocked on the bathroom door. "It's me, baby."

Olena walked to the bathroom door and pulled it open. "I'm sick."

"What's wrong?"

"I don't know. I want to go to the hospital.

"What's wrong?"

"I'm throwing up, and I'm dizzy. I just don't feel right."

Jason had a strange look on his face. "Do you think it was something you ate?"

"I don't know. I just need to go to the hospital…to emergency. Will you please take me?"

"Yeah, I'm going to take you right now."

Thirty minutes later, she sat on an examining table inside of Piedmont Hospital on Peachtree Road. The nurse took her blood and gave her a cup to urinate in. Olena gave them permission to test for everything. Thirty minutes later, a doctor entered the room with Olena's chart in her hand.

Olena tried to read her expression, but the doctor's face was like stone.

"You're pregnant."

"No."

"That wasn't a question. I'm telling you that you are."

"Oh." She sat stunned. "I am?"

"Yes, you're pregnant. Now the blood test will take a little longer to come back to confirm it, but based on the urine test you're pregnant. Our urine tests are quite accurate. So congratulations. Were you and your husband trying?"

"I'm not married…yet. And no we weren't trying."

"Then consider it a blessing."

"A blessing?"

Olena walked through the double doors that led to the waiting room.

Jason stood and took a deep breath. "Did they find out anything, baby?"

"Why do you keep calling me, baby? Can you just call me by my name, please?"

"What's wrong? I can tell something's wrong. What did the doctor say? Did you find something out?" She didn't know what to tell him. She never wanted to lie to him, so she nodded. "What is it? What's wrong?"

"I'll tell you in the car."

They walked out slowly through the sliding glass doors.

Olena's head faced the ground.

They waited a few minutes for the valet to pull Jason's car around.

Her mind raced the entire time.

"Can you tell me now?" he asked as they continued to wait for his car.

She shook her head.

The valet pulled Jason's Bentley around.

Jason held the passenger door open for Olena and walked around to the driver's side, tipping the valet before Jason got behind the wheel and drove off. He turned left on Peachtree Road northwest. "Baby, I want to know what the doctor said."

"I'm afraid to tell you," she said as her voice cracked into pieces.

"I need to know. We can work through whatever it is. Do you have an STD or something?"

"A what? No. Why would you ask me that?"

"I don't know. I'm just wondering why you're afraid to tell me."

When he pulled into a Chevron gas station, she said calmly, "I'm pregnant." There were a few seconds of silence. "Did you hear what I said?"

He nodded as he clenched his jaw and strangled the steering wheel.

"Are you going to say something?"

"Is Desmond the father?"

"No. I never had sex with him."

"Is Porter?"

She nodded and said softly, "Yes, but it was before you and I started seeing each other again."

"Does he know?"

"No, I didn't know. I just found out."

"When's the last time you've spoken to him?"

"It's been awhile."

"What's a while…a day…a week?"

"A few days after the reunion show. He called to wish me well."

"You haven't spoken to him since then. Please don't lie."

"Briefly."

"Do you love him?"

"I love you."

"My question was do you love him because I know it's possible for someone to love more than one person."

"Possible to love more than one person, I agree. Not possible to be in love with more than one person because when you're in love that person has all of you—mind, body, spirit—everything."

"How many times did you have sex with him?"

"What difference does that make?"

"I just want to know."

"Once."

"So you had sex with him one time and you got pregnant? Please don't lie to me. Just be honest."

"It's possible to have sex with someone one time and get pregnant."

"I know it's possible. I'm not asking about what's possible. I'm asking about what actually happened. Did you only have sex with him one time?"

"One day not one time…multiple times in one day."

"Multiple times in one day." He shook his head. "What is your definition of multiple?"

"More than once."

"Be a little more specific. How many times…two…three…ten?"

"Stop it. I can't remember." So many thoughts were running through her head, but the one thing she didn't want to think about was what Jason was asking her.

"Did you have sex with him at your condo? I just want the truth. I need to know. Did you have sex with him there?"

"Why does that matter?"

"Just answer my question, please."

"Yes! I had sex with him there. Okay?"

"No, it's not okay. Where? In your bed," he said raising his voice, "The one you and I sleep in together."

"But you and I are hardly ever at my condo."

"But when we are." When she didn't answer him immediately, he shouted. "Answer me!"

"Yes," she screamed, "I'm sure you had sex with at least one woman while we were separated. Didn't you?"

"No, I didn't. You know what my situation was like at that time."

"But it's not like that now, so maybe it wasn't like that then."

"It's been like that until recently."

"And you're not lying to me."

He shook his head. "I don't want anyone else. No one, and I do mean no one, is going to love you the way that I do."

She was pregnant, and if she said, "I do," soon she'd be married. But the decision between Porter and Jason wasn't as clear cut as the one she'd made between Matthew and Jason. And, if she were to let the truth be told, she still couldn't get Mr. Washington out of her mind. "Somebody for me," that's what Porter had become—someone for her.

She looked over at him. Her eyes couldn't lie.

Jason shrugged. "I'm in love with you. So that baby you're carrying is mine too. If momma asks, we'll say you had in vitro. That's all anyone has to know. Okay?" He turned to look at her. She nodded. "Nothing can come between us."

Olena thought she'd feel relief. Jason knew and didn't care. Nothing would stop the two of them from being together. But what about Porter? What he didn't know wouldn't hurt him, but what she knew tore her apart.

"I—"

"You, what?" He held her hand. "It's just a lot right now, but once I get you home—to your new home—and you get all settled in, it's going to be fine. You'll be around the boys and Momma."

"It wouldn't be fair if I didn't tell Porter."

"Life's not fair," Jason replied. "He wants fame. Not a baby and not you." But Olena wasn't quite sure of what it was she wanted until Jason said, "Remember when you first told me about the reality show, and you promised you wouldn't let it come between us?" Olena nodded. "Well, Olena. None of this would have happened if you'd done as I asked and didn't go on there. Now, I need you to be a woman of your word, and don't let that show come between us." She nodded again. That's what she would do; she would be a woman of her word.

He got out of the car to fill up the gas tank.

She checked her cell phone. It had been on vibrate all day, but she felt a text message come through a few minutes earlier.

Olena, please call me. We still need to talk. I don't think it's the end for us.

She started typing her reply, but decided to delete her message. As much as she didn't want to, she deleted his contact information too. She and Jason were meant to be together.

Everyone else was incidental.

READERS GUIDE FOR

by CHERYL ROBINSON

DISCUSSION QUESTIONS

1. In the beginning of the novel, Olena has a hard time sleeping. On her mind are the two men she's been seeing, Matthew and Jason, as well as, the impending operation Jason is scheduled for. What is your first impression of Olena and does it change over the course of the book? If so, when and why?

2. Jason is a single father dealing with a serious illness that has caused him to become affected by erectile dysfunction. Regardless, he wants to marry Olena. Do you think that a marriage without sex can survive? Please explain your answer.

3. Olena goes against her personal beliefs regarding reality TV in order to gain exposure in hopes of securing a publishing contract. In your opinion, is that the action of a woman who is trying to succeed by any means necessary or someone who is confused and unsure of what she wants? Please explain your answer.

4. Of the ten eligible bachelors, only two, Porter Washington and Desmond James, seem to catch Olena's eye. Both are public figures. While it is known that Desmond was booked to appear on the show through his sports agency, what do you think of Porter's motives? Do you think he truly cares for Olena? Did you think he was on the show for a similar reason as Desmond?

5. What is your opinion of reality TV? Is it merely entertainment, or do you think the consequences of some of the antics being displayed can be harmful to young girls, in particular? Do you think reality TV negatively portrays black women, or, do you think, in general, reality TV portrays women, regardless of race, negatively?

6. Discuss reality TV dating shows past and/or present. In your opinion, do shows such as these get women fixated on the idea of finding a "knight in shining armor"? What do you think is the impact of dating shows on young women?

7. If given the opportunity to participate in a reality show of any kind, not just one focused on finding a mate, would you do it? Why or why not? Do you think reality shows are scripted as the novel portrays?

8. Deanna Knox sees herself as a victim of reality TV. Do you fault Media One producers for what happened to her? Please explain your answer.

9. As part of the reality show, Olena is filming in the ten "most romantic cities" in the world. Do you agree that those cities are the most romantic? What city do you think is the most romantic city in the world? Why?

10. Olena is a woman who has made many mistakes in the past, especially as far as men are concerned. Low self-esteem was an issue she dealt with in her past. Do you think a person's character is shaped by past experiences, or do some people become unnecessarily stuck in the past? Is Olena justified with her worries over what was reported in the tabloids? Should she have simply brushed it off as something from her past? Please explain your answer.

11. Who would you have chosen between Jason and Porter? Please explain your answer.

12. LaRuth considers herself a "faithful Christian" who carries the Bible, quotes scripture, wears a cross and casts harsh judgments on others all the while hiding her own skeletons. Have you ever met someone like LaRuth? What is your overall impression of someone like her?

13. Who was your favorite character? Why?

14. What did you think of the ending of the novel? What do you think this means in the long run for Jason and Olena?